CLARISSA WILD

DEDICATION

For all the book sluts who crave to be chased by masked villains
with a 10" D…
Open wide.

AUTHOR'S NOTE

Vile Boys is a dark bully romance that warrants a warning.

This book is incredibly violent and ruthless, and is filled with terror and carnal desire. You will hate these boys with all of your being, then fall in love with them so hard you'll forget how to breathe.

This book will destroy your heart. But it will also stitch it back together piece by piece.

I will ask you to trust me.

I promise you it is worth the fall.

And if you won't surrender willingly ... well, these devilish boys will definitely drag you down to their degenerate, hedonistic hell and claim your heart anyway.

Because you don't like villains who ask nicely.

You like villains who make you beg.

NOTE: Vile Boys takes place on the same timeline as Evil Boys. Both books can be read as a standalone.

TW/CW for Vile Boys can be found here:
https://www.clarissawild.com/vileboys-tw/

PROLOGUE

Crystal

"You will take all of me, every piercing and every throbbing inch," Ares groans, slowly lowering me onto his length. "And when I am done with you, *they* will have their way with you."

I glance down at Caleb and Blaine, as their two tongues roll around us both, their fingers flicking across my most sensitive spots.

But it is Ares's grip on my body that turns me meek.

"Everyone will see, and everyone will know what a filthy girl you are," Ares whispers. "And you will do it all for me."

I can't think, can't even breathe as these boys, these killers, drive me to the edge of insanity.

Each touch, each kiss, each thrust makes me stray further and further into their depraved claws.

"Because you're my fucking good girl, aren't you?" Ares murmurs as he sinks deeper into me until my entire body begins to shiver. "Say it."

Even if I denied it, I know deep down in my heart it's true.

I never imagined I would willingly give myself to killers like them. These boys have corrupted every inch of my heart until nothing but sweet, delicious hatred was left.

Hatred for how badly I want them to own me.

So let it fucking flow.

"I'm your good girl."

I can feel him smile against my ear as my eyes nearly roll into the back of my head. "Now let your God take you to purgatory."

Someday, they will know my wrath.

Even if I want to beg them to use me, even if I crave nothing more than their fingers on my slit while being denied over and over, even when I come so hard I can feel myself ascending into heaven … *hatred* is the only thing I'll carry with me.

To the end.

ONE

Crystal

The roses on the bushes next to me shimmer in the eerie lights dancing in the sky above. The dew drops on their leaves fall to the ground as I walk through the maze, wondering why my heart pounds like I'm slowly headed toward death.

Electric lanterns are all I have to light my path, but the music guides my way through the maze as I focus on the noise.

When I make a left turn, a ton of people dance in a small courtyard in the middle of the maze. People are strewn all across the path, leading up to a gloomy-looking house almost entwined with nature. The branches of several invasive trees almost run through the building, and the roof is so pointy it makes me want to shiver. If evil built a house, that's what I'd imagine it would look like.

Suddenly, someone's hands lock onto my shoulders from behind. "Crystal! You made it!"

Just as I spin around in my heels, Kayla hugs me tight.

"It's so dark and gloomy here," I say.

"I know! Isn't it perfect?" She's glowing right now.

I look around at the decorated trees and bushes, the expensive outdoor furniture all across the courtyard, and the food, which looks

7

like it was made by a Michelin-star restaurant.

"They've poured in a lot of work," I say.

"Tartarus always throws extravagant parties. Or so I've been told. I've never actually been invited to one … up till now." She squeals with excitement.

"How did we even get an invite to this party?" I ask.

Suddenly, Penelope throws her arms around my shoulders. "Perks of having friends in high places."

"Nice to see you finally made it," I say, winking.

"So Felix got us in?" Kayla asks her.

"Dylan. One of these guys is an old friend of his. I don't know who, and I don't care. As long as I don't have to ever associate with any of them, I'm good."

"What do you mean?" I ask.

Kayla leans in. "Tartarus guys are dangerous. More than the Phantoms because they don't even care who they do business with as long as it gets them more money and fame. Good guys, bad guys, they don't differentiate. I don't trust them." She grabs my shoulders and turns me around. "Look. There they are." She points at three boys standing on the balcony.

One is as tall as can be, with long black hair with a soft curl in it, who looks like he just stepped out of a haircare commercial. He's clutching a glass of champagne as he stares off into the distance with that God-like chiseled face of his, thin lips smiling arrogantly, like he knows everyone thinks he's handsome as hell.

Another one grips the banister behind him tightly as he chats away with someone inside the house, while his other hand runs through his undercut and dark blond hair. His cheerful demeanor and upturned grin complete with lip piercing are in stark contrast to all the scary tattoos marking his skin.

The last one stands with his back toward us, his black hair styled in a comb-over, arms casually draped over two girls like they're his entourage. And even though I see the least of this guy, he has a certain threatening aura around him, like he could turn around and choke the life out of those girls if they said a single thing that displeased him.

"Ares." Kayla points at the one with the two girls and the black, comb-over hair. "Caleb." The heavily tattooed one with the blond hair. "Blaine." The one with the long, flowing hair who looks like he just stepped out of a commercial. "ABC. That's what some people here call them because they're always together, but I prefer devils from hell."

Penelope snorts. "Appropriate."

"Right?" Kayla says. "People don't just join Tartarus for the fun of it. They're literal demons." She looks up at them standing on the balcony and whispers, "If you interfered with their plans, they would make you beg to forget it ever happened."

I gulp.

I'm starting to think coming here was a bad idea.

"Ahhh, don't worry." Penelope throws her arm around my shoulders and tugs me away from Kayla. "They won't bother with us if we just dance and have fun. So are you two up for some drinks?"

Someone turns up the music even louder, and the crowd behind us bursts into cheers. The music fills my bones with excitement, and my limbs move automatically to the rhythm.

"I wanna dance!" I say as I throw Penelope's arm off me and drag them to the dance floor. "C'mon!"

Dancing like this makes me feel like I'm floating to the moon, so I let myself go on the beat, dancing away like a girl high on drugs, but I don't care what I look like. I just wanna have unbridled fun and turn off my brain so I don't have to think anymore.

"God, I'm getting thirsty," Penelope yells over the music after a while. "Anyone wanna grab some drinks from that table over there?"

She points at the table filled with delicate bites and small drink glasses.

"Sure, let's see what's on the menu." Kayla rubs her hands together like she's hungry.

But when I look at the table near the door to the house, those three boys walk out, and my blood runs icy cold. On Ares's shoes is an emblem of fire and horns, and my mind stops working for a moment. Images of blood splatters on the pavement and fire mix into one, and then disappear a second later.

I swallow.

"I'm gonna stay here and vibe to the music some more," I tell the girls, clearing my throat. "I don't wanna stop dancing. You go ahead."

Kayla and Penelope nod and head to the table, and when they're out of sight, I turn around and walk toward the same pebble path

9

those boys just headed down through the rose maze. The path goes all the way around the house to the front, where a gate blocks out anyone who dares to step inside.

The three guys standing on this side instantly make my heart pump faster. Their ominous figures cast a shadow on the road behind the gate, and one of them clearly carries a weapon.

"You know who we are," one of the guys behind the gates says.

"We don't care," Caleb growls, running his fingers across his undercut and through his dark blond hair.

"Let. Us. In," the other guy says, and he flashes a gun behind his coat.

"How about …" Blaine replies, swooping his long, dark hair over his shoulder. "No."

"Fine."

The guy pulls out his weapon.

BANG!

He shoots off the lock with his silenced gun, and the three boys jump back to avoid the shot.

"Motherfucker," Caleb yells, enraged. "You fucking shot at us!"

The gunman kicks open the doors straight into the boys.

"Move!" one of them shouts as they barge right through the boys like they don't exist.

I should run.

As fast as I can, far away from here, before anyone sees me standing here.

But when the middle one of the three boys turns around, I feel frozen to the ground. Eyes gray and devoid of life, a face with features so sharp it could split mountains, and soulless pupils burning into the men's backs as they run toward me. Pure, unfiltered rage hides deep inside, fueled by something far greater than just the intrusion into his domain. And it makes my heart pick up in fear.

Ares.

"Over my dead body," he growls, his voice low and just as deadly as the gun he pulls out of nowhere.

BANG! BANG!

Two silenced shots. One blink.

My hand immediately slams into my mouth.

Just one blink between me and the one guy who lived a sliver of a second longer than the other. They both sink to the ground, bullet holes in their heads.

Oh my God.

"I guess they got it coming for them," Caleb says, biting the piercing in his lip.

"Did you have to do that?" Blaine says as he stares down at the bodies.

"When you send a message, you send a clear one," Ares says, his voice still void of any emotion.

But then he raises his head.

Piercing, haunting gray eyes stare straight into mine.

I swiftly turn and run as fast as I can.

I don't know where I'm going. I just know I need to get out of here.

I go through the rose bushes and into the maze. But panic seeps into my veins the second I come across the courtyard. Any of these guys could be from Tartarus. If they realize what I saw ...

I can't risk it.

Bypassing the courtyard, I head straight into the other side of the maze up ahead, my heart racing in my throat. I keep running, despite the fear creeping further and further into my veins, crippling my muscles.

An overgrown path up ahead narrows quite a bit, but I still push through, desperate to get as far away from the scene as I can. But when I misstep, I fall sideways into the prickly roses.

"Ow!" I groan, retracting my arm covered in cuts from the thorns.

I rub my arm and face, smearing some of the blood on my dress before I continue. But the second I make a left turn, I come to an abrupt halt in front of a crossing.

Right as three guys approach from the left.

The same three guys I just saw murder two people in cold blood.

Ares. Blaine. Caleb.

Their stride is so frigid it makes my entire body shiver. I'm frozen to the ground as they come closer, unable to move a muscle except that damn heart of mine that beats uncontrollably fast.

I can't even breathe.

It's as though Ares's rage controls my very soul with one piercing look, and I'm merely a puppet dancing to his command.

Caleb and Blaine move right past me without even throwing me a glance, the cold breeze that follows them making my blond hair drift in the wind.

But I notice too late that Ares has stopped right in front of me. He towers over my petite four-foot-nine-inch frame. He must be at least six feet and seven inches, if not more.

He takes a step closer, and I can literally feel the electricity zing through the air.

He's a killer.

My eyes flick to the gun glinting in his belt buckle.

Take it. Steal it. Use it. Make him pay.

But my body refuses to move.

His hand rises to touch my face, and my eyes widen in shock. On his thumb is a single droplet of blood, which he inspects like it's made of gold.

When his eyes connect with mine, a slow but docile smile spreads on my lips.

An actual smile.

I can't look away from those haunting gray eyes sparkling with curiosity, even if I wanted to. Caleb and Blaine have stopped a few feet away and watch him with keen interest.

Ares's eyes twitch and narrow as they lock in on my smile, and he aggressively wipes his finger on his sleeve and walks off, following the boys back to the party in the courtyard.

But I can still feel the prickle of his thorns.

***

ARES

I clutch my cup filled with vodka as I stare at the partygoers dancing away while I'm casually draped over my seat. But the people in front of me are like shimmers in a dream, fading into the back of my mind.

My thoughts have drifted off along with them, possessed by a certain blond-haired girl in a little beige lace dress with bloodied cuts all over her skin. A girl who watched me kill.

I let her run.

I watched those little feet dash off into the darkness beyond the maze, awakening the violent animal caged inside me.

Something about that soft face with plump cheeks like apples made me want to sink my teeth into her and taste her sweetness.

God, I wanted nothing more than to chase her all the way through the entire fucking maze and make her scream. Become the force of terror everyone sees me as.

Until I saw that smile.

That sweet, innocent pink-lipped smile that could make a man fall to his knees and beg.

I take a sip of my vodka, but the alcohol does nothing to quench my rage.

I've never hated anything more in my life ...

Until I saw that fucking smile.

No one fucking *smiles* at me.

Especially not after they just witnessed me kill.

And she fucking *smiles*?

My fingers dig into the glass so harshly it breaks underneath their strength, shattering into a million pieces onto my lap.

People look at me like I've lost my damn mind.

"Are you okay?" Caleb asks. "Dude?"

But I don't even care if I'm bleeding.

All I can think about is how I'm going to crush that smile ... and destroy that girl.

TWO

Crystal

Later that week

In class, I can barely focus on what the teacher's trying to say. I hear his words, but they go in one ear and out the other, and the words on the board in front of me are a jumbled mess in my mind.

I close my eyes to take a breath, but all I see are those piercing gray eyes staring back at me.

I swallow away the lump in my throat and look at my mobile phone to check the time. I feel like I'm a sitting duck, waiting to be hunted and killed.

I can't stop thinking about what I saw.

Ares saw me. I know he did.

So why didn't he confront me?

He didn't even say a word. Even though I know he must've seen my guilt-ridden expression when he brushed that droplet of blood off my face.

It's almost as if he was … taunting me.

They killed those two men like it meant nothing.

And now I can't help but wonder … what will those boys do to their only witness?

***

I scroll down on my laptop, taking in all the information I can find on those boys. Blaine Navarro's whole existence revolves around some kind of dojo. Apparently, he's a black belt and teaches people next to his college studies, but I don't know what kind of martial arts or what it even means.

Then there's Caleb Preston, whose father is a successful businessman, but in every photo, Caleb looks miserable. And his mother is nowhere to be seen.

"Hey, what's up?"

The sudden intrusion makes me slam my laptop closed real quick.

Brooke, my friend from a different sorority, sits down beside me. "Wait, were you looking at someone's profile?" Her eyes glitter with interest.

"No one in particular. Just some old friends," I lie.

Her eyes narrow. "Sure." She places her hand on my shoulder. "You don't have to lie to me. I recognized Caleb Preston."

My eyes widen. "Shhh. Don't say it out loud."

"Wait, don't tell me you have a crush on him?" She makes a concerned face.

Blood drains from my face. "No."

She giggles. "I won't tell a soul, promise."

"I don't!"

Her smirk only grows bigger. "Want me to introduce you to him?"

"Ladies. Keep it quiet, please," the librarian calls to us.

Brooke hides her face behind her hand and whispers, "Oops. My fault."

"Hey guys, care if I study with you?" Kayla asks as she smacks her books down on the table right beside me.

"Sure, no problem," I reply, hoping it'll keep Brooke from asking more questions.

"Don't think we've met before," Brooke says, and they shake hands. "Brooke."

"Kayla, I'm her friend."

"Same." Brooke smiles. "We met at a party during summer break."

Kayla pulls out a chair. "Oh, so you're the girl who taught her how to drink."

"Oh God." I bury my face in my hands.

"What? That's a good thing." Kayla bumps into me with her hips. "You need to relax more."

"Exactly what I said," Brooke says, getting up and packing her things. "But anyway, I have a class soon. See you later, okay?"

I wave as she walks off. "See ya!"

Kayla sits down and opens her books. "You know, I heard the Phantom Society is having a party soon."

I put my laptop away. "So?"

"Wanna go together?"

I sigh. I really don't want to put myself in more danger.

She smiles and jerks my arm. "C'mon. It'll be fun."

When she puts it like that, it's hard to say no.

"Fine, fine, I'll come," I whisper.

"Yay," she says with a grin. But when she glances over her shoulder and spots an angry librarian ready to kick us out, she says, "Sorry! We'll be quiet now."

***

CALEB

I chuck my bag on the table in the hallway and make my way to the common room. "Man, I'm beat."

"I don't know, Father, figure it out," Ares barks into his phone before he ends the convo.

I throw myself onto the couch and lean back, snatching some peanuts out of a bowl on the side table.

"What was that all about?"

He places his phone in front of him on the table and stares at it for a moment, and I can tell shit's not going good at all.

"Doesn't matter," Ares says.

"Well, obviously it does, since you're already brooding over just one phone call," I retort, throwing more peanuts into my mouth.

"I ask for help. Once. Just one time. And he gives me shit." His nostrils flare. "And he wonders why I don't wanna come to the family dinners." He leans back and slams his hands into the armrests of his seat. "Fuck."

"Help … as in …?"

He stares me down with that chilling glare of his. "Bodies."

I swallow my peanuts. "Right. Those."

"I thought those were already taken care of?" Blaine asks, striding in with flair. "Ares?"

"I'm working on it," he says.

My eyes widen. "Wait, don't tell me they're still in the freezer outside."

"Where I keep my ice cream?" Blaine scowls. "Ew."

"Stop complaining," Ares growls. "Unless you have a better idea."

"I'll have to throw out that whole tub of perfect chocolate goodness," Blaine whines, rubbing his forehead.

Ares tilts his head at him. "Shall I put the bodies in your bedroom instead?"

I almost choke on my handful of peanuts. "Oh my God."

"On second thought, you can have the ice cream," Blaine murmurs, throwing his hair to the side. "My stomach can't handle all that dairy anyway."

"Fragile," I joke.

"Darling, I prefer it when my ass doesn't squirt, unlike yours."

"Fuck you," I retort.

Blaine tilts his head. "You asked for it." He winks at me, and we both laugh.

"Is something funny about this whole situation?" Ares asks, all serious, clutching the armrests like he's going to rip them off. "Because I don't get it."

"Oh, lighten up," Blaine murmurs, approaching him from behind. "You've been far too tense ever since that party." Blaine massages Ares's shoulders. "Relax. Throw it out. Kiss a girl. Fuck it out of your system. And then let's do what we do best."

"Fuck shit up? Kill people?" I say.

Blaine looks up at me. "Well, I was going to say party, but I guess that could work."

I throw some peanuts at him, and he catches them with his mouth. "Good one."

"I know I'm a catch, darling, thank you," Blaine muses.

"Jesus, you're so annoying," I say, laughing.

Ares shoves Blaine's hands off his shoulders and gets up.

"Enough."

"What is going on in that mind of yours?" Blaine asks.

Ares approaches the window, staring out at the front gate. "We weren't alone that night."

I stop eating immediately. "What?"

"When I killed those dudes at the front gate … There was a girl. Just for a moment. But I know she saw me kill."

I swallow, but my throat feels raw.

Fuck.

If he's right, this could get ugly real fast.

"A girl from this university?"

He nods, still staring outside like he's waiting for her to reappear.

"We actually crossed paths when we went back to the party again," he adds.

"Wait …" Blaine narrows his eyes. "That girl with the beige dress who made you stop?"

Ares turns. "So you saw her too."

"I wasn't sure," he says, folding his arms. "I figured you just got enamored by her beauty. I mean, she did look like an angelic deity in that dress."

"She watched us murder two men, and you let her go?!" I shout at Ares.

"What was he supposed to do?" Blaine raises his brow at me. "Kill her too?"

I wasn't going to suggest it, but now we have an additional liability.

"She was bleeding," Ares mutters, rubbing his fingers together like he's savoring the memory of her blood on his skin. "And for some reason, she smiled at me. It threw me off guard."

My lips part. "Smiled? She *smiled*? At you?" I snort, biting my piercing. "Why do I find that hard to believe?"

"Do you think I'd lie?" he grits at me, making me shut up immediately.

"No, of course not."

Usually, girls pretty much run away from him the second he even so much as looks at them. He's definitely got this killer aura that rarely anyone dares to come close to. Except maybe a handful of fearless girls who crave it because he has two of the most valued things in this world. Money and a big dick.

But never just because they enjoy his company. So I get why it would bother him that the girl who actually saw him kill two people would smile at him.

"Did you catch her name?"

Ares shakes his head. "But we'll find out soon enough."

"Do you think she'll tell?" Blaine asks.

It takes him a while to answer, but when he does, a chill runs through my veins. "Most definitely."

"We gotta stop her," I reply.

"Hold up, if we go after someone from this university, this will not end well," Blaine says, approaching Ares. "We cannot risk our already precarious position after those killings here on Tartarus ground. If there's another body ..."

"I know," Ares replies. "Which is why I'll need you two to help me."

I bite my lip piercing and drag it into my mouth. "You're scheming."

Blaine's smile stretches from ear to ear. "Tell me more."

Ares throws us a glance over his shoulder. "We can't kill her. It's too risky."

"But ...?" I lean forward, eagerly anticipating his next words.

His eyes flash with excitement. "We can make her regret she ever looked."

"Oh ... make her fear us," I say, rubbing my hands together. "I like that."

"But how do we find her if we don't know her name?" Blaine asks.

"There's a party at the Phantom house in a couple of days," I say.

They both look at me like they're wondering why I'm even mentioning it.

"I saw the girl talk with Nathan the other day," I add. "They might be friends. Maybe he dropped her name, and I just can't remember?"

Ares suddenly rushes at me, jabbing his finger into my chest. "Pry it out of him."

"Wow. Calm down, darling," Blaine says, placing a hand on his shoulder. "We're all friends here. No one's your enemy in this house."

Ares's nose twitches, but he does pull away, and I finally feel like I

19

can breathe again.

"If Nathan invites her, she'll definitely be there," I tell him.

"Good." He grabs his jacket off the chair and throws it over his shoulder. "Then we'll be there too, waiting until she's all alone …" His fist clenches. "And drowning in fear at the thought of crossing us."

THREE

Crystal

"You made it!" Nathan hugs me tight, barely clutching his glass enough not to spill it over my pink dress.

"I didn't even realize it was you," I mutter. "These white masks make it so hard to recognize anyone."

He pulls away and winks. "It adds a bit of flair, don't you think?"

I smile. "I suppose it does. I should've guessed this would be your theme, considering the name of your frat house."

He smirks. "Phantom kinda gives it away, don't you think?"

He throws his arm over my shoulder and points at all the rooms. "That's where the drinks are, and that's the kitchen. You can get fabulous homemade sushi there, courtesy of our amazing in-house cook."

Someone clears their throat behind me. "Milo. Just say Milo." The guy with the lanky frame and red hair sticks his hands into his pockets, sporting a mischievous grin. "And if you want, I can even make them fresh on the spot for a beautiful lady like yourself."

He attempts to grab my hand, but Nathan swiftly pulls it away so he can't reach it.

"Not her."

"What? I wasn't doing anything."

Nathan lifts his brow. "Of course, you weren't."

Milo shrugs and walks off, waving. "Have fun at the party, Crystal!"

"Thanks," I tell him. "How does he know my name?"

"My boys know who I'm friends with," Nathan replies. "We don't keep secrets from each other."

"Admirable."

"Anyway, where was I? Right, the dance floor is right through that door in front of you. And upstairs are some bathrooms you can use if you need them. That's about it." He pats my back. "Anyhow, I gotta run. Text me if you need anything!"

I wave as he runs up the staircase, and I take a breath before I start looking around. The place is so crowded, I don't even know where to start. I was still indecisive about whether I should even come tonight because of what happened the last time I went to a party. Plus, I still have a ton of studying to do. But Kayla practically begged me to come, and I can't say no to her.

I pull out my phone and text her.

Me: Where are you?

It takes her a while to reply.

Kayla: Dance floor! Purple dress. Hard to miss.

Me: I'm wearing a pink dress. Wave if you see me.

My scarf slowly pulls off my shoulder, but I swiftly pull it back up so it stays put, and I walk toward the dance floor. The whole place teems with people, and the music booms through the speakers.

I look around to see if I can find Kayla, and when I see a raised hand waving at me, I grin and walk over.

"Crystal!" She hugs me. "I was already wondering where you were. I'm glad you came. It wouldn't be a party without you." She grabs my hand and pulls me back to the dance floor. "Now c'mon, let's dance."

***

CALEB

I sit on a chair in the back of the dance floor next to a masked guy wearing a suit, but I know exactly who it is.

Nathan Reed, Phantom and definitely one of the organizers of this party.

He immediately sighs out loud. "What are you doing?"

Apparently, I'm easy to recognize too. "Sitting down next to you. Is that a problem?"

He throws me a glance. "Yes."

"Why?"

"We're not friends anymore."

"But we were. We could be."

"Not interested."

"What do I have to do to make it up to you?"

"Ask Ares," he growls, taking a sip of his drink.

I sigh out loud too and look around the room until I finally spot her dancing with a friend. A cheerful smile adorns her sharp face, blond hair sweeping back and forth across her shoulders, her thighs almost in perfect ratio to her ample breasts hiding in that pink dress of hers, and for a moment, I'm struck in awe at her beauty.

I totally understand why Ares wants to play with her.

"Are you staring?" Nathan mutters, pulling me out of my thoughts.

"No," I retort.

"Yeah, you are." He snorts.

"I was just wondering who she was. That's all."

"Crystal Murphy. She's a friend." He leans forward and glares at me, flashing a knife in his pocket. "Stay away from her."

My eyes narrow at his warning, which I intend to fully ignore. "Do you think a knife is gonna make me listen?"

A smirk slowly spreads on his lips as he retracts his knife again and pulls his hand from his pocket. "You never fuckin' listen."

"Nope," I retort, smiling right back at him. "But I'll leave her alone."

For now.

"Good. She's too innocent for you anyway," he adds.

"Innocent?" My brow rises.

"Yeah. Doesn't hurt a fly. Doesn't deserve to get her heart crushed by the likes of you." He tilts his head at me. "I know what you and those other Tartarus guys can do to people."

I thrust an imaginary dagger into my own heart. "Wow."

"I'm just saying … you hurt her, I'll hurt you back." He winks, then gets up and saunters off through the crowd.

But I keep my gaze fixated on the blond-haired girl with the bubbly smile. Because that smile hides a dirty, dark secret … and I will make sure she doesn't tell anyone.

As she twirls, her beautiful green eyes briefly make contact with mine, and I suck in a breath, mesmerized by her beauty, until I remember she saw us murder two people.

And judging from the way she narrows her eyes at me, she hasn't forgotten.

That's right, Crystal.

We'll be here, watching you, always listening, always waiting.

Waiting until you slip up.

Waiting until you part those pretty lips and spill our filthy secrets.

Waiting … so we can swallow you whole.

***

Crystal

For a moment, I'm taken aback by the stranger in the seat, staring at me like he wants to rip this dress right off my body, but then Kayla grabs my hand and drags me into the middle of the dance floor, and I've forgotten all about him.

We dance against each other, bumping asses, showing off, and sure enough, some guys start watching our moves. Kayla loves the attention. Me, not so much, but I'll happily assist in making her shine. I'm not here for boys, though. I'm just here to take my mind off an upcoming test … and two dead bodies.

I gulp and spin around so we're butt to butt, but when my eyes connect with two haunting gray eyes hiding behind a white mask near the door, I pause.

Streaks of black hair peek out from above the mask. With that casual white button-up with two loose buttons that barely cover his muscular pecs and a pair of tight black pants, he draws all the attention of the girls around him.

But he doesn't seem to notice any of them looking except me.

My blood feels like it's gone icy cold.

It's him.

"C'mon, dance with me." Kayla grabs me and twirls me around.

By the time I can finally look back, he's already gone.

Shit, where did he go?

I unfurl myself from Kayla's grip and stumble over my own dress, but she catches me before I slip and fall.

"Whoa, you okay?"

"Yeah, just got a little dizzy there," I murmur, laughing it off like it's no big deal. "I think I'm just gonna go get some fresh air."

"All right, I'll come with you."

"No, no, you stay and dance. I'll be fine," I say, stepping away.

"You sure?" she asks, concerned.

"Yeah, yeah, go dance. I'll be right back," I reply before I disappear into the crowd.

The music blasts in my ear, but my senses feel numb.

Like I've just been confronted with saying the biggest lie.

But I couldn't possibly tell her the truth about what really made me sweat. I don't want to put her in danger if Ares comes after me. And those deep-set, devilish eyes told me enough with a single glance—he's coming for me.

***

ARES

The moment I crossed the doorstep, I knew I'd found her.

That curly blond hair and those pinkish lips along with those stunning green eyes instantly gave it away.

She's the girl I've been looking for, the one who saw me kill.

The second our eyes connected, her entire body tensed up, and my cock stirred into action at the thought of trapping her on that dance floor and forcing her to come with me.

God, the amount of fun I could have chasing an innocent girl like her ... making her fear me and erase that wretched smile off her face.

Suddenly, someone grips my shoulders and pulls me back away from the dance floor and into a wall. By the time I process what's happened, I'm about ready to gut them like a fish until I realize who it is.

"Kai?" I growl, throwing his hands off my shoulders.

"So it is you. Thought I'd recognized that awful stench of your ego," he says, smirking.

"Fuck you," I spit back, jerking my shoulders free. "Don't touch me."

He holds up his hands. "Relax. I'm just trying to talk."

"About what?" I bark back.

"You haven't been replying to any of my messages."

"Intentionally," I reply.

"Figured," he retorts, snorting. "Look, I don't know what the hell your deal is, but I'm gonna need you to stop. Too much is at stake here. Put whatever shit you're holding against me behind you, please."

"Not even thinking about it," I say, leaning back against the wall so I can keep an eye on the door in case she walks out.

"What is your fucking problem?" Kai growls. "You know I need your help, and you're blatantly ignoring it."

"Deal with your own shit," I say, glaring over his shoulder. "I have better things to do than help you and these Phantoms fight some imaginary enemy."

"Look at me. Is this how you're going to treat me?" he says, tilting his head. "You can't even look at me when we're talking."

"Not if I can avoid it."

"Fine. Fucking hate me, whatever, but I'm not the one who'll suffer if you don't help," he says, pointing his finger at my chest as if I'm the problem here. "You came here into my fucking territory to enjoy my fucking party. The least you can do is return the favor when I ask for help."

"Fine. You want me to leave?" I raise a brow as I push myself off the wall to get up in his face. "Because I'm fucking fine with that. Don't worry."

"No, I'm not saying that," he says. "I'm just saying, I help you out, you help me out."

"Since when have you *ever* helped me?"

His lips part, but he doesn't respond as quickly as before, which means he doesn't know the answer.

Checkmate.

"Thought so," I quip, and I move past him.

"Nathan's going to be destroyed if you don't help," he says, his voice all serious.

I pause and think about it for a moment. "Your guy ... not mine."

"So you'd let a fellow student die?" he adds.

I swallow. "If that's the lesson, then so be it."

And I walk off, leaving him seething with rage.

But I don't care. His emotions do nothing to me. They haven't for a long while.

Brushing it off, I walk back to the dance floor, but to my surprise, her friend is alone, and she's nowhere in sight.

Where did she run off to?

I look around at the couples in the hallways smooching, but none of them are her. I'm obsessed with finding this girl.

"Ares." Caleb's voice makes me stop in my tracks as he whispers into my ear from the side. "Her name is Crystal Murphy."

A devilish grin spreads on my face.

Of course, it is.

Crystal fucking Murphy.

Such an innocent name for such an innocent girl …

It's a pity I'll have to destroy her.

"Thank you," I reply.

"She's out on the terrace beyond the kitchen," he adds.

My tongue darts out to wet my lips. "I'll deal with her."

I walk through the crowd toward the kitchen. Another door at the other end is wide open, so I head out. There's a small fenced-up stone terrace with seats, and the music is still audible out here, albeit far less loud.

But the one thing that makes me pause is the girl in the pink dress, staring off into the distance like she's waiting for a certain someone to come and whisk her away.

A wicked smile forms on my lips.

There she is.

FOUR

Crystal

I take a deep breath and close my eyes to calm my unsteady heart. It's dark outside anyway, so there's nothing to see. Just a few minutes away from the dance floor is all I need to calm down.

Suddenly, a hand snakes around my waist, and all the adrenaline comes flooding right back in.

"Are you afraid of death?"

My eyes burst open at the sound of his voice.

It's him.

My body tightens as he moves closer, my fingers thrumming against the pocket in my dress, where I keep the small knife I've always brought everywhere since that night.

"You know who I am, don't you?" he whispers into my ear, breath lingering near my skin, creating goose bumps all over. "Say my name."

An air of darkness slowly envelops me.

"Ares." His name rolls off my tongue like I'm summoning a demon from hell.

"Good girl. So you've heard what people say about me." He grabs a strand of my hair and lifts it. "Yet you still smiled at me. Why?"

"Why … I smiled?" I'm flabbergasted that this is the question he'd ask.

"You've seen what I'm capable of. Why aren't you terrified?"

I suck in a breath through my teeth, staying put despite his looming presence towering over me. "I don't break for anyone."

I've been broken too many times to let anyone shatter me again.

His fingers dig deeper into my dress. "We'll see about that."

I stick my hand into my pocket and grasp the handle of my knife.

"You can't kill me in front of all these people," I mutter, sweat drops trickling down my back.

I can hear him snort away a laugh. "You think I want to kill you?"

"You killed those men," I whisper.

It's out there now.

"I did kill them."

How he so easily admits to it makes my blood boil.

"Aren't you going to ask me why?"

I bite my lip, wondering what I should say. Every word feels like a maze, and each answer leads into his carefully laid out trap. "Does it change the outcome?"

There's a pause. "You have a way with words."

I grasp the banister of the terrace, ready to kick back. "And you destroy people because of the words they speak."

"Don't pretend to know my business," he says. "I don't think you understand what it takes to lead the Tartarus House. But I do."

A knife suddenly prods into my waist, making my heart jump.

"You know my secret. But I'm not here to kill you, Crystal."

My jaw drops.

How does he know my name?

"I don't want you to die. Not this sweet, innocent soul who smiled so happily at a killer." He plays with my hair, coiling it around his finger like I'm a shiny, new toy to play with. "No, what I want is something far more sinister."

I hold my breath to stop his blade from piercing my skin.

"Your fear."

I can't breathe. Can't swallow. Can't even flinch without feeling the tip of his knife bore into me. But I will never give him the thing he wants most.

His free hand trails a line from my neck all the way down to where my dress covers my breasts, and when he hovers over it, I grasp his

29

hand.

"Oh ... so the little innocent girl does have some bite to her," he murmurs. "Good. A chase isn't fun without a challenge."

The knife pushes farther into my skin with each passing second, as if he's taunting me to see how far I'll take it, until I can no longer hold his wrist. The moment I let go, the knife stops digging into me, and I let out a breath.

"Good choice," he murmurs into my ear.

His hand lingers near my chest, electricity humming between us like he's testing the waters, seeing how easily I'll bend to his will. Just like everyone else in his world.

I should stab him. Thrust this knife into his cold, detached heart. He deserves it.

But then his lips suddenly come down on my neck, and all my thoughts of murder dissipate.

I'm frozen to the ground as his lips freely roam my skin, planting kisses wherever he goes, and I can barely breathe.

"You taste as sweet as you look," he murmurs, his heady voice luring me into the abyss with him. "I wonder if your blood does too."

His teeth sink into my flesh, and a strangled cry escapes my mouth, the sound blocked by his hand, which swiftly moves to cover it.

What the hell? He actually bit my shoulder.

His teeth retract, and my skin surges with blood and pain, but when his lips cover the wound, I gasp. His tongue dips out to lick the blood, kissing my skin before he licks his lips against my ear.

"Sweet as fucking sin."

He's sick. Completely deranged, and—

"Don't scream. Unless you want this knife to make you bleed too," he whispers, the tip of his knife reminding me of my precarious situation. "And I will certainly lick the blood off the blade as well."

"You're insane," I murmur when he finally removes his hand.

"Insane ... perhaps." His hand moves down my neck. "Or perhaps you just haven't seen anything of this world yet."

His hand dips into my dress from the top where he cups my naked breast and squeezes.

"Perhaps you haven't experienced enough of it yet to differentiate between pleasure ..."

I suck in a breath to stop the moan from spilling out when he pinches my nipple between his index finger and thumb and rolls it around.

"And pain."

He pinches it so hard I bite my tongue. "F-fuck."

"Ah-ah. Quiet," he whispers, pushing the tip of the knife into my side. "Or I will have to cut our little bout of titillation short."

"Titillation?" I squeak. "This feels more like, like…"

My train of thought is interrupted by each twist he applies, as it's sending currents of arousal straight to my pussy.

What is happening? Why am I letting him do this to me?

"Like you want to submit?" he says.

He pulls his hand out, only to slide it down my dress and creep in underneath. Within seconds, he's reached my panties, and he slides them aside with ease.

"Have you ever been touched by a god?"

"What?" I mutter, confused.

But then his fingers slide across my slit, and I'm as much at a loss of words as I am at a loss of my thoughts.

Ares actually slides his fingers down my slit underneath my dress.

Right in front of everyone on this terrace.

"Wait," I mutter, feeling delirious with need.

But he doesn't stop. "Why? Afraid someone will see you squirm from my fingers?"

Shit. He's trying to get me to feel the fear. I won't let him.

He swirls his fingers around like he knows exactly what he's doing, carefully avoiding the most sensitive spot like he wants to coax the pleasure out of me. And something about that makes me clench the knife in my pocket so harshly I worry the handle might break.

"I know you're thinking of using that knife on me. It won't stop me."

What? How does he know?

"I can feel your hand tensing around the handle."

I immediately loosen my grip.

"And I will definitely use it against you if you try."

"How?"

His knife pokes into my belly. "You bringing a knife here makes for an awfully good story when people suddenly find you stabbed, wouldn't it?"

I stay frozen to the floor, unsure what to do. But his fingers, good

31

God, those fingers will be the death of me before his blade ever punctures my skin.

He swirls around, wetness pooling between my legs as I struggle not to moan. But he's listening, waiting for the moment I cave in, and I don't want to give it to him. All I can do is accept and let the pleasure slowly take over while my mind spins in circles, trying to make sense of all this hatred and lust mixing into one.

I can't call for help. If he hears so much as a single word, he'll kill me just like he did those men and use his charms to persuade people it was all self-inflicted.

He slides back and forth, stopping right before he hits my clit, almost like he's avoiding it on purpose, and I'm on the edge of just begging him to do it.

What is wrong with me?

"Go on, then … make a sound. I dare you," he whispers, turning up the heat, fingers splaying before they dive straight in.

I gasp in shock when he enters me, feeling me up. Not just because of his sudden invasion but also because of the wetness that pours out of me.

"You're so wet for me already," he says, grinning against my skin. "You don't stand a chance."

"Fuck you," I grit, trying to ignore the lust flooding my mind.

"Are you angry with me?" he muses, thrusting in a finger and keeping it there as if to remind me of the fact that he can do anything he wants to me as long as his knife pokes into my skin. "Or angry at how good it feels when I pet your little pussy?"

"You want me to hate you?" I hiss through my teeth. "Job done."

A low, rumbling laugh emanates from deep within his chest.

"You think I will settle for that?" he groans, circling around inside me. "Oh no, I want you on your knees, begging for a break from the terror I will instill in your heart at the thought of being owned by me."

He thrusts in another finger, making me swallow a mewl, and I clutch the banister of the terrace with both hands now to keep steady so I don't fall.

"I refuse," I mutter, as he keeps on filling me with his fingers until I'm dizzy with mounting arousal. "I will never give you what you want."

He pulls out his fingers, leaving me bereft, wanting something I shouldn't.

His fingers slide up and down achingly slow, lulling me into complacency with his groans close to my ear as his body leans into mine. His cock hardens against me, thick and long as it prods into my ass, and I can't ever imagine it being inside me.

"I beg to differ, Ambrosía," he groans.

Ambrosía? What does that even mean?

I can't focus on his words because of what he's doing to me.

Right as the pad of his thumb touches my clit, his lips cover the wound on my shoulder, and he bites down again, his teeth even more painful than before. And fuck me, I can't differentiate between the mounting pain and the aching pleasure between my legs as he slowly circles around my clit, making me want to squeeze my legs together.

But the moment I flinch, there's that knife again, reminding me of my place.

Knock his teeth out.

Kick him.

Punch him.

Stab him with his own knife.

Beg for more.

Every violent thought coursing through my head is replaced by desire with each stroke of his fingers.

His tongue dips out once more, circling the fresh wound, sucking up the blood as his fingers go faster and faster. And it's becoming harder and harder to hold on. To resist. To exist without wantonness.

Too late.

"See how wet you are for me?" he whispers into my ear. "Even when I hurt you, you still want for nothing more than to come on my fingers right now."

"F-fuck," I groan, unable to keep the moan from slipping out too. "Why are you doing this?"

"You call me insane, yet you're the one driven to insanity," he muses.

"Toying with me isn't going to make me fear you," I say, breathing heavy breaths to try to keep the orgasm at bay.

"You think fear can only be achieved through terror and violence?" His finger circles my slit faster and faster. "I will make you fear the day you come for me. Because you will never want for anything more than an orgasm from my touch."

33

I gasp as he suddenly retracts his fingers, my clit thumping with need, my heart practically screaming at me when he pulls them from underneath my dress dripping with my wetness.

"See for yourself how badly you wanted that," he whispers, bringing them closer to my face.

"Remember my teeth, Crystal. Remember how they felt as they sank into your skin. Remember what you felt when I penetrated you with my fingers, because the next time you feel it, it will be the cock of a god thrusting into your wet, aching pussy."

"Crystal! I've been looking everywhere for you!"

Kayla's voice makes my eyes widen, and I glance at her over my shoulder, pleading with her in my head not to get close.

What if he kills her too?

Suddenly, he steps aside, and the knife disappears from my waist. I look around, confused. He now stands next to me on the terrace, clutching the banister as though he was never messing with me.

And the knife is nowhere to be seen.

What the …?

"Are you okay?" Kayla asks. "You look a bit pale."

My eyes flutter over to Ares. He glances at me over his shoulder through his ghostly mask, and my whole body heats from that one look.

Kayla hooks her arm around mine and drags me away from him. "What were you doing there? Did you recognize that dude? That was Ares."

"Oh … I didn't realize," I lie.

I swallow back my pride.

But as we head back inside, my whole body feels like it's about to combust.

And when I turn to throw a final glance at him, he's turned around to face me. A devilish smirk adorns his face as he brings his fingers, the fingers that were just inside me, to his lips and actually licks them off while staring right at me with those smoldering gray eyes.

My eyes begin to twitch.

I hate him.

I've never hated anyone or anything, but I hate him more than anything in the entire world.

FIVE

CALEB

"C'mon, let's go home. You're shaking," some girl tells Crystal as they hurry off through the front door while I watch them from a chair in the lobby.

Interesting.

I tap my lighter against the table and fiddle with my cig until finally Ares appears from the kitchen.

"What did you do?" I ask.

He's got his hands down his pants as he casually strolls to my table. "What needed to be done."

A filthy smile forms on my lips as I look up at him. "You played with her, didn't you?"

Without responding, he grabs a cig out of the package lying on the table, puts it in his mouth, and steals the lighter from my hand to light it up.

"We're inside," I say.

He just stares at me while he takes a whiff and blows it out in my face. I inhale the leftover smoke like it's a gift. God, I love it when he's his usual sadistic self.

"Let's go."

"What? Already?" I frown. "But we just got here."

35

"I got what I was after," he replies. "We're done here."

"But the party—"

He pushes his own cigarette into my mouth. "Stop moping around."

I take a big drag, my dick twitching from the fact that this cig was just in his mouth.

He takes off his jacket and throws it over his shoulder. "This place is musty. Where's Blaine?"

"Upstairs banging some randos, probably," I say, snorting.

"Typical." Ares pulls out his phone and texts him. Then he flicks his fingers at me and holds them out until I hand back the smoke so he can take another drag.

"Hey, you can't smoke in here. Take it outside. There's a designated smoking area."

Some Phantom fucker with a white mask approaches us with folded arms. I don't know who it is, and I don't fucking care. And seeing as how Ares blows the smoke out in the dude's face, neither does he.

"Okay, you're done. Leave. Now."

"Already planning on it," I respond, walking off.

Ares follows me and throws the cigarette at the guy without even glancing at him.

Outside, I can still see Crystal and her friend.

"Should we follow her?"

"I'm good. Do what you want," Ares replies, and he saunters off into the night, leaving me to myself.

But I can't stop from turning in the other direction and following the girls as they cross the road. The pull is too strong to ignore. I want to know what kind of girl we're dealing with and if she can really keep her mouth shut.

I don't know what Ares did to her to get her to run from the party, but I can definitely deduce it was something filthy enough to make even my cock twitch.

And dammit, I want a taste of whatever he had too.

I follow them back to a recently renovated sorority, Alpha Psi, making sure they don't see me. When they head inside, I smile.

Found you.

I look around to see if anyone is watching before I run to the back of the building and hide, waiting for some men to pass on the street.

Don't want anyone to see what I'm about to do.

When the coast is clear, I climb up the ladder on the back of the sorority. The whole thing is shoddy as hell, but I make it work. I head up to each window and peer inside to see if she's there. There are girls in every room, but most of them are either sleeping or busy with their homework, so they don't spot me taking a peek.

I head farther up and pause when I spot a door opening up in the back. I lean against the wall and listen through the open window.

"I'm fine, Kayla. Don't worry."

"Are you sure? Because you don't look like it. Did Ares do something to you?"

Bingo.

"I just wanna take a shower."

"All right. Well, I'm right next door, so yell if you need something."

My heart thrums in my throat as I listen and wait until her door closes.

Kayla must be gone now, which means she's all alone.

At least, that's what I want her to think.

***

Crystal

I step under the shower, but I can't even feel the droplets falling onto my numb body.

I lift my hands, but they're shaking with vigor still, even minutes later.

Why can't I shake this rage?

I slam my hand against the wall and focus on the sound of the water pitter-pattering down and disappearing into the drain, along with my sanity.

I should've stabbed him.

He was right there. I had my knife, and I had the opportunity.

Yet ... I didn't.

I close my eyes, trying to get the image out of my head, but no matter how hard I try, all I can see is my hands clutching the banister while his hand dives into my panties, coaxing out a dangerously lewd

37

side of me I've never felt before.

Why did I let him touch me like that?

Anger coils around my heart, suffocating its happiness until my smile is replaced by a grimace. I grasp the faucet and turn up the heat, burning my skin with the scalding water. But the pain is nothing compared to the hatred I feel.

I've never felt anything like it before.

It's not just because of the way he touched me, but that he actually made me want it.

I can still feel him down there, between my legs, sliding through my slit, circling around, almost making me combust. And then he stopped.

Leaving me wanting to finish the job right here, right now.

I grumble in frustration and turn the faucet to the other side, icing my back. The hot-to-cold change causes me to hiss, but I have to do something to get rid of this feeling, this need to both strangle a person and have their hands all over me.

God.

He called himself a god.

Who even does that?

And why did it make my pussy throb?

I grab the soap and start scrubbing it into my body to rid myself of his marks, but no matter how hard I brush the soap into my skin, I can't get rid of the marks he left on my mind.

Fuck him.

I rarely swear, but he makes me want to curse at the top of my lungs.

Because after all this, all this hot and cold water, this soap, all this time, I can still feel the pleasure I felt when his fingers were on me as though it's still happening.

I turn off the faucet and step out to dry myself off, then put on a long-sleeved nightgown I brought with me.

I have to do something about this. Make it stop so I can focus on more important things.

Grumbling, I march to my window and close the curtains, then throw myself onto my bed and cover my face with my pillow, screaming into the void. I'm going insane.

Insane with anger.

Insane with a lust I don't want.

Insane with the idea of bringing my own fingers down my body until I can feel the thrumming of my heart right down there between my legs.

***

CALEB

When I turn to look again, there she is, lying in her bed like a porcelain doll.

Her curtains are closed, but a small sliver remains open. Enough for me to peek through. She's wearing a long-sleeved black nightgown, but her neck and legs are still exposed.

Her hands start to touch her breasts, and I'm completely mesmerized. My lips slowly part as she squeezes and tightens her own nipples right through the fabric.

I'm rarely affected by women, yet …

I instantly harden.

Fuck.

Her hand slips down her nightgown, all the way between her legs, and when she rubs herself, I suck in a breath.

She's touching herself right in front of me, and she doesn't even realize she's being watched.

A slow, decrepit smirk spreads on my lips as my tongue darts out to wet them while my pants get tighter and tighter from the growing bulge. I don't know why it gets me going, but it does, and I can't get enough.

She keeps going, circling her pussy right through the fabric of her nightgown, and fuck me, I want nothing more than to open this window and crawl in to help her out.

But that would never happen without her squealing for help. And then I'd lose my chance at watching this sexy show.

Instead, I bring my hand down too and start rubbing myself straight through my pants. I get even harder at the thought of her watching me too.

But she doesn't know I'm here. Doesn't pay attention to anything except those fingers rolling around, faster and faster, her breaths coming out in short gasps. The sounds she makes are like music to my ears, and my shaft strains against my pants, so I unzip and pull it out.

She won't see me here. Her eyes are closed, and she's too busy pleasuring herself to even notice someone watching her. Yearning for her. Getting turned on by her.

God, I never imagined myself doing this, let alone because of a woman, but here I am, pleasuring myself all because of a honeydew-looking girl playing with herself.

I groan with excitement as I jerk off in the dark of night, my heart rate shooting up from the idea that someone could catch me here. The sliver I peek through is like taking a quick glance into heaven itself, and I can't get enough of watching her squirm on her bed, of seeing her get closer and closer to the edge.

Small puffs of air leave her puckered lips, and her moans get louder and louder. My hand follows her movements, quickening the pace as my tip begins to drip with pre-cum.

If she looks this way, I'm screwed, but I don't even care anymore.

I'm playing with fire, knowing full well what kind of inferno it could unleash, but I can't stop.

Fuck, I need her to continue. Need to watch her writhe on that bed from her own damn hands, wishing she was writhing onto mine.

I jerk off faster and faster while she circles her clit right through the nightgown.

I wonder what she's thinking of, if it's Ares who got her so hot and bothered, if she's imagining his hands all over her, almost like he's touching me too through her.

Somehow, the thought only gets me harder, the veins in my shaft pumping with vigor.

I can't hold it any longer.

Groaning, I release myself, cum shooting out against the window, covering every inch.

By the time I'm spent, she's stopped wriggling her fingers, and I peer inside, panting heavily.

Why did she stop?

***

Crystal

Shit.

I can't do it.

I tried. I tried so hard. Back, forth, left, circular motions, everything.

None of it worked to get me to a climax.

My breaths come in short gasps, my clit still thumping from the unkempt desire, yet I can't get off.

Why?

Why can't I do it?

I'm doing everything I always do, yet ... all I can think of is how Ares touched me down there and how my fingers can't even come close to what he did.

I should not be thinking about him, yet that's exactly what I'm doing because I can't come any more thanks to him.

I grab the pillow again and scream into the void.

CRACK!

A loud bang against metal pulls me from my thoughts, and I tear the pillow away.

What was that?

I get up from my bed and stare wide-eyed at the window.

Is there ... someone out there?

Swallowing, I walk up to the window and shove it open wide, but I don't see anyone out there in the dark. Only one streetlight is on, but I don't see anyone walking around. Maybe it was the wind blowing off some twigs from the trees around the house. Yes, that must've been it.

My eyes travel down to the fire escape next to my window to find a few translucent droplets on the railing, and I rub it off, rubbing the droplets between my fingers.

I look up at the sky, searching for clouds, but there are none.

Weird.

I grab the window and shut it again, but my fingers are almost glued to the windowsill, my pupils dilating.

From the top edge of the window outside, a translucent whitish liquid slowly drips down.

I swallow as my hands begin to shake when I turn them around and look at the droplets on my fingers.

Sticky white glue.

I bring them to my nose and smell a familiar scent.

My eyes widen.

Oh God.

It's cum.

Blaine

"So ... you're late," I mumble as Caleb stumbles into the Tartarus House and chucks his white mask aside.

Closing my book, I toss it onto the table next to me and get up, yawning. "How was it?"

"What?" he mutters, confused.

"The party," I add, just as confused. "The one we just attended?"

"Oh, I don't know," he mutters.

My eyes narrow, and I fold my arms. "You don't know?"

"Yeah. Boring. Fine. What do you want to hear?"

I tilt my head at him. "You know ..." I tap my cheek to hide the decrepit smile on my face. "I was there too, in case you forgot. You guys kind of left me there all by myself."

"Right. You know, I did forget. Sorry." Caleb shrugs. "Does it matter?"

"You sound awfully distracted," I reply.

"And you were awfully busy sexing up some people upstairs, weren't you?"

Cheeky little bastard. "I do what I do best. You know that."

"So do I," he retorts, making his way to the kitchen. "Are there leftovers? I'm famished."

"Arlo left some egg sandwiches in the fridge from his trip to the store," I say as I follow him inside.

He rips open the fridge and grabs the egg sandwich without even asking if it's okay to eat them, and he tears open the package and goes to town on them. He eats like an animal devouring prey, unpretty, disgusting, actually.

"Can you at least use a fork? Peasant," I say, throwing him one.

"A fork? On a sandwich?" He scoffs. "You're ridiculous."

"You eat like a pig," I retort as he rams the fork into the sandwich and picks it up from the counter, shoving it into his mouth in one go. "Good God, can you get any filthier?"

"Oh, you don't even wanna know." He snorts a little too loud to my liking.

I sigh out loud. "Darling, what are you hiding?"

"Nothing," he mumbles, grabbing himself a drink too.

I plant my hands on the counter. "You came home fumbling like an idiot, and you're distracted as hell. What. Are. You. Hiding?"

He chugs down some juice and throws away the empty carton. "We found the girl."

Now he's got my attention.

"You know her name?"

"Oh, I don't just know her name." He paces around. "I know where she lives. I know what she wears when she sleeps. I know what she looks like when she plays with herself."

My eyes widen. "What? Are you insane?"

"Yup. Definitely." He stops momentarily to stare at me. "Don't tell Ares."

"But you two were looking for her at that party, right? He knows you were there."

"Yeah, and I think he toyed with Crystal at the party."

Crystal...

What a precious name for a precious jewel.

"Because when she got home, she got under the shower immediately and then started getting herself off in bed."

"How did you find her?"

"Followed her, then snuck up onto the fire escape behind her sorority."

I slap my own face and rub my forehead, but then I'm reminded it

44

creases your skin and ages you, so I stop immediately. "You could've been caught."

"I know, but I wasn't. Well, maybe." He taps his fingers against each other. "I may have actually shot my cum against her window."

I burst. "What?!"

"Shh!" Caleb hisses. "Not so loud."

"You left evidence at a crime scene, and you're expecting me not to get pissed off?" I growl. "Darling, you should know better, honestly."

"Fuck off with your 'darling.' I did what I wanted. Who are you to judge, Mr. Fucking-all-holes-he-can-get-his-dick-into?"

"I would be mildly offended if it wasn't *you* who was saying it," I spit back.

He smirks. "Then you can't blame me for being a little raunchy."

"Still, that girl watched us kill, and now you went over to her house and left spunk all over her window? If she calls the police, we're done for."

"She won't. Not after whatever Ares did to her. Really spooked her," he says. "Besides, she doesn't know it was me who left that cum."

"What if she thinks it was him, hmm?" I ask. "Ever thought about that possibility?"

"So? He wants her scared. Job accomplished."

I fold my arms. "I don't think it will be that easy."

"Why not? Threaten her. Make her keep our secret, or else. She's seen what we're capable of now. Might as well commit to it," he responds. "She's the kind of girl who wouldn't hurt a fly. There's no way she'd rat us out."

"I don't know, darling," I muse. "Something about this feels off, and it's not going to be pretty."

"Whatever," he says, shrugging it off like it's no big deal. Then he raises his finger. "Don't tell Ares."

I raise my brow back.

"Promise me, Blaine," he asks. When I don't reply, he adds a pout. "Please."

I roll my eyes. "Fine. But if he asks, I won't cover for you either. I'll just pretend I know nothing and be done with it."

"Sounds good to me," he says, walking off, leaving the kitchen one giant trash can. "Have to go shower now to get rid of this stain in my pants. Bye."

"Go wash your ass, you filthy bastard," I tell him, and he actually winks at me.

God, I need a rinse too after this conversation.

I grasp an apple from the basket and lean back against the counter, throwing the apple up and down as the pink sheen reminds me of the glossy cheeks of the girl from the maze.

I wonder if she knows what she's up against.

If she's prepared for what's to come.

Maybe it's about time I paid her a visit.

***

Crystal

At school, I feel antsy, clutching my bag close to my shoulder as though someone might steal it from my hands. Of course, no one would. It's a ridiculous thought, yet … What if those boys want something from me?

I mean, Ares made it very clear he wanted me scared, and then that same night, someone came to visit me and left cum on my window.

I'm not losing it. I know it was there because I touched it.

This means someone was watching me while I was playing with myself, and I can only think of three people who would do such a thing: those Tartarus boys.

I gulp and walk past the people chatting away in the hallway, blissfully unaware that a murder has taken place on campus soil and the perpetrators visit these very same classrooms.

But right before I enter my next class, the door closes in my face.

A big, flat hand rests on the door as a figure approaches from the shadows, hair as dark as the skull shirt he's wearing, with only the jewel on his belt buckle glinting in the dark on top of his purple pants.

I twist on my heels, but he grabs my shoulders and pulls me back, cornering me in the hallway underneath the stairs where no one ever comes.

And when I look up, there he is. A glorious man, who looks

almost seven feet tall, chiseled and sculpted like an angel fallen from heaven, flexing his muscles as he flicks his hair back.

"Blaine," I mutter.

"Oh, how adorable, you already know my name," he muses, his voice awfully chipper and … zesty. "So nice to make your acquaintance."

He grasps my free hand and pulls it up to his face, pressing a gentle kiss on top, and I'm too shocked to even say a word.

What are you doing, Crystal?

I swiftly pull my hand back.

"What do you want?" I have trouble looking away from his gold-colored eyes.

"Can't we have a little chat?" He leans in to casually play with my hair, twirling it around his finger like he's petting a dainty doll. "I'm curious as to why you were at the Tartarus party *and* the Phantom party."

"It's none of your business," I reply with a smile so I don't anger him too.

"So direct, yet you're still sporting a polite smile," he muses, his eyes landing on the tips of my lips. "No wonder they've taken a liking to you."

They?

I frown. "What are you talking about?"

He slowly plants his hands behind me on the wall, trapping me inside.

"Hey—"

He leans in so close I can smell his fruity cologne, and I can't even finish my sentence. For some reason, it's becoming harder and harder to breathe when his nostrils flare against my skin. I can hear him suck in a few breaths.

Is he … smelling me?

Within seconds, he leans back, staring straight into my eyes for a good ten seconds, and this could not get any more awkward.

What is happening?

With a single finger, he tips up my chin and inspects my face like he's determining the value of cattle, and quite honestly, it's making me feel weird.

What is wrong with him?

When his finger slides down my chin and neck to the bite mark visible on my shoulder, I slap him away.

"Stop it," I say.

"Hmm … interesting."

I tug my puffy pink shirt farther over my shoulder. "What is? Do you have something to say to me or are you just going to feel me up like Ares did?"

"Feel you up?" The tip of his mouth quirks up into a smile. "Oh no, if I was actually touching you for pleasure, you'd know."

My cheeks flush with heat.

He did not just say that.

He grabs my shoulder and leans in again, getting a little too close for comfort. "You're curious. I like that."

I frown, completely confused as to what's happening here.

"But you gotta learn to defend yourself, darling. Do you want me to teach you?"

"Defend myself?" I parrot.

"Yes," he adds with a bright but slightly ominous smile. "Because they'll never stop until they have what they want."

They. He's talking about Ares and … Caleb?

"What do they want, then?" I ask, pretending I don't know exactly what I witnessed … and the warning Ares gave me.

But the deadly smirk on Blaine's face makes my entire body erupt into goose bumps even before he says the word out loud. "You."

My whole body feels like it's running a fever.

"Now go on." Blaine pulls me away from the wall. "Get to class." He adds a gentle nudge like he's egging me on to keep walking.

But all I can do is glance at him over my shoulder and see the sinister look in his eyes after that warning.

A warning of what's yet to come.

SEVEN

When I get out of class, I immediately head into the girl's bathroom and lock myself inside. My heart is still racing from that encounter with Blaine.

They'll never stop until they have what they want.

Me.

I can still hear him say the words out loud, and they make me shiver.

I close my eyes and take a breather, squeezing my own knees until they hurt.

You can do this, Crystal.

You promised Dad.

I nod and take one last breath before I pick up my bag again and exit my stall. A girl with pretty long black hair applies bright red lipstick in front of the mirror.

I wash my hands and splash my face with some cold water.

"Rough day, huh?" she muses.

"You don't even want to know," I mutter.

I don't know her, but I guess she can sense my unease.

"If it's boys bothering you, I always make sure they get exactly what they give," she says, winking at me through the mirror. "You can do this."

"Thanks," I say, smiling.

She sticks out her hand. "Lana."

"Oh, hey. You're Felix's sister, right?" I say.

She frowns. "How'd you know?"

"His girlfriend, Penelope, she's my friend. She's dropped your name once or twice."

A smirk forms on her face. "Did she now? Hope it was good."

"Oh yeah, she called you a tough bitch not to be messed with."

She laughs. "Sounds about right." She holds out her lipstick. "Here. Put this on. Makes you feel like you can conquer the world."

I stare at the lipstick for a second before I pull it out of the cap.

"Promise," she adds.

Maybe it's worth a try.

I put it on in the mirror and rub my lips together.

"See?" She stands behind me and then puts my hair in front of my shoulders instead of behind. "A queen in the making."

I hand her back the lipstick, and she tucks it into her purse. "Destroy their hearts before they kill yours," she says, winking. "Good luck."

She leaves the bathroom while I take one more moment to admire the girl in the mirror.

This is me.

I'm me in all my beauty, pain, and endless devotion.

And no boy will ever take that away from me.

With my head held high, I march out of the bathroom to the cafeteria where I know they'll be. It's lunchtime, and guys like them always hang out with the popular crowd, so I know they must be in there.

When I walk through the doors, I pause and look around. My eyes settle on a group of guys sitting at a far too large table in middle of the room with just the three of them. And my heart immediately begins to pound.

One of them wears a white cotton tank top that's almost see-through, and he laughs as his tongue darts out to lick his piercing, just one of many that adorn his face and tattooed body. Another one leans back against his seat, his chiseled face almost angelic as he brushes aside his long black hair off his black skull shirt. And then we have the most devious of them all; a black-haired guy with a sharp nose and equally sharp eyes, veins protruding through his skin as he leans into the table to explain something, his black shirt half-open at the top.

It's *them*. Those Tartarus boys that make all the hairs on the back of my neck stand up.

They're just chatting away like nothing ever happened between us. Like they didn't threaten me because I saw them kill.

I just know it was one of them who stained my window with cum. Was it a threat?

I swallow away the lump in my throat and head for the boys, knowing full well I'm walking straight into the lion's den. The closer I get, the more that same aura of darkness falls over me, and I bury my hand in my pocket to fumble with the knife like it's my only lifeline.

I march up close to their table and clear my throat. They only stop talking when I plant my hand on the edge of the table. Only Caleb and Blaine look at me even though I'm right in front of Ares, who's seated to my left. He's clearly ignoring me.

"Uh-oh," Blaine mutters, a smile slowly forming as he shoves Caleb with his elbow.

After I've gathered my courage, I say, "One of you was at my dorm."

Caleb tilts his head, a daring look on his face. "Are you accusing us of something?"

My eyes narrow. "One of you knows what they did."

"Oh boy," Blaine says, snorting. "This is going to get juicy."

Caleb leans back so far his ripped abs become visible underneath his white cotton tank top, and they make me do a double take. "Say it then. What did one of us do?"

I swallow, a blush creeping up on my cheeks. If I say it out loud, everyone will hear.

"You left ... cum on my window."

A wild smile forms on Caleb's face, and Blaine laughs. "What?"

"Don't deny it," I say. "One of you three did it. I'm sure."

Blaine leans into his own hand as he perches his elbow on the table. "That's a wild accusation, pretty jewel."

Jewel.

My heart almost stops beating.

I haven't heard anyone say that word in such a long time. And I hate that it's coming from his mouth.

"Crystal," I tell him.

"I know." He smiles coyly at me, and for some reason, it makes me blush.

I should not be blushing at these guys, shit.

"And what makes you think we did that?" he adds.

Am I going to say it?

"Because … it was right after the Phantom party. And you guys threatened me not to—"

Suddenly, Ares grabs my wrist, fingers digging into my skin as he finally looks up at me with those bright, devilish eyes.

"Not another word."

His menacing look makes me cower in my boots, and I almost instantly regret coming here to confront them.

I don't even know which one of them it was. They won't tell me, obviously.

But I need them to know … I won't go down without a fight.

"I told you to be careful," Blaine mutters, licking his lips.

"You want to do this here?" Ares's low voice makes goose bumps scatter on my skin. "Fine. Have it your way."

Suddenly, he tears me away from the table with one big swoop and pulls me toward him. I can't even react, let alone fight him off. It all happens so fast.

One second, I'm standing my ground against them …

And the next, he's got me pinned to his lap.

His actual fucking lap.

And he wraps one arm around my belly while the other snakes up my neck to my mouth, preventing me from making a sound.

"I warned you not to speak about it," he whispers. "And I make good on my threats."

He presses me into his body, and I can feel all the rock-hard abs behind his black T-shirt while his fingers splay against my belly. All the courage I gathered in the bathroom instantly dissipates while panic takes over.

"Now tell me again why you are here," Ares murmurs into my ear.

When my lips part, his hand slowly dips into my white skirt from underneath, and I can barely breathe.

With his hand on my mouth, I can't even squeak as he rubs me right through my panties. "Go on. Say it."

This is insane. He's literally playing with me in the cafeteria, in front of all these people.

"You think one of us soiled your window?" he muses, flicking his index finger back and forth. "Yet you deliver no proof."

I whimper as he presses down on my clit, trying so hard not to let anyone notice what he's doing. But he's going faster and faster while his hand keeps pushing me further into him until I can feel his bulge poking in my ass.

I can't let him do this. I have to stop this.

I reach into my pocket, but the second I do, he swiftly takes his hand off my mouth and grasps my wrist.

"Ah-ah, little rose, don't even try," he whispers. "You're mine now."

"Why are you doing this?" I say.

"You tried to expose me in front of everyone here," he answers, his fingers lifting up from my panties only to slide them aside. "So now I will expose you."

My lips part, but nothing except a suppressed whimper escapes as his fingers slip between my pussy lips, and I can't freaking breathe.

How is this happening right now?

"So tell me, girl, how do you know what it was?" he asks, circling my clit. "Did you feel it?" His sharp nose rests against my neck, hot breath fanning the flames of the fire being stoked in my body. "Did you taste it?" I can feel him grin.

Caleb licks his lip and bites on his piercing. "How did it taste, little slut?"

"You're sick," I hiss.

But Ares only applies more pressure to my clit, making it hard for me to focus on what they're saying as the lust courses through my body.

"Don't make a sound," Ares whispers. "Unless you want everyone to hear you moan."

"Don't be shy. Tell us how you came to the conclusion," Blaine muses. "I'd love to know."

"It obviously looked like cum," I answer.

Ares's shaft twitches against my ass, and I can feel it grow harder and harder, even when I thought it couldn't get any bigger. Oh God.

No wonder he warned me to fear him.

"You think you know what our cum looks like?" Caleb muses.

Blaine sticks his finger into his dessert and licks it straight off his finger. "Interesting."

"You're messing with me," I say.

"No …" Ares says, his dark voice lulling me into slow and gradual despair as I'm forced to face my own arousal from his fingers rolling around my slit. "You're the one playing with a god."

A god?

The arrogance.

I—

Suddenly, he exposes my clit and touches the tip, and an actual moan leaves my mouth.

I swiftly cover my mouth with my hand to prevent other noises from spilling out. But the damage is already done because I can definitely see the arrogant grins on Caleb's and Blaine's faces.

"I warned you, you would fear the day you would get your first orgasm from me," Ares whispers, his fingers expertly teasing me, circling around until it almost feels like I'm going up a roller coaster of sexual ecstasy. "I'll make you wish you never looked at me."

He flicks his finger across my most sensitive spot over and over in a way that I've never felt before, not even by my hand.

What is this? How is he doing this?

I can't even think straight. That's how consumed I am with what he's doing to me. What he did before during the party was only a mere tease compared to this.

And it's just his hand.

I can only imagine what his dick can do.

It prods into my ass, and I realize just how thin the layer of fabric is between us. The thought nearly drives me insane.

I should not be thinking about him like this at all.

What is wrong with me?

Ever since he touched me at that Phantom party, I've been unable to touch myself without thinking of him, and now he's forcing me to go there again, with his fingers swiveling back and forth across my slit.

All in broad daylight, in front of everyone here.

And he won't stop.

"Wait," I mutter, feeling the rush as I go higher and higher toward that cliff.

"No," he hisses, going faster and faster until my clit throbs with need.

The edge of no return ... and it's too late to stop.

My body tenses up against his, and when his lips drag along the back of my neck, I nearly faint from the amount of arousal coursing through my veins.

Oh God. I don't want to do this in front of all these people.

His lips quirk up into a smile.

Suddenly, he pulls away, leaving me on that edge, desperate and ready to plead.

"What ..." I mutter, confused.

His hand splays against my thigh, fingers still wet, a reminder of what he just managed to do to me.

"How does it feel to be brought to the brink of destruction by a god?" he murmurs. "Does it make you want to plead and beg for mercy?"

I'm writhing in place from the mounting orgasm waiting to be unleashed, but he's leaving me hanging, just like before, and I'm about ready to pull the knife from my pocket and jam it into his chest.

But then I'd be branded a murderer ... In front of all these people.

He grins against my neck. "Then beg."

"F-fuck you," I say through gritted teeth.

He releases my wrist, only to shove two fingers so far inside my mouth that I gag. "Bite, and I will rip these panties to shreds and fuck you right here on this very table."

My heart begins to race at the idea of his length slamming into me.

"Now suck."

"I can't," I growl back.

He slaps my thigh so hard I squeeze my legs together.

"Suck."

I do what he says, but only because I have no choice. I can still feel the sting of his hand and my own desire pooling between my legs.

But the groan that emanates from his body nearly makes me explode without even being touched.

"How does she suck?" Caleb asks, licking his bottom lip. "Like a good little slut?"

Holy shit. A slut? What is wrong—

My thoughts short-circuit when Ares's tongue draws a line from my hairline to my collar. "Better."

Caleb groans too, and his hand dives underneath the table. I can only imagine what he's doing down there, and I gulp when he narrows his eyes at me, watching me intently as Ares's dips his fingers in and out of my mouth.

I cough when he finally pulls them out. "Every time you deny me, I will make you remember to fear me. Understood?"

I shudder in place as his hand slides down my chin and curls around my throat, squeezing enough to remind me not to reach for my knife.

"Do you want me to have a hard-on in the middle of the cafeteria?" Blaine murmurs at Ares. "Because it's too late now."

"Take care of it later," Ares growls. "I want to prove a point here."

His hand that was on my thigh slowly trickles down my legs again and slips underneath my panties, causing a wave of desire to flood my body.

"You've thought of me, haven't you?" he whispers. "You fantasized about these fingers dipping in and out of your pussy just like that night at the Phantoms. Admit it."

"No."

That's a hard lie.

But I couldn't possibly admit to myself that I tried to finish myself off after he left me hanging and couldn't. Let alone the fact that I could never admit it to them.

Caleb grins like he knows more about it than I want him to. Is it that visible on my face?

"You're a terrible liar," Caleb muses.

"F-fuck—"

Before I can finish my sentence, Ares sinks his teeth into my shoulder, but he stops right before he punctures me in the same spot as before.

"You remembered me," he says. "I can feel you tense up." His fingers pause despite my body wishing he'd continue. "Terrified I might bite you again?"

"I don't fear anyone," I say through gritted teeth.

"No? Let's see if you can still sport that smile after I'm done with you." He teases me so much I'm beginning to sweat. I look around at the people walking by, wondering if they notice or can even be bothered by what these boys are doing. But I'm too far gone to even care anymore, as the arousal takes over my body.

"That's it. Feel that need coiling around your heart?" he whispers. "The one that begs for you to let go and give in to me?"

"No," I say through gritted teeth, staring at Caleb, who's still rubbing himself in front of me.

"Liar." Ares rolls the tip of his finger around my entrance, making me yearn for it, and I hate it. But he won't give it to me. "I can taste your fucking fear on your skin, Crystal."

"I'm not afraid," I hiss back, trying to ignore the swirls of his finger as he coaxes out my wetness.

"No? Are you not terrified to show everyone in this room just how badly you want to come?" He pulls away and leaves me feeling bereft. "Because you will. You will show all these people what it looks like when you fall apart. Your only choice is how loud you'll be."

He swirls around my clit again, making it thump with need, and I'm so close to falling apart that I clutch the table in front of me, trying to keep it together.

His dick bobs up and down against my ass, and he moans into my ear. "Now, what's it going to be, little rose? Are you going to come for me? Or should I fuck it out of you?"

Oh God, no. Please, anything but that.

"God, this is too hot," Blaine murmurs, his Adam's apple bobbing up and down.

"We're watching you," Caleb muses, biting his lip as he jerks off underneath the table. "Do you want others to look at your pussy too?"

"No," I swiftly respond, barely able to focus on his voice because of what Ares is doing to me.

Ares's raspy voice almost pulls me over the edge. "Then beg."

I can't. I can't take it anymore.

"Please …"

He's already pushed me beyond what I can handle.

"Please, *what?*"

I'm falling apart at the seam.

"Please … let me come."

The groan he lets loose makes me shiver in place.

He pulls out his left hand, releases my throat, and dips his right hand between my legs, shoving my panties aside so he can finger my clit.

Oh my God. All this time, he was toying with me with his non-dominant hand?

Just a couple of flicks is all it takes for me to reach the peak.

I shove my own two fingers into my mouth and bite down as I come so hard I nearly squeal out loud.

My head tilts up as the lights on the ceiling turn into stars in my eyes, my whole body feeling like it just floated away into space.

Good God, I don't want it to stop.

Ares slows his pace, and it's almost like I'm being dragged from heaven by the devil himself.

He pulls out of my panties and grasps my fingers, tearing them away from my mouth, only to bring them to his. I'm too shocked to even react as he licks off the blood with a wicked grin on his face.

He leans in to whisper, "You will never have enough. Like an addict, you'll spend the rest of your life wondering when you can get another hit. And you will get … *nothing*. Unless you beg. Because that is your punishment for looking at me and giving me that rotten smile."

His hand vanishes from between my thighs, my pussy still quaking from the orgasm.

My brain finally kicks into gear, and I shove him away, jumping off his lap so swiftly I stumble and fall to the floor.

He tilts his head at me, gazing down at me with disdain, while his bulge protrudes through his pants like it's ready to rip through me.

"Look around you," he says.

And when I do, my whole face turns as red as a beet.

Everyone's looking at me.

Gossiping.

Laughing.

Talking.

About *me*.

I swallow and crawl up from the floor, scrambling away, but I still can't help but glance over my shoulder at him.

"Go on. Run, little rose. Run." His dark face haunts my very fucking soul as he makes a fist with his hand. "Before you get plucked and crushed."

EIGHT

ARES

I watch her run off like a flower losing its petals to a harsh wind.

She's almost too pretty to taint.

Almost.

But she's seen death with her own eyes, and the price she pays is heavy; keep my secret or be destroyed trying to reveal it.

I might end up doing it anyway, just for fun.

My tongue darts out to lick my lips, her blood hardening my dick. I really can't resist the taste of her. No wonder I'm having such a hard time holding back.

"Did you really have to go that hard on her?" Blaine asks, picking up his coffee and taking a sip.

"She needed to learn a lesson," I reply, wiping my hands on a napkin in front of me, and I chuck the thing in the bin ten feet away from us. "She knows not to speak out loud about our business now."

"Lest anyone know what kind of bastards we truly are," Blaine muses.

"Bastard and proud," Caleb says with a grin.

"Caleb."

My voice immediately makes him drop the wretched smile.

I get up. "Come with me."

"Don't be too hard on him either," Blaine tells me.

I throw Blaine a glare, but when he pouts, it's hard to stay mad.

"Please, darling," he adds.

I ignore him and march off, hiding the hard-on in my pants as I strut out of the cafeteria and head straight for the old bathroom that still has a lock on it. I hold open the door until he's here.

"Get in."

He reluctantly follows me inside, and I lock the door, waiting until he's perched against the sink.

"What's up?"

I pull my gun from my pocket and aim it straight at his head.

His eyes widen, and he slowly lifts his hands in the air.

"It was you, wasn't it?"

His Adam's apple rises and falls in his throat. "I couldn't help myself. After she got back home, she started playing with herself in her bed, and I kind of got carried away watching her."

My nostrils flare.

He got carried away? That motherfucker…

I pull back the safety.

"Do you know what it could cost us if word got out?" I rasp.

"I was just messing with her head. Like you," he says, shuddering, but more with delight than actual terror. "You scare her so well."

"Just messing with her …" I parrot, narrowing my eyes as they slide down his body, settling on the bulge in his pants. "Yet you're hard as a rock."

His face shows all kinds of emotions. "So are you." His eyes flutter down, and his tongue pushes up against the inside of his cheek.

I grasp his throat and shove him all the way to the wall. An *oompf* leaves his mouth as his back hits the tiles, and my gun recoils, leaving an imprint on his skin.

My fingers squeeze tighter and tighter until I can feel his heart pulse beneath my thumb, and his breath is in my hands.

And then I lower the gun and smash my lips onto his.

I take his mouth, tongue and all, consumed by fury and arousal. A toxic combination for a poisonous need.

"Fuck," he groans into my mouth.

"Shut up," I growl as I roll my tongue around his. I grasp his bulge right through his pants and say, "You can't stop, can you?"

"No," he responds, making my blood boil.

I release my grip from around his throat, and he sucks in a deep breath before I place them on his shoulders and say, "On your knees."

I lower my zipper while he looks up at me with greedy eyes.

"You walk around with that hard-on for the rest of the day," I growl as I part his lips and bring my cock to his mouth. "She made me hard as fuck. That's your fault. Now fucking take care of it."

His pierced tongue rolls around my shaft, and I tilt my head back when he says, "Yes, Sir."

***

Crystal

I keep walking without looking back until I finally reach the exit and head out into the open air and sun, trying to breathe.

Don't let it get to you. You're stronger than this. You can take them.

I suck in a fresh breath of air and focus on steadying my heart rate.

No one saw what Ares did under the table. They just saw you fall from someone's lap, that's it.

But what if they heard me moan?

What if they heard me beg?

Something touches my shoulder, and I shriek out loud.

"Crystal?"

I barely register that Penelope's standing behind me.

"Are you okay? Did something happen?"

I snap out of it. "I ... uh ... I just had an accident in the cafeteria."

I don't know why, but I don't want to tell her the truth. She already got hounded and chased by those boys of the Skull & Serpent Society because they wanted her so badly they just took her for themselves. I don't want to put this on her plate too.

"Talk to me. Tell me what's wrong," Penelope says.

"No-nothing," I lie.

If I told her the truth, she'd get swept into their madness along with me, and if push comes to shove, and they end up hurting her, there will be an all-out war between the Tartarus and the Skull & Serpent. I can't have that on my conscience too.

"I'm okay," I say, nodding. "I just had a panic attack from being stressed out. That's all."

She grabs me and hugs me tight, and it grounds me.

"Thank you," I mutter.

"Do you want me to grab you a drink? A bite to eat?" she asks.

I shake my head, smiling. "No, I'm good. Thank you. I just wanna go back to my room. Maybe lie down for a bit."

"Of course," she replies. "If you need me, call me, okay?"

I nod, and she smiles back. "Will do. Thanks."

"I'm always here if you need me." She gives me another hug.

"I know."

Dylan waves at Penelope from the bench they're sitting on, and she runs off. "See ya!"

I wave at her. She seems so content with those boys even though they hated each other's guts last year. How easily things can change. You never know who you might fall in love with.

I walk across campus, sauntering across the pavement while trying to ignore the thumping in my pussy.

Ares really did a number on me.

I don't even know how he did it. One moment, I was dead-set on confronting them with what they'd done, and the next, I was on his lap, getting toyed with until I came so hard I could barely stay put.

It was wrong. So damn wrong.

Yet my body can't stop tingling from the way he touched me.

I sit on the bench near the second building and grasp my bottle of water from my bag, taking a huge gulp. Gotta cool myself down somehow.

After what Ares did, I'm surprised I can even walk.

I can't believe he did that. All just to frighten me into silence.

I shiver. It worked all right. But I will never, ever let anyone know, and definitely not him.

Fearing him is exactly what he wants.

After I've taken a fifteen-minute break, I continue on to the sorority. But when I turn a corner, the sight of a guy covered in tattoos and piercings leaning against the building makes me freeze in the middle of the sidewalk.

Caleb.

His fist rests against the wall, muscles bulging as he supports his own weight, thick slabs of muscle only protected by his thin tank top. I'm glad he's wearing a pair of jeans because I definitely don't want to see what's underneath there.

He's talking with someone on the phone, but it takes me a while to register what he's saying because I'm so far away and still trying to listen in.

"No, not today. Dad wants to meet up at Fi's Cups and Cakes for some coffee in about three hours and then head to our supplier, so I'm out."

Who is he talking to? One of those other guys?

He lowers his phone as well as the fist that's perched against the wall.

But before he looks my way, I'm already long gone.

***

Later that day

I race down the mountain on my bike, holding the flowers I plucked tightly, swallowing away the tears that sting in my eyes. The road curls around the corner, and I let my worries blow away in the wind that meets me on the way down.

When I'm back in Crescent Vale City, I look up the mountain at the gates of Spine Ridge U, dark clouds gathering above it. It truly is a gate straight to hell.

Taking a deep breath, I continue my biking journey until I get to my destination; Crescent Cemetery.

I get off my bike and place it against a tree near the entrance. I stare at the entry and all the graves beyond. Every time I'm here, it feels like my throat clamps shut.

Breathe, Crystal. Just breathe.

I walk across the path, sauntering past the dead. The sun creeps through the trees above me, scattering light across the stone pebble path and every marker mounted on each grave. It's a warm welcome home for those who linger and stay.

My mother always said she doesn't believe in ghosts, but I do.

I see the flecks dance in the light, watch their spirits mingle, longing to connect in the endless solitude of death.

I take another deep breath when I finally reach the grave at the top of the small hill. The flowers from last time have already wilted.

I go to my knees, remove them from the glass vase, and put in the new ones. A few I plucked from the field beyond the college and one additional bright red rose. Just like the rose he always gave to me.

I place it on the grave, separately from the other flowers, and then close my eyes.

"I brought you some new flowers," I mutter into the wind.

The wind blows into my ear, brushing past my hair.

"I miss you, Daddy," I whisper.

The faint sound of the wind pushing through the leaves of the trees above almost makes them sound like they're whistling, and somehow, the tune puts me at ease.

It's almost like he's actually here with me.

Tears form in my eyes, and I let them run.

I need him.

I need him so desperately I can't breathe.

But he isn't here anymore, and nothing I do will bring him back.

But his soul... still lingers. I can feel it. And it gives me all the strength I need to push on.

Fight, Crystal. Don't ever give up.

Flashes of a symbol with bones on it flicker in front of my eyes, and I look up at the building at the end of the graveyard. But the symbol vanishes.

It only exists in my memories. Just like my father.

I swallow and make the tears stop.

"I will make it right," I say, placing my hand on the grave. "I promise on my life."

***

An hour later

"How are your studies coming along?" my mother asks.

I was drinking my coffee, but I pause halfway through, swallowing after a while. "Oh, I'm doing fine."

I don't want to lie to her.

It's not going well.

But if I told her the truth about my latest issues with a couple of boys, she'd have a heart attack, for sure.

"I heard that the university has been having some problems with certain individuals making a whole scene and the police being involved. Have you heard anything about that?"

"Um, no, not particularly." I take another quick sip.

That's also a lie.

I did hear about it from Penelope because there was a huge fight between the Skull & Serpent Society and the Phantom Society. Supposedly involving the previous dean of Spine Ridge. But I don't know the full gist of it, and I don't think I want to. I just know that it's over now, so I don't want my mother to worry about it.

"I just wonder if Spine Ridge University is still a safe place," she mutters.

"Of course. It was probably just a one-time thing, and the cops handled it. The school itself is fine," I say. "Besides, it's not like I'm gonna change now that I'm already in my second year there."

"It's always a possibility." She reaches out for my hand and gently rubs it. "You know you're always allowed to quit."

"I know." Never happening.

She smiles at me. "You're always welcome back home."

My heart fills with warmth. "Thanks."

My eyes flutter out the window to a peculiar car parked outside Fi's Cups and Cakes. It's an Aston Martin, the same model some of the rich guys at school have, but for some reason, I feel like I recognize this one. The license plate on it looks familiar.

"Well, better eat this cake before it's dry," Mom says, pulling me from my thoughts.

I take a forkful of my cake and shove it in my mouth. "Delicious."

"Oh my God, you're right," Mom says, grinning as she swallows her piece. "Why didn't we come here sooner?"

"I don't know, actually. Penelope recommended it to me last year," I reply. "I don't think I can ever go anywhere else now that I've tasted their cakes and pies."

The bell at the top of the door rings as more customers come in. The place is so busy there's a line at the counter, but no one seems to mind because they know the wait is worth it.

But as I take another bite from my cake, a man with neatly combed dark blond hair in a suit standing in line catches my attention because next to him stands an equally dark blond-haired guy with tattoos all over his arms, hands, and neck. And all the hairs on my body stand up straight.

"Crystal?" Mom mutters, but I can barely hear her over the sound of my own breathing as it picks up.

I swallow my piece of cake but almost choke on it, and I knock over my coffee.

"Oh God!" my mom says, swiftly grabbing my mug so it doesn't spill over more.

I cough a little and look up at the guy whose eyes are locked on mine like a missile ready to strike. His piercings rise and fall with each of his steady breaths, but the one in his eyebrow twitches.

"Are you okay?" my mother mutters.

I scoot aside and look at the coffee on the floor. "Yeah. I didn't get any on my lap, luckily."

"Let me go grab some paper towels."

She immediately rushes off toward the counter, pushing past the suited man with slick blond hair to grab some of them, and I watch intently as she smiles at him.

He talks to her and then grabs the towels himself, handing them to her with a smile. She blushes and says something back, but I can't hear it over the hubbub from the other customers.

Caleb narrows his eyes at my mother but doesn't say a word.

When he looks at me again, I grab the menu on the table and hide behind it. Even though he's already seen me, I don't want to give him more reasons to come close.

I peek over the menu. My mother continues talking to the man, seemingly forgetting about the coffee spill on the floor beside our table and her half-eaten cake. They're laughing and exchanging looks, and Caleb seems awfully annoyed by the whole ordeal.

A smile forms on my face.

But she seems enamored by the man beside Caleb, so much so that she pulls out her phone and shows something to him. I can't tell what, but he immediately pulls out his phone too.

Are they exchanging numbers?

I push the menu to the side to get a better view, but the second I do, Caleb grabs the man's shoulders and pushes him away from my mom.

"Let's go, Dad. The line is way too long, and I know a better place."

He ushers his dad away, but not before his dad says goodbye to my mom.

Right before Caleb exits, he throws me a final glance, a warning of sorts, but I let it slide off my shoulders. I just stare back until they've disappeared through the door, and the bell rings again.

I breathe a sigh of relief.

I'm glad they didn't order anything because the only free seat left is next to us.

My mom strides back with a gleeful smile on her face.

"What happened?" I ask. "You look like you're radiating."

"That man. Oh, he was so handsome," she murmurs, and she practically falls into her chair, dreaming away.

"Mom." I gently pry the paper towels from her hand.

She shoots up from her chair. "Oh, I'm sorry, sweetie, I completely forgot."

I chuckle while we both get on our knees to clean up the mess. "It's fine, Mom, I get it. You got swept off your feet."

She sniggers like a schoolgirl. "It's been a while since I last hit it off. Do you mind?"

"No, not at all," I say as we rise again, and I ditch the soaked towels on the table.

It's been a while since my mom last dated anyone.

I mean, not since …

I swallow away the lump in my throat.

"It's fine." I wave it off like it's no big deal even though I know full well who the man she just gave her number to is attached to. "When are you two meeting up?"

NINE

CALEB

A few days later

I chew my cucumber stick vigorously, swirling my tongue around the stem while watching her intently.

The cafeteria is noisy today, but I filter through the chatter just to focus on the girl in front of me.

She's wearing that same beige dress again from the night of our party at the Tartarus House, and the more I look at it, the more I remember it vividly from those few seconds I saw Ares approach her in the maze.

Crystal Murphy.

A girl so innocent yet …

That pretty blond hair and picture-perfect face are such a distraction that I'm starting to wonder if I should do something about it. Make it messy, with pretty pink lipstick and black mascara smeared all over her face while her hair is a bungled mess from all the cum.

My dick twitches in my gray sweatpants at the thought.

I normally never get so excited about girls. But I have to control myself.

She sits beside those bastards from the Skull & Serpent Society, the actual fucking leader Felix and his girlfriend, Penelope, along with some more friends.

It's them versus just me. Blaine and Ares have classes.

But if I approach her now in front of all of them, they'll probably kill me for even trying to get near.

No, I need to wait until she's all alone.

Defenseless.

Scared.

So I can punish her for showing up to that same goddamn café I was at with my dad.

Was it a coincidence?

I could've sworn I saw a few blond hairs disappearing behind a wall the second I ended my conversation with Blaine. But when I went to look, no one was there.

Was it all my imagination?

I take another bite and finish up the sticks until nothing is left. But I'm still hungry as hell, so I continue to my little bowl of pudding, scooping up some of the strawberry whipped cream and dipping it into my mouth.

My favorite.

When I take a lick, she briefly looks my way and finds my eyes hidden underneath my black hoodie.

I roll my tongue around the spoon without looking away. Her eyes are almost glued to my mouth as I slowly push the spoon filled with cream inside and swallow.

She swallows too.

Does she know I was the one who stained her window?

God, I wish I could've seen her face when she discovered it.

A tainted smile makes its way onto my lips.

Is she even aware of what she's unleashed?

She picks up her half-finished food tray and walks to the bin, putting it in the trash before making off to the hallways. I immediately jump up and go for the pursuit.

Adrenaline races through my veins as I make my way through the doors and see her disappear down a hallway to the left. I follow her around the corner, and the moment she glances at me over her shoulder, I know I've gotten her right where I want her.

Her pupils dilate, and she makes off to the right, her pace

increasing. But I'm prepared for a chase.

She runs up the staircase, and so do I, until we reach the top level, and there's nowhere for her to run except toward the dean's office.

Slowly, I stalk up the staircase so she doesn't try to bolt again.

She drops her bag and turns around to face me. "What do you want from me?"

If only she knew ...

We're about to devour her whole.

***

Crystal

A guy in a black hoodie and gray sweatpants slowly walks up the stairs, each step thudding as hard as my heart until he's at the top. My body instinctively leans away from him as he towers over me, his hands moving to his hoodie to lower it, tattoos peeking out. Underneath, a familiar set of hazel eyes bore a hole into my chest. His dark blond hair falls over his strikingly handsome, square face, but something about the upside-down cross dangling from his ear makes me swallow away the lump in my throat.

Shit. I should really have taken a different turn when I ran upstairs to avoid him.

"What were you doing at that café?" he asks, his voice gruff and hazy like he's been smoking.

"The same as you," I reply staunchly.

His jaw flexes, and he rolls his eyes, almost like he already knows why I was there but just wants to hear me say it out loud. "Okay ... Why were you at our party?"

I hate being interrogated like I did something wrong. "To dance. Why else?"

I try to move past him, but he follows my step to the side. I stare up into his cold, hazel eyes, which turn more threatening the longer I look into them.

"Are you going to let me pass?"

He tilts his head to the right, the left side of his lip turning up into a mischievous, lopsided grin. "No."

My nostrils flare. "I can scream. You know that, right?"

"Do it," he retorts, the smile disappearing from his face. "Who do you think is faster?" He steps closer. "Security … or my hand curling around your throat?"

I gasp, and a squeak nearly escapes my mouth, but I force it back down.

"I'm not going to let you threaten me," I say. "I did nothing wrong."

"Then why were you there?" he repeats.

"I was invited," I answer, folding my arms.

He takes another step until he's right in front of me. "Not the party … the gate."

The gate. Does he mean the one beside the Tartarus House?

My blood runs cold.

So they all know I was there.

"I wasn't."

Suddenly, his hand is on my throat, and he pushes me until my back hits the wall, and I can't fucking breathe.

What the hell?

"S-top," I hiss.

"What did you see?"

"N-nothing," I lie.

Everything.

I stare him down equally harshly, consequences be damned. His grip around my throat tightens, fingers digging into my skin until I can't help but claw at his hand, but his grip is unrelenting.

He leans in, hot breath on my skin as he whispers, "The first lie is my fingers around your throat … the next one is my fingers *down* your throat."

Shit. He can't be serious. Would he actually do that?

"So you choose, Crystal." His eyes flicker with excitement. "If I know you well enough, I know you'll pick the safer option."

"You don't know anything about me," I hiss.

I can feel his smile against my cheek. "I already know more about you than you want me to." His body presses up against mine, bulge hardening against my thigh. "I know who your friends are. What your room looks like. What you look like when you come on someone else's lap." He pauses, his grin deepening. "What you sound like when you play with yourself."

My eyes widen.

"What?"

A dirty smirk forms on his face. "Do you really not know?"

And then it dawns on me.

The white stain on my window.

His fingers slowly loosen so I can speak. "It was you."

I can feel his hot breath against my neck, and when his tongue darts out, I nearly faint.

"Who were you fantasizing about while you fingered yourself? Ares?" he whispers, his tongue dragging a line all the way up to my ear. "Did you come thinking about him? Or did he leave you craving so much more you couldn't even finish?"

I try to shove him away, but I'm no match for his strength. "You're disgusting. Watching me? Coming all over my window?"

A low, rumbling laugh emanates from deep within his chest. "That was just a taste of depravity. A warning." His free hand hovers over my body, lingering dangerously close to my nipples without actually touching them, yet it's still causing electricity to surge through my body. "Make no mistake, slut, we know exactly what you've been up to, sneaking into our lives. Don't think for a second you'll be able to evade our grasp."

"I'm not sneaking into anyone's life," I growl.

"If you hold your life dear, you'll keep your nose out of our business," he says.

"You're the ones who killed someone," I hiss.

He leans back and gazes into my eyes. I don't know why, but I can't stop looking at the way he's tugging at his piercing with his teeth. "True."

He says it with such conviction and zero regret that it makes goose bumps scatter on my skin.

His fingers loosen, but only a little. Just enough to allow me to breathe. "You will forget what you saw that night."

I look him dead in the eyes. "No."

His eyes narrow. "Are you that desperate to be punished again?" His free hand dives between my legs, feeling me up, and I struggle to keep my legs together when he pries them open. "Because I can arrange that just as well as Ares did."

"You're just as insane as him," I say, trying not to react even though his hand rubs me right through the fabric of my pants.

"You think that's an insult, but it's the greatest compliment I could receive," he murmurs, still rubbing me, making me dizzy with heat. "Did you know insanity is only one step behind euphoria?"

He toys with me like he's done this a million times before, fingers splayed against my slit, circling my clit like he knows every inch of my body's triggers without ever having touched it. And I'm now not just struggling to breathe but also struggling to stay upright. Shit.

"You think this is the worst we can do to you? Playing with your pussy?" he murmurs, going faster and faster. "You haven't even seen the worst yet. But you will."

Suddenly, someone comes up the stairs, and Caleb abruptly lets go of me.

"Mr. Preston? What are you doing up here?"

It's Dean Rivera!

Caleb moves away and folds his arms. "Just having a chat with a girl."

I struggle to even stand as I grasp for my throat, coughing and heaving, my clit still thumping with the desire Caleb managed to coax out of me so easily it should be illegal. I'm still sucking in air, trying to regain my senses.

Shit. I should say the truth. Expose them right here, right now.

But then … they'll definitely get me killed before the cops would even show up.

"Well, do it somewhere else, please," the dean says. "This is the office floor."

There's no time. This is it. If I'm gonna make it out of here, I have to do it now.

I shove Caleb aside. He's caught off guard as the dean walks past us.

I storm down the stairs, only looking back to see his tongue dart out to wet his lips, seemingly amused by my escape.

He towers over the banister to gaze at me, and all the hairs on the back of my neck stand up while I keep running farther and farther away from him.

The look on his face tells me exactly what I'm up against …

Pretty boys who hide unfathomable demons, waiting to strike.

And I've become their next target.

TEN

Crystal

Weeks later

"Oh my God, these cookies are amazing," I mutter as I stuff another into my mouth.

I'm not often at my mom's place now that I'm studying, but she always bakes these amazing cookies and cakes for me when I am.

"Don't eat all of them!" mom yells from the kitchen. "Save some for our guests."

I frown. "Guests? Who?"

"You'll see," she says, chuckling.

Now I'm even more confused as I grab my glass of Coke and take a sip.

RING!

The doorbell almost makes me choke on my drink.

I hear a bunch of clattering sounds coming from the kitchen. "Shit!"

"You okay in there?" I ask. "Need some help?"

"No, no, I can clean it up. Can you open the door for me, please?" she asks.

I get up from the couch and put down my Coke before I open the door. But I don't know what to say when I see the same chiseled blond man I saw at Fi's Cups and Cakes standing in front of me with a bunch of flowers in his hands.

"Hi. I'm here for Abigail—your mother. She must've told you we were coming, right?" He sticks out his hand. "Jonathan. I met her last week at Fi's Cups and Cakes. She was getting paper towels for you."

"Right ..." I mutter. "I remember that." My eyes narrow. "Wait ... did you just say *we*?"

"Jonathan!" My mother's squeal from the kitchen makes me step aside as she forces her way through to hug him tightly.

Wow.

That was quick.

"I'm so glad you're here," she says.

"You look beautiful today, Abigail," he says, making her blush.

My mom hasn't blushed since my dad last called her pretty.

"Are these for me?" my mother asks as he hands her the flowers, and she takes a whiff. "Thank you." She pecks him on the cheek while she ushers him inside.

But my eyes don't just widen at the sudden affection they're showing to each other after having only known each other for a single week.

It's the fact that Jonathan didn't come alone.

And when the second guy's eyes settle on mine, there is nothing but fire raging behind them.

"Crystal, this is Jonathan and his son, Caleb."

***

CALEB

My face darkens, eyes growing wickedly sharp the second I lay eyes on the daughter of my father's new fling.

It's her.

Crystal Murphy.

Her mother is my dad's fucking crush?

My fist tightens as I struggle to contain the anger flooding my veins.

"Aren't you going to say hi?" her mother asks when the whole

75

house has gone quiet.

A slow but dubious smile forms on her lips. "Hi."

The softness in her voice makes it hard to breathe.

This is her doing. I just know it is. How else could this happen? Her mother came up to my father after she dropped her coffee. Their meeting wasn't a coincidence. She shouldn't have been there in the first place, yet ...

My father pushes me forward. "Go on."

My eyes narrow. "Hi."

She tilts her head at me in such a mischievous way that it makes my cock twitch.

That look on her face ... she's pretending she doesn't know me?

Fuck.

She's definitely doing this on purpose.

And my dick is definitely hardening in my pants from the sheer audacity.

"Well, who's hungry?" her mother asks to break the ice.

She scurries off into the kitchen while my dad places his coat on the rack and sits down at the table.

"Sit, sit!" her mother tells us as she comes back inside with a tray filled with freshly baked potatoes. "Dinner's all ready."

"That was quick," my dad says.

"She's been prepping all day," Crystal muses.

I grasp the chair beside my dad and sit down reluctantly despite Crystal staring at me like she's too afraid to even say a single word.

I pick up a piece of bread and shove it into my mouth while my dad grumbles.

"Caleb. Behave."

"I am," I retort. "And I didn't ask to be dragged here."

Crystal sits down opposite me and casually pours my dad some water before pouring herself a glass. So I grab the water when she's finished and slowly pour my own glass while glaring at her, then pick up my glass and take a huge gulp, my eyes still locked on hers.

She did this, and I want her to know I'll make her regret it.

My father clears his throat. "Caleb, I just wanted you to meet my girlfriend."

I spit out my water. "Girlfriend?!"

Her mother steps in with a plate filled with pork loin and sauce, a blush creeping onto her cheeks when she sees my dad and me.

"Oh ... you told him?" she mutters.

He nods. "Yes. I have no reason to hide." My father stretches out his hand, and she puts down the plate before offering her hand. He presses a gentle kiss on top that makes me want to vomit. "You're too lovely not to share."

She chuckles and blushes some more, and the sight makes me want to roll my eyes.

I haven't seen my father act like this in a long time.

She leans in, and he kisses her right in front of me, and Crystal's jaw is nearly on the floor.

"Wow. That was quick."

"Sorry, we can't help ourselves," her mother says, giggling like a schoolgirl. "Sparks have been flying since I first laid eyes on him."

"I couldn't help myself. She was that beautiful," my father says.

"O-kay ..." I mutter. "The food's getting cold, though."

"Oh, right, let's eat, everyone!" her mother says and sits down beside Crystal.

But as her mother scoops up potatoes onto my plate, all I can do is stare at Crystal, who seems blissfully unaware of how much I want to punish her for letting all this happen.

But I won't let her get away with this.

***

Crystal

I haven't eaten. I nibbled at my food.

I guess that's what happens when a muscular, tattooed, threatening guy stares at you with each bite you take.

He's wearing a pair of expensive-looking black pantaloons and a white button-up shirt, complete with a jacket. His dad must've told him to dress nice for the occasion, which means his dad thinks my mom is a big deal. But he's still got those piercings and that upside-down cross dangling from his earlobe to rebel.

Caleb's eyes are on me like a hawk still, watching me swallow down my drink, and it still makes me choke up. His tongue darts out to wet his lips when I put down my glass, and I almost make it tip over.

"Abigail," Caleb suddenly says slickly. "Would you mind telling me where the bathroom is?"

"Oh, unfortunately, the bathroom is being renovated right now. But we have another one upstairs. Crystal can show you," Mom says.

Oh shit. I hadn't thought about that at all.

Caleb scoots back his chair and towers over the table in a menacing way.

"Uh …"

My mom prods me, and I practically feel forced to stand.

"Sure."

Sweat drops begin to form on the back of my neck as I slowly push back my chair and step away.

Caleb meets me halfway near the edge of the table, and says, "Lead the way."

The only bathroom this house has left is out of sight of both his dad and my mom.

And definitely far enough to muffle any sounds.

Shit.

The walk upstairs is agonizing, my heart beating faster and faster as we get closer to the hallway and farther away from safety. I can hear his footsteps behind me, like a looming shadow creeping up on me.

I clear my throat and touch the handle of the door once we get there, but the second I try to open it, he pushes me up against the door and plants two firm hands against the wood, trapping me between his arms.

"You did this." His voice is gruff. Unsteady.

"Did what?" I mutter.

He leans in closer, throwing me a menacing glare. "Don't play innocent."

"I don't know what you're talking about."

"They're dating."

I raise a brow. "So?"

"They barely even know each other."

"Love works in mysterious ways," I respond.

When I try to move away, he won't let me.

"Don't pretend you weren't the cause of this." He points at my chest. "You and your mother weren't supposed to be there. And now my dad can't stop talking about your mom."

I shrug. "I don't see the problem."

His finger slides down my chest, and my breath catches in my throat when he lingers near my nipple, barely grazing it. "I don't think you understand, so let me make this fucking crystal clear for you." I hiss when he pinches my nipple with his index finger and thumb. "My dad is a catch, and if they get together for real, there's a considerable chance they'll get engaged and married."

I try not to react as he twists harder and harder. But it's really, really hard.

"And that means we become something neither of us wants."

I gulp back the moan stuck in my throat when he finally releases my nipple.

"Do you get the picture now?"

I know what he's trying to insinuate.

I narrow my eyes. "You seem awfully opposed to your dad falling in love with someone and actually being happy."

He scoffs. "My dad *is* happy. He doesn't need another woman. Especially not *your* mother." He taps my chest like I'm some kind of bug he needs to squash.

"I can't stop them," I say.

He leans in, growling, "Make them."

"How?"

His nostrils flare. "I don't care how. Break. Them. Up."

"No."

"No what?" he retorts.

"No, I'm not going to tell them to split."

His eyes look like they might start shooting darts at me.

"You *will* do it," he grits.

"Or what?" I taunt. "You're not going to hurt me." I pause and raise a brow. "Your dad won't let you."

His face tightens. "Tell me no again," he says through gritted teeth. "Swear to God, Crystal, I will make you regret it."

I gather my courage, knowing full well what these vile boys are capable of. But if my mom and his dad being together hurts him so damn much, then I'm going to be their biggest cheerleader just out of spite.

He knows I'm right.

If my mom and his dad are together, he can't hurt me.

"No."

79

Suddenly, he pushes down the door handle and shoves me inside the bathroom, locking us both inside within mere seconds.

My heart is racing in my throat as I back away while he keeps stalking toward me. But when my legs hit the tub unexpectedly, I fall...

His strong hand grips around my forearm, keeping me from crashing headfirst into the wall. But the air feels too thick with tension as I stare into his hazel eyes, thick lashes lowering over them as his gaze intensifies. I struggle to even breathe properly.

My eyes flick across the sink, looking for something to grab and use as a weapon. A toothbrush, a comb, a toothpick, the ... scissors.

"Don't even think about it," he growls.

His nostrils flare, the piercing glinting in the dark as the only light that comes into the bathroom is from the little window at the top of the door. "Whatever game you're playing, you won't win."

My eyes slowly dip down his face to look at the intricate tattoos on his neck, a spiderweb filled with roses. "What game?"

A wicked, upturned grin spreads on his face. "The one where you pretend you didn't purposely come to that café with your mother because you knew I'd be there." He licks his bottom lip, and my eyes briefly dart up to the glimmering piercing on his lip. "The game where you pretend you're an innocent girl who tries her best to stay away from the bad boys her mom no doubt warned her about. You think hurting you is the only way I can make you do what I want?"

Suddenly, he reaches for my pocket and steals my phone with ease.

"Hey!" I shout as he swiftly turns around and dials some number.

A phone starts ringing.

He chucks my phone into the sink, and I jump on it to see if the screen isn't cracked. "You asshole! Why'd you steal my ph—"

He holds up his phone. "I have your number now."

An icy cold shiver runs up my spine as he tucks it back into his pocket. I drop my phone right back into the sink while he keeps getting closer and closer to me. Before I know it, his hand has snaked around my neck.

"This girl has been very, very bad, hasn't she? She can't stay away from danger."

"I have no idea what you're—"

He squeezes, and I can't breathe.

His other hand cracks open my jaw, and he pushes in two fingers until I gag, tears forming in my eyes from the sheer fullness in my throat.

When he takes them out again and releases me from his grip, I cough and heave.

"Another lie and it'll be my cock in your throat next."

"Jesus!" I say.

"Don't call out his name. He's not here, and he definitely won't be watching what I do to you."

I have to put a stop to this.

I lunge at the small scissors lying on the sink, but his hand wraps around my wrist the second my fingers touch the handle. And he shoves me into the tub, grabbing my neck so it doesn't snap.

RIP!

With his free hand, he tears the shower curtain away and twists it around my wrist, tying it to the pole.

My eyes widen. "What the f—"

He snatches my free wrist and grabs the flexible shower hose from the left, twisting it around my wrist, then seals it back in place.

In two fell swoops, I've been tied up in my mother's tub.

And a villainous boy towers over me with such a wretched smile on his face that it makes my body feel numb.

Oh God.

His blond hair falls over his forehead as he leans in to whisper, "I warned you that you'd regret it."

I thrash around in the tub, kicking him in the belly. "Let me go!"

He pulls a knife out of his pocket and holds it across my neck. "Not so loud, little slut. Don't want your mother to hear you scream and see you like this, do you?"

As much as I want either of them to free me, I worry what it would cost me.

"Do you think I wouldn't use it?" he asks, pushing the blade into my skin.

"You're insane," I say through gritted teeth.

He tips up my chin with the knife. "Because of you."

And even though I want to say he's lying, something about the way he looks at me stops me from saying the words out loud. I'm strapped to the freaking tub, completely at his mercy.

I can't let him do this.

He's the guy who tried to threaten me …
Who came all over my window and watched me play with myself.
He tilts his head, and I begin to thrash again out of spite.
But the knife reminds me of my place as it pushes into my neck.
"Do you have a death wish?" he taunts.
"No, just a wish to kick you in the balls," I retort.
He snorts. "Still ready to fight, even after I've tied you up."

He grips my ankles tightly and spreads them on the edge of the tub, dragging me toward him. My head hits the bottom of the tub while my thighs fall over. Towering over me, he perches between them. "But your resistance is only a turn-on for me."

ELEVEN

CALEB

When I lean in and take a whiff of her scent, I almost groan out loud with excitement.

After seeing her play with herself, I've wondered what it would be like to touch her ... to taste her. And now that I'm so close I can't resist it any longer.

Ares already had his turn. Now she's mine.

My fingers slide along her legs and up her thighs, underneath that dainty skirt she's wearing, and I can feel her skin erupt into goose bumps.

She jerks the shower hose to no avail. "What are you doing?"

RIP!

Before she can shriek, I cover her mouth with my knife, and I tear away what's left of her panties, chucking them into the corner of the bathroom.

"You won't need those anymore," I say, her eyes boring a hole into my head. "Ever again."

Her eyes widen. "What?"

"You heard me," I say. "You won't wear these again."

"Like you get to make that decision." She scoffs.

I slide the knife across her lips and her cheeks and watch them

83

puff with repressed anger. "Yes. Or has my knife not made that clear yet?"

She sucks in a ragged breath through her nose but doesn't respond.

Good. It's about time she learned to behave.

I pull back the knife and place it on the tub's rim, just out of reach of her feet so she doesn't get any ideas.

My hand slides across her pussy, and she shudders in place, then jerks the shower hose once more. "That's not going to work, little slut."

"Don't call me that!" she hisses.

When the pad of my thumb slides across her clit, she slams her lips shut to stop the moan from slipping out, but I saw. I definitely fucking saw.

"Because you don't like it?" I say, rolling my thumb around until her cheeks start to flush. "Or because it makes you feel like you want to submit?"

"Not a chance," she spits, her thighs flexing when I run my fingers along the inside.

But she's already dripping, and when I dip my thumb into her wetness, she definitely struggles to maintain her composure.

This is why she's been chasing us despite knowing exactly what she saw.

She likes the danger. The thrill of getting hurt.

I push up her skirt until it reaches right above her pussy, licking my lips at the sight, the memory of the night I watched her play with herself flickering through my mind.

"Don't look at me like that," she says.

"I like to look at you," I respond, and her eyes find mine in the dark. "I enjoy watching you—"

"Suffer?" she interjects.

I bite my lip. "Beg."

"Never."

The corner of my lip tips up, and I run my thumb across her clit to see her squirm in place. "We'll see about that."

"Do you do this to everyone you've barely met?" she retorts. "Tie them up in a bathtub?"

I smirk. "No, just you."

She shudders in place as I slide up and down her slit, spreading her wetness all over.

"Did Ares touch you like this?" I ask.

"You saw him?" she rebukes.

"Oh yes," I groan, picturing his dick poking her in the ass. "I saw you too, writhing on his lap, desperate to come."

"He forced me," she responds.

I throw her a glare. "You begged for him, and you will beg for me."

She scowls, visibly struggling with how good my thumb feels on her wet pussy. "How long are you going to keep this up?"

I flick her clit and watch her tense from my touch. "Forever if I must."

"Why? To get a point across? To get a rise out of me?"

I lick my lips. "The only thing rising here will be my cock."

Her cheeks turn bright red. "Ridiculous. My mom is downstairs. She'll check on us at any moment now."

"Then you'd better not make me wait long," I say.

I circle around her clit with my thumb achingly slow until she slowly begins to understand we're not going anywhere.

"Why are you doing this? Just to punish me?"

She made her decision when she repeatedly denied me and told me she wouldn't get her mother to back off. This is her fault, and now I'll force her to face the consequences.

"I gave you a choice," I growl back, swatting her legs open when she tries to close them on me. "You chose wrong."

When she tries to kick me again, I grip her leg tightly until my fingers dig in, and I bring my lips down to her ankle and press a delicate kiss onto her skin. She wriggles in the constraints, her body slowly erupting into goose bumps as I go higher and higher ... and higher up her silky smooth legs.

"Did you think of him while you played with yourself?" I ask, dragging my piercing along her skin. "Did you imagine it was his hands touching you?"

"If I'd known you were behind my window, I would've never done that. You watched me like a creep," she says, struggling to breathe through what I'm doing.

She's still pretending my touches do nothing to her.

Pity for her, I see right through that lie too.

"You watched us," I muse, throwing her a devious glance as I lick her skin and circle around her most sensitive spot. "It's only fair I watch you too."

Her lips part. "That was diff—"

I put one finger against my lips and press my other hand back onto her pussy to play with her while watching her try so hard to resist the building arousal in her body.

"You're going to give me everything he gave you," I say, biting my lip when her clit begins to throb under my touch. "And then you're going to watch me do the same."

She frowns. "What?"

Enough talking.

I grip her knees with both hands. Her head rises as I perch myself between her legs and lean in.

"What are you—"

Her words turn into a strangled moan as I press my tongue onto her clit.

No wonder Ares got so turned on by the taste of her on his fingers.

A grin spreads on my face.

He may have been the first to taste her … but I will be the first to feast on her.

***

Crystal

I can't believe it.

Caleb is actually licking me.

And not just that … Something hard and metallic rolls against my clit, and it's driving me insane to the point that I can't stop the moans from spilling out, even if I wanted to.

Is that … a barbell in his tongue?

He flicks it around my clit, and I'm instantly sensitized to the point where I feel like I can't breathe. I've never felt anything like it before. It's out of this world amazing, yet …

Caleb looks at me from underneath those thick eyelashes, hazel eyes brimming with the type of arrogance that would make any girl want to shove their boot in his face.

He knows exactly what he's doing.

He's trying to get me to surrender.

To call him out as the winner of this game I didn't know I was playing until it was too late to back away.

Fuck.

I jerk the chain and the fabric around my wrists, but it's too tight, and I can't get it to loosen. I'm stuck in a weird position and half-naked, completely at his mercy.

But damn, it feels so good. The way he rolls his tongue around my slit and gently flicks the tip along my sensitive spot has me writhing with pleasure in these binds.

Who would do this to another person?

And what is happening to me?

"You like what I'm doing, don't you, little slut?" he groans, lapping me up. "Think hard about lying to me because I will punish you."

Fine, then I won't answer at all.

"If you let me go, I'll give you the truth," I say.

"Good try, but no," he murmurs against my pussy. "You haven't learned your lesson yet, so let me make it very clear to you." His tongue rolls around my slit, and I can't help but bite my lip in response to the way his barbell touches my clit. But then he bites into me.

I swallow down a shriek to prevent my mother from coming up the stairs to check.

"What is wrong with you?!" I hiss. "You bit me."

"Do you even have to ask?" he says.

His tongue slowly circles over the painful bite mark he left. "Don't worry, I didn't make you bleed. But this pussy has got to learn not to stick its nose into other people's business."

"I didn't do anything! I was just there, just like everyone else," I reply.

But I'm so confused by the way he laps me up, coyly rubbing over my clit with that barbell that I can't even remember what I just said. Or what he just said.

"You followed us. Multiple times. Admit it."

When he flicks back and forth, I almost lose it. My wrists strain against the fabric and metal, trying to resist, but it's hard.

"Answer me, Crystal, or I will punish you again," he says.

"It was an accident," I grit.

He nips at my clit again, and I jolt around in the restraints.

He grabs the knife and holds it over my belly, placing the tip between my thighs so it points down at my pussy.

"You want to do this the hard way?" he asks, still licking me like he never intends to stop. "Because I can make it even harder on you."

"Doubt that," I rebuke.

Maybe a little too soon.

Because he plucks the knife off my belly, holding the sharp end in his hand, while he slips the handle down my slit.

"You're going to regret not telling me, little slut."

He pushes it into me, and I gasp in shock, but then he begins to twist it around along with every stroke of his tongue, and the shock turns into pure and utter denial.

Because I don't want to be feeling this intense arousal, this need to shove my body further into his face.

What is wrong with me?

"You thought you could resist, but I will bring you to the brink," he warns, twisting the knife's handle inside me while licking like a man obsessed. "And you're going to come all over this knife."

"No," I hiss. "This is wrong, and you know it."

"Wrong? No. Fucked up? Yes," he says, grinning against my skin as his tongue dips out to playfully curl around my clit. "Now beg."

"Not a chance," I say.

"Beg like you begged for him," he growls.

"No," I respond.

He bites me again, and I bite my own cheek in response to prevent the squeal from leaving my mouth.

"Fuck you," I say through gritted teeth.

He chuckles and thrusts the knife handle in and out even faster. "Every time you swear at me, it will only make me harder."

He's getting hard from me?

Shit, why am I even thinking about this?

Caleb pulls out the knife, and his tongue hovers over my thumping clit but doesn't press down, making my whole body quake with need.

How is he doing this? I don't understand why my body has this reaction to him when I barely even know him. He's just a goddamn bully, and here I am, wishing he'd finish the job.

His tongue slides across his bottom lips, the tip barely brushing past my slit, and I'm about to combust.

"Go on," he whispers.

"F-ff..."

He fans a breath across my sensitive area, making it throb so badly I cave.

"Please," I mutter.

"Please, what?"

"Please ... make me come."

Oh God.

I'm embarrassed ... and he's managed to make me hate him.

"What ...?" A devilish smirk forms on his lips. "Never had to beg?" Now, I really want to slap him. Hard. "Don't worry, you'll have plenty more opportunities."

"F—"

I can't finish what I was going to say because when his tongue lands back on my pussy, I fall apart just from the sheer pressure he applies at the right moment. My whole body convulses from the ecstasy that follows, and my eyes roll into the back of my head. And when he pushes the knife's handle back inside, I see actual stars on the ceiling.

"So wet ..." Caleb murmurs when he slowly pulls it out again and brings it to his lips to take a lick. "Fuck. It's such a shame."

When I finally get down from the high, I mutter, "A shame?"

He licks the knife clean before standing. "A shame ... that you refuse to tell your mother to back off." He steps into the tub between my legs, towering over me, peeling away one of the buttons at the top of his shirt so a part of his muscular, tattooed pecs are revealed, and it makes me do a double take.

He brings his hand down to his zipper and slowly lowers it. "I guess I have no choice but to paint your face as beautifully as I glazed your windows."

My jaw drops, but then he pulls out his dick, and I'm momentarily too stunned to speak.

There's a piercing right through his shaft, as well as one at the tip, poking through the opening, with a little ring attached, and then another one near his pubic bone.

I've never seen so many piercings on a single human being in my life, let alone three in the dick.

The smirk on his face only widens as he grips my chin and makes me look at him. "My eyes are up here, slut."

I hate him.

I hate that he made me look.

And I hate that he made me come so hard I saw stars where there are none.

"You look like you've never seen a pierced cock before," he says. "Have you ever even seen a cock at all?"

"Of course, I have," I spit back. "I never asked to see yours."

"Pity for you, you won't just be looking at it," he says, and he goes to his knees right on top of my belly. "Open your mouth, Crystal."

I grimace. "Not a chance."

He grabs the knife and tilts my chin up. "You will give me what I want."

"What *you* want ... is that why you're so eager to chase my mom away?" I retort.

He stares me down for a moment, the blade pushing into my skin, and I worry I may have said my last words there.

But I swore an oath to myself that I wouldn't let anyone break me, so I won't, no matter what.

Not even for a guy with that many piercings and such sick, twisted needs.

"Why I want her gone is none of your business," he says.

"If you don't give me a reason, I'm not going to interfere."

"I will give you a reason," he says, and he pushes the knife into my mouth and parts my lips. "You either get your mother to end things ... or I will use your body to my heart's content."

My heart shoots up a notch in speed as his length bobs up and down in my face.

Good God. How am I supposed to choose?

I can't do this. I can't.

But I can't get between my mother and her new crush either.

And if I tell her the truth, he'll surely kill her.

"So what's it going to be, Crystal?" The knife slides across my tongue. "Destroy your mother's heart ... Or your body belongs to me."

I shake my head gently to stop the knife from slipping down farther.

"Crystal?"

All the blood drains from my face.

Mom.

"Crystal and Caleb, are you okay up there?" I can hear her yelling from downstairs.

"Lie to her," he whispers, pulling the knife from my mouth.

"I'm giving him a tour of the house, Mom!" I yell back.

There's a pause.

"Okay! Don't take too long!"

Judging from her footsteps, she just walked away from the stairs.

Caleb just stares at me, but the tips of his lips certainly quirk up into a lopsided smile. "Good girl," he says, his dick still right up in my face. "Now choose."

"No."

"I will leave you hanging here until she finds you if you prefer." He tilts his head. "But then I'd be forced to silence her too."

My breath falters. "Don't."

"Then choose," he grits.

I swallow away all the resistance I had left.

"Fine. Do what you want."

His eyes narrow, and he pulls back the knife. With his thumb, he tips down my bottom lip. "Beg."

It takes me a while to utter the word. "Please."

The wicked grin that forms on his face makes me want to punch him.

"Good ... you're finally learning." He pushes my chin farther down. "Now open up, little slut, and taste me on your tongue like I've tasted you."

He slowly pushes in the tip, and I can feel every one of his piercings as they slide across my tongue. I gag when he reaches the end of my mouth and touches my uvula, but he doesn't relent, forcing his way through until my eyes grow watery.

"Good girl. Look up at me while you take it deep."

I never knew it could be possible for a guy to be so depraved, so cold and vicious, and that I would actually beg him to take me. I should've known guys like him would find a way to make me yield. But I will not break. Not for him. Not for Ares. Not for anyone.

So I take him in with a smile on my goddamn face.

Caleb's nostrils flare, and he goes in even deeper until I struggle to breathe.

"That's right, little slut. This mouth belongs to my cock now."

When he finally pulls out, I suck in a breath.

"Again," he says, pushing right back in, farther than before.

I can feel his piercings scrape along my throat, forcing me to swallow him down.

"Are you crying, little slut?" he muses, biting his lip. "I'm not even halfway in."

I want to bite. Hard.

"Ah-ah. No teeth." He tilts my chin up and makes me look at him and the glinting knife in his hands. "Remember this little friend? Hurt me, and I hurt you."

So I stop resisting as he slowly enters me, and my tongue wraps around his length, touching every barbell as they go down, but I still struggle with every inch.

I've never done this before.

Never.

But I would rather die than admit that to anyone, let alone a devil like him.

"Take it deep. I know you can do it," he says.

When he finally pulls out, I heave and gasp for air. "I can't."

He pushes back in again, forcing me to take him deeper with every thrust.

"Yes." *Thrust.* "You." *Thrust.* "Can."

Before I know it, he's in to the base, and I can't. Fucking. Breathe.

But the worst part about it all isn't my lack of oxygen.

It's the fact my pussy can't stop throbbing.

What is wrong with me?

He pinches my nose shut. "How does it feel, Crystal? Does my cock make your pussy clench with need?" He leans back to touch me, dipping his finger inside, and my thighs clench against his arm as he pulls out a finger covered in wetness.

"So goddamn wet for me," he murmurs. "I wonder how much wetter you can get."

When he finally releases my nose, I suck in a much-needed breath, only to be overcome by the giant dick inside me. He thrusts into my mouth much faster, allowing me no time to catch my breath as he forces me to take more and more of him. I look around to catch my bearings, but he grips my chin.

"Keep your eyes only on me. I want you to imprint this face on your retina so you'll see me instead of him every time you make yourself come."

Is that what this is about? Rivalry?

He groans wildly and buries himself inside me to the hilt while thrusting two fingers into my pussy.

"Oh fuck," he moans.

That's when I feel it.

Thick ropes of cum shoot down my esophagus. I can taste his saltiness on the back of my tongue as it keeps coming.

I'm helpless to resist because he's pinched my nose shut again and growls, "Swallow. All of it."

I push my tongue against the ridges of his shaft, the barbells scraping along my throat as I swallow down the salty cum, the same cum that was on my window, now inside me.

When he finally pulls out, I heave and cough out my lungs, trying to suck in the oxygen. Cum and saliva dribble down my chin and my cheeks. But the worst part about this all is that I can still feel my pussy throb, waiting, wishing for more.

Fuck.

Caleb stands up and looks down at me, licking his top lip like he's admiring his artwork. But the harsh look on his face slowly begins to change into something less violent, more … aghast. Eyes bore a hole into my face and chest, his facial muscles tightening and releasing as he grimaces.

What is going through his head?

And why do I even care?

"Caleb?"

The sound of his father's voice has both of us on edge.

He swiftly tucks his dick back into his pants, steps out of the tub, and snatches the knife off the edge.

RIP!

He slices through the shower curtain and then unfurls the shower hose from my other wrist, releasing me from my bond.

He bends over and grips my chin. "Don't ever say a word about this to anyone. Ever."

But before I can even open my mouth, he's already opened the locked door and marched out, slamming it shut behind him.

TWELVE

CALEB

She's consumed me already.

With just one look, one touch, she's beguiled me.

Fuck.

I should've known following her that night of the party was a bad idea, but I just had to go and stalk the girl Ares was obsessing about … and now I'm obsessed too.

I have to get out of here.

I storm down the hallway in her mother's house, angry as hell.

I should not have fucking done that.

But fuck, I wanted to so fucking badly I couldn't stop myself any longer.

She pissed me off with her Little Miss Innocent ruse and her incessant need to say no straight to my face, but most of all, that delicious fucking body I just can't get enough of.

I knew I would one day go this far when I saw her touching herself.

That I would take without asking.

That I would taste her in my mouth and be so overcome by the desire to claim her as my own that I wouldn't be able to stop myself.

I hate her for it. I hate what she's done for me. I hate that I barely know her and still want her to think only of me.

If Ares finds out, he'll definitely kill me.

And there's no way Crystal will be able to clean up the fucking mess I made and still look presentable. Dad's gonna see her and know what I did.

Fuck.

I have to get out of here.

I storm down the stairs and walk straight past the dinner table.

"Caleb?" my dad calls as I head for the front door. "Where are you going?"

"Away."

Her mom looks at me like she's seen a ghost.

"But we haven't even finished dinner yet," Dad says, frowning at me. "What happened?"

"Have fun," I growl. "I'm out of here."

And I slam the door shut behind me.

***

Crystal

I steady myself against the wall as I step out of the tub, but I pause when I see the girl in the mirror. A pretty face ... destroyed by a boy who wanted to teach her a lesson.

I fish my phone from the sink and tuck it into my pocket. I open the faucet and gurgle to spit out his taste, then grab my toothbrush and clean my teeth and tongue, but nothing I do can rid me of the stain that is Caleb.

My mother invaded his dad's life, and now he's invaded mine as a punishment.

But I never gave up, and I won't.

I clean my face off with a paper towel and throw it away, then I brush through my hair with my fingers and get rid of any last blotches. But my face still looks like I got run over by a freight train.

And the girl underneath is far from the one I remember.

His little jewel… slowly cracking.

***

95

Two years ago

"Dad," I mutter, yawning as I open the door to his workshop. "What are you doing up so late?"

He cuts the last few stems of the roses and places them down on his workbench. "Oh, just finishing up this order. Did I wake you?"

I saunter into the shop and marvel at all the beautiful bouquets he's made that weren't here a day ago.

"You did all this tonight?"

He nods. "A fickle customer. They decided to change their order at the last minute, and I wasn't prepared."

I look at the clock in the corner. It's already way past midnight. He should be sleeping too.

"Dad …" I sigh. "You need your sleep too."

"I'll be fine, don't worry," he replies.

Always the stubborn one. He can never say no to an order, no matter how hard it is to create or how many bushels of flowers it'll take. Despite earning only so little on his craft …

I touch the red and white roses, which smell like perfume and feel as delicate as silk against my fingers. "If they're so difficult, why not just cancel the order?"

He places down the knife he was cutting them with. "Oh no. There is no canceling. Not with this customer." He swallows, almost as if he finds it hard to admit. He approaches me and grabs my face, placing a gentle peck on my forehead. "But you don't need to worry about that. I'll make it work. Just go to sleep."

"I do worry about you, Dad," I murmur. "These customers sound like they need to be told no."

He shakes his head. "Impossible."

"Then why did you take the job?" I ask, and I grab his hand. "We don't need their money. We can do without. I can get a job too, and we can—"

"Oh, my pretty little jewel," he interrupts, a gentle smile on his face. "So concerned about other's well-being." He grabs a rose off one of the bushes he created and plucks it, then tucks it into my hair. "I raised you right."

I smile and blush, feeling the prickles against my ear. "Yes, you did, Dad."

Tears well up in my eyes. I can't help it. He sacrifices so much to keep this family fed.

He catches one of the tears with his thumb. "Don't cry, my jewel. Your face is far too pretty for those tears to stain it."

I laugh it off. "I just worry too much."

"I know you do." He looks down at me from underneath his eyelashes. "But I need you to go to college. Okay? And you need to make sure you study hard, and to do that, you need your sleep." He grabs my shoulders and turns me around so I face the door again. "So go back to bed, little jewel, and we'll see each other again at breakfast in the morning."

He pushes me forward, so I keep walking, but I can't help but glance over my shoulder. "Promise me you'll go to bed too, Dad. I know you want to take care of us, but you have to take care of yourself too."

He picks up the bouquet he was working on again. "I promise I will take care of ... everyone."

Even now, he can never choose himself.

"Sleep tight, little jewel."

***

Present

His pretty little jewel.
Tainted.
But not destroyed.
Dad wouldn't want me to give up that easily.

I grab some of my mom's foundation and smear it on my face to conceal the splotches and tap on some of her pink blush. Then I grab her mascara and put some on.

There. Much better.

I turn toward the tub, which is a complete mess, and grasp the shower curtain and put it all into the big bin in the corner. No way we're going to use that ever again.

I open the door and blink a couple of times from the brightness of the light.

I hadn't even realized I spent so much time in the darkness with him.

I take in a deep breath and go downstairs. Gloom overwhelms me at the thought of having to see him sitting there with a grin on his face, knowing full well what he just did.

But when I finally get to the dining room, he's gone.

"Crystal? What's going on?" my mom asks. "Is everything okay?"

"Um … yeah," I mutter, trying to put up a fake smile. "I just showed him around and put on some makeup while I was upstairs too."

"O-kay." My mom frowns.

God, I hope she believes my lie.

"You sure took a lot of time showing him around upstairs," she says.

I blush and avert my eyes. "Yeah … Anyway, where's Caleb?"

"He left," she responds.

"I don't know what's up with him. I apologize for the rudeness," his dad says, clearing his throat.

"It's fine," my mom replies with a polite smile. "It happens. I know how difficult it can be to raise kids on your own."

"Right, thank you," he responds with a smile.

"Um, Mom, you're gonna have to replace the shower curtain," I mutter.

Her brows furrow. "What? Why?"

"I accidentally leaned into it, and it broke off. Sorry." I rub my lips together. "I put it in the bin. I'll buy you a new one."

"It's okay. Thank you for telling me. Do you know why Caleb left?"

"No." I lie, shrugging. "Did he say something?"

"No, he just ran off," she replies.

"He does that sometimes," his dad adds. "Things have been difficult on him ever since his mom …" His dad swallows away the lump in his throat. "It doesn't matter. I'll talk to him later. Promise."

My mom reaches for his hands. "Thank you. I'd love that. I really want this to work."

So quickly falling in love already. I'm impressed.

"Me too," his dad says. "And for what it's worth, I think you cooked a lovely dinner."

They smile at each other, and my mom blushes. "Thank you." Then she looks at me. "Let's eat, Crystal."

I nod and sit back down again like everything's normal.

She'll never know what I did for her and never find out what I plan to do. Because I'll take my secrets with me to the grave.

***

ARES

The next day

I'm glad we finally managed to get rid of those damn bodies in the freezer, but it was far too much trouble for my liking, with Blaine's connections being iffy at best. Too many men asked questions they shouldn't be asking, but there is no way in hell I would ever ask my dad's men to take care of it, so I guess I'm content.

"Hey, don't be so pouty," Blaine muses as he sits beside me just as class starts.

"I'm not. I'm just contemplating the best course of action now that those men are dead," I say.

His brows furrow. "You think they'll come after us?"

"I don't think it. I *know* it." I lean on the table on my elbows and tap my fingers together. "It's only a matter of time."

"But they were just peons," Blaine says. "They shouldn't have stepped onto our territory if they wanted to live."

"They're lures," I respond.

He frowns. "What … like …?"

"Bait," Caleb adds as he flops down onto the bench. "To get us to react. And we did."

"You're late," Blaine mutters, casually filing his black-painted nails.

Caleb shrugs and ignores him. "Anyway, there's no trace of those bodies or the kills. If anyone asks, we'll just deny we're involved. Easy."

"You're a fool if you think that will stop those fuckers," I tell him, leaning back in my seat and fishing my vape out of my bag.

The teacher narrows his eyes at me as I take a drag right in front of him, but I don't care. He won't kick me out. He knows the power our family name holds at this fucking university.

That's the only positive thing about it.

99

"What do you want to do about it, then?" Blaine asks, snorting. "Face them head-on? That's a massacre."

"No," I say, taking another deep drag of the vape. "Let them come to us." I hand the vape to Blaine, who seems eager to take a drag as well.

"Oh, cherry flavored. My favorite," Blaine muses like a happy bird.

Caleb's phone keeps buzzing, and I look over at him as he continuously scrolls on a social media profile without a care in the world that people are texting him. But the pictures I see floating by make me narrow my eyes.

Crystal Murphy.

I tilt my head and watch him scroll faster and faster, as though he's memorizing each photo until they blend into one. A perfect photo for a perfect girl.

Too perfect to destroy …

Yet neither of us can help ourselves.

I lean in to whisper into his ear, "Her?"

He stops and slams his phone down on the desk like he got caught masturbating.

"Don't worry," I say, placing a hand on his knee. "I won't tell a soul."

He doesn't respond, merely quivers when I slowly raise my hand up to his thigh.

"When?"

"After I watched her play with herself," he responds.

"When you came on her window?"

He nods. "I couldn't stop thinking about her." He breathes out a sigh and makes a fist with his hand. "She followed me."

I stop moving. "How do you know?"

"I saw her and her mother at the Fi's Cups and Cakes store at the same time I was there with my dad. She was waiting for me. I'm sure of it."

"Oh, this is getting interesting," Blaine muses, taking another drag of my vape. "Tell us more."

Caleb grinds his teeth. "My dad took me out to dinner to meet his new girlfriend, and it turned out to be her fucking mom."

My eyes widen, and my fingers dig into his flesh. But he doesn't even flinch.

"She sent her mom to my dad. I know she did," Caleb grits. "It's too much of a coincidence, but she won't admit it."

"Hmm …" A smile forms on my lips. "So the rose turns out to be prickly after all."

Blaine watches us with amusement. "You know, I quite like you two getting obsessed over something other than each other for once."

I ignore him and grab Caleb's phone so we can both look at the pictures he was obsessing over. "She's an enigma, isn't she? A beautiful mystery you can't wait to crack open and uncover." I lick my lips at the sight of her gorgeous face, wondering how it looked from his point of view when she came from my fingers.

He and Blaine are the only ones who saw.

But I will have my chance to see what her face looks like as she falls apart soon enough now that I know what she's been up to.

A wicked grin spreads on my cheeks as my hand slides up even farther across Caleb's thigh.

"Oh boy, here we go," Blaine mutters. "You've made her your target now, haven't you?"

Caleb slowly nods, nails digging into the wood of his desk as I reach his cock.

"She made herself a target when she hurled her mom at your dad," I whisper, poking at his thick length, which bobs up and down in his pants. "She deserves to be punished along with her friends."

He glances my way, the desire in his eyes so fierce it's hard to ignore, and it makes me want to slam my lips onto his. But I'll let him simmer in his heat for a little longer.

"That girl …" I whisper into his ear, "We're going to destroy her, and she's going to beg us to do it."

THIRTEEN

Blaine

With my romance book in one hand and a cup of steaming hot cocoa in the other, I sit on a bench outside the Tartarus House and enjoy the evening. It's far too noisy inside right now, and sometimes I just want a little me-time away from their crazy shit.

Besides, these novels don't read themselves.

I flip the page and lick my lips as the guy is about to kiss the girl for the first time, only she doesn't know it yet. I always get giddy when I get to this part. It's one of my favorite books, and I can just read it over and over without ever getting bored.

With a stupid grin, I take a sip of my hot cocoa when I spot a blond-haired girl in a little blue dress stomping toward the cars parked out front beyond the gate with a knife in her hand.

"Oh dear …" I mutter as I place the cocoa back on the little table beside me.

She walks past each one with the knife held out in front of her until she finds the car she's looking for. An Aston Martin. And I know just who it belongs to.

She scratches along the paint without a single care whose car she's damaging. Or maybe that's exactly the point. She slices through the metal and punctures the tires, then looks up at me with disdain.

I just keep drinking my cocoa, shrugging as I lift my book to hide my face behind it, even though she's already seen me.

When she's finally gone, I breathe a sigh of relief.

I'm so glad she didn't come up to the gates looking to fight me. I don't want to hurt her.

At least not in a break-your-fingers kind of way.

I shut my book and place it on the bench beside me, then pull my phone from my pocket and start the convo.

"Caleb?"

"What do you want?" he barks.

"Well, I thought you'd like to know a certain girl just slashed your tires."

"WHAT?"

"Yeah, you might want to come downstairs," I reply.

"Is she still there?" he growls.

"Nope. Sauntered away with that little knife of hers like it was no biggie." I gaze at my nails, wondering if I should do a different color because black might not suit me after all. "She also kind of ruined your paint job."

He hangs up without saying another word.

I scoff at the phone. "Rude."

I place it on the bench beside me and pick up my book again to finish.

The door slams open. "Why the fuck didn't you stop her?" he yells.

"I don't know. It's not my problem." I shrug.

He grabs my open shirt and knocks the book out of my hand. "You let her do that to my car?"

"Get your hands off me," I growl back. Only when I narrow my eyes does he finally do what I say. "This Gucci is far too priceless for you to tear holes into it."

"I'll tear holes into your body if you don't fucking tell me where she went right now," he barks back.

"Oh, don't threaten me with a good time, please," I muse, chuckling.

He attempts to slap me, but I grasp his wrist and twist it until he's locked in a place where he can't move.

"How many times must I tell you? You can't win this, Caleb," I say.

"All right, all right, I'm sorry," he splutters.

I slap him on the ass and release him. "Good boy."

He gets all flushed as he pats himself down and pretends I didn't just easily subdue him.

Sometimes he forgets I'm a black belt in both ju-jitsu and Kendo.

Hell, I even forget it myself sometimes.

"She walked back down the street she came out of," I say, pointing him in the right direction. "Looks like it's on the way back to her dorm."

He walks toward the gate and throws it open, then runs to his car, the panic settling in his eyes when he sees how badly damaged it is. "My fucking baby." He caresses the car. "She ruined you."

"It's just a car," I yell across the lawn.

"It is not just a car, asshole!" he yells back. "She just got a fucking paint job!"

"Well, maybe you shouldn't have pissed that girl off as much as you did?" I shrug.

Now he's really fuming.

Oops. My bad.

He slaps his own car a little too harshly. "She's gonna fucking pay for this."

"Do you really think that's the smart thing to do?" I ask him, casually sipping on my hot cocoa. "You know, seeing how she pretty much knows something no one can find out?"

"I don't fucking care. She ruined my car."

"And what did you do to deserve it?" I muse, taking another sip while he's almost exploding like a hot air balloon being fed too much fire.

He slowly marches back into the property. "She followed me. So I gave her a piece of my mind."

My eyes narrow. "You mean an inch of your dick."

The smirk says it all.

He leans in to whisper into my ear, "Every fucking inch. And if you want to know … She also tasted divine."

Now why did that make my dick bob up and down in my pants? I'll never know.

He turns around and saunters off, waving at me. "Don't tell Ares."

104

"You know I'm terrible at keeping secrets, darling," I warn him. "I might let it slip."

He sticks up his middle finger at me. "Then tell him the truth and let him know how good she felt while she came all over my fucking tongue. I'm sure he won't mind that I played with his shiny new toy."

***

Crystal

I put my bag in the corner of my room and take a deep breath.

There. Much better now.

I shrug off the leftover anger and grab my study books so I can prep for a quiz before I have to go to sleep.

However, when I turn around, the shadowy figure in front of me makes me scream.

Right into his hand that covers my mouth.

Caleb.

My eyes widen.

How did he get in?

A cold breeze follows him into the room, and my eyes immediately lock onto the open window.

Shit. I knew I should've closed it before I left.

"Shh … don't want to wake your friends now, do we?" he whispers, eyes filled with rage.

I kick him in the balls, but he swiftly grabs my arms and wraps them together, body pressed against mine as one hand is still snaked tightly around my mouth to prevent any sound from coming out.

"Do you really want to do this, Crystal?" he asks. "After you've already been such a bad fucking girl, slashing my tires?"

I knock my head back into his so he loses some of his grip, and I tear away from him.

But he holds my arm and drags me right back to him, this time with a knife pointed right at my neck.

I stop fighting and hold my breath. "Now are you going to behave? Or should I make you feel the same pain you gave my beautiful car?"

"You ruined my face, so I thought it'd be fair game to ruin your

105

precious car in return," I spit. "An eye for an eye."

His fingers dig into my skin, jaw tensing up.

Suddenly, he shoves me up against the door, one hand firmly planted on my belly.

"An eye ..." he growls, holding the knife closer to my face, lifting it up high. "Is that what you want me to take?"

Panic fills my bones, but I stay put, trying to remain calm.

Don't show them any weakness. Zero fear.

"You do that, and my mother will know exactly what kind of family she's attached herself to," I tell him.

His hand slowly lowers between my legs, and I struggle to stay put. "Is that before or after you tell her about how you writhed all over my tongue?"

I spit on his face.

He deserves it.

His nostrils flare, eyes looking more incensed than ever. And all it does is make me smile.

He wipes his hand along his face and gathers my spit while lowering his knife until it touches my bottom lip.

"Open your mouth," he growls.

When I slowly part my lips, he pushes his own two fingers inside and gives me back my own spit.

"Pretty girls like you don't need to act dirty," he says.

He spits back.

Right into my mouth.

"I'll be the one to *make* you fucking dirty," he groans. "Now swallow."

Oh God.

The knife tips up against my lips. "Go on."

I do what he says despite the humiliation and swallow down both of our spit.

"Good girl."

He lowers the knife and leans in, his lips hovering so close to mine, and I suck in a breath. Instead, he reaches for the doorknob and locks the door, stealing the key. A wicked grin spreads on his lips as he leans back and watches me for a moment.

Then he steps back, tucking the key into his pocket.

"Give me back the key," I grit.

With a smug smile, he steps back until he reaches my bed. He sits down, palms behind his back. "Come and get it then."

I lean against the door and look for a way out, but the only other option is through my window, the same way he came in.

"Don't even think about it," he says. "I will catch you before you make it halfway across the room."

My teeth clench together.

Shit. He's lured me into a trap in my own room.

"Now, come here, Crystal."

"No."

My eyes flutter to my bag. My knife is in there. If I can grab it, I might be able to fend him off.

WHACK!

Caleb's knife lands right beside my head into the wood.

He threw an actual fucking knife at my head.

"Grabbing your knife will do you no good, Crystal. So go ahead, grab mine. See if you can hit me."

He's completely insane.

Still, I grab the handle, the blade much heavier than mine as I rip it out of the cracked wood. I clutch it tightly, slowly walking toward him while keeping a careful eye so I don't misstep.

And then I strike.

He swiftly grabs my wrist and twists my hand until it hurts, and I drop the knife. Right into his other hand.

"What did I tell you?" His voice is low, gruff, almost like he's warning me not to overstep his boundaries. "You can't win this game."

He pulls me to him and lifts me from the floor, only to throw me over his lap.

"What are you doing?"

He slides his calloused hand underneath my blue dress. "Giving you the punishment you deserve."

"Let go of m—"

THWACK!

A sharp pain hits my ass cheek, and I yelp.

I try to shove myself off him, but he holds me steady with one hand. "Stay."

Another hit to the other ass cheek almost has me flying off the bed.

Oh my God ... He's actually spanking me.

107

FOURTEEN

CALEB

"What the hell is wrong with you?" she hisses.

I know exactly what the hell is wrong with me.

This girl.

This girl right here who couldn't keep her hands off my beautiful car, that's what.

I spank her again, and each of her cries gives me pleasure.

God, I'm really just as fucked up as she said I was, but I don't care. I need her to feel my rage.

"What the f—"

I slap her again. She keeps thinking she can fight back, but she already lost the moment she started playing. And it's about time I silenced her pretty little mouth.

My fingers slide underneath her panties, and I rip them off. "What did I tell you about these?" I hold the destroyed panties in front of her face. "Stop wearing them, or I will keep destroying every single pair."

I slap her ass again, and her back arches from the sizzling pain, her mouth opening wide to let out a cry. Instead, I stuff the panties inside and clamp her mouth shut.

"Quiet, little slut, or your friends might hear you," I groan.

I gently pet her sweet little ass, rubbing her skin to prepare her for what's to come.

All she'll feel is the burn of my strikes.

"You've been a naughty fucking girl."

I slap her again, this time gentler than before but still harsh enough for her to bite down into her own panties.

"This is your punishment for destroying my car."

THWACK!

My hand comes down on her ass again, leaving a fine handprint.

"Asshole," she muffles through the panties.

She thinks insulting me is going to save her? Wrong.

The next hit is sharper, and she thrashes around again, but I keep her steady with just the palm of my hand on her back.

"You can't escape this, Crystal," I say, rubbing her sore ass. "One way or another, you will pay for what you've done."

THWACK!

Her skin burns underneath the palm of my hand. Another hit makes her yelp against the panties in her mouth, and my cock twitches in my pants from the sound.

"Fight me, and I'll only spank you harder," I warn.

My hand comes down on her other ass cheek again, her skin reddening under my touch. Her ass looks so nice covered in my handprint.

I rub the spot to soothe her pain, but only for a moment. She'll need to learn to savor these seconds.

"What do you want?" she asks, her voice sounding more desperate with every passing second.

I lick my lips and slide my hand across her ass. "I want you to lie here and take it like the bad girl you are."

THWACK!

Her toes curl against the bedding, and she shoves her knees into me, but it doesn't faze me one bit.

I spank her faster and faster until there's barely any break, and each one of my strikes produces a louder moan. I'm relentless, swatting her pretty little ass with a flat hand until I can see a clear outline.

Until I know for sure my mark, this lesson, will stay with her for days.

"Please ..." she murmurs.

My hand hovers right above her skin.

Good God.

The sound of her voice just now.

Pleading with me.

Begging for mercy.

I didn't think there was anything I could ever want from a girl, yet ...

My hand slowly dips down between her thighs. She tenses up as I circle her pussy, sliding two fingers up and down her slit.

She doesn't strike me as a girl foolish enough to go up against three of the most dangerous guys on campus. She knows what people say about us. That we're murderers who take no sides, devils in disguise who play for whatever team they fancy. We don't fucking play by the rules.

She followed me, and after the harsh warning I gave her, she still keyed my car.

There has to be a reason behind her madness. And I want to find out what it is.

"You knew I would come to you. Before you keyed my car, you knew exactly what it would do to me," I say, teasing her pussy. "Yet you did it anyway. Just to spite me? Knowing full well I would come for revenge?"

I spank her ass again, the burn hitting twice as hard after I just convinced her I'd be nice.

"You wanted me to come to you, didn't you?" I murmur, slowly slipping down farther into her slit.

When I touch her clit and circle around it, she sucks in a breath and shakes her head.

SLAP!

"Lie."

She spits out the panties and growls, "I wanted you to pay for what you did at my mom's house."

I shove the panties back into her mouth. "But you knew exactly what it would cause if you went through with your little plan." I flick the tip of my fingers across her most sensitive spot. "Because deep down inside you, you're yearning for someone to give you those orgasms you so desperately crave."

SLAP!

I spank her when she least expects it, just above her pussy, and I know she can feel it there, awakening an arousal she didn't know existed inside her.

Because I know how it feels, this position she's found herself in, this submission of one's very fucking soul. I know it so well that I don't understand why I crave to dominate her. But I do.

I want to break down that barrier filled with lies and make her see there's no hope. Break her until she's a whimpering slut at my knees, ready to suck and swallow.

Just like Ares once did to me.

"You see, you and I are not so different. We enjoy the thrill of danger. The threat as we're forced to submit…" I groan, slipping my fingers down between her thighs again, spreading her wetness all over. "Admit it."

She shakes her head.

SLAP!

"Stop." *SLAP.* "Lying." *SLAP.* "To." *SLAP.* "Me." *SLAP!*

Each slap is alternated by a swipe across her clit, mixing pain and pleasure until even she can't tell them apart. Until she can't control herself any longer and moans freely to each of my strikes.

"I can feel your pussy throb, slut. You love this. You love being punished and used," I murmur, pushing two fingers inside her while she gasps in shock.

God, her pussy is so fucking tight and wet. Perfect for a wicked sinner like me.

"So I will give you what you crave so badly."

I curl my fingers and play with her G-spot until she writhes on my lap. And then I spank her again, the palm of my hand reverberating in her pussy.

When she tries to sit up, I grasp her hands and pin them behind her back, then pull out my fingers to spank her again.

"You're a bad girl," I growl. "Say it. Say you're a fucking bad girl for damaging my car like that."

"I'm a bad girl," she whimpers as I spank her again until she finally yields.

I slowly push my fingers back inside and circle them until her toes curl and her breath becomes unsteady. I go knuckle deep and curl my fingers up, then spank her little red ass until she mewls with delight.

"That's it, slut. You're going to come while I turn this ass red for my enjoyment," I groan, watching her slowly come undone.

Something is so fucking powerful in knowing she's helpless to defend herself against the impending orgasm, and it turns me on so fucking much to just watch her plead.

"Please ... let me come," she murmurs, moaning when I slap her again.

But she doesn't deserve me touching her little clit.

No, she's going to come from the palm of my hand on her ass and my fingers inside her alone.

"Then come," I say, thrusting in and out of her pussy with two fingers. "Come all over my fingers just from being spanked."

THWACK! THWACK!

The last two spankings send her over the edge, and I can feel her pussy contract around my fingers, a long-drawn-out moan slipping out of her. The panties slowly roll out of her parted lips as she lays her head down on the mattress, defeated.

I pull out my fingers and bring them to my lips, dipping out my tongue to taste that sweetness once more. Fuck. So fucking delicious.

Too delicious to say no to.

Too delicious for this to be the last time.

God, what have I gotten myself into?

One glance at her in that blue dress and that red ass underneath, and I'm already rock hard.

The last time I had any interest in girls was years ago.

Why this one? Why now?

Is it only because Ares wants her?

Or is it ... something more?

I plant a flat hand on her ass and say, "Don't ever touch my car again."

I release her from my grip and get up, but she flops down onto the bed like a limp noodle, completely spent from the amazing orgasm I just gave her.

Someone knocks on her door. "Crystal? Can you help me out with my homework tonight?"

I swiftly throw her key onto her bed.

Before she unlocks that door, I'll be long gone, slipping into the dark, cold night where demons like me thrive.

FIFTEEN

I blew off the girl who knocked on my door and said I couldn't help her with homework. I'll make it up to her when I feel normal again, not like I got hit by a hurricane.

There was no way in hell I was going to open that door after just having my ass spanked. What was I supposed to say? Sorry, I can't even sit right now, but sure, I'll help you with your homework? There would be questions I don't want to give the answer to.

So I stayed put in my room and waited until the morning before I finally had the courage to get out. I swiftly slipped away while they were having breakfast under the pretense that I was going to work on homework in the library.

Now I'm here in school, walking down the giant staircases, carefully holding the banister so I don't slip. My legs are still stiff, and every time I take a step, I can feel my ass clench. It still burns from his hand, which left an imprint on my skin. Even now, it's still there, buzzing, humming, reminding me of the wicked pain he inflicted on me.

Pain that quickly turned into a sinful pleasure I should not have been feeling.

God, why can't I stop thinking about it?

When I finally get to the bottom of the stairs, I breathe a sigh of relief, then straighten my skirt so no one can see the palm of his hand on my ass. This short pink skirt was all I had left to wear today.

My mind isn't fully there as I head across campus to the grassy area where I normally eat with my friends, but the moment I see them happily chatting away in our usual spot, I freeze.

I can't go over there.

How am I supposed to face them after what happened?

How am I supposed to sit there with a straight face knowing my ass burns so hard I can still feel my pussy throb just from the memory?

I can't lie to them.

But I can't tell them the truth either.

I need to clear my mind. Sit somewhere where I can think without anyone to distract me.

I walk toward the benches near the rose garden, but then I spot a familiar black-haired guy with a killer aura walking right in my direction. Ares. Even though he's looking at his phone, I can't risk bumping into him, so I spin on my heels.

Only to see another guy wearing a hoodie, with familiar streaks of blond hair peeking out, staring right into my soul. He bites the piercing in his lip when he sees me, then takes a drag of his cigarette and chucks it on the ground.

Oh God. Caleb.

Did he follow me?

Or is he just waiting there, lurking in the shadows, watching me to see if I mess up and spill their secrets?

I swallow down the lump in my throat.

I'm locked between them with no way out.

Except right into the maze.

Without thinking, I bolt, heading straight into the rose maze. I don't care where I'm going. All I know is that I need to get away from those guys as fast as possible.

At a split, I take a left turn, and then another, and then a right. I have no clue where I am or which path to take, so I recklessly pick without thought or reason. The only thing driving me forward is the handprints on my ass and a promise of more to come if I don't stay the hell away.

But it's too late now.

It's too late to run from those bastards who've made it their mission to destroy me.

CRACK!

The snapping of a twig behind me sets me on edge, so I run like hell into the next bend and around another corner. Swaths of roses hang down from unkempt bushes, and I shove them out of my way as I run through a part of the maze barely anyone visits. There are scratches on my face, but I don't care as I keep going, desperate to escape this harrowing feeling in my heart that it's about to be swallowed whole.

I spin on my heels and listen for footsteps, waiting for them to come out of the bushes behind me. A few bluebirds hover above me, and my heart rate shoots up just from the fluttering of their wings.

I'm really losing it.

I'm totally and utterly losing my shit here.

I don't even know if they followed me … or if I'm making it all up in my head.

Were they even there to begin with? Or was it just my active imagination taking hold of me?

I take in a deep breath and turn around.

Only to run face-first into the chest of a giant.

My hands slowly creep up his chest, fingers trembling across each thick slab of his muscles that protrude right through that white button-up shirt he's wearing, as my own heart rate shoots up while I listen to his. Time almost comes to a stop.

But I still manage to lift my head and gaze up, following a trail from the partially opened buttons to the shark tooth necklace dangling from his neck, all the way up into the eyes of the most handsome man I've ever seen, his chiseled jaw and sharp cheekbones in stark contrast to the flowy, curly hair on his head.

Oh God. It's Blaine.

"Hello there, darling."

***

Blaine

I have never been more pleasantly surprised than I am right now.

What a coincidence. I come here to read a sexy smut scene in my new romance book, and the second I'm about to sit down on the bench underneath this tree in the middle of the rose maze in a place no one ever visits because it's too damn hard to find, this gorgeous girl bumps into me and falls head over heels for me, and then we kiss in the moonlight.

Oh no, wait, that was just my overactive imagination.

But I can make it work.

She looks up at me like she's seen a ghost and swiftly shoves herself out of my grasp. Not so violent now, after that whole scene with Caleb's car.

"Aw, don't be afraid," I muse. "I won't bite." A devilish smile worms its way onto my face. "Unless you want me to, of course."

"What are you doing here?" she asks, getting all flustered.

I frown, smirking. "Well, I could ask the same from you, no?" I tap my finger against my cheek. "This is public property, after all."

"I ... I ..."

She sure has a lot of trouble finishing her sentences around me.

"You, what?" I tilt my head and step closer. "You were looking for something?" She seems frozen to the ground as I tower over her. But this girl almost looks like a goddamn princess when she's scared, with those big doe-like eyes and that pink skirt.

I grab a strand of her hair and twirl it around my finger, mesmerized by her beauty. "Or maybe you were looking for... someone?"

"I wasn't," she says, her breath faltering when my fingers reach her collarbones.

"You and I do a lot of bumping into each other, don't you agree?" I muse, brushing past her chin so it lifts, and I can look into those gorgeous green eyes of hers. "It's almost as if it was fate."

Ares and Caleb truly have no clue what kind of a jewel they've tried to defile.

My eyes slide down her body, and my tongue briefly darts out at the sight of that long-sleeved white cotton top through which her nipples peak and that short, bright pink skirt underneath.

116

"What a feast for the eyes you are," I murmur.

She blushes and looks down, but then tugs at her skirt, her hands briefly skimming past a red mark near her thighs, and my eyes narrow.

That mark … it definitely looks like fingers.

Poor girl really didn't know what was coming for her.

I did try to warn her.

"He hurt you, didn't he?" I ask, curious if she'd tell the truth. "Are you trying to hide?"

Her lips part, and she sucks in a breath, but she immediately attempts to step away from me, so I grab her wrist. "Please. Don't go."

She pauses, conflicted.

"I won't hurt you."

She swallows, visibly concerned. "You're a part of their group," she says. "I can't trust you."

"I understand," I say. Still, I pull her closer and lift my hand to tear a rose from the bushes, and I tuck it behind her ear. "If it were up to me … I'd treat you like a queen." I lift her wrist and press a soft kiss on the top of her hand.

She doesn't jerk away as I slowly lower it again, and the blush on her cheeks clearly gives away she's enamored by me as much as I am by her.

She can't be any taller than five feet, judging by how small she seems compared to my six feet nine inches. She even looks fragile, just like the roses surrounding me. But just like them, she is a bud ready to bloom, something to admire and cherish. Ares and Caleb don't appreciate her beauty. All they want to do is crush it in the palm of their hands just so they could be the last to hold it.

I lean over to whisper into her ear, "Now, take a left, then a right, go straight ahead, don't stop until you see the red lantern, then two more rights. That'll get you to the side exit near the gates."

I press a gentle kiss on her neck. "Now run away, darling."

She looks like a ghost when I spin her on her heels and push her in the right direction. Almost like she can't believe I'm helping her. But I don't play by the rules, and especially not Tartarus ones.

I step back and sit on the bench, opening my book while she darts off into the maze, fluttering away with that little rose still stuck in her hair.

She'll come running back into my arms soon enough, but until then … I'll satisfy myself with this dirty romance.

***

CALEB

I could've sworn I saw her run into the maze, but I can't find her anywhere. Maybe I'm imagining things.

Fuck. This girl really is doing a number on me.

I push some roses out of my way and make my way back, but when my phone rings, I pause.

"Yeah?"

"Caleb, finally. I've been trying to call you all day."

"Sorry. Been busy, Dad," I mutter, walking out of the maze.

"Studies, right?"

"Um … Yeah." I lie, but there's no way in fucking hell I'm going to tell him about Crystal.

My dad would die if he knew what I did to her.

And then he'd kill me too.

Nope, not happening.

"So here's the thing, I'm going to a barbecue next week, and I want you to come with me," he says.

"A barbecue?" I frown. "Really?"

"Yeah," he responds. "Is that so odd?"

"You haven't done that in years."

"I know, but I thought it'd be fun. So what do you say, boy?"

I roll my eyes. "Do I have a choice?"

"C'mon, humor your dad for once," he says, chuckling. "It's not often we get to do things together."

"Because you're always working," I reply.

"Exactly. So it's a date, then. I'll text you the address because I haven't memorized it yet."

Memorized?

"But I'll see you next week. Also, don't stay up too late."

He hangs up before I can say another word.

That was weird.

A barbecue? He's literally not shown any interest in that since I was a kid.

What's going on?

My phone buzzes, and in comes the text with the address. The second I see where it is, my skin begins to crawl, and my fingers cramp around the phone from holding it too tightly.

The same place we went to when he told me who he was dating.

Crystal's mom's house.

"Fuck!"

SIXTEEN

ARES

A week later

I roll the dice and lean against the wooden table to see them settle. Loud cheers erupt from the women behind me, one throwing her hand around my face and kissing me on the cheeks.

"And another win for this fine gentleman right here," the dealer says.

I take the chips and give one to the dealer, then walk off, the two girls flocking behind me like birds flying to a feeder.

Walking up to the guard near the VIP area, I show him my ID, and he swiftly removes the line for me. "Welcome, sir."

Everyone here knows who I am. Perks of being the owner's son.

I nod at the guard, and the two women follow me inside. I settle down on a red velvety couch in the back of the VIP room and stack my chips on the table.

"Champagne, sir?" a server asks me.

I take a glass off the tray, and so do the women, then they settle down beside me, snuggling up against me like they want to rip the skin off my body. And I'm not even sure I'd mind.

"That was such a good game," the left one says, running her fingers over my thigh.

The other one hangs her legs over mine, trying to claim me. "We brought him some good luck, don't you think?"

I take a big sip of my champagne, the heat keeping my rage at a minimum while the ladies start to feel me up, kissing my neck and cheeks. I just know they want me to bring them up to my private room here at the casino.

But I'm not in the mood right now.

I grab a chip and stare at it, the pink color on the backside making me think of a particular pink-lipped girl who's been a thorn in my eye ever since she stepped foot on this campus.

She's been following Caleb and me around, and I know it's not just to catch us in another kill.

I came here to distract myself, yet …

I flip the chip, annoyed that I worry so much about just one girl.

Why all of these kisses and touches remind me of her.

Why they make me want to push them aside and walk out of here so I can hunt her down and give her the chase she's been quietly begging for.

Maybe I should.

I take my last sip of the champagne and look up, only to see a shimmer of a figure walking past the VIP section, our eyes connecting in the same instance as wild rage becomes me.

"Kai?" I mutter.

What is he doing here?

I get up and walk off.

"Wait, where are you going?" the girls ask.

"Out."

"But your chips—"

"Buy yourself something nice." I leave them with a literal gold mine, but it's mere pocket change to me.

I march out of the VIP area and catch up with him. I grab his shoulder and make him turn around. "What the fuck are you doing here?"

He smirks. "You know why I'm here."

My nostrils flare. "He invited *you*, didn't he?"

His eyes drift off to the room in the back that's well guarded, the one no one but highly privileged staff and trusted people are allowed

121

to enter.

Yet … *he's* invited?

"It's just a conversation," he replies.

My fist balls. "Give him my warm fucking regards." I chuck a remaining chip at his face.

"Ares … really?" Kai scoffs, picking it up from the floor.

"Have fucking fun with him," I growl back. "By all means. Stoke those flames some more."

"I can't help that he wants to talk with me. You know that," he replies.

"You could tell him to eat a bag of dicks," I growl back.

"And then what?" He raises his brow. "You think that's gonna go well with him?"

I snort. "Like you have any clue what it looks like when he pops off."

"I'm just saying, I'm trying to keep the peace here," he says, shrugging.

"Yeah … you're running to him like a toothless dog with its tail between its legs," I grit.

"Says the eternal coward," he retorts.

That's it.

That motherfucker is dead.

I grasp his collar, lifting a fist, ready to strike.

"Go on. Do it."

I glare him down, wishing I could cut him as deeply as my father cut me.

"Do it. Hit me," Kai eggs me on.

But if I did, I'd give him another reason to become a martyr.

I swallow my rage and put him back down.

"Should've just punched me," he says.

"Yeah. But then I'd be just like you," I spit. "And I'm not that kind of man."

I shove him away and out of my reach before I do something foolish.

"That's a low blow."

He's right, but I don't care.

He pats down his shirt. "Do you always have to be such a raging animal?"

"You know why," I quip back at him.

122

His mellow face slowly changes into something more sinister, darker, and I don't like it one bit. Not because it looks just like how I see myself in the mirror, but because it's turning softer and softer. Unlike him.

Like he's actually starting to pity me.

And I fucking hate how it looks.

"I'm so—"

"Don't." I raise a finger. "Don't you fucking dare. Fuck you, I'm out of here," I growl, fishing a cig from my pocket to light up in the middle of the fucking casino. Fuck the rules. "Give him this."

And I stick up my middle finger as I turn around and march off.

When I get outside, my phone rings, and I pick it up so fast I nearly crush the screen when I press the button. "What?"

"Ares?"

Caleb's voice takes off the edge a little, and I take a drag of my cig and blow out the smoke.

"What's up?"

He sounds at the end of his rope. "Fuck. I need your help."

I toss my cig aside and walk straight to my car. "On the way. Tell me where."

***

CALEB

Thirty minutes ago

I sit back in my chair and shove my fork into the piece of meat lying on my plate without ever taking my eyes off her.

Crystal fucking Murphy in her cute little button-down onesie with wildflowers on it. She looks like she walked straight out of a picture book. Like a magical creature that doesn't exist.

She's casually drinking a Coca-Cola while ignoring my stares, pretending she doesn't care when she's clearly affected by my mere presence.

I can't blame her. I feel the same way.

Especially after getting my hands all over her ass the last time I saw her.

But something about this whole get-together in this suburban home puts us both on edge.

"There you go," her mom says as she puts a salad on the table. "Jonathan will have more steaks ready in a few minutes."

So they're on a first-name basis already. Great.

I cut into my steak like I'm butchering someone, and I think Crystal knows just as well as I do who I'm imagining here.

"No need to destroy your steak like that, dear," her mother says, giggling when she sees me go to town.

I just shove the biggest piece into my mouth and watch her be abhorred by my chewing habits.

"Do you have to act like a pig?" Crystal asks, picking up a magazine and hiding her eyes behind it.

I smirk. "You should know best of all." And I take another big bite. Nothing beats Dad's steaks ... except maybe when I have to fucking share them with the most vexing girl on the planet.

"You're disgusting," she says, rolling her eyes before she lifts the magazine back up so she doesn't have to look at me.

"Yet you happily moaned to my filth," I muse.

Her cheeks turn the same color as the beets in the salad. "Can you not say that out loud? Jesus," she hisses, looking around to see if her mom heard, but she's still in the kitchen busy with the spatula in some atrocious dish to impress my dad with mediocre cooking. Why he bothers coming here to eat when we've got cooks back at home is beyond me.

"And for the record, those weren't moans. They were gasps of shock."

"Right." I shove the last piece of steak into my mouth. "Just like that wetness between your thighs were just tears of joy."

Her jaw drops so far I swear it's going to hit the table, and all I can do is grin.

She promptly pulls up the magazine again to block me from looking at her, but I've seen enough already to know the goddamn truth.

She's still thinking about my handprint on her ass, and so am I. In fact, I haven't been able to stop fantasizing about it and jerking myself off to the mere memory, wondering when I can fuck around with her next.

But this whole barbecue thing with my dad and her mom is really making it hard.

124

Harder than my dick ever will be.

Fuck.

"You're imagining things if you think I enjoyed that," she hisses from behind her women's magazine.

I plop some cherry tomatoes in my mouth. "And you're lying to yourself, so I guess we're both delusional here."

"I am not," she retorts.

"Yes, you are." She glances over her magazine just when I swallow, and her eyes immediately follow my Adam's apple as it moves up and down. "Want me to prove it?"

"You're despicable," she hisses. "And I'm trying to read."

I snort and pick up more cherry tomatoes. "Didn't know you could read upside down."

She smashes the magazine down on the table and growls at me. Actually fucking growls. And I don't know why, but I love the sound coming from her pretty little mouth.

Which is fucked up because I fucking hate her for inserting her mom and herself into my life.

I start laughing.

"What are you doing?" she mutters.

"What does it look like?"

She swipes her blond hair to the back. "Stop laughing at me."

"You make it hard not to laugh," I retort, biting my lip piercing when I see the anger in her eyes.

I've always had a thing for people getting mad at me. I can't help it. It eggs me on and gets me hard. And she makes it so damn difficult not to get excited.

She picks up a cherry tomato and chucks it at my face. "Stop. Just stop it."

Right then, her mom comes back out with a pitcher of cold water and a whole lot of silence, which seems to overwhelm everyone here.

"Well, you don't have to stop talking because of me," her mom muses. "Go on, talk with each other."

"I have nothing to say to him," Crystal says, piercing a sliced strawberry with her fork.

My eyes home in on her fork as she brings it to her lips, and I can't help but focus on that delicious tongue as it wraps around the strawberry and plucks it off the fork.

Good God.

125

"Crystal, that's not nice," her mom scolds.

I shift in my seat to hide the boner and clear my throat. "It's fine. I don't want to be here either."

"Caleb!" my father growls from right behind me.

He leans over me to place a plate with more steaks on the table.

"Can't you two get along?" he asks me. "You'd do me a big favor if you could just be a gentleman for once."

"Him? A *gentleman*?" Crystal scoffs, snorting loudly.

I tilt my head as she stares right back into my eyes, and fuck me, it makes me want to grab her and bend her over this very fucking table to show her just how much of a fucking gentleman I can be.

"Bitch," I retort.

"Caleb!" My dad shoves me.

Crystal scoots her chair back. "Let me help you in the kitchen, Mom."

Crystal throws me a snooty look, but I ignore it as she heads to the kitchen.

"Really, Caleb?" my dad scolds me.

"What? I don't fucking like her. Big deal."

"Don't. Don't fucking do this." He breathes out a big sigh. "Not today. Please."

I roll my eyes.

"Go make up with her," he says, pointing at the kitchen. "Now."

Reluctantly, I scoot my chair back too and saunter into the kitchen. She's cutting a cucumber lying on a wooden board, maybe a little too hard.

The closer I get, the harder her cuts become, like she's trying to slice through the board itself.

Or me.

I lick my lips and watch her seethe.

She's probably still thinking about all the things I did to her to make her filthy as hell.

Just as filthy as me.

I approach her from behind, placing both hands on the counter so I can look over her shoulder.

"You're bad at this," I say.

"Probably not as bad as you."

I grab her hand that's holding the knife, and she freezes in place. I guide her hand across the board and cut through the cucumber so thinly that the slice that's left is practically see-through. I keep going, each slice causing her to take a ragged breath as I push up closer and closer, my cock growing harder and harder.

"That's how you do it," I whisper into her ear.

She takes another ragged breath, her hand tightening around the blade while mine tightens around hers. Her body quivers against me, and I'm wondering if I just made her pussy wet.

"I want to skewer you," she murmurs.

My cock twitches.

"Do it," I whisper into her ear.

She spins around on her heels, poking the knife straight into my belly. "Do you always beg like that?"

"Do you see me on my knees?" I grip her hand and push the knife even farther into my belly. She's taken aback and flinches. "It will take a knife to get me there."

"You're an asshole," she grits.

"Only to people who annoy me," I reply.

"Why are you so protective of your dad?"

Fuck, is she really trying to interrogate me right now while I'm so close to busting a nut all over my pants because of her presence alone?

I lean in. "I hate you for interfering in my life."

"This isn't about you," she replies. "It's about our parents' happiness."

"Except it isn't. This *was* about me. Because you weren't there in that café out of pure luck. You were there to find *me*."

She retracts the knife so fast, my hand lingers near the blade, and it cuts into my hand.

"Crystal, Caleb," her mother says as she walks in, but her pupils dilate the moment she spots the blood drops running down the palm of my hand. "Oh no, you're bleeding." She grabs my hand and inspects the wound.

"Cut myself," I lie.

Crystal narrows her eyes at me while her mom starts dabbing the wound with a towel. "Let me go grab a Band-Aid."

"No, it's okay," I say, smiling at her to add an extra level of fakeness. "Thank you."

She smiles back. "Can you guys come back outside? There's something we want to share."

I frown when she turns around and heads back outside, and

127

Crystal seems equally confused. She shrugs and places the knife back on the cutting board before she follows me outside.

Her mom and my dad hold hands and hug while they stand near the edge of the table, and I have a sense of overwhelming dread.

"Crystal. Caleb," my dad begins, smiling awkwardly. "You might want to sit down."

Crystal grabs a chair. "What's going on?"

"Crystal …" her mom mutters, rubbing her neck, which has become red.

"Tell us," I say.

Her mom looks at my dad with complete devotion, and it makes me want to puke.

"Abigail and I …" my dad begins, breathing out a loving sigh as he grabs her hand. "Are engaged."

SEVENTEEN

CALEB

Abigail grins like she's on drugs and shows off the ring to both of us.

I'm gonna be sick.

I'm not listening to this shit.

I immediately jump up and walk off.

They can't be fucking serious. Are they for real? Is this a joke?

"Caleb! Wait. Hold up," my dad says.

"No," I growl, and I open the front door and head out.

"Caleb. At least talk to me!" He grabs my arm and makes me stop.

"Don't." I jerk my arm free.

"Jonathan," her mom mutters as she runs to him and clutches his arm. "Let him be. I think he needs some… time to digest it."

I stare them both down with disdain.

I can't fucking believe this. They barely fucking know each other.

I fish my phone from my pocket and waltz off down the street, while dialing the only number I've memorized. I don't know where I'm going or how long I'm going to walk. All I know is that I needed to get the fuck out of there because I was about to explode.

My dad. Married to a new woman?

Even though my mother's still here?

Fuck that.

And fuck that fucking girl who made it happen.

***

ARES

I find Caleb drifting somewhere in the middle of fucking nowhere outside the city. He was halfway across the road near the base of the mountain, and I signal him to come to the parking lot while I park the car.

When I step out, he's already screaming. "Why? Why the fuck did they have to do that?!"

"What happened?" I ask as I shut the door.

"I was at a fucking barbecue, my dad, he invited me to her mom's house," he rants.

A barbecue? His dad? That's out of character.

"And then they fucking told us they were getting fucking married!"

He roars out loud and punches the fucking lantern, leaving a dent. But he won't stop.

I walk over and grab his hand before it hits again, then point it at my chest.

"Stop. Punch me instead," I say.

He looks at me for a moment, bottom lip quivering. "No."

Tears well up in his eyes, but before he begins, I drag him to me and hold him tight. "Don't. Don't do it."

"It fucking hurts," he says, burying his face into my chest.

I run the palm of my hand over his back, and I can feel him slowly release all the tension stored inside his body. "I know. But you can't let them win."

"How do you even fucking deal with this?" he mutters. "How do you keep going when you just want to fucking give up?"

I grab him and push him back, holding his shoulders, leaning my forehead against his. "You walk … step by step."

He smiles and suddenly leans in to press a kiss onto my lips.

Flustered, I lean back and stare at him for a moment.

His lips part. "Sorry, I—"

130

I grab his face with both hands and kiss him back, smothering him with all the love he's been trying to die for. But when I inch back, I don't know if it's enough.

If I'm enough to keep him sane.

Tethered to this world.

While he dances the line and exists on the brink of destruction.

"Thank you," he mutters, swallowing. "I needed that."

I hold his face and make him look into my eyes. "Now tell me. Who are you?"

"Caleb Preston," he says.

"No, who are you?" I repeat, slamming my forehead into his. "Who the fuck are you really, Caleb?"

"A fucking devil from Tartarus." The grin that slowly forms on his face is magnificent.

"Exactly. And what do we fucking do?"

"Maim hearts, mutilate bodies, murder souls."

He knows precisely what it means to be part of Tartarus.

We rule the darkness, the inhospitable, and make it our own. We don't fucking bow to anyone.

I grin right back at him. "Good boy. Now what are we going to do?"

"Maim hearts, mutilate bodies, murder souls," he repeats.

"Starting with that fucking girl … who drove your father to her mother and tangled your lives." It's about time we dealt with her.

When he drifts off, I keep his eyes focused by gripping his chin. "She caused this, right? Then let's fucking punish her."

"How?" he asks. "When she's about to become my—" He retches from the idea. "Fuck. I can't even fucking say it, let alone think about it. I already covered her with cum. We can't go back from that."

My eyes narrow. "You covered *her* with cum?"

"I meant her window," he says, swallowing again.

I lick my lips, but he doesn't say another word, so I let him go.

"Let's go," I say, marching back to my car.

"Where?"

"Back to the Tartarus House," I reply, opening the door. "So we can discuss all the bad things we're going to do to her to make her pay."

A wicked grin slowly spreads on his face. "Now you're talking."

***

Crystal

I barely got home in time before a storm broke out. I blow out a sigh of relief when I finally close my bedroom door and flop down on the bed.

God, it was a long fucking day.

I'm so glad that whole barbecue thing is over. Nothing more awkward than hearing your mom's about to marry your enemy's dad.

I shiver at the thought of Caleb Preston becoming part of my family.

But if it makes my mom happy to be with his dad … who am I to get in the way of that?

I grab my study book and open it to the page I left it on. It's about time I had a proper study night.

However, my buzzing phone distracts me so much I can't focus, so I grab it to see what's going on.

Penelope: *Wanna come and hang out? Go to a club?*
Crystal: *Sorry, I got studying to do. Nxt time?*
Penelope: *Aw … I miss u!*
Crystal: *How about tomorrow?*
Penelope: *Perfect! I'll ask the boys too.*
Crystal: *Cool, see you tomorrow!*

I click away the convo and eye my study books, but then my phone buzzes again. I'm starting to wonder if she just needs someone to chat with.

But when I see the text, my face turns white.

Anonymous: *You shouldn't have come close.*
Me: *Who is this?*
Anonymous: *I want you to pay for what you did.*
Panic sweeps me up.
Me: *WTF?! I didn't do anything.*
Anonymous: *Then why were you there, watching us kill?*
Oh shit. It's them.
Me: *Whichever Tartarus guy this is, leave me alone.*
Anonymous: *Like you left us alone? No. You will pay.*
My heart's beating faster and faster.

Me: For what?!

Anonymous: Think. Think hard, because you won't get another chance.

Me: This isn't funny.

Anonymous: It wasn't meant as a joke.

I suck in a breath through my teeth before I edit the anonymous number and add a nickname. This has to be Caleb. He's the only one who stole my number when he got ahold of my phone.

Crystal: I'll block you if you don't stop.

Prick: Try it. See if it works out well for you.

He's threatening me? That motherfucker…

My finger hovers over the block button, ready to push. But I don't know if I have the balls to actually go through with it. They've already warned me not to, and I know they're not the kind of men to mess with.

Me: What do you want?

Prick: Those pretty lips … begging for mercy.

I swallow back the lump in my throat.

Me: Don't. Don't fuck with me.

Prick: Or what? Will you tell your friends? Go ahead. Tell them where we are. We'll be waiting …

Shit, I don't want to put them in danger either.

What do I do?

Prick: Right outside.

My heart almost comes to a stop.

Me: Stop.

Prick: I can see you.

A cold chill fills my bones.

I slowly turn around on my bed and blink at the window.

When thunder strikes down on the earth, it illuminates a ghostly figure standing on my balcony, a golden, demonic-looking mask complete with horns covering half his face. In his hand is a knife that glints in the dark.

My eyes widen.

Oh God.

My phone buzzes again, and I can't fucking move as I watch the text come in.

Prick: You look a little pale, little rose. Don't worry. We'll give you back your red glow. Run. Run as fast as you can, and

let's see who wins this game.

One look over my shoulder at the man behind my window, just one look, and I'm gone.

I rush through the door and down the stairs of the sorority, trying to get away from him as fast as I can. I don't know where I'm going. All I know is that I need to be as far away from him as I possibly can.

EIGHTEEN

Crystal

I run straight into the pouring rain. There's no time to grab a coat, no time to grab anything.

Because he's right there, climbing down the steps of the fire escape next to the balconies.

Oh God.

Sheer panic forces me to move as I run toward the main area of the campus in the middle of the night. Hardly anyone is outside, and by the time I do finally come across a student, I can barely speak.

"Are you okay?" they ask, lifting their umbrella.

I suck in a breath, wondering what to say. "Just going for a run!"

"In the rain?"

I pick up my pace even though I must look insane.

If I told them the truth, they'd be implicated.

Mutilated.

Killed.

Just for knowing.

It's not a question of if but a question of when. And I don't want anyone else's life to be in jeopardy.

I turn around the corner of the street but come to an abrupt halt when I see another stranger in a hoodie slowly walking in my direction. In one hand is a phone with open texts, and in the other is a knife just like the guy on my balcony. And on his face is the same eerie gold demonic mask.

Oh God. There are two of them.

That's why he said we.

My phone buzzes again, and I hold it up, rain pitter-pattering down on the screen, which I swipe away to read the text.

Prick: Run ... hide ... wherever you go, we'll find you.

My whole body begins to shake.

I dash to the right, away from the guy in the hoodie and run all the way across campus through the pouring rain, my clothes soaking wet when I finally get to the big doors of the main building. They're closed off, and when I try to pull them open, they refuse to budge.

Everything's closed. It's midnight.

No one's still here except maybe a guard just to shoo away any unwanted guests.

Shit. What do I do now?

When I look over my shoulder, my breath falters.

There are two of them now, staring me down from the far end of the main campus grounds, and I can't help but wonder if they're smiling behind those damn masks.

I run away as fast as I can in the only direction that's still safe; the Spine Ridge gardens. My heart's going a million miles an hour, and it almost feels like they can hear it. Like it fuels their desire to chase me even faster.

Every time I glance over my shoulder, at least one of them is right behind me, slowly catching up with me.

Shit.

Rain trickles down across my cheeks, and I brush my hair out of my face to see better in the darkness. There has to be somewhere I can go where they can't find me. But before I know it, I've run all the way to the rose gardens.

My phone buzzes, and I take a quick glance.

Prick: Tick tock, little rose. What will you do? Run and hide? Or face your demons?

My feet almost tumble over themselves when I spot a guy in a gold demon mask with horns standing mere feet away from me, casually tossing a lighter up and down, the suit he's wearing

136

completely soaked through.

But none of it seems to matter.

Not when their mission is to destroy me.

I gulp and turn around, but I almost drop my phone when I see the other one standing right there, equal feet away as the other, his hoodie hanging over the mask as he pushes the tip of the knife into his index finger, looking like he's wondering what I'll do. Which arms I'll run into and meet my inevitable fate.

I shudder in place and look to my right.

The entrance to the maze.

I gulp.

I will definitely get lost in there, but I have no other choice if I want to have even a shot at escaping their grasp.

So I tuck my phone into my pocket and bolt inside.

I don't know which way to go—left, right, right, left, two further, another left, then a long way ahead, and another right. I have no clue where I am or if I'm going in the right direction, but as long as it's far away from them, I'll be fine.

I run through the maze until my feet can barely take it anymore. But their laughter in the background makes all the hairs on the back of my neck stand up.

"We know where you are … We can hear your steps, Crystal."

Is that … Caleb? It has to be. His voice sounds the same.

"One. Two. Three."

Another voice I can't place.

But each time I walk, I hear it.

"Four." Another step. "Five. One to the right."

He's counting my steps?

They know which direction I'm going?

"Go on … keep running away. The more you run, the more excited we get," Caleb calls. A deep, rumbling laugh follows, making goose bumps scatter on my skin.

I keep going left and right, trying to maintain a silent pace while also hurrying so they don't catch up.

CRACK!

I spin on my heels to look, but no one is there.

Thunder flashes in the background, making my heart beat just as loudly.

I step back, cautious of my surroundings. But when I turn around to look, I'm precisely back in the middle of that little hidden area with the big tree and the bench where I saw Blaine.

But the exit that was once there in the back is now blocked off with several big wooden beams and a sign that says renovation.

Oh God.

I'm trapped.

CRACK!

The snapping of twigs makes me spin on my heels again, the cold of the rain settling in my very fucking bones as two masked individuals emerge from the maze. But I don't know if it's the rain turning my body cold or their maddening stares through those demonic golden masks.

"Found you."

Caleb's voice grates my soul, but it's definitely him.

"Caleb," I grit.

The one with the hoodie claps. "Good job. You figured it out."

"Stop the jokes. This isn't a game."

"Oh, but it is. You made it one." He points his knife at me.

"You're crazy. I didn't ask for any of this," I retort.

"No? Then why were you so keen on running?" he muses, stepping closer.

I take a step back. "Because you told me to."

"Hmm …" I can barely see the devilish smile appearing behind those scary teeth, but it's definitely there.

"You were the one who texted me." I hold up my phone to show him. "You're the one playing games here. Not me."

"Prick … apt name," he murmurs. "But you're wrong."

I frown. "What?"

The other masked man pulls out a phone and shows me the texts. The texts I sent *him*.

"Wait, so you …" I mutter.

He tilts his head, and the low voice that follows makes my pussy throb, not out of free will but from the memory of his fingers alone. "Hello, little rose."

I'm too stunned; I don't even know what to say. "But how … You gave him my number?"

"He *is* a prick, I'll give you that," Caleb muses, snorting while Ares throws him a damning glance.

"What do you want?" I growl, trying to defuse.

Ares tucks his phone back into his pocket and pulls out his knife instead. "We already told you … do you need a reminder?"

They're here for me.

There's no way they'll let me pass.

There's only one other option.

I fish my knife from my pocket and chuck it at Ares's head.

He avoids it, and it flies into the bushes, but I still turn around and make a run for it.

I bolt toward the closed-off exit and rip at the wood, trying to tear it away. But within seconds, two strong hands pull me away and drag me toward the middle.

"Let me go!" I yell.

They set me down on the bench, and one of them, Ares, holds a knife against my throat.

"I told you that you would regret the day you'd come for me."

"Because you have to threaten girls with knives to make them want you?" I retort.

I don't know what's gotten into me, but I want to make him feel as powerless as he's trying to make me.

He tips up my chin farther, the knife etching into my neck. "Nothing you can say will change the course of tonight." He forces me to look at him. "Before this night is over … you will give me your fear."

I hiss when the blade cuts into my skin just a little, a tiny droplet running down my neck before he retracts his knife.

"Caleb. Do what it is you came here to do."

He steps away only for Caleb to replace his spot in front of me.

"Your dad will never allow you to—"

He grips my throat, squeezing so I can't say another word.

"You're the reason this is all happening. You're the reason they're together."

"That's why you chased me here tonight?" I croak, his fingers squeezing off my airway.

"I told you … my father doesn't need a new woman in his life. And now they're engaged." His fist balls. "Make your mother pull back her claws and call off the marriage."

He only slightly releases my throat so I can properly talk.

"It was their choice. They should be allowed to—"

"Do it. Or I will do it for you," he growls, staring straight into my eyes.

"What? How?" I mutter.

"I have my ways," he says, tilting his head as he holds up the knife to show me. "Do you want to see for yourself?"

I shake my head. "Don't hurt my mom."

His voice is gravelly as he says, "Then break. Them. Up."

"You're a monster," I tell him. "You'd rather destroy your father's happiness than see him with a new wife."

His hand slowly rises from my neck to my chin, his thumb brushing my bottom lip. "I can destroy you too if you're not careful."

"No," I say.

He frowns and looks at Ares who beckons him, and he slowly steps away so Ares can confront me again.

"Oh, little rose …" Ares murmurs, towering over me. "Haven't you learned yet we won't stop until we have what we want?" I can see him smirk through that demonic mask. "If you won't split them up, I'll make it happen." He holds up his knife, gazing at it like it's some kind of toy. "It's been such a long time since this blade last tasted some fear-drenched blood, and I'm sure your mother will be more than eager to run just like you."

My eyes widen. "No. Don't hurt her."

I try to get up, but Ares shoves me down.

"Sit. Down," Ares commands.

I swallow at the sight of his knife almost boring a hole into my forehead.

"Don't hurt my mother, dammit," I growl back.

Ares tilts his head. "And how are you going to stop me? Hmm? Indulge me."

"You're sick," I hiss, the rain making my teeth chatter.

"You have no idea of the depravity I'm capable of." He pushes the knife into my forehead, and I swallow away the lump in my throat as the blade slowly slides down my cheek and chin, as though Ares is carefully trying to peel away any resistance remaining in my body.

But I will not fucking fear him. I will not. I refuse.

And I will never, ever let them lay a hand on my mother.

"Take me."

The knife pauses near the base of my neck.

"If you want to hurt her for her choice to love Jonathan, hurt me instead."

The rain begins to subside while the two boys stare me down, their masks glinting with each strike of thunder.

"Crystal," Caleb growls from underneath the mask. "Don't fucking tempt me. Break. Them. Up. Or I will."

"No," I repeat. "They deserve their happiness." I swallow down the cowardice building inside me. "And if you hold that much hatred against her, give it to me instead."

A low, rumbling laugh emanates from deep within Ares's chest, and he leans away, lowering the knife. "Well, isn't this an interesting turn of events? The innocent little rose, offering her body up to the two most vicious men on campus." His laugh abruptly ends as he pushes the knife into my chest. "You won't survive."

I take in a hampered breath. "Then I'll die saving my mother."

"Crystal ..." Caleb groans, raising his head to the sky as droplets of rain still pitter-patter down occasionally. "Fine. Choose. Your mother or you."

I take another deep breath before I sign away my life as I know it. "Me."

Ares laughs again, the laughter almost turning into a moan. "So much courage ..." A smoldering smile follows as he rips off his mask and stares me down with amusement glimmering in his bright gray eyes. "I can't wait to drain it all from you with just our hard cocks while you whimper for forgiveness."

NINETEEN

ARES

I have her right where I want her.

SLICE!

I cut through the bands that keep her outfit together, and her tits spill out. She desperately tries to keep the soaked fabric together, but I push the knife underneath her wrists and force her arms to spread so we can take a look.

"Fuck ..." Caleb groans at the sight of her perky tits.

Finally, I can look at this beautiful prickly rose, her nipples peaking from the cold rain, and my eyes can't stop ravishing every inch of her pale body, those pink buds practically begging me to suck on them.

But there will be plenty of time to enjoy her body later.

First, I want to see what has gotten him so riled up about her.

I tuck my knife away and step away as I say, "Caleb. You do the honors."

"My pleasure." Caleb grips her by the hair, tilting her head back. "Now say a fucking prayer, slut, because you won't have anyone to save you from us devils while we drag you to hell."

He pushes her chin until her lips part. "Open your fucking

mouth."

When they're wide open, he spits inside and shuts them again. "Now swallow."

God, I love it when he gets all riled up. It's not often he lets himself go like this.

It definitely makes my cock hard and ready to fuck.

"Fuck you," she spits.

He tilts her head back even farther, forcing her to look at him. "Show me how far you're willing to go to save your precious mother."

With a keen eye, I watch him, waiting for him to go down those steps to hell. I'll be right there with him, enjoying the sight of her quivering wet body until she finally utters the words I've wanted to hear since I first saw her here on campus.

I want her in complete and utter subjugation, whimpering with fear.

And then I'll take her to my fucking domain.

But first, I'll let him have his way with her.

"As long as you don't touch my mother," she grits, droplets of rain still tumbling down her lips.

"Open your mouth, Crystal," he commands.

"Did you hear me?"

He parts her lips with his thumb and presses the blade against her lip. "Whether or not I touch her is entirely up to your skills … to satisfy me."

He pushes the blade inside just far enough for her to feel it on her tongue, and watching her fight the feeling is making my cock twitch.

"Now keep that mouth open wide," he says.

A smirk forms on my face.

Oh yes, I will definitely enjoy watching him ruin her.

Caleb pulls out the knife only to unzip his pants and take out his dick, and her face contorts at the size of him. Or maybe it's his ample jewelry, I can't tell which.

She might have a heart attack once she sees mine.

"What's the matter, little rose? Were you hoping we'd go easy on you?" I muse, zipping down too.

"No," she replies. "I'm just annoyed I have to see this asshole's dick again."

I pause halfway through the zipper.

Again?

My eyes immediately jerk up to Caleb, who throws a glance at me.

"Oh, you didn't tell him you fucked me in the bathroom of my mother's home?" she says, snorting. "Guess the cat's out of the bag now."

That girl ...

"Shut up," Caleb growls at her, clamping his fingers around her throat to keep her quiet.

But all she does is smile. "Too late to keep it a secret now, Caleb."

My grin grows wider.

I'm impressed.

"When?" I ask Caleb.

"When our parents first had dinner together. I couldn't help myself. She was taunting me."

"Bullshit. I said I wouldn't break them up, and you couldn't take it," she retorts.

"Interesting," I reply.

"So ... guess your secret's out there now," she muses, eyeing me. "Your buddy here went behind your back to get to me."

I tilt my head at Caleb, who looks at me now, his fingers deeply entrenched in her neck. The same throat his dick slid down mere days ago. He's already gotten to her before I did. Twice now.

"He even tied me up to the bathtub," she adds.

I should be mad. Punish him like we're punishing her now.

Yet the idea of his cum slipping down her throat makes me wild with lust.

"All right then ... show me how you fucked her," I say.

Her eyes widen. She made a mistake thinking I would step in out of pure spite.

I would love to know why he'd go that far for a girl he barely even knows.

Especially one he clearly knows I've set my eyes on.

Caleb licks his lip and the piercing, and it almost makes me want to smash my lips onto his and bite them too just to taste his blood.

Instead, I lean away and watch him from a little farther, stroking my dick right through the fabric of my pants so he gets the picture.

He rips off his mask and chucks it onto the ground too, a deliciously wicked smile forming on his face before he brings the tip of his dick to her mouth and says, "You asked for it, so let me fucking give it to you."

He slowly enters her mouth, taking ample time to feel her tongue as her eyes begin to water the deeper he goes. By the time he hits her throat, she struggles to move.

"Regretting your choice?" he asks as he goes even deeper.

She shakes her head even though she's clearly struggling.

Hmm … maybe I underestimated her tenacity.

"Caleb. Go to the base," I tell him, my eyes glinting with desire as I watch her struggle not to panic. "Now."

"I'm only halfway in," he says.

"Now," I tell him. "One. Thrust."

He does what I say and buries himself inside her to the hilt, the sight of her pupils dilating while her face turns red from the sheer force he applies is magnificent to watch.

"Do you feel the fear yet, little rose?" I ask. "Settling deep within that chest?" I lean over to whisper into her ear. "Do you wonder how long it will last before you can take another breath?" Caleb squeezes her throat. "If we'll even let you?"

When he finally pulls out, she sucks in a breath, wheezing.

"Don't stop," I tell him as I rub myself.

I want him on the edge, just like I had her, and then I'll intervene.

"Keep fucking that eager throat until nothing is left of her but a whimpering mess," I tell him, egging him on.

He goes faster and faster, the look on his face growing more menacing with every passing second, while she looks like she struggles to take him whole.

When he pulls out again, she yelps, "God, I can't take it."

"Yes, you can," he groans, thrusting right back in again. "You'll take me and then some, and you'll do so without complaining because that's what you asked and begged us for."

I love this new raw side of him. Very dominating.

I wonder where he learned it.

A smug grin spreads on my face.

"Fuck, your throat feels so good," Caleb groans. "You wanted it, so now, take it. Take my cock deep, slut."

He fucks her face like he wants to own it while she slowly averts her eyes to meet my gaze.

But then he grips her chin and says, "Eyes on me. I'm the one fucking you, not him."

"Don't worry, little rose. You'll get the chance to feel my cock on the tip of your tongue soon enough."

Caleb pushes in to the hilt, his balls squeezing, and I know what's coming.

A vicious smile tips up the side of my lips as his cock hardens inside her mouth, but when he begins to moan, I grasp his shoulders and tear him away from her.

"What the f—" He groans wildly as he's unable to stop the impending orgasm from taking over, and he spurts his juices all over her face, but without a throat to milk it out of him. When he attempts to rub it out, I swat his hand away.

"Let it fucking spray," I growl. "A ruined orgasm is all you deserve now."

He mewls as the orgasm slowly subsides, and I push him farther away from her. "Fuck, that wasn't enough. I need mo—"

"Later," I retort, throwing him a glare that shuts him up. "You will get another turn when you learn not to play with what's mine." I grip her chin and look at the mess he's made. "He stole your throat before I had a chance … so now he will watch while I take this throat back and make it mine."

"Stole my throat?" she gasps.

But my fingers are already curled around her neck.

She wants to taunt the devils? Well, she's summoned us now.

"Open your legs," I growl.

When she doesn't do it fast enough, I spread them open with a single hand.

RIP!

A mewl escapes her lips when I rip the remaining fabric of her outfit out of my way. I push my fingers right up against her slit. "Remember these fingers, little rose?"

"Like I want to—"

I push two fingers against her clit, circling around. "Hmm … His cock made you wet already." I chuckle.

I swivel my fingers, and I can feel her struggling not to writhe on this goddamn bench.

I warned her, told her what I would do if I ever got my hands on her. Now that she's here in my grasp, I'm not fucking letting go until she's covered in cum, wasted on lust, and completely overcome by exhaustion.

My fingers roll around her needy little clit, her pussy growing wetter and wetter under my command. Her thighs try to push together, so I squeeze her neck even harder until she stops.

"That's it. Try to fight me, and I'll only give you more. Pain. Pleasure. An intricate, intoxicating mix, don't you think?" I murmur, swirling her clit until it begins to thump with need. "Getting close already?" I twist and turn my fingers and spread her wetness all over her slit. A devilish smirk forms on my face. "Then fucking beg for it."

I release the tension around her neck enough so she can speak, and her whimpers tell me enough.

"Please …"

"Such a willing little slut," Caleb murmurs, his shaft bobbing up and down again at the thought of a second turn.

She's on the edge of another orgasm, so I retract my hand, and the whimpers that follow make my dick so hard it can barely be contained. I bring my fingers to my lips and taste her on my tongue.

Such a delicious taste. Who could pass on that?

No wonder Caleb was so desperate to try her out.

"You want to save your mother?" I ask her. "Then you will be at our beck and call. Any time, any day, anywhere …" I swipe my free hand across her face, picking up all of Caleb's cum along the way with two fingers. "No limits. Complete submission. Just like a good little fucking whore."

***

Crystal

I can't breathe while Ares's fingers are around my neck, squeezing tighter and tighter as he rubs all the cum across my face and picks it up with his fingers like it's something to play with.

Still, I manage to utter two words of defiance. "Fuck … you."

His eyes burn with passion as he brings his fingers up to his lips and opens his mouth. His tongue rolls around his cum-covered fingers, and he actually swirls it around in his mouth.

I'm too stunned to even say a word.

What the hell?

147

The following groan sets my whole body on fire despite the rain drenching my clothes.

His hand moves up my chin, and he pushes down. "Open your mouth."

When I do, he dribbles Caleb's cum right back into my mouth straight from his tongue, then pushes my chin so it closes. I can taste him on my tongue just like before in the shower, only with Ares's added saliva, mixing salty and sweet together.

"Now swallow," he growls.

I'm almost contemplating spitting it right back in his face. But what good would that do me when he's the one holding the knife? Ares will definitely punish me, and I've already seen what Caleb's punishments look like … I can't even begin to imagine what Ares would do.

Slowly I swallow back the cum, the saltiness still inside my mouth after, like an everlasting reminder of their domination over my body that no longer belongs to me … but to them.

"Good girl."

His gravelly voice makes my whole body erupt into goose bumps.

His eyes briefly rise to meet Caleb's gaze. "Are you watching?"

Caleb nods.

"Good."

Suddenly, Ares grabs my cheeks and smashes his rough lips on mine.

I'm too stunned to even speak, let alone bite back, as he devours my mouth like it always belonged to him.

TWENTY

Crystal

I've never gotten a kiss this consuming, this overpowering.

His lips roam mine, piercing through them with his tongue to claim that too. I'm helpless to stop him, weak against his rough lips that leave scorching kisses on my mouth. His tongue rolls around mine as he moans against my lips, and my pussy vibrates with a need I never knew I could have.

But this man ... is a monster.

I shouldn't let him kiss me.

Not like this.

Not ever.

I bite down on his tongue, and he pulls out. "You bit me."

He licks up the blood like he's reveling in the fact that I did. But his eyes immediately flicker back up to Caleb with intensity, almost as if he wants to tell him something with his eyes alone.

A word even I can discern just from the look on his face.

Mine.

"Get on the bench," he tells me. "All fours."

My eyes narrow, settling on his pocket where I know he keeps that damn knife.

Steal it. Gut him.
Make him bleed.

But no matter how hard the knife in his pocket is luring me to act out on the vicious thoughts swirling through my mind, I can't get myself to actually do it. If I tried … they'd kill my mother.

I have no choice.

Crawling back to the bench, I slowly lift myself while both their eyes gorge on my naked breasts like ravenous animals.

I feel humiliated as I kneel on this wooden bench, shivering from the cold rain clattering down. But when Ares stands before me, I don't feel nearly as cold anymore because of those icy gray eyes staring me down.

"Unzip me."

I don't know why, but his voice alone can command my body, and I move my hand to his zipper. He grabs my wrist. "Slowly."

Only when I nod does he release me.

I zip him down slowly as he demands, my eyes briefly flicking to the knife in his pocket.

Don't do it. Not now. Not yet.
Do it when he least expects it.

But my eyes instantly flick back toward the giant cock that immediately pops out. Not just because it's much larger than Caleb's was, but also because of the numerous piercings in the head. Four metal buds all aligned in a cross all inside the glans, and then another one underneath the tip.

My God. It has to be at least ten inches, if not more.
That thing will never fit inside me.

"Are you surprised at my piercings, little rose?" he murmurs, and he tips up my chin with a single finger so I look at his eyes instead. "Or my size?"

"Probably both," Caleb murmurs, but Ares ignores him.

He smirks. "Say my name."

"Ares."

He sucks in a breath through his teeth, his lip quivering with delight as his dick bobs up and down in my face.

"And what am I?"

I know what he wants me to say.

"A man who thinks too highly of himself."

I couldn't help myself. I just had to say it.

A filthy, decrepit smirk spreads on his face. "Just as you will, once you've felt these King's Crown piercings go down your throat."

He grips my wet hair, tilts my head back, and plunges in.

No remorse.

Not an ounce of hesitation.

I gurgle and choke on his size, feeling each of his barbells deep within my throat, his cock throbbing with both pleasure and pain as he consumes my very throat like it was made for him and him alone.

"You are not the only one with thorns, little rose," he grits, pulling out, only to thrust right back in again. "Can you feel them scraping your precious throat?"

Not a second for a breath, nothing except the plunging of his cock into my mouth over and over again while my eyes almost roll into the back of my head just from the sheer amount of throbbing between my legs.

He left me on the edge of an orgasm on purpose, to make me want this, to make me want to plead and beg for mercy.

Fuck. I never thought I could feel hatred as badly as I do now, but I hate this man with every fiber of my being.

"That's it. Give me all your loathing and turn it into despair," he groans, thrusting in faster each time. "Because you will never, ever be freed of this chain you've put around your own goddamn neck, of which the only tether is in my merciful hands. You belong to me now."

He drives in and out, coating my tongue with both Caleb's cum and his own pre-cum, the two salty tastes mixing into one.

He's even more of a savage than Caleb was.

"More," he groans, pushing even farther, far beyond my uvula and down my actual throat, and tears spring to my eyes.

"You thought I couldn't go any deeper?" he says, sounding amused. "*More.*"

He goes so far down my throat I can no longer breathe, all while keeping my eyes up to meet his gaze, as though he wants to instill in me the knowledge that I no longer belong to myself.

My entire being … is theirs.

From the corner of my eye, I watch Caleb jerk off, his semi-hard-on still making me anxious.

"Caleb." There's a glimmer in Ares's eyes. "Take her pussy."

Ares pulls out of me, and I mutter, "What?"

Two of them at the same time?

Ares grips my chin and forces me to focus on him. "He will take your pussy, and you will enjoy every inch of him inside you while I plow into your throat."

***

ARES

"Oh God," she mutters.

"No," I grit, burying myself inside her balls deep. "You have a new lord and savior now. Me. And you will bend to my fucking will."

It's too late for takebacks. Her body belongs to us now, and we will use it however we see fit.

Caleb positions himself behind her on the bench, and her legs quake when he pushes them apart. She tries to turn her head to look, but my dick is stuck in her throat, making it impossible.

Slowly, he pushes in, and her loud moans vibrate against my shaft, sending delicious shocks up and down my body.

She will make a fine toy indeed.

"Every inch, Caleb," I groan, pulling out to allow her to breathe as he forces his way in.

"Oh fuck," she mewls.

I know she can feel every inch of him inside her. The same piercings that were in her throat before now push into her pussy, making her feel all the things she never wanted to feel.

Lust. Betrayal. Hunger.

I move along with Caleb, matching his rhythm, piercing her on both ends, creating an intoxicating blend of pain and bliss.

I pull out for a second and watch the raindrops enter her mouth instead. "That's it, little rose, take it like a good girl," I say. "One breath and your mouth is mine again."

She sucks in a breath right before I dive back into her while Caleb does the same, and lust almost bursts from my very fucking veins. A guttural groan emanates from deep within my chest.

Fucking him gives me life, but fucking her … feels like I've died and gone to heaven.

"She's so fucking wet," Caleb groans, fucking her like an animal in heat.

And I'd be lying if I said it didn't make me want to bury my cock even deeper in this velvety throat.

Rarely have I felt anything so delicious as being able to taint something so pure, so fucking perfect.

"She likes this," Caleb murmurs, slapping her ass. "With every stroke, she gets wetter and wetter."

"You hear that, little rose?" I lift her head while I'm deep inside her, forcing her to swallow back those tears. "You're a natural at being spit-roasted."

She moans when we both drive in and out of her.

"Fuck, I can feel her tightening," Caleb groans.

"You're close, aren't you?" I ask.

She nods, trying so desperately not to fall apart. But her body already belongs to me, and that orgasm she thinks she can withhold is mine for the taking. All I need to do is find her trigger … push the button … and watch the magic unfold.

And there will be no choice.

She'll have to endure as many as I desire and as much cum as I wish for her to swallow.

Because that is what she is now …

A puppet to my every whim.

***

CALEB

I've never in my life fucked any pussy this fucking good. And I fucking have had chicks by my side, occasionally. None as vexing as this girl right here, though.

I could never have imagined she'd fit this snugly around my dick.

Or that I'd be so fucking hard for a girl I hate.

I admit, I'm a bastard, but I don't fucking care. She made her choice. Her body belongs to us now, and I won't fucking stop until she's paid for her mother's mistake.

She wanted to take the fall, then so be it.

When Ares momentarily pulls out to allow her to breathe, she mutters, "Fuck … please."

It almost sounds like she's begging me to fill her up.

153

A grin spreads on my cheeks. "No worries, slut, I will give you what you so desperately want."

I plow into her, every stroke harder than before, enjoying myself on her sweet pussy, which feels fucking divine around my shaft. She's so goddamn tight and wet that it almost makes me want to pull out and stick my tongue inside instead.

But I don't want to catch any more of Ares's ire, so I'll play along to his whims. As long as this fucking pussy is mine to use, I don't care.

I flick my hair to the side in the pouring rain and watch the droplets roll down her perfect body. I grip her ass and slap it so she mewls out loud while he's still inside her mouth.

"Fuck yeah, make that sound again," I groan.

I slap her other ass cheek too so I can hear more of those noises she makes, the sound exhilarating.

My balls slap against her thighs as I thrust into her mercilessly while raising my eyes to meet Ares. I can see everything he's doing to her from here, how his cock slides into her throat, how he makes her cough, choke, and whimper, how he grips her hair and tilts her head back, and fuck me, it makes my cock even harder while it's inside her.

"You like watching me fuck her mouth, don't you?" Ares asks.

I bite my lip and nod, my fingers digging into her ass.

"Do you remember how her tongue felt as it wrapped around your shaft?" he asks.

I gulp, remembering those vivid images of her tied to her bathtub as she swallowed my seed. God, I fucking loved every second of my own depravity … until I remembered I was supposed to hate her.

"Fuck, yes," I groan, burying myself inside her pussy to the hilt right when he does the same to her mouth.

My dick throbs inside her, on the verge of bursting again.

But then Ares's face tightens with rage. "Pull. Out."

"What? But I'm about to—"

His lip twitches. "Now."

I can't hold it any longer, but I still do what he demands. My piercings slide across her pussy, and I moan as I hit that edge.

I can't put a stop to it. "Fuck, I'm coming."

My cum spurts out onto her slit and ass from a distance, but the second I try to move my hands to my dick to ease the orgasm, Ares growls, "Stop. Don't fucking touch it."

I pause, my shaft still bobbing up and down with pure need. But he won't let me give in to it.

"But I'm coming," I groan, desperate to touch myself.

"Good. Enjoy your second and last ruined fucking orgasm while I fill up this precious little throat," he retorts, burying himself inside her once more.

Ares lowers his eyes to meet her gaze, her body quaking on the bench as he tips up her chin and says, "Now come while your mouth is full with my cum."

Her whole body begins to shiver while his back arches and his balls squeeze together.

She moans out loud, and her legs squeeze together, hands desperate to hold something while she falls apart. They swiftly move to her pussy, but I grip her hands and keep them away.

"If I can't, you won't either," I tell her.

Ares smirks as he groans with pleasure, pushing in again for good measure while he fills her to the brim with his seed.

When he pulls out, she coughs and heaves, splotches of cum dripping out of her and onto the ground.

"Filthy little rose," Ares says as he goes to his knees in front of her. "Next time, you will drink up every …" He swipes up some of his own cum from her lips. "Last …" He pushes the dollop inside and rolls it around her tongue. "Drop."

Then he gets back up and tucks in, zipping up while my cock is still heavy from two ruined orgasms.

We fucked her so good, she's still hanging over the bench like a rag doll.

"What now?" she mutters.

"We're done here," Ares barks, glaring at me.

I swallow and push away the need to come again as I tuck my cock back inside.

I'll get my turn again someday.

She lifts her head to look as we walk off. "Wait … you're just going to leave me here?"

Ares halts and glances at her over his shoulder. "Your body belongs to us now. You will be ready for us whenever, wherever, however I see fit." His fist balls. "Do you understand?"

She slowly nods, wiping away some of the cum off her face.

A slow but hot grin spreads on Ares's lips. "Good girl."

155

Then he waltzes off back into the maze, and I follow suit, but I stop halfway across the area to pick up our masks. I can't help but gaze at her over my shoulder, wondering if she even knows what she's gotten herself into.

What kind of trade she really made.

When we leave, she'll be all by herself, with all the time in the world to think about her fucking sin ... And all the ways we're going to make her repent.

TWENTY ONE

My body feels icy cold as I lie on the bench and breathe.

Just breathe.

In and out.

Over and over.

It's all I can do. All I'll ever do until it's time.

Time for them to meet their fate.

I don't know how much time has passed since they found me or since they have left, but I don't care either. All I want to do now is lay my head down and rest on this hard bench for however long I need.

I pause and listen to the sound of my heartbeat while slick saliva and cum slowly run down my face and neck, covering my already wet clothes and body.

The rain starts again, but I welcome the downpour, washing away my sin.

I sold my soul to devils.

But I will gladly pay the price.

A single tear rolls down my cheek.

Not from fear or sadness or regret … but a tear filled with rage.

I stare at the knife lying in the bushes, glinting in the dark, beckoning me to get up and move.

You can do this.

You made your choice.

Now stick with it.

I sit up straight even though I can still feel the pounding in my own pussy that betrayed me and came from all the reckless thrusting on both ends. I was practically begging for it, pleading for them to let me come.

I never imagined I would willingly give myself to killers like them. And that I'd be left in such a lusty mess.

But I did it for all the right reasons, and someday, they will know my wrath.

I stand, a slow but vicious smile spilling onto my face as the rain destroys what was left of the mask I put on before I went outside.

A world oblivious is a world asleep, but I am wide awake to the horrors of this world.

Even fucking gods can bleed.

I bend over and pick up my knife from the bushes, the rose emblem flickering in the only light inside this maze. A slow, drawn-out laughter emanates from deep within my chest as I push away whatever I felt while they fucked me.

Even if I wanted to beg for them to fuck me, even if I craved nothing more than their fingers on my pussy while being denied over and over, even when I came so hard I could feel myself ascending into fucking heaven … *hatred* is the only thing I'll carry with me.

To the end.

Wherever it may lead me.

I've already taken the first step. And I intend to finish the stairs all the way down to fucking hell just so I can make those devils disguised as gods pay.

***

Blaine

I lather my body with soap and rinse it all off before I throw a quick glance at the mirror and smile at myself. These long locks really shine well with a little sprinkle of water. Maybe I should carry a spritzer around in my pocket to keep them moist and pretty.

God, I look fucking amazing today.

It's probably not the weather, just me.

My hand slides down my body as I feel myself up, my mind drifting to previous encounters with my lovers. There are so many; I can just pick whichever I like to fantasize about. There's no limit to my mind nor to my body, as I can never get enough of all the delicious men and women this world has to offer.

I admit I'm a slut, but I don't care in the slightest bit. What use is a world if we can't fuck around in it? And in my fantasies, oh boy, am I the fucking center of multiple people.

I groan as I wrap my hand around my ample cock and stroke it like it's nobody's business. And it isn't because I'm all alone with no one to look inside my brain and see that a blond girl slowly begins to push her way through the crowd. Her petite, curvy body dances to the rhythm of the music in a skimpy, see-through dress, her eyes settling on mine, pulling me closer.

And I rub myself harder and harder as she begins to undress in the middle of the dance, rubbing her pussy and tits, smearing wetness all over, and I can almost picture myself coming all over that beautiful body.

She stops and wags her finger, then kisses two other boys right in front of me. And the smile on my face widens even more.

"Oh, Crystal … you naughty girl," I mutter, jerking off faster.

"Wow."

I stop abruptly as the door to my bathroom is opened.

"Can you not?" I mutter, disappointed. "I'm busy."

"I can see that," Caleb says as he marches inside.

I raise a brow as his eyes travel down my majestic body to my dick. "Oh …" My smirk deepens. "Well, if you'd like to, I'm sure there's more than enough water for the two of us."

He snorts and washes his hands in the sink. "I don't think that's going to work, Blaine. My dick's already spent. Twice actually. But thanks for the offer."

Twice? What has he been up to?

"Then why did you come into my bathroom? You have your own."

"I just wanted to let you know that Ares and I went after her."

His eyes meet mine in the mirror, and the water suddenly feels too hot under my feet.

"What do you mean?"

"Her mom came onto my dad, and she refuses to break them up," he explains.

"Yeah, I know about all that." I wave it away, bored that this is the reason he got my dick to go flaccid after all that effort. "Get to the point."

"She actually fucking traded us her body to keep her mom safe," he says, licking his lips.

I narrow my eyes. "Did she now?"

"What? You don't approve?" He turns around and folds his arms.

"I would've used different means to get what I wanted," I reply, folding my arms too.

He smiles smugly. "I'm not you, though."

"Good," I retort, running my fingers through my hair. "Wouldn't want those filthy hands touching my perfect body."

He rolls his eyes. "Whatever."

"You don't sound at all sure of what you did with her," I say.

"It's too late. She's already made her choice," he says. "And we made good on our promise to give her everything she asked for."

My cock bobs up and down from just that sentence alone. "Please elaborate."

He shrugs. "We just fucked her. That's it. We didn't hurt her."

I sigh out loud. "It's fine. I don't need the details."

"You're just mad we didn't invite you," he says.

I scoff. "You wish. I don't involve myself in petty squabble."

"Petty squabble?" he barks. "I'm pretty fucking sure she set her mom up with my dad on purpose."

"How are you so sure?" I ask, turning off the shower.

"Stop with the cryptic shit," he retorts. "Can't you just ..."

"What?" I grab a towel and wrap it around myself. "Absolve you of your sin?"

He sucks in a breath, refusing to let it go until he can no longer hold it forcefully. "Look, forget it." He walks off.

"Why did you come in here, Caleb?" I ask. "Just to make me feel jealous? Or to revel in your devious ways?"

"I just came here to…" He halts near the door, hand lingering near the handle. "She's in the maze. Your favorite spot." He swallows, eyes finding mine through the fog.

Aha.

Feeling guilty already?

A decrepit smile forms on my face. "Run to your master, doggy. I'll take care of your mess."

His lip twitches, and he gives me the middle finger. "Fuck you, Blaine."

"Aw, I love you too," I say, throwing him an air-kiss.

He marches out and throws the door shut behind him so I can focus on getting my dick to go back down.

God, if only I could just finish what I started, but alas, it'll have to wait.

I have a blond-haired goddess to find among the roses.

***

Crystal

Rustling noises in the back of the maze make me turn around abruptly, knife clutched tightly in my hand.

A tall figure emerges from the route through which Ares and Caleb disappeared, a simple bathrobe all that separates his naked skin from my eyeballs. But even that fails to hide thick slabs of muscle on his pecs and calves as he steps forward.

Blaine.

I swallow and step back, holding the knife out in front of me. "Don't."

He holds up his hands. "I'm not here to harm you."

"Sure, just like your friends weren't," I retort.

He runs his fingers over his robe. "Does it look like I'm carrying weapons to you?"

I take another good look, gulping because of all the effort it takes not to gawk at the muscles that flex with each of his movements.

161

"Maybe you're hiding them."

"Do you wish to look underneath?" He starts peeling away the robe.

I swiftly cover my eyes and look away. "No, no, it's fine. I believe you."

"I'll be happy to show you all I have with me, which is not more—or less—than the well-endowed body I've been gifted with."

His smooth voice makes it so damn hard not to. But I've seen enough dicks for today, so I keep my eyes closed.

"All right, suit yourself."

"Is the robe on?" I ask when I hear shuffling.

He chuckles. "The robe is on."

When I slowly open my eyes again, he's right in front of me. He grabs my hand and peels it away from my face. How did he move so quickly? I was blindsided so swiftly I didn't realize he'd already made his way over to me.

And now he's holding my hand, and I'm too mesmerized by how he looks at me to even pull away.

His free hand rises to meet my face, but I flinch the second he tries to touch me. He pauses, studies me, before his knuckles softly caress my cheek, dulling my senses and lulling me into submission.

"Are you all right, darling?"

He talks so … affected.

Yet it doesn't feel at all unnatural with him.

I don't even know how to respond because he's looking at me so intently, so up close, it almost feels like he's peering straight into my soul.

He smiles. "You can speak."

My face heats. "Oh, right, yeah … I guess."

He pulls his hand away and looks at it, the back of his hand covered in saliva and … cum.

Oh God.

For a second, I almost forgot what Ares and Caleb did and that I was still drenched with all the evidence.

I try to run off, but he grips my wrist. "Don't go. Please."

The softness in his voice makes me stop in my tracks, and I let him step closer.

"You look like you could use some help with cleaning up," he says, smiling gently before he tugs me along. "Come."

Before I know it, I'm dragged away, barely able to hold my ragged clothes together as well as the knife in my hand while we zigzag through the maze. I can't keep track of our route, but within a minute, we end up right at the same spot I first saw the Tartarus boys at during the party they threw.

The paved area in front of their backyard door along with that same balcony they once stood at.

It all seems like such a distant memory.

"C'mon." Blaine drags me forward.

"Wait, isn't that the Tartarus House?" I yelp.

"Yes, it's fine," he replies, opening the door and pulling me in.

"What do you mean fine? That's enemy territory."

"Enemy?" he parrots, pausing as the door closes behind me.

Shit.

I'm already inside.

My hand tightens around the knife as I hold it out in front of me, ready to strike whoever tries to come at me.

Blaine turns around, his chiseled face so strikingly different from the gloominess of this building's interior that it catches me off guard when he looks me dead in the eyes. "Is that how you see me?" he asks, his hair cascading down his shoulder as he tilts his head.

"I ..."

I don't even know what to say.

Is he my enemy? Or is it just because he's friends with them?

Blaine leans over, still towering over me with that huge frame of his, and he taps my cheeks. "Made you blush."

The mischievous grin that follows makes me blush even harder.

I swallow away the lump in my throat and tuck my knife into my pocket. "I don't know what you want from me."

"Darling, my intentions have always been very clear." He tips up my chin. "I came because you needed help."

Now, I'm even more confused.

Why would someone from the Tartarus House want to help me?

And especially someone so close to Ares and Caleb?

"C'mon." He grabs my wrist and drags me through the gloomy, purple-painted hallway. Everywhere I look are erotic paintings and statues, tongues, nipples, dicks, everything together all at once. Music blasts upstairs, but it reverberates through the entire house. Every light is gloomy like they intentionally want to cast shadows inside their own home, and everywhere I look are bottles of liquor, books, drugs, and sex toys littering the cabinets. Nothing's hidden. Everything's out in the open, and when I blink once, I swear I spot a couple having sex in the back of the kitchen.

We go up the double stairs that lead around the building in a square, the loud music near us making me search.

"Pay no attention to the noise. People love to throw lewd parties here," Blaine says as he pulls me into a hallway down the left. "In here."

He swoops me into a room completely covered in royal green from head to toe. The walls, the ceiling, even the rug on the hardwood floor, as well as the expensive furniture and the bedding all look like it cost as much as my mom's house. "Holy shit ..." I mutter, looking around at all the expensive decorations. There's even an Adonis statue in the back next to a floor-to-ceiling gold mirror.

"Like my room? I did the decorating myself," he says all proudly, and he throws off his bathrobe, catching me off guard with those impeccable glutes. "Be right back, darling."

I'm frozen to the floor, staring ahead while wondering what the fuck is going on, and if I'm really losing my mind right now.

I probably am.

What am I even doing here?

Why did I let him lure me into this devil's den?

"There." He returns wearing a dark red robe covered in jewels and a thick gold rope around his waist. "Much better. And comfortable."

"You just switched bathrobes."

"Darling, that one was for outside strolls, not inside," he replies, spraying himself with a bottle of aftershave before he walks over to me and grabs my face.

He inspects me up close, and I'm almost inclined to swat him away.

"Turn around." He spins me on my heels with ease, his finger dipping underneath my dress.

I tense up and try to reach for my knife, but his hand gripping my wrist stops me.

"Relax."

His calm voice makes me unwind, and I let go.

He slowly lifts my dress until my ass is visible, and I suck in a breath when his hands slide over the red marks Caleb left behind.

"Handprints," he mutters. "Who did this to you?"

"Caleb," I say.

His hand lowers my dress again, and he grips my hand. "Come with me."

He drags me into a white and gold-marbled bathroom and shuts the door behind him. The place is so bright and spotless, it makes me blink. There are several rain showers in the back and a giant tub lined with gold in the middle. Everything in here, even the little table and candle, is made of gold, and it makes me wonder just how fucking rich this dude really is.

His big hands come down on my shoulders, and I jolt up and down.

"You don't have to fear me like you fear them," he murmurs.

"I don't fear them. I'm not afraid of anyone," I swiftly respond.

His breath tingles against my neck. "Good. Hold that feeling for as long as you can."

"As long as I can?" I repeat.

"They'll break you eventually."

When his hands leave my shoulders, it feels like a ghost flying away, leaving me with shivers all over.

He grabs a bottle off his top shelf and sits down on the bench in front of the bathtub, patting his thigh. "Come here."

I swallow and shake my head.

He raises his brow. "Are you afraid I'll bite?" A smirk forms on his lips. "Oh right, I forgot … you're not afraid of anything. So why don't you come?"

Shit. He got me there.

He opens the jar and shows me the contents. "It's just cooling gel. See? Nothing dangerous."

I swallow and push back the apprehension to get closer.

He grabs me by my thighs and pulls me in, easily pushing me down onto his giant lap.

"Now, that wasn't so hard, was it?"

He fingers the jar with his index finger and middle finger, and I don't know why I focus on it, but I can't take my eyes off him as he brings them to my ass and rubs the gel into my skin. The cool glow it applies feels nice against the red marks Caleb left.

"Feels good, doesn't it?" he murmurs, and he blows cool breath into my ear, making goose bumps scatter on my skin.

What am I doing? Why am I letting him do this to me?

He swiftly turns me around so I'm looking at him instead of the door, my legs over his, and I can feel his package underneath my ass, twitching behind that robe.

But instead of poking me with it, he grabs a towel, dips it into the half-filled tub, and wipes it along my face, cleaning up the filth.

"There … much better," he murmurs, gently dabbing my face with the towel.

And something about that softness in him breaks me.

Tears well up in my eyes, but only one manages to roll down before I push them away again. He picks up the one tear with his index finger to stop it from falling.

"If you want me to hurt them, all you need to do is ask," he says. "And I will oblige."

"They're your friends," I say. "Aren't you supposed to defend them?"

"I am, and I can't actually kill them, but sometimes they deserve an ass-whooping just as much as anyone else, which I am more than happy to provide," he says, making me chuckle. "Well, I'm glad you can still laugh about it."

"I'm sorry."

"Don't be. I love how you laugh," he says.

God, why is it so warm in here all of a sudden?

"I don't understand. Why are you so nice to me?" I ask.

He raises a brow. "Am I not allowed?"

"No, that's not it," I say. "I just … didn't expect it."

"Because they're my friends," he says. My eyes drift off, but he tips my chin back so I look into his eyes. "I may be part of the Tartarus House, but I will *not* stoop to their level."

"Won't they get mad that you're doing this?" I ask.

A devilish glint in his eyes makes him look cocky as fuck. "Darling, I'm not afraid of their madness." He grabs my hand and presses a kiss onto the top. "And I'm not afraid of what I want either."

The kiss turns into a lavish one, leaving several heated marks on my skin near the wound on my arm from the rose bushes. And when his tongue dips out to lick the blood, I actually feel my pussy thump. His groan sets my body on fire.

Oh God.

166

What am I doing?

I stumble off his lap as he licks off his lips like he savored my taste.

All of the boys who live here are devils in disguise.

They're all so … sexual. And this guy is no different.

I can't trust him.

"This was a mistake," I mutter, turning around.

"Where are you going?" he asks, tilting his head. "Don't you want a shower and clean clothes?"

I snatch a bathrobe off his rack and put it on.

"I have that at home, thanks," I say, opening the door.

But I still can't help but glance over my shoulder at that gorgeous tall body and those sensual eyes that are almost enough to lure me right back into his arms.

"You know, the offer still stands," he says, with legs spread wide, his hands behind on the tub to support himself. "If you want to learn how to defend yourself against them, I can teach you."

I swallow away the lump in my throat and open the door.

I have to leave. Now. Before I make a grave error in judgment.

But when I close the door behind me, his voice still haunts me all the way to the stairs that I bolt down.

"I'll be waiting for you."

TWENTY TWO

CALEB

Music blasts in my ears, the noise only partially drowning out the arousal still coursing through my veins.

Fucking her was the best aphrodisiac in the world, I'm not gonna lie.

I've never felt anything close to it before, not even when I'm with Ares.

And that … that's a hard pill to swallow.

I take a big gulp of my whiskey on the rocks.

My door bangs open, and Ares barges in, slamming it shut behind him.

What is he doing here? I thought he said he wanted time alone after we left her in the maze?

He pulls the plug on the music, so I yell, "Hey!"

He waltzes over to me and smacks the glass out of my hand, shattering it to a million pieces before gripping my shirt and pulling me in for a kiss so possessive it melts every inch of my resistance away.

His kisses are about the closest thing one can get to peace.

Before he takes it all away again.

When his lips unlatch, he murmurs, "Go behind my back again,

168

and I will kill her."

"What?" I mutter, blinking rapidly.

"Have I ever lied to you?"

But I'm too flustered to even respond.

He'll … kill her? But that doesn't make any sense. He's the one who's obsessed with her.

He's lying.

"Answer me."

"No," I reply swiftly.

"Then don't ever try to fuck her again without my permission," he says, tilting his head as his tongue darts out to wet his lips.

He shoves me back into my seat, still towering over me like a goddamn god raining down thunder.

I adjust myself in my seat. "Is that why you didn't let me finish twice?"

"She was not yours to take," he seethes.

My brows furrow. "I thought you wanted to punish her?"

"Together." He balls his fists. "Not separately."

I swallow as he gazes down at me with disdain.

Is he upset that I used those pretty lips for myself?

Or is he jealous I wanted her instead of him?

He grabs his zipper, and my cock bobs up and down as he slowly unzips.

"As a matter of fact, I don't want you to touch her at all," he says, pulling out his long, hard cock that makes my mouth salivate. "Until I give you permission."

He grips my chin and pulls me off the seat.

"On. Your. Knees."

I go to my knees in front of him willingly.

"Now wrap your hand around my shaft and make me come all over that goddamn filthy mouth of yours."

"Yes, Sir," I moan, and I do what he asks of me, desperate for more—like a beggar looking for scraps.

***

A day later

I pull out a cig, light it, and take a deep whiff. Not enough nicotine in the entire fucking world would be enough to still the boner in my pants.

But Ares made it very clear I will know hell on earth if I touch it.

I blow out some smoke and try not to look antsy even though I'm getting so aroused just from the mere memories plaguing my mind.

I can still see her in front of me on that bench, pussy fitting so snugly around my cock it made me want to claim her all for myself. But then I saw that rage in Ares's eyes, and I couldn't fucking do it.

She isn't fucking mine, and she never will be. He made her his obsession, and he's intent on destroying her. The only question is … do I want to go along with his every whim?

I take another whiff.

All I've ever wanted was him. Even when I was with other men, I still desired Ares so much that the moment he let me have it, I caved and broke things off with another.

I know I'm hated for it.

But no one understands me the way he does.

No one understands *him* the way I do.

But now there is *her* … Crystal … A girl who's managed to capture both our possessive souls. A girl hell-bent on making us her enemy. Even if she denies ever sending her mother to my father, she's the reason they're together, and she will pay the fucking price.

She made her choice … her body belongs to us now.

I take another drag.

Us.

Which means I can do with her whatever the fuck I want.

I don't need Ares's permission.

When she walks out of the building she had her first class in, I hold the smoke in my mouth and fix my eyes on her. With those jeans and that thick sweater, no one could ever tell she was railed into oblivion last night.

A smirk forms on my face as I wait until she finally lays eyes on me, and the terror in her eyes makes me breathe out the smoke through my nose like a goddamn dragon.

Destruction looks gorgeous on her.

She skitters off across the pavement, away from me, and toward her friends sitting in the grass, clutching her bag tightly like she's afraid I might steal that too.

Don't worry, Crystal, we'll only steal your fucking soul.

Nothing more, nothing less.

And when we're done with you, you won't even want it back.

My phone rings, pulling me out of my thoughts.

Dad's number makes me swallow, and I throw my cig away before I answer.

"What's up?"

"Hey, Caleb, your dad here."

"Figured as much from your name on the screen."

"Very funny," my dad jests. "Anyway, I just wanted to call and ask how you're doing?"

"Fine."

"And your studies?"

"Also fine."

"You're not very talkative, are you?"

"No." I kick a little rock lying near my feet.

I know there's always a reason when he calls me, and it's never to catch up.

"So you're not gonna ask how I am?"

"How're things?"

"Right ..." He clears his throat. "Anyway, I'm going to go on a date with my fiancée tomorrow..."

"*Fiancée*, wow," I parrot, rolling my eyes.

But my father continues. "And I want you to entertain Crystal while we're away."

"What?" I bark through the phone.

"Caleb ..."

"No. Fuck no."

"Caleb, I'm trying to ask you nicely."

God, I have to put a fucking stop to this before he asks something from me I cannot do.

"She's a terrible liar and a shitty person, Dad."

"Caleb!" he yells through the phone. "That's no way to talk about your—"

"Don't. Don't say the word," I interject. "Don't call her that. She won't ever be that to me, and her mom won't ever be my fucking mother."

171

"No one said that."

"Then why the fuck are you trying to forget my actual fucking mother still exists?"

I hang up the phone before things get even more heated, but damn, I really can't control myself.

My phone buzzes.

Dad: I really wish that conversation could've gone differently.

Me: Maybe stop seeing that woman, then.

Dad: You know she'll be my wife whether you like it or not.

Me: You're pretending Mom doesn't exist.

Dad: I'm not. But I have to move on. And so should you.

I almost crush the phone in my hand.

Dad: I want you to get to know her. Spend some time with both her and her mother. Who knows, maybe they'll grow on you.

The only thing that'll grow is my dick the second I get my hands on that fucking girl who caused all of this.

Me: Doubt that.

Dad: Try.

Me: I'm not going to entertain her like some goddamn clown.

Dad: If you don't have the time, fine, but you will be nice to her, and you will behave from now on.

Me: And what if I don't? What then? You're just going to force me?

Dad: Do you want me to take away access to your bank account? Because I will do it.

I'm really trying hard not to chuck my phone into the nearest tree.

Me: Fine. I'll be fucking nice to her. Happy now?

Dad: Good. It doesn't have to be this way, you know? You could just try to put in some effort.

Me: I'm going to class. Bye.

I turn off my phone before he can send any more texts, and I look at all the unmarked skin on my wrist, wondering if I should get another tattoo just to take the edge off the rage inside my heart.

***

Crystal

I knew I had to run in the opposite direction the second I saw those hazel eyes.

I couldn't look at them for one more second without immediately being reminded of all the dirty things Caleb and Ares did to me on that bench in the maze. I can still feel them too … inside my pussy and throat, the mere memory enough to make my clit throb, and I hate it.

I hate it so much I don't want to think about it one more second as I barge across campus grounds.

"Hey, Crystal!"

Penelope's voice stops me in my tracks. She and our friends are having a picnic in the grass, and all the guys from the Skull & Serpent Society are there too, though they don't seem pleased to be there at all. I snort to myself.

"Hey," I say, waving back, and I grin at Kayla, who's there too. "Hi, Kay!"

"Come sit with us," Kayla says, pointing at the blanket.

I suck in a breath and try to push away the evil thoughts floating through my head. I can't keep avoiding them forever. I've already gotten so many messages asking where I've been and what I've been doing. I don't want to lose the last semblance of normalcy I have at Spine Ridge University.

I blow out a sigh and approach them in the grass. "I forgot it was lunchtime. I didn't bring anything."

"We've got extra sandwiches," Penelope says.

"Yeah, want mine?" Dylan holds up a half-eaten one.

"Dylan!" Penelope swats his hand down. "Gross."

Alistair snorts, and Dylan throws him a foul look. "What? I was just being nice."

"Thanks, Dylan," I say. "I appreciate it."

"See? At least someone's nice about it," Dylan says.

"Go cry about it." Felix rolls his eyes.

Dylan's face scrunches up, and he pulls out his lighter and holds it underneath Felix's jacket. My eyes widen when the fire immediately burns a hole into the fabric.

"Jesus F—" Felix pats down the jacket until the fire is out. "What the fuck did you do that for?"

"Well, if that isn't a warm welcome," I mutter.

Alistair laughs out loud, and everyone looks at him like he's gone insane.

But then slowly, more people begin to laugh, even Dylan.

"Bitches," Felix adds, but then he briefly laughs too.

"It's been madness since they've joined our picnics," Kayla says.

"Tell me about it." Penelope rolls her eyes. "If only they would behave."

"Hey. I behave," Alistair says, taking a bite of his sandwich. "And I like this. What is it?"

"Salmon," Kayla says.

He immediately spits it out. "Why the fuck would you let me eat this, Dylan?"

"Don't look at me." Dylan shrugs. "Wanna swap?"

Alistair sighs out loud and swaps their sandwiches.

"See, I'm nice," Dylan says in a chipper voice.

Penelope holds out a box toward me. "Here, pick out whatever you want."

I grab a peanut butter and jelly sandwich. "Thanks."

My stomach growls, and Kayla and Penelope look at me like they're about to burst into laughter.

"Guess we got you just in time," Kayla says.

I take a bite out of my sandwich. "This is delish. Reminds me of how my mom used to make them."

"Same. That's why I bring them to class." Penelope winks. "So ... got any plans tonight?"

"What?" I swallow down the peanut butter.

"You know, the text I sent you?" she asks. "About the club?"

Wait, did she?

I pull out my phone and check the texts.

Shit. She's right. I completely forgot I said yes.

But that was yesterday ... before those two devils came to knock my world upside down and steal my literal breath away.

"Sorry, I forgot." I swiftly take another bite and chug down my water. "I've been busy."

"With what? I haven't seen you in the library in days," Kayla says. "It's almost like you've got some kind of secret lover."

I almost choke on my water. "No, no, nothing like that. Just some stuff going on with my mom. Nothing big."

"Your mom?" Penelope frowns. "Is she okay?"

"Yeah, yeah," I say, putting on a big smile to hide the lie. "Anyway, what about the club?"

"You still up for partying with us?" she asks, biting her lip. "We're going to Club RIVERA. Felix has a VIP pass because it's one of his father's clubs. Anyway, it's gonna be a blast."

"I can't come." Kayla slams her lips together. "Family thing. But you go have fun."

"Are you sure?" I ask. "Because I'm more than fine sitting this one out."

"Yeah, of course!" she says. "I'll come next time you go. No worries."

"Perfect!" Penelope says, wrapping her arm around my neck. "This is gonna be a fabulous night. I can't fucking wait."

"Same," I say.

Maybe I should just do it. What harm would it do to just have a little bit of fun? Besides, I could use the pick-me-up after everything last night.

My phone buzzes, and I check the messages.

Brooke: Hey, wanna come hang out at Club RIVERA? My friend got sick so now me and Lana are all alone. We'd love it if you'd come along.

"Wow."

"What?" Penelope asks.

"A friend, Brooke, just asked me to come to Club RIVERA too." I look up into their bewildered eyes. "She says Lana is going with her too."

"Wait, what?" Felix frowns and steals my phone away. "What the fu—"

"Felix," Penelope warns him. "Give back the phone."

Felix's nostrils flare, but he still hands it back to me. "She's my *fucking* sister. I didn't give her permission."

"She doesn't need it," Penelope retorts, lifting her brow. "She can enjoy her free time any way she wants to. If she wants to come to the club, that's her choice."

"She's not going alone," he barks back.

"She's not," I say. "Brooke's with her."

He seems really on edge. "That's not enough."

"We'll be there too. It's fine," Penelope says.

"What could happen?" Dylan mutters, taking another bite of his sandwich.

"Did you fucking forget about the Phantoms?"

Phantoms ... I think Felix means Kai, Nathan, and Milo, as I heard from Penelope they were beefing. But I tend to stay far away from fights. At least, I used to.

"No, absolutely fucking not," Felix growls.

"What if I went with her?" I've already said the words before I realized it. Everyone's looking at me now. "I mean, Brooke asked. I could just ... join them?"

Penelope sighs. "But I miss you. I really wanted to dance together."

"It's fine. Nothing's stopping you guys from dancing together," Kayla says.

I smile at Felix. "If Lana and Brooke want me there, I can join them. I'll keep an eye on her."

"You sure?" Penelope asks me, grabbing my hand. "You don't have to sacrifice yourself."

"Yeah, it'll be fun. Besides, you're with plenty of people already, while they're only with two. It'll balance the groups a bit if I go with them instead." I wink.

"Only if you're sure," Kayla says.

I text Brooke back.

Me: Sure! Would love to.

Brooke: Awesome! Meet us at Club RIVERA around eight.

Then I put my phone down. "There. It's a done deal."

***

ARES

I straighten my collar and clear my throat, then knock on his door. "Come in."

I push down the handle, the metal feeling like it weighs a ton in my hand as I open the door.

Five guys with tons of tattoos and piercings stand in front of his desk, their heads turned as their gazes fixate on me.

"Ares. Glad you could finally make room for me in your schedule." It's hard not to miss the sarcasm in his voice. My father points at a chair in the back. "Sit."

I walk past the men and sit down, their gazes still upon me like hawks ready to strike their prey.

"*Mi hijo* ... care to explain yourself?" my father asks.

"No." I fold my arms.

"These men have told me you've been killing some of their guys. Is that true?"

I avert my eyes. "I don't remember."

My father's fist comes down on the table, and my eye twitches in response.

"Speak the truth, now."

"They came onto my property," I say, crossing my legs too. "I have the right to defend myself."

"They were there with orders," one of the men in front of my father's desk growls. "You had no right."

"I had *every* right," I retort, my fist balling. "I paid for that lot of land Tartarus was built on out of my own pocket. I *own* it." I zero in on the men standing in front of my father's desk, all high and mighty. "And I will defend it when someone trespasses."

My father's nostrils flare. "Regardless. They were there for a purpose."

"Oh really? On campus grounds?" I rebuke. "Because I'm more than willing to explain to the dean what they were doing there. I'm sure the board members will be curious to know all about it."

My father's eyes widen, and the men seem on edge.

Good.

I know he's been scheming with them, but I won't allow it to happen on Tartarus grounds.

"I will make reparations," my father tells the men, ignoring me. "You have my word." He holds out his hand.

"Your word better be worth something," the main guy says, shaking his hand. "Because if not, our mutual understanding will be over."

"I will not risk any of our lucrative deals over my son's indiscretions." He throws me a brief glare. "You are valuable business partners." He adds a snakelike smile before handing them a check. "I know it will not replace the lives lost, but please take this as

177

an olive branch."

"Thanks," the guy says before he flicks his fingers at his other men. "You'll hear from us."

"Of course," my father says as they turn around. "Rest assured, I will deal with my son."

When his gaze settles on me, I can practically see the fire blazing behind his eyes, and as the door closes, the darkness surrounds us once again.

And the only sound is my heart as it beats wildly out of control.

TWENTY THREE

Crystal

I dance to the rhythm of the music, trying to get lost in the sound of this fabulous song they're playing in Club RIVERA. Lana and Brooke dance alongside me, and we bump our butts and swirl around each other in a sultry manner. Lana's hair sways from left to right as she dances to the rhythm, her moves attracting so much attention that it's hard not to get flustered. I'm not used to all the attention being on us, but I can live with it as long as it's not Tartarus boys glaring at me from a corner.

But I doubt they'd come here to a club owned by the Rivera family, the father of the leader of the Skull & Serpent Society.

Felix, Penelope, Dylan, and Alistair all chat, dance, and drink in the VIP section. I briefly said hi to them before I went to the dance floor with the girls.

Tonight, the club wanted everyone to grab a red mask at the entrance to hide their identity, and I have to say it does make me more outgoing and more willing to let go in the music.

I take some more sips of my alcohol, feeling the buzz rushing through my veins. But suddenly, Lana begins to wobble, and she nearly falls into me.

"Wow," she murmurs.

"You all right?" I ask.

"Yeah, yeah, just getting a little tipsy," she says.

"I'm gonna go to the bathroom. You wanna come?" Brooke yells over the music.

Lana shakes her head. "I'm good. You go ahead."

But my bladder is filling up quickly. "I have to pee." I adjust my dress as it's crept up from all the dancing we did. "I'm coming with you."

Brooke hooks her arm through mine, and I put my drink on the table somewhere, then we head off to the bathroom. The place is filled with girls chatting about the latest drama while doing their makeup. I do my thing in a stall and wait for Brooke to finish too.

"Oh God … I'm gonna be sick."

I can hear Brooke throwing up in the stall, and I rush inside to hold her hair so it doesn't get all sticky and filthy.

"Fuck. I'm sorry, Crystal," she says.

"No, no, it's okay."

She goes on and on with no end in sight, then begins to cry. "I didn't wanna ruin the evening."

"You didn't ruin anything," I say, comforting her. "We had a good time. We just drank too much."

I'm feeling dizzy too, but I didn't drink nearly as much as she did.

"I always get too excited," she says before throwing up more.

"Just get it out of your system," I say, rubbing her back. "You'll feel much better soon."

After an hour, she's all done and slumps against the toilet. I grab some paper towels and rinse it under the water so she can dab her face with them.

"God, I'm so glad it's finished," she murmurs. "Thanks for helping me."

I smile. "Of course. That's what friends are for."

"You think … we could keep dancing?"

I snort. "If you want to, sure. What's stopping us?"

She grins, and I help her get up. "Lana's waiting for us. Better get back in the game before she steals all the hot boys from under our noses."

I laugh as we exit the bathroom and head back to our spot, but Lana's nowhere to be found.

"That's weird. I could've sworn we left her here. Right?" Brooke asks.

I nod and look around, but I don't see her anywhere, not even near the VIP area where her brother is. *Where could she be?*

We check the bar as well as the top floor and several exclusive rooms, but we can't find her anywhere.

"This is making me nervous as fuck," Brooke says. "Felix told me to watch her."

Brooke pulls out her phone and texts her while I watch.

Brooke: Where R U?

But Lana still doesn't appear to have read it.

I sigh out loud and open the bathroom door and call out her name, "Lana?"

No response.

Brooke: Hello? Earth to Lana?

Brooke: This isn't funny.

"Do you think she's playing hide-and-seek?" she mutters.

"Why would she?" I retort, confused.

"I don't know."

"We must've missed something," I say.

"Well, these red masks we're forced to wear don't fucking help either," Brooke says, getting more and more annoyed.

So I grab my phone too and send her a message.

Me: Lana, please RE! Are u OK? You disappeared on us.

"Oh God," Brooke panics. "What do we do? If Felix finds out she's missing, he's gonna kill me."

"Calm down. No one's missing," I say. "We just lost sight of her. She's gotta be in here."

"We were gone for so long without an explanation," Brooke says, shivering. "I should've told her I was feeling sick, but I didn't wanna ruin the evening."

She grabs her phone and begins texting her again.

Brooke: Tell me ur in the bathroom, or I swear to God I'll walk over to your brother and tell him you're missing. I don't want no fuckin trouble.

She waits and waits, chewing off all her nails while she's at it.

Lana: Sry, got sick so I got home on my bike. Don't worry bout me.

We both breathe a sigh of relief.

Brooke: O shit. That sucks.

"Maybe it wasn't the alcohol after all?" Brooke asks. "I mean, if she got sick too."

"Maybe," I respond, then focus on my phone again.

Me: Are you sure? I can come. I don't want you to be alone.

Lana: Yeah, I'm fine. Go party! But also, pls don't tell my brother.

Brooke: Don't want him to worry, huh?

Lana: Yeah. Did he notice something?

Brooke: No, they were still in that exclusive area for a good while. I don't even wanna know what they were doing in there. TMI.

Lana: Pls just don't tell him I was gone.

Me: We won't tell him, don't worry. As long as you're safe.

Lana: Thank you.

Me: DM us if you need us, and we'll be there in a min, OK?

Lana: GO dance. Don't worry about me.

Me: OK, get better soon!

Brooke: K, feel better!

I tuck my phone away again and smile at Brooke, who's no longer incessantly chewing her nails. "Thank God. I would've died if I had to go talk to her fucking brother."

I laugh. "That's what you're worried about?"

"Have you ever talked to him?" she asks. "He's a scary guy."

"True," I reply. "Anyway, wanna dance?" I wink.

She grabs my hands and tugs me along. "Thought you'd never ask!"

***

When the night is over, Brooke's lost to a guy at the club, and I don't want to tear her away from him and ruin the rest of her evening, so I decide to head out by myself. She's not ready to leave yet, but she's sober enough to make her own decisions, and I've told Penelope to keep an eye on her while also making sure she didn't say anything about Lana to Felix so she wouldn't get in trouble. Because that's what good friends do.

I hold my shoes in one hand while I have my phone in the other as I try to get a cab, but apparently, things are quite busy around this time in Crescent Vale City. I'm not having any luck securing a ride back to Spine Ridge U.

"Damn," I mutter to myself, strolling through the streets.

I can still hear the music blaring in the background, along with several groups of girls and guys having fun outside. People are laughing, screaming, shouting, and doing all sorts of stunts to grab attention. But a particular group of guys follows me, making me feel on edge.

"Hey, beautiful. Where are you going?"

I ignore them and head straight across the street. It'll be a few more blocks before I get to the road that leads up the hill. If I can't find a cab soon enough, I'll have to walk all the way back to Spine Ridge U.

"Hey," the dude behind me says. "Care to answer, or are you always this obnoxious?"

There are five of them in total following me, and not the kind of guys I'd ever want to associate with. Definitely from the wrong side of the tracks and most definitely drunk as hell.

"Please leave me alone," I tell them before I saunter off.

"Hey, that's not fucking nice," another one yells.

I increase my pace, but within minutes, they've caught up with me, and now fear really is coiling its way around my heart.

"Hey. We're talking to you, bitch!" one of them yells before gripping my jacket.

"Let go of me!" I yell, jerking free of his grip.

They laugh and surround me, preventing me from moving another step.

Shit.

I'm cornered.

"I don't want anything from you," I tell them. "Please, just let me be."

One of them laughs. "I don't think so. You insulted us."

"I didn't say anything," I say.

When I try to move past them, one of them shoves me back into the middle of the group.

"Don't even think about it."

"Let me through," I say through gritted teeth, my hand diving into my pocket.

He raises his brow. "Or else?"

I pull out my knife and point it at them, and they begin to laugh.

Fine. If they won't take me seriously, then I'll make them.

I attack him, running my knife through his hand.

"ARGH!" he screams.

I pull it out and try to bolt.

"Grab her!" the wounded one shouts.

Another guy grabs my waist and pulls me down to the ground.

"Get off me!" I shriek, and I slice around to get him to back off, cutting into his arm.

"What the fuck is wrong with you?" he spits, trying to steal the knife from my hand.

"No, no, no!" I scream, holding on to it for dear life. "That's my father's knife!"

"She fucking cut me!" the guy I hurt yells. "How about we teach her a fucking lesson for that, boys?"

"Oh, now we're talking," another guy says, and he steps over to me and grips my hair, pulling my head back so tightly I shriek.

"I can't fucking wait to play with you."

A car comes veering down the road, tires screeching left and right, headlights blinding me.

"What the f—"

I shut my eyes as it's headed straight toward us.

"Watch out!"

SCREECH!

A loud thump makes me hold my breath.

Yelps are all around me.

My eyes flash open, but the blinding lights stop me from seeing anything except the damaged metal and leg sticking out from underneath the wheel.

Oh God.

BANG!

I jolt up and down against the ground.

Was that a ...

Another shot goes off.

My eyes burst open.

Someone in a hoodie tucks a gun away and pulls out two big knives, slicing into the men one after the other like he's cutting through butter. With ease, he fights them off, jumping around their attacks, cutting into their flesh instead. Their screams fill the void of the night.

One by one, they all go down, blood spattering all around me, and I close my eyes, waiting for my impending doom.

I can hear the clicking of the metal before it goes off, and I open my eyes to await my final moments.

BANG!

My heart jumps along to the sound.

The guy who was on top of me, holding me down, has a giant hole in his head.

I shove him off me, and he flops onto the road like a sack of potatoes.

But now I'm staring straight into the barrel of a gun.

A puff of smoke appears from beneath a hoodie, and the gun is retracted, replaced by a hand covered in tattoos.

"Get up."

I can't even properly process what happened as my legs move on their own, my whole body shaking as I crawl up from the ground.

Unsteady, I fall into him, but he holds on tight.

Two familiar hazel eyes bore a hole into my head when I look up. And for a second, I almost forget how to breathe … until he reminds me.

"Breathe."

I blow out a single shell-shocked breath. "Caleb? What are you doing here?"

I gaze at the bodies surrounding me, and my knees begin to quake. There's blood everywhere, on the ground, on his Aston Martin, and even on my dress.

He tucks away his knives.

"Saving your ass," he replies as he opens the car door. "Now get in."

"What?" I mutter, utterly lost in the violence that just happened.

"I said get in," he grunts.

When I don't respond, he grabs me and shoves me into the passenger's seat himself. "That wasn't a fucking question, Crystal. Get in."

One of the bodies gurgles and groans.

"Wait," I say, pointing at him. "He's still alive. We gotta—"

Caleb pulls out a single small knife and throws it at the man, piercing his bone right between his eyes.

"Not anymore."

The man slumps to the ground.

Another body on top of the pile of bodies he left.

Caleb fishes all the knives out of the dead bodies, wiping them on his hoodie like it means nothing to him. And as he tucks them all away, he marches to my door and shuts it tight, sealing me in silence.

I swallow the lump in my throat when Caleb gets in right next to me.

"Did they hurt you?" he asks.

I shake my head. "No."

"Good. Next time, you call me." He slams the door shut. "So I can chop off some fingers before I kill them."

He starts the car as panic coils around my heart.

Don't show fear. Don't ever fucking show it, Crystal.

"What are you doing?" I ask.

"Getting us the fuck out of here," he growls. "I don't wanna get the cops on my ass."

I glance at the place he hides his knives. "You killed them."

"Because they tried to fucking touch you," he retorts, glaring right back at me. "No one fucking touches you except us."

He did this for me out of pure possessiveness?

His foot hits the gas, and the car races off.

"Thank you," I mutter after a while.

There's a pause. "You're welcome."

He's still looking at me, not just in an angry way, but in a way that almost feels … protective.

I grab my coat and pull it tighter.

"I don't understand how you were even there to save me?"

"I was watching you," he retorts.

My eyes widen.

He followed me? The entire night?

"You shouldn't have gone there," he adds. "RIVERA clubs are dangerous."

"I just wanted a night out with my friends, that's all," I say.

"It took every ounce of self-control for me not to drag you out of there myself, you hear me?" he says, looking at me sternly.

My lips part, but I don't know what to say.

"I let you play around in that club because you needed the release after last night, but don't think for a second I'm letting you out of my sight."

I swallow. "Why?"

"Because my dad told me to," he growls.

I roll my eyes. "Sure."

"Believe what you want," he quips, jaw tensing.

"So where are we going, then?"

He glances back and forth between me and the road. "I'm taking you the fuck home. Where else?"

I rub my lips together and look away. "Impressive. I don't believe a single word you're saying."

"Then don't," he growls, shifting gear so fast that I almost fall over.

"You don't have to protect me. I'm not your fucking girlfriend," I retort.

"I will protect what belongs to *me*," he grits back, eyes fixated on mine for a moment. "You knew what you signed up for when you made that deal with us."

"Out of necessity," I add.

"You're ours." He continues. "To play with. To use as we see fit." His eyes trail down my body and the short dress I'm wearing. "And you will do as we say."

I pull the coat even tighter, but it won't cover up all my skin.

Fuck.

He drives faster and faster through the city, not giving a shit that he's running red lights.

"You're going too fast," I say.

"I don't fucking care," he growls, shifting gears again.

"Why are you in such a rush?"

"I need to get the fuck away from there," he grits. "Before I turn around and run over the rest too."

My breath falters. "The rest?"

"You thought those five fuckers went to that club by themselves? It was a group of twenty dudes," he says, grinding his teeth. "They all frequent that club looking for easy chicks to score and dump while they're intoxicated."

"Shit," I mutter, moving in my seat to grab the door. "Brooke's in there."

His hand suddenly grips my thigh, fingers digging into my skin to keep me in place. "She's not with one of them. I checked," he says.

"You're not going back there."

I gulp, but he doesn't remove his hand, and for some reason, I can't stop focusing on how each finger splays against my inner thigh and how much my heart rate picks up with every passing second that his fingers touch me.

Slowly, his fingers start to inch up.

"Caleb. You're speeding."

"I can't help it. I want you out of my fucking car as fast as possible," he grits.

I try to swat his hand away, but he won't let go.

"Do you even fucking know why?" he says, throwing intense glances my way.

I swallow and shake my head, the alcohol making me feel dizzy.

Or maybe it's from the obsessive way he's looking at me.

And the possessive way his fingers inch closer and closer to my most sensitive spot.

"Because since we chased you into the maze, I've been living with a goddamn raging hard-on."

I clench my legs and look down.

My pussy throbs.

It actually fucking throbbed.

Oh fuck.

TWENTY FOUR

CALEB

I slowly slide my fingers underneath that partially see-through black dress she's wearing, her skin damp with sweat, body glitter making her skin look so goddamn edible I just want to take a bite.

I swallow back the lust, but it's impossible to stop as my fingers slowly dip between her thighs.

I know I'm not supposed to do this because Ares wants to share her.

But I can't help myself.

Whenever I'm around her, all I want to do is touch her, taste her, lick her, consume her, impale her on my rock-hard cock until she mewls my name.

Goddammit, what the fuck is happening to me?

I shake it off, but I don't take the palm of my hand off her pussy.

She whimpers when I push the pad of my thumb down.

She hates me just as much as I hate her, yet ...

I nudge her legs apart and circle around her pussy with my fingers, sliding across her panties until I can feel the wetness straight through the fabric.

She averts her eyes, but I can see her bite her lip, and the mere sight alone makes my cock strain.

I straighten my jeans, but none of it helps to get rid of this

189

growing need to hit the brakes, grab her face, and smash my lips on those rosy lips of hers.

God-fucking-dammit.

What the fuck has she done to me?

I hit the gas even harder despite going far beyond the speed limit, but nothing's gonna stop me from getting to my goal as fast as possible.

But my fingers have a mind of their own as they play with her pussy, circling her damp panties until her breath comes out in short gasps. And fuck me, that sound alone could make me come right here, right now.

And I hate it. I fucking hate how much she makes me want her.

"You're going too fast," she mutters as I slip across the road.

But I couldn't care less about safety right now.

"Unzip me, Crystal," I growl.

She briefly glances my way with shock riddling her face.

So I push her panties aside and swirl around her clit, making her squeak.

"What about the speed limit?" she mutters.

"Didn't you hear me? Take out my cock."

Her hand swiftly moves to my zipper, and when my dick is finally released, I groan out loud from the pent-up lust raging through my body.

"Are you going to slow down now?" she asks, swallowing as I slowly dip down her slit.

"Hold your hand below your mouth," I command.

She does it while eyeing me like I'm going insane.

"Spit."

When she dribbles it, I command, "Wrap your hands around my shaft."

"Are you kidding me? You're driving," she says.

I hit the gas even harder. "Fuck me."

"All right, all right," she mutters, finally wrapping her hand around my shaft.

As her fingers squeeze and move up and down, they are the closest thing to heaven I'll get right now...

Before I'll drive us straight into hell.

"Caleb," she mutters, wriggling around in her seat from the heat as I push my fingers inside her. "You've gotta slow down."

"Fuck that," I growl, swirling my fingers inside her pussy and then on top of her clit, spreading wetness all over.

"We're on the road," she murmurs, struggling to jerk me off.

"Don't stop," I tell her.

Her thumb rolls across the top of my dick, making it hard to focus on the road.

But at this point, I don't even fucking care if we make it home.

Living on the edge like this keeps me sane.

Her thighs clench together as her body begins to shiver from my touch, but I swat them open. "Don't fucking close your legs. Keep them wide open."

"But someone might see if they drive by," she says.

"Fuck it. Let them fucking see what kind of bad little slut you are for me," I groan, my cock twitching against her palm.

God, if I'd asked her to suck me off instead, I would've busted a nut within a second.

But I need to fucking resist.

I can't.

I fucking swore it to him.

But this girl ... this girl is going to be the death of me.

And if she's the one to kill me, then fuck my life, I'm going to drag her with me.

A soft moan escapes her mouth. "Oh fuck."

"Yes. I'll fucking finger you any way I want, any fucking time I want."

I flick her clit fast and hard. Feeling it thump underneath the pad of my finger is a fucking aphrodisiac, and I can't fucking get enough.

I don't want it. I fucking *need* it.

I need the rush so bad I can't fucking live another fucking day if I don't have it.

"Caleb ... please," she whimpers.

"Please, what?" I grit. "What are you?"

Her eyes almost roll into the back of her head, and fuck me, I physically have to hold back my orgasm. I want it so badly I could fucking scream.

But I want something else far more than just a quick release.

So I hit the gas as we head up the mountain and drive into the dark night.

"Caleb, it's too fast. We're gonna crash," she whimpers while I dip my fingers right back into her pussy again.

"You're gonna give me everything you have to give."

"What?" She gasps.

"Your orgasm or your life."

"Are you joking?" she squeals.

"Do I look like I'm joking?" I stare her directly in the eyes. "I'm gonna keep fucking driving until you give me what I want."

"You're insane," she says, but her wet pussy clenching around my fingers begs to differ.

"Who's gonna bust first, you or me?" I say as she jerks me off. "Because I've been edging for days now, and I still want your fucking orgasm more than mine."

She sucks in a breath.

"What's it going to be, slut? Make me come and die, or come for me and live?"

"Oh fuck," she mewls as I pull out only to toy with her clit instead.

"That's it. I'll only go faster and faster until you surrender."

She's still holding it back, still trying to keep her body to herself, but she doesn't understand what she traded us for.

A life for a life.

Hers belongs to us now … and I intend to use it as I see fit.

"Oh God."

"Don't fucking beg to him after you struck a deal with boys who came straight outta hell."

"You're a fucking demon," she grits.

It only makes me laugh because she's still jerking off this fucking demon like she's on a mission to make me come even faster than her. "Fuck yes, that's right. Hate me. Loathe me."

She struggles to withhold her moans, but I know she's getting close. I can feel it.

"Caleb, stop the car," she mutters.

"No." Her begging only makes me hit the gas harder.

"Why? Why are you doing this?"

Because I'm not supposed to be fucking doing this.

I'm not supposed to have my fingers inside the pussy of the girl I hate.

The one girl my father told me to be nice to.

The one girl my best friend, my lover, wants to keep for himself.

The one girl responsible for all of my fucking misery.

I'm not supposed to want her …

And it makes me want to kill and die.

"Doesn't fucking matter," I say through gritted teeth. "All you should worry about is the fingers between your legs driving you insane and your hand stroking my dick. Now give me your orgasm."

I'm high on the adrenaline fueling my growing lust as we race up the mountain, the edge of the road coming into view.

"I can't," she murmurs, shaking her head.

"Yes, you fucking can. Give it to me. Now," I growl, circling her clit fast and hard until she finally releases all of that pent-up energy, filling my car with so many fucking moans that I combust with her.

I can feel her clit thump against my fingers as my balls squeeze, and I let out a harsh groan while my cum shoots out over my steering wheel.

"Fuck, keep going," I tell her.

Her hand slides up and down my shaft, saliva and cum mixing together as I empty my balls and finally don't feel like I wanna die anymore.

"Caleb, the cliff!" she screams.

Right before the road stops in front of a steep drop down the mountain, I hit the brakes, and the wheels screech against the gravel.

When the car comes to a stop, we've already gone past the last curve. A certain death was avoided just at the last fucking second. The bright lights from the city down below almost makes it feel serene.

Crystal slowly untangles her hand from my cock. Her chest rises and falls with every deep breath she takes, and for some reason, I home in on it, my eyes flickering past her ample breasts hiding beneath that thin black dress, that sparkling little neck, and those luscious lips practically begging me to kiss them.

So I pull my hand out from her pussy, grip her chin and smash my lips onto hers, claiming her mouth just like Ares did. For a moment, she's too stunned to react, but when my tongue pierces through her closed mouth, I can feel her kiss me back.

Even though I can taste her hatred on my very fucking tongue, I need more, I need so much fucking more, and it fucking scares me to the point where I can't fucking breathe.

I lean away and look into her eyes, searching for answers she can't fucking give me because all I see is the hatred I've instilled in her reflected right back at me.

SLAP!

A harsh hand comes down against my cheek.

"How dare you," she hisses. "How fucking dare you actually kiss me after almost driving us off a cliff?"

A smirk forms on my lips. Not just from the way she's raging, but also from the sting of the palm of her hand. This girl can hit hard.

"How dare I fucking kiss the girl who sold her soul to me?" I say, tilting my head. "Sounds to me like you regret your decision. Too bad your pussy doesn't agree."

A blush creeps onto her cheeks. "That wouldn't have happened under normal circumstances. And you literally threatened to kill my mother if I didn't do what you wanted."

The smirk on my face only deepens. "Then why did you kiss me back?"

Her face contorts, and she gasps in both annoyance and shock. "I did not."

"Lie."

"Whatever." She jerks open the door handle.

"What are you doing?"

She hops out. "Leaving."

"Crystal. Get in the car."

"No." She slams the door shut.

I push the button so the window goes down. "Get. In."

"No, thanks. I'd rather not die."

"We didn't die."

"No thanks to you," she retorts and starts walking.

I back up my car and drive alongside her. "Because you finally let yourself go. Stop walking."

She continues her strut. "Leave me alone."

"It's dark. We're almost there. C'mon. Let me drive you."

"I don't want to be anywhere near you," she hisses.

"Your body still belongs to us whether you want it to or not."

"You've had your fill, haven't you?" she says, peering inside at the cum all over my steering wheel.

I wipe it off, then lick it off my hand. Watching her eyes almost bulge out of her head is the best thing I've seen tonight. Okay, maybe second best, after the orgasmic face she made.

"You underestimate my lusty needs," I say.

"Whatever. You can take care of them yourself. I'm done. I'm not willing to risk my life too. I didn't sign up for that."

I keep driving beside her despite her walking off. "I won't kill you."

She stops in her tracks. "You almost did. I'm no better off with you than those dudes you shot."

Now that ... that fucking hits hard.

"Crystal ..."

"I don't fucking trust you." The look in her eyes is so cold it makes me recoil, and I don't fucking understand why. "You wanted me to hate you? You got your wish."

I've never cared about any girl before.

But those words she just uttered make me turn my car around.

"Fine. Suit yourself. Fuck you."

And I drive off to get as far away from her as fast as possible.

I dropped her off at Spine Ridge U safely. What more could she want?

I slam my hands against the steering wheel and yell, "Fuck!"

None of it will curb my rage.

For a moment there just after we both came, all the coiled-up emotions that had entangled around my heart were released ... just for a moment ...

Before it all came crashing right back into my chest the second she opened her mouth and told me she hated me.

Fuck her.

Fuck that woman who I've been trying to haunt so badly I didn't realize she started haunting my soul instead.

TWENTY FIVE

ARES

I lean over the banister to watch Caleb strut into the house in the middle of the night, clothes covered in blood.

Where the fuck has he been?

I slowly march down the steps and approach him from behind as he hangs his coat. "You're late."

He pauses and waits a second before answering. "I was busy."

"I can see that," I reply, ogling the blood up close. "Whose blood is that?"

"No one that matters."

I step closer so I'm within an inch of his face. "What were you doing out there? Think hard before you answer. Lie to me and we're done."

His nostrils flare. "Crystal needed help. She got attacked. I protected her. The end."

My eyes narrow. "You were following her."

"So what if I was?" He passes by me, but I won't let him get away this fast.

I grip his arm and stop him mid-track, but the scent that comes from his hand makes me fixate on his fingers. He shudders in place as I bring them to my nose and take a whiff, then dip out my tongue to take a lick.

"You …" His eyes widen as rage becomes me. "You *fingered* her?"

He swiftly retracts his hand and says, "I d—"

I grip his collar. "Don't. Lie. To. Me."

A ragged breath leaves his mouth. "Yes."

My nostrils flare.

I can't fucking believe he went behind my back and fingerfucked her on his way back.

How dare he?

I drag him with me to the bathroom downstairs and throw him in. I don't even care to close the door before I start interrogating him. "Where?"

"I tried to resist, I fucking swear on my life. But I just fucking couldn't. She was sitting right beside me and—"

"In the fucking car *I* gifted you?" I growl.

He backs away until he hits the wall. "She drove me insane. *You* drove me insane with lust."

"Insane?" I parrot, closing in on him. I plant a hand beside his head on the wall. "Insane? You don't even know the meaning of it if it was staring you right in the face." I tip up his chin. "You betrayed me."

He shakes his head. "I couldn't take it anymore. You were edging me for so long, and then she needed my help and ended up in my car, and I … let myself go." He averts his eyes. "I knew this would happen. I knew you'd be mad."

"Of course, I'm fucking mad." I make him look at me. "I told you not to fucking touch her without my permission, and then you went and fingered her pussy."

"I'm sorry," he mutters, his eyes filling with regret.

And I fear I may have pushed him too far.

"I almost … drove off a goddamn cliff," he adds.

I sigh out loud.

Fuck.

"I didn't want to fucking do it."

Yet he did.

"You … couldn't help yourself, could you?" I say, looking down at his bloodied clothes. "You just had to go and kill some more … and then feel her pussy after." I lick my lips.

"I was consumed," he says. "By rage and a need I've never felt."

"Did murdering them make you feel good?" I lean in to lick the droplets of blood off his neck. "Did it make your cock hard?"

I lower my hand and grip his cock instead, which is still throbbing in his pants from the aftermath of whatever the fuck they just did in that car.

"Is that why you wanted her so badly?" I ask.

He groans. "Ares ..."

"Did she make you come so hard all over yourself you saw stars?"

I zip down his pants and he leans into me, moaning.

"Not just that. The steering wheel is ruined."

"Were you so overcome by desire you couldn't stop yourself from soiling the fucking car *I* gave you as a present?" I squeeze his dick until it hardens in my hand. "Answer me."

"Yes!" he mewls.

I spin him around and smash his face up against the wall. "I made a grave mistake allowing you to simmer in your own lust," I growl as I yank down his pants. "But don't fucking worry, Caleb. Your punishment won't be like teetering on the edge of bliss any longer."

I grab a bottle of lube from the top shelf above the sink and rip down my zipper, pulling out my hard cock.

"If you're not going to listen when I don't give you what I want, then I'll fucking give you everything you'll ever want and more." I slather it all over my cock. "You'll come so hard for me you'll never even think about her without wanting my goddamn hard cock up your ass."

I thrust inside with no remorse, and he yelps in surprise, then moans as I deepen the stroke.

"Now coat those fucking walls instead."

***

Crystal

Barefoot, I make my way back to campus, wishing I could kick some rocks on the way, but that would hurt my toes. Goddamn that motherfucker. He almost got us killed, then shrugged it off like it was nothing.

What the fuck is wrong with him?

And how dare he make me come so easily when all I wanted to do was bite his head off?

Groaning out of frustration, I slap some tree branches out of my way as I storm across the lawn.

"Everything okay there?"

The low, booming voice makes me turn and look.

"Here."

A hand rises from the fountain, and I swear I'm seeing the dead rise.

Or maybe I really am drunk.

I step closer to get a good look because I swear I recognize that voice.

A guy in a pair of purple pants, a black top, and a shark necklace dangling from his neck lies on the fountain stones.

"Blaine?" I walk up close. "What are you doing here?"

He drops a book on the ground. "Reading."

I frown. "In the middle of the night?"

"Couldn't sleep." He smiles.

I pick up the book. "How do you even read here when it's dark outside?"

He raises his phone and shines the bright light in my face, making me squint.

"It's not easy, but I make it work," he says, chuckling. "Come. Lie down with me, darling."

I sit down on the fountain and sigh out loud. "I don't know if I want to."

"Do you have somewhere to be?"

"Nowhere in particular," I reply.

"Then why not just lie down for a second?"

Hmm ... can't refute that logic. And I could really use a breather if only for just a moment.

"I'm not asking you to bare your soul," he says. "Just lie down for a moment. Take a breath. It's worth it."

"But why?" I ask, placing my bag on the ground.

"You'll see." The deadly smirk on his face makes it hard for me to trust him. But he's the only guy out of the three with a sliver of chivalry, so I decide to lie down after all.

But when I blink, it's so hard to believe my eyes I have to rub them with my hands.

"Wow," I mutter, gazing at all the stars above.

With the water cascading down the fountain sounding like a rippling stream, it almost feels like we're somewhere off in the mountains far beyond the human world.

"Beautiful, isn't it?"

It is. It's gorgeous. Like out-of-this-world divine.

And looking at all those stars beyond almost makes whatever I'm going through feel so tiny compared to the vastness of outer space that it calms down my racing heart.

"No wonder you wanted to lie down here," I say.

"Obviously. Reading these books is so much better under starlight." He chuckles again. "Well, I mean, the stones are harsh underneath my head, but all these stars make it worth it."

"Why not just lie on the ground?"

"In the dirt? With my hair? Ew," he says, making me laugh. He briefly glances at me before continuing. "There are bugs in the grass too, and I don't want those squiggly legs crawling all over me."

Now I'm laughing even more, picturing him shrieking when an ant crawls over his gorgeous face.

"I'm glad I could make you laugh, darling," he says. "You looked like you needed it."

I nod and wipe a single tear away. "Thanks."

"You don't have to tell me anything, and I won't ask," he says. "I just want you to know I'm here to listen if you want to talk."

"Thank you," I say. "I don't know if I want to. Tonight was … heavy."

"Hmm … Well, judging from the car I saw drive past a few hours ago, I assume it was Caleb?"

I nod, and he looks away.

"I'm surprised you haven't pummeled him in the face yet," he says. "I have. Many times."

I laugh again, and he smiles at me. "Believe me, I wanted to. Several times. Almost every day, actually."

"I can imagine," he says.

"You're not awfully fond of your own friends, are you?" I muse.

He turns around on the stones to look at me instead of the sky.

"I don't choose the life they lead, but that doesn't mean we're not friends. I belong to Tartarus as much as they do."

"Why? Why do you want to be with those ... those demons?"

He chuckles again. "We have a long history."

"Hmm ..." A long history, which he obviously won't tell me.

I wish I could understand these boys, but they've shrouded themselves in a cloak of mystery that I can't seem to pull away because they're desperate to hold it while simultaneously attempting to destroy my life.

"You know, I think you're holding your own pretty well," he says.

"You think?"

"Yeah. You're tenacious. And even in the face of danger, you still smile."

My lips part, but I don't know what to say.

"You don't trust me, yet you're lying right beside me," he says.

A blush creeps onto my cheeks. "You asked me to."

"Regardless of the odds thrown in your face, you stay gentle. Humble."

Now I'm really blushing like crazy. "Thanks. Gentle, though? I don't know."

"Nonsense," he says. "You just don't see yourself the way I do."

He does have a way with words.

"But you will ... someday."

I smile. "I appreciate the sentiment. I just wish I could see it that way."

"That's because of them, isn't it?"

He sits up, looking at me intently, which makes me want to look away.

"If I could do something about it, I would. But my hands are bound. I can hurt Caleb, and I might be able to slap Ares, but that's about it. I couldn't ever kill him, though." His hand drifts through the fountain water.

"Why?"

He snorts. "Believe it or not, Ares saved my life."

***

Blaine

Ten years ago

I sneak into the casino and hide among the crowd, hoping to find some unwitting people too busy playing their chips to notice me. I wait until one of them strikes a pose and laughs, then snatch away a chip lying on the table.

But when I turn around, I bump headfirst into a security guard.

I drop the chip.

"Oh no ..."

He grabs my collar. "What are you doing in here? Where are your parents?"

"Not ... here?" I reply.

I don't want to tell him my whole life story.

Suddenly, he drags me with him. "You're coming with me."

"I'm sorry, I won't do it again!" I yelp, but the guard ignores me and drags me all the way through the main hallway and into a remote area where a single door is blocked off by a dozen guards.

We pass through it, and he chucks me inside.

In front of me is a desk with a menacing-looking man sitting behind it. A boy my age sits in the chair in front of it with a piece of paper he was obviously reading from before the guard interrupted.

"This little dude was caught stealing chips from guests," the guard says.

"Was he now?" the man behind the desk says, clasping his hands.

"Do you want me to punish him?" the guard asks.

I squeak. "Please, don't."

"No. I will do it myself," the man replies.

The guard leaves, closing the door behind him, and the man behind the desk stands and approaches. I crawl away into a wall as he towers over me with narrowed eyes, his face reminding me of death.

"Please, it was just one chip. I just needed some cash."

"To do what?" the man responds. "You're too young to work at your age. You should be in school. So why are you here?"

202

"My parents can barely make a living wage. I'm just trying to help," I respond.

The boy in the chair turns around and looks at me, his piercing gray eyes making this dark room feel a little lighter.

"You should know better than to steal from one of the richest men in town," the man in front of me barks.

Suddenly, he pulls out a knife, and my eyes widen as I hide in the corner.

"Please, don't hurt me!"

A chair is kicked over.

The knife comes down.

But it isn't my flesh that it stabs. It's the boy's back.

He cries in pain but maintains eye contact with me, and I shudder in place against the wall, desperate to prevent imminent death, while guilt floods my veins.

He saved me.

"Ares!" The knife is pulled out, and the boy groans. "What were you thinking? I could've killed you!"

"Don't ... hurt him," Ares says, turning around to face his father. "Please."

His arms are open wide, but all I can focus on are the droplets of blood rolling down his back.

The man in front of us points the knife at me. "He is a thief. He deserves—"

"Pain?" Ares quips.

Fuck. I didn't want him to take this for me. I didn't ask him to.

"You ..." The man narrows his eyes. "I would've killed him if it wasn't for you."

"Don't. Please," Ares begs. "He won't do it again."

"No. He won't." The man wipes his knife on his pants. "Because you won't ever *let* him do it again."

What?

"This boy is your responsibility now. Make sure he never, ever tries to steal from me again," the man growls. "If he does, I'll make both of you pay, and it won't just be another scar."

"Yes, Father."

His father?

His own damn father stabbed him with a knife, and it doesn't even faze him?

The boy turns his head to me, and the look in his eyes is all I'll

203

ever need to know.

Just one act of righteousness and my life has been forever chained to his.

***

Crystal

Present

He lifts his hand and gazes at the droplets of water running down. "Our lives are entangled by a debt I can never repay."

I sigh out loud.

Ares, saving a life?

Why does that sound hard to believe after what I witnessed?

"I know what you think about Ares, but he isn't all evil," Blaine says.

"I'm just … surprised, I guess," I say. "But wait, you said something about Ares being responsible for you after that incident."

"Ares took me under his wing. He showed me how to hustle, and in turn, I was able to protect both him and my parents." He takes a deep breath. "I've cultivated a strong mind and body to make sure of that. And with a generous donation on his side, I was able to start my own business too."

"I'm impressed."

"Thank you," he responds, giving me a smug smile. "Regardless, I can't really hurt him as you can tell," he says, glancing my way with those devilishly handsome eyes of his. "But that doesn't mean *you* can't."

The glimmer in his eyes makes a fire in me burn brighter than ever before.

Maybe, just maybe … I should give this a chance.

"All right," I say, sitting up too. "If your offer is still on the table, teach me."

A wicked smile makes his face light up in the dark like a ghost come back to haunt the living. "I thought you'd never ask."

TWENTY SIX

Blaine

Days later

"So what do we do?" she asks as she stands in the open grassy area, looking all fine and fancy.

God, it almost makes me pity her.

She's got a long road ahead of her.

But I will be there every step of the way.

I chuck a wooden stick her way, and it lands in front of her feet.

"Pick it up."

She does what I say and holds it like it's filthy, but if you ask me, it's the finest wood around. The trees here in Priory Forest are old and provide the best sticks one could ask for while training.

"What am I supposed to do with this?" she asks.

"Hold it. Tightly, but not too tight."

"Like this?" She holds it in front of her.

I nod and tilt my head to look at her stance. We'll have to work on that.

"Now what?" she asks.

I straighten my back, positioning myself sideways while I pull off my belt buckle and toss it aside so she won't hurt herself. Then I raise my hand and beckon her. "Come at me."

"What? With this?" She looks at the stick like it's a piece of rubber.

"Mm-hmm."

She laughs. "You want me to hit you with a stick?"

"Did I not make myself clear, darling?"

"Oh no, you did. I'm just wondering what this will teach me," she murmurs.

"It'll teach you the basics of fighting with a weapon," I say, still beckoning her. "Now come. See if you can hit me."

"*If?*" Her eyes narrow.

I grin at her. "Give it your best shot."

The shimmer in her eyes as she bolsters herself is nothing short of magnificent.

She runs at me, clunky at best, swiping her little stick left and right, but none of her hits actually land because I know how to avoid them. Her moves are like how a child with no training would attack.

"Jesus, how are you making this look so easy?" she mutters, breathing raggedly after what seems like the fiftieth try.

"Experience," I muse.

She makes a snooty face. "Well, you didn't say I'd start with a stick. I might actually be able to hit you with something real."

I snatch the stick from her hand and swipe it under her legs. She falls down immediately, and I point it at her face, then say, "Anything is a weapon if you know how to use it. I'm not going to give you a weapon you aren't ready to use."

She scowls, and I raise a brow in response, then hold out the stick so she can take it back.

"Yet." She surprises me with a swift swoop while getting up, and I avoid it by jumping away.

"Clever girl," I mutter. "Again."

She keeps on trying to strike me instead of going for the obvious.

"Hit me," I say.

"I'm trying," she barks.

"C'mon," I say, still easily avoiding each of her strikes.

"Stop moving so much!"

"You think your enemies will just stand still and let you hit them?" I retort.

206

"Enemies?" She pauses. "Who said anything about enemies?"

"You assume Caleb and Ares are the worst people out there. They're not."

She tries to strike me again, but I don't have a black belt for nothing.

"The question isn't if you can win in one-on-one combat. You can't," I say.

"Then why are we doing this?" she yelps between breaths, on the edge already.

"The question is, can you outsmart them?" I tilt my head and smirk when her eyes narrow.

Finally, she's beginning to understand.

"Hit. Me."

She swoops in from underneath and repeats my own move right back at me.

SNAP!

The stick breaks in half against my thick calves, and the sound makes me look down.

PUNCH!

Her fist strikes my chin out of nowhere, making me lean away and rub my chin.

She gazes at me with a smug grin on her face. "That good enough for you?"

Oh my ...

So there is spice in her after all. I like it.

"Good. You're starting to understand the art of distraction."

She tries to hit me again, but I grab her fist and twist her wrist so she's forced to spin around, and I easily subdue her. "Don't get cocky now. I can bend you to my will with little to no effort."

She huffs and puffs, her body snugly fitting into mine as I hold her down.

But she stomps on my feet and shoves her elbow into my midriff, making me buckle in pain. She breaks free when I try to take a breath.

"Well ... you got me there," I say, huffing as she steps away with a giant smirk.

To be honest, I kind of let her have that win.

But she doesn't need to know that.

"You're a swift learner."

Her face begins to radiate, and it makes my heart throb.

That's the face I'm looking for.

The spirit of persistence is what she'll need to cultivate.

"You want me to win using dirty tricks," she says, rain slowly beginning to pitter-patter down from the sky. "I want to learn how to fight fair."

"Darling …" I sigh out loud. "The fight was never fair to begin with."

I grab my umbrella and open it. "Ready to head back?"

She frowns. "Already? We've only just started."

I point at the sky.

"It's just a little rain," she says. "I'm not made of sugar."

"You sure about that, darling?" I taunt.

She narrows her eyes. "You say the fight isn't fair, but you won't even make it fair."

I'm intrigued. "How so?"

She grabs a new stick off the ground and holds it in front of her. "You said they have weapons, and I need to prepare for that. You have nothing. I have this stick. That isn't a fair fight."

A dark smile slowly forms on my face. "Nothing?" I close my umbrella again and point it at her. "I beg to differ."

Her face contorts as a smug grin appears. "An umbrella?" She snorts, droplets of rain rolling down her cheeks, making me lick my lips at the thought of lapping them up.

She emboldens her stance and grips the stick tightly. "Like you said … it was never fair to begin with." Her lip quirks up into a lopsided smile as if she thinks she's already won this fight. "So bring it on."

Too bad for her I still have a trick up my sleeve.

I tilt my head and pull the handle of my umbrella outward, opening the secret compartment. And as I slowly take out my katana, her smile dissipates swiftly, her eyes glinting in the harsh glimmer of my blade. The complete and utter shock on her face as her pupils dilate and her jaw drops was worth every second of this encounter.

"Now, darling … are you truly ready to fight me?"

TWENTY SEVEN

ARES

I cut through my apple and stick it onto my knife, shoving it into my mouth while staring at the two guys sitting at the table in front of me. We finally have time to talk in private in the comfort of our own house, and they refuse. They've been avoiding my gaze all day long while in class, and I don't like it one bit.

"What's going on?" I ask. "Why aren't you talking to me?"

Caleb grabs his Coke and takes a sip. "Should I be?"

I raise a brow. "You never know when to quit, and now you decide to be quiet?"

"He's just been ... busy," Blaine muses, picking up a grape and throwing it into his mouth.

"Busy. With what?" I grit.

"Work. School. His father." Blaine laughs. "*Her* mother."

I sigh and pick up another slice with my knife. "Has she made any efforts to break them up yet?"

"My father's only gotten more determined." Caleb rolls his eyes and takes a bite out of his sandwich. "I gave him an earful."

"Her mother really is asking for it, isn't she?" I push my knife through another apple slice. "Maybe we should visit her house sometime. Bring Crystal along too."

Caleb pauses mid-bite. "You mean ..."

"You know exactly what I mean," I muse, tapping my fingers on the table. "Apparently, we didn't make ourselves very clear."

"But we made a deal with her," he says.

"So?"

"Why not enjoy it a little longer?"

My eyes narrow. "Stretch it out?"

"What deal?" Blaine asks.

"She traded her body in exchange for us not killing her mother," I respond with a coldhearted look.

Blaine grabs his drink and sighs out loud. "Oh boy. That explains a lot."

"I didn't ask for your judgment," I hiss.

Caleb frowns. "He didn't say—"

"He doesn't need to say it. His face tells me enough."

We both look at Blaine now.

"Wait ... you don't think we should?" Caleb snorts. "Since when have you started being a saint?"

Blaine shrugs it off. "I'm not. I'm simply saying ... maybe you should try other methods."

"Like what?"

He waves his hand around. "I don't know. Use your charm and wit. You have that."

"Not as much as you," Caleb says.

"Speak for yourself, Caleb," I say. "And Blaine ... he's right. You haven't been yourself lately. You've been sneaking off an awful lot. Care to explain?"

His face grows a little redder than usual, and he shoves a handful of blueberries into his mouth. "I've been training."

"You're a black belt. You don't need training," I point out.

"That's not for you to decide," he responds, folding his arms. "Besides, I'd like to be prepared for the worst. You make a lot of enemies during your business dealings, especially when it concerns your father's company."

Hmm ...

Well, that much is true.

Still, I feel like he's not telling me the full truth. But I can't make him tell me either. Blaine only talks when he wants to. Thanks to his impeccable training, no amount of torture could ever compel him.

"Fine. I guess you two have been busy," I say, folding my arms too. "All the more reason to let off some steam. There's a girl out there who knows what we do and could spill details at any moment. The only hold we have over her is her mother. It's time to crush her last remaining resistance. Why don't you join us this time, Blaine?"

He swallows, and it takes him some time to respond. "Well, I mean ... if it's necessary."

"Of course, it is." I grimace at his apprehension. "Since when do you not like fucking around?"

"You know what? I feel like it's time we threw another party," Caleb suddenly says.

"Fabulous idea, Caleb!" Blaine says with flair. "I could use the distraction. And a real freakish party has been long overdue." He throws his arm around me. "C'mon, what do you say, Ares? We could even invite that girl, Crystal."

"Hmm ..."

I do admit I love the kinky parties we throw here at Tartarus.

Everyone on campus and beyond knows us as the place to experience the best kind of high.

"What kind of hedonists would we be if we didn't indulge ourselves every once in a while?" Blaine muses.

"Hedonists?" Caleb mutters.

"Darling ... Tartarus?" Blaine snaps his fingers. "Gates of hell, through which every sinner enters the glorious lands of devils incarnate. They don't call it the seven sins for nothing." He licks his lips. "Lust is one of them."

"Yeah, yeah, we all know you got plenty of that, reading your filthy little books," Caleb retorts.

"Hey, who are you calling filthy, pig?" Blaine spits back.

"Stop," I say, silencing them both. "Fine. We'll have our party. And you two will make sure she attends."

Their eyes light up.

"But once she steps foot inside these halls, you won't touch her until I give my permission. Is that understood?"

They both nod.

"Good." A devilish smile forms on my face. "Let's plan the greatest party this campus has ever seen."

211

***

Crystal

After finishing an exam, I make my way out of the main building, texting.

Me: Finally done with the exam. Coming!
Penelope: Hurry up. Kayla is about to devour your cake.
Kayla: Lies.
Me: You can have a bite.

Grinning, I grab my bike at my sorority, then race off. It's been so long since I last drove this thing. It's a bit unsteady, but I manage. I head down the hills and into Crescent Vale City below, where Kayla and Penelope wait for me at Fi's Cups and Cakes.

"I'm here!" I shout, announcing my arrival like an idiot when I step into the shop.

Everyone's looking at me like I've lost my mind, but I don't care.

The girls sit in the back, and Kayla's hand hovers over her fork as she opens her mouth. I speed my way over to their table and steal the fork, then swiftly take a bite out of the strawberry cake piece they ordered for me.

"Aw, I got so excited," Kayla says.

"Too bad," I say, winking. "This cake is mine."

She grins. "I love it when you get all aggressive."

"Aggressive?" I scoff.

"Who doesn't get aggressive over food," Penelope says, snorting as she takes a bite of her carrot cake.

"Excuse me, I don't get aggressive," I respond.

"Sure, you don't," Kayla says, laughing before she sticks a fork into my cake. I literally pull the plate away and protect it with my life.

She raises a brow. "See?"

"Mine."

"Hold up," Penelope mutters as she looks at the front door. "Isn't that one of those Tartarus boys?"

My heart immediately sinks into my shoes.

Oh God.

I hope it's not Caleb again.

I really don't want to look.

212

"Oh my God, you're right," Kayla says. "That's Blaine. With a guy."

Wait, what?

I turn around in my seat, the wavy black hair and extravagant clothes giving it away. He's actually groping someone's ass in front of the counter while they place an order.

"What is he doing here?" I ask.

"Getting cake, obviously," Kayla says, snorting. "And not just the one behind the display."

Penelope gasps. "Oh my God, Kayla."

"What? Look at them. They are so dating," she says.

"Blaine?" I mutter. "Dating?"

It hadn't crossed my mind that was even an option with those Tartarus boys. I always thought they only cared about their own pleasure, not to date other people.

But then the two turn sideways, and my jaw is on the floor because Blaine smashes his lips on the guy's mouth in full view of everyone in this shop. And not just a simple kiss—no, an actual straight-up French kiss where he grips his throat and makes sounds.

"Good God, is it hot in here?" Kayla fans her own face with the napkin.

And I struggle to even breathe.

Because the first thing he does as their lips are still tethered to each other is look at me.

I immediately turn around and pretend I don't exist, shoveling my cake into my mouth like it's nobody's business.

"I wonder who it is," Penelope mutters.

"They're coming this way," Kayla hisses. "Act natural."

I'm sweating like crazy, and it doesn't relent.

Two hands curl around my seat.

A piece of cake lodges in my throat.

"Crystal. How nice to see you here too."

Oh God. Now I have no choice.

He literally spins around my seat so I'm facing him and his ... boyfriend, I guess.

The guy holds a little bag filled with cake and drinks, but his lovestruck eyes focus solely on Blaine. And honestly, I don't blame him.

"Um, hi," I say, waving awkwardly. "I didn't know you went to

Fi's Cups and Cakes too."

"Of course, I do. Everyone in this city does," Blaine muses, leaning back against the guy he just kissed. "They have the best cake."

"Right," I mutter, not knowing what to say. "Well, I just didn't expect you to enjoy them."

I gulp when his hand slowly lowers to the guy's butt, and I struggle to stay focused.

He lowers himself so he's on my level, eyeing me up while I lean back in my chair, desperate for air. "Am I not allowed to have my cake and eat it too?"

Kayla giggles behind me.

"By the way, I wanted to invite you to a party at the Tartarus House," he whispers into my ear. "Don't tell your friends."

"Why?" I squeak.

"It's not safe for them."

Blaine smiles and checks out my friends before he steals a strawberry from my cake. His tongue dips out to curl around the strawberry, licking off the whipped cream before he bites off the entire thing right in front of me, then moans—actually moans—as he swallows it down.

And for a second there, I almost wish I was that strawberry.

But then the thought is immediately banished from my head.

He grins again and leans back, throwing his long black hair over his shoulder. "Well anyway, I'll text you the time and date. Have fun at your little get-together with your friends, darling. Bye."

He strolls off and slaps his date on the ass before they leave the shop.

But I can't even get myself together ... as the two girls behind me begin to squeal.

Kayla wheezes. "*DARLING?*"

I turn around in my seat and chuck the remaining strawberry at her face. "Shut up."

TWENTY EIGHT

Blaine

Later that week

She throws her knives at my face, and I narrowly avoid them as they hit the tree behind my head. But the second I turn, she's right in front of me, knife at the throat, and I can't help but gleefully smirk.

"That's my girl," I muse.

"Learned from the best," she says, winking before retracting her knife.

"Let's take a break," I say as she pulls the knives from the tree.

I grab the bottle of water off the bench and chug it down while she sits to take a breather. I hold out my bottle and offer her a sip, which she gladly takes, chugging it all down until only a few droplets are left. And as she pulls the bottle away, my eyes can't help but home in on the few droplets landing on her lips and the tongue that dips out to lap them up.

What I wouldn't give to suck them off.

She hands back the bottle, and I immediately chug down the remaining water, but the mere thought her lips were on this bottle just seconds ago makes my cock twitch in my pants.

215

"God," she murmurs, leaning her head back. "This training thing sure takes up a lot of energy."

I chuckle. "If it feels easy, it won't do anything. It's supposed to be hard work."

"I know." She sighs. "I just wish it could've been different. That I wouldn't have had to learn any of this, you know?"

I smile and pick another rose from the nearby bush in this maze. It's the only place we've been able to train in peace and quiet during the day without people looking at us. I've seen her performance with and without people watching her, and she's ten times better if no one can see how good she is.

It's like she automatically downgrades her own skills just for the sake of appearing weak.

And I understand. This world is harsh on women and especially those who don't conform to the norm she tries hard to be a part of.

But I see through that thin veneer of perfection, the innocent, sweet girl facade she's made into her core being. Underneath all that hides a fighter, a fierce creature determined to protect the ones she loves … and herself.

Her parents may have called her after a crystal, but she's like a diamond in the rough to me.

Beautiful, not in spite, but *because* of the sharp edges.

"We've been at it for so long," she mutters. "It's already gotten dark again."

"Good. It's better to train at night," I reply.

"Why?"

"Because then no one can see how you fight." I wink.

I mean, that's what she wants, isn't it?

"Can I ask you a question?" she asks, catching me off guard.

"Well, you may ask, but I can't guarantee a satisfying answer," I reply. I roll the rose between my fingers to get rid of the thorns, but her eyes are fixated on the spinning move. I wonder what she's thinking about—if she's trying to decipher the thoughts in my head like I'm trying to unravel her. If she thinks about untying my clothes slowly, meticulously, wondering about every part that will appear from underneath, just like I do with her.

She swallows. "Ares helped you, right? Did his family force you to fight for them?"

"Oh no, fighting was my own choice," I say. "Out of honor. And spite, of course. But mostly so I could stand on my own."

I'm curious that was the question she wanted to ask.

"What … what was it like being near him?" she asks tentatively.

I smirk. She wants to know more about me?

"Sorry if I'm being intrusive," she mutters, waving it off. "Forget I asked. It doesn't even matter."

"No. I won't forget."

Her face flushes.

"Since you worked out so hard, I'll reward you. But …" I raise a finger. "You must promise me you will tell me something about you too."

She gulps but still nods, and a wicked grin spreads on my cheeks.

My history is boring, but hers … now that sounds like something I definitely want to dive into.

***

Five years ago

"Faster!" my sensei barks while I swoop my stick around and knock the dummy off balance.

Sweat drips down my forehead as I fling the katana around and around, trying my best to be as fast as he is.

"C'mon, Blaine. You gotta put more effort into this if you want to get as good as I am," he grits.

I know I need to perform better than my best. There's no other option. No other choice.

I owe it to Ares to be the strongest I can be so I can fight for him when he needs it to repay the debt.

SLICE!

With a quick slash, I cut through the dummy's head and knock it off.

"There you go," my sensei says, clapping his hands. "See? You can do it if you put your mind to it."

But his appreciation isn't the only reason I want to get strong.

I need to become someone no one can ever beat, no matter the cost.

I have nothing left in my life to give to the guy who saved me, so the only gift I can give him is my life itself.

My sensei snaps his fingers. "Again."

When my training is done, I head to the showers and rinse off the sweat and hard work.

The door squeaks. "I see you had your daily bout of fun again."

"Is there anything you need, Ares?" I ask, lathering myself with soap.

He always comes to watch during my training at the dojo, but never this late.

"I'm just wondering why you refuse to use a gun instead of such a clunky weapon," he murmurs while looking at my katana lying on top of my clothes.

"I'm proud of what I do," I reply.

"A gun would kill so much faster," he responds.

So I tilt my head as I look him straight in the eyes and say, "But a gun wouldn't allow me to taste my victim's blood on my tongue like a savage killer, now would it?"

He snorts, and we exchange vicious smiles.

"Dad's asked if you can accompany us tonight. He's striking a deal with a new party in town. Don't know if they're trustworthy. We need the extra defense."

I wash off the soap and turn off the shower.

"Your father asked for me?"

He nods. "I guess it's finally time to put those skills of yours to the test."

A grin slowly spreads on my cheeks as I wrap my towel around my waist. "Cutting into wood is exciting but not half as thrilling as cutting into flesh."

He flashes a gun behind his back. "Want to count bodies?"

***

Present

"Wait ... Ares was there when you trained?"

"I didn't mind. I got used to it eventually."

"Wasn't it ... hard to grow up with him?"

I snort. "Are you implying he's been rough on me?"

Her eyes widen. "Oh no, I just meant that—"

I chuckle. "Relax. I'm only trying to poke the bear."

"Oh ..." She breathes a sigh of relief ... as though she was worried there for a second that I might be insulted, meaning she cares about my feelings.

Interesting.

I sit beside her, but the second I do, she inches away, retreating into herself as though she's unsure what to think of me. As if my size alone and the strong hand that grips the back of the bench makes her fear me.

So I lean in and softly place the rose behind her ear, whispering, "You'd rather die than fear Ares, yet you offer it to me freely. Why?"

She licks her lips and averts her eyes. "I ..."

I gently catch her chin between my fingers and make her look at me. "You promised to tell me a truth about you too."

"I'm not scared of you. I'm scared of myself."

I frown. "Because of me?"

"Because of what you're teaching me."

Oh ...

I'd almost hoped it was because of something else.

Her eyes darken. "Because I don't want to become as cruel as they are."

"You? Cruel?"

"You think I can't be?" A hint of mystery tugs at her lips, and my God, does it harden my cock.

"You're learning how to defend yourself," I say.

She fishes her knife out of her pocket and stares at the blade. "And how to kill."

My whole body almost erupts into goose bumps just at the thought of her slicing her way through her enemies. Good God, I was right. She does have a violent streak to her.

"What?" She scoffs. "You don't think I could kill?"

"Oh no, that's not it ..." I muse, tilting my head so I can look at her. "I'd pretty much sell my soul to see you kill."

Her eyes find mine in the dark, glimmering with a burning curiosity that makes it so hard to look away.

Lord, I know those two fucks want her, but I could never deny her if she ever gave me a chance.

Slowly, she leans in and gives me the softest peck on my cheek, and I swear I've never cherished anything more.

"Thank you," she mutters. "For helping me."

The way she looks up at me, with that gaze of adoration …

Fuck it.

Without thinking, I grab her chin and smash my lips to hers.

God, her taste is divine. No wonder those two couldn't keep their hands off her. She's like a sinful little package waiting to be unwrapped, and I groan into her mouth just from the sheer desire that's been roaring through my body ever since I first saw her on Ares's lap, mewling to his touch.

Maybe I should steal her from him.

Would he kill me if I tried?

She pulls away from me and stares at me, eyes flickering back and forth between both my eyes and lips, as though she's contemplating whether to kiss me back … or kill me for daring to try.

I wouldn't blame her if she did.

I might not even stop her if she tried.

But I will never, *ever* regret kissing those beautiful lips.

TWENTY NINE

Crystal

Without thinking, I slam my lips back on his, his groans lighting a flame.

I've never kissed this passionately, this fiercely before. It's like a fire consumes my soul.

My hands entangle around his thick neck, curling through his silky hair, desperate to get closer. And he answers my greed with fervent licks, rolling his tongue around mine, equally as needy to get closer while his hands snake around my waist and trap me.

But then I remember who he is and what house he belongs to, and I instantly regret what we just did.

I swiftly jump up from the bench, the shock finally settling in.

"Oh God," I mutter, swiftly grabbing my stuff. "This was a mistake."

"No, it wasn't. It was anything but a mistake." He gets up from the bench too. "I fully intended to kiss those pretty lips, darling, and I'm not going to say I'm sorry."

Wait, what?

I thought I'd convinced him by kissing him on the cheeks.

Has he wanted to kiss me all this time?

I gulp as my eyes slowly trail down his body, settling on the hard-on in his pants clearly visible through the fabric.

"Fuck," I mutter, biting my lip before looking away. "God, I should've known."

"What?" He snorts. "That you'd kiss me back?"

My jaw slowly drops, and my cheeks begin to glow. "No, I was overcome by …"

"Lust?" He grips my arm as if he could sense I was about to turn and run. "I know exactly what you felt because the same need courses through my veins."

I shake my head. "But I saw you at Fi's Cups and Cakes with someone."

He steps closer, leaning in to get on eye level with me while licking his top lip. "Ask me what you want to ask. You can say it out loud."

"I thought you were gay?"

God, I can't believe I'm asking this question.

He smirks. "Call it whatever you like, but I don't care what appendage someone has as long as they're just as greedy as I am."

Oh wow.

He leans back and taps his chin. "But if you need a name for it, I guess you could call it pansexual?" He clears his throat. "Regardless. That wasn't the question you wanted to ask, was it?"

I'm still so flabbergasted by what just happened that I don't even know what to say. "What?"

For every step he takes toward me, I take one back until my ass hits the sharp roses.

He grips my arm and stops me from falling into them.

"Ask me what you really wanted to know," he muses.

I swallow away the lump in my throat. "That guy in the shop was your boyfriend, right?"

He shakes his head. "Not a boyfriend. A boy toy. A plaything."

"But you—"

"Entertain myself with him." He interjects. "What can I say, darling? I'm a sexual creature. I need pleasure, and I need a lot of it."

"Oh … and you think I'm your next victim," I muse, rolling my eyes before I push myself off him.

"No, wait," he says, gripping my arm so I won't leave. "You're not. I've not made myself very clear, have I? Oh dear." He sighs out loud and runs his fingers through his velvety black hair. "I've been keeping myself busy ... with others ... so I could get you off my mind." The gulp that follows makes me stop resisting. "I've wanted nothing more than to kiss you, and I couldn't help myself any longer."

Suddenly, I hear clapping from the corner, and my entire body erupts into goose bumps the second I hear his voice.

"What an epic show."

I gaze at the only exit through which Ares appears, his bright eyes shimmering in the moonlight.

"Too bad the only audience you had ..." He smirks. "Was me."

***

ARES

I stop the slow clapping even though I quite liked how they both reacted the second they heard me.

It took every ounce of self-control not to intervene when he kissed her. Seeing his lips on hers made me want to shoot him on sight. But then I remembered I wanted her in a vulnerable position. Needy.

And looking at the way she yearned for his kisses, she's almost ready to submit.

The problem is ... it's not to me but to him.

My nostrils flare.

If it wasn't for the fact that he's my right hand, I probably would have killed him on the spot for even daring to touch her. But I need him alive and on my side. Which is why his falling for her, out of all people, complicates everything.

"Blaine," I mutter, "you disappoint me."

He immediately lets go of her and steps away.

"Sneaking away and playing with *my* little toy?"

"*Your* toy?" Crystal scoffs.

My eyes fixate on hers, but she refuses to look away, like a deer staring straight into the headlights despite knowing its end is near.

"Have you forgotten the deal you made?" I fish my phone from my pocket. "I'll be more than happy to call your mother since Caleb sent me her number. See what she prefers."

Crystal's pupils dilate, and she shakes her head.

Satisfied, I tuck my phone back and focus on Blaine. "You went behind my back to seduce her."

He sinks to his knees in front of me. "I will not deny it. But I will not apologize for it either."

My eyes narrow. "How long?"

"Just tonight," Crystal interjects, and we both look at her. "He only kissed me once."

"Once?" I parrot, insulted she'd think it wouldn't matter to me.

The thought alone turns me blind with rage, and I pull out my gun and aim it at his head.

"No!" Crystal tries to jump in.

"Crystal, don't," Blaine warns her, keeping his gaze fixated on mine.

"But he'll kill you," she says.

"He saved me from death long ago, and ever since, my life has belonged to him," Blaine says. "If he wishes to take it, then so be it."

His Adam's apple moves up and down when I push the metal into his forehead.

"If he only kissed you once, why would you care whether he lives or dies?" I ask her.

She parts her lips, but there's no answer, so I say it again. "Tell me, do you care so much about this man who kissed you once that you would save his life at all costs?"

I'm curious what she will pick.

"Yes," she replies.

My eyes twitch. "You want to save his life?" I take off the safety and watch her panic. "Then kiss me the way you just kissed him."

"What?" she gasps.

I push the barrel into his head. "You heard me. Kiss me like it's the end of the fucking world because it will be the end of his if you don't."

She swallows and makes a fist, then slowly steps closer, eyeing Blaine once before she grips my face and softly plants her lips onto mine. The kiss is extraordinary, fluffy light yet filled with so many hidden desires, it's almost as if it was meant for me.

But I know it isn't.

Yet when she pulls away again with those rosy stained lips of hers, it almost makes me want to drop this gun and grasp her face to smash them right back on.

No wonder he's fallen for her so easily, so desperate to throw away his soul for a dangerous girl.

I lower my gun and tuck it away. "You're lucky," I growl at him.

"Thank you," Blaine mutters. "I will not disappoint you again."

I grip her chin and make her look at me. "Next time you let him touch you ... my hands will be there too, curling around your throat while you beg for mercy from my cock. Do you understand?"

She nods softly.

When I push her away from me, she mouths, "Asshole."

A smug grin forms on my face, my hand wrapping around my gun. "Care to say that again?"

But instead of a glimmer of fear settling in her eyes, all I get is another damn insufferable smile.

My nostrils flare.

She fucking knows exactly what she's doing.

"I will see you at Tartarus House," I tell Blaine as I turn around and waltz off. "We've got a party to prepare for." I glance at her once more, savoring the sight of her in those tight little yoga pants. "And I will see you there tomorrow night."

THIRTY

Crystal

The doorbell rings, and I grab my bag and hurry downstairs.

Kayla approaches, but I swiftly intervene as she opens the door.

Blaine steps inside in a pair of black PVC pants and a see-through black mesh shirt, along with a silver necklace, and I swear, every time I see him, he looks even sexier than before. His hair is styled in a curly wave, half of it in a bun, while loose strands fall beside his defined jaw.

He grabs the doorpost and checks out my short red dress with puffy shoulders, his eyes slowly skittering across my body like a spider draws a web, ensnaring me. "Well, hello there, gorgeous." He pulls me into his arms.

"Holy shit ... Blaine Navarro?" One of the girls behind me squeals, making me turn my head.

Some others gasp in shock, and one nearly faints on the couch.

"What the hell is he doing here?" another one asks while they all try to get up close. "Oh my God!"

He winks. "I'm just here to pick up Crystal Murphy, ladies. But I appreciate the sentiment."

A collective disappointing sigh follows from my fellow sorority girls.

"Don't pay attention to them. They're just jealous," Kayla says, winking before she slaps my butt. "You have fun with whatever you two are going to do."

"Thanks," I mutter, trying not to blush as he escorts me outside.

"I won't bother you ladies any longer," Blaine muses, blowing them an air-kiss. "Enjoy your evening!"

When the door closes, half of the girls behind me squeal their heads off.

"Sorry," I mutter.

"Ah, don't worry. I'm used to the attention that comes with looking as good as I do."

God, the arrogance of this guy. It's insane yet … kind of endearing.

With a giant smile, he offers me his arm. "Care to take a walk, darling?"

I hook my arm through his. "Do I even have a choice?"

"Well, you could always try to outrun them," he says. "Take your mom on a long vacation."

"Nice fantasy you got going there," I reply as we walk across the road.

"Ahh, we all know Ares and Caleb would probably chase you and your mother to the end of the world."

I snigger to myself. "Sounds about right. I still don't understand why he wants to get rid of her so badly he'd threaten to get her killed. It can't be just to protect his dad."

Blaine sighs. "He has … issues."

"Evening."

Caleb's sudden intrusion makes all the hairs on the back of my neck stand up. But when I turn to look at him, I'm momentarily too flabbergasted to speak. I've never seen him wear a dark red shirt, but the color suits him well. It makes all of his tattoos and piercings jump out … especially with that unbuttoned part at the top. Of course he paired it with some black jeans and a ton of intimidating jewelry.

I wonder if he's brought that knife of his along, too.

"I didn't know you were also coming to pick me up. Am I that much of a threat?" I ask.

"No." He wraps his arm around my waist. "I just don't trust Blaine here to keep his paws off you."

"Paws?" Blaine scoffs, throwing back his long hair.

"Now tell me who has issues?" Caleb muses, sticking up a middle finger covered in skull rings.

"Excuse me, this manicure was way too expensive for you to insult it like that. The only paws here are those chewed-up nails," Blaine says, wincing.

I chuckle as we head toward the front entrance of the Tartarus House. "You know, for two men forcing me to come to a party, you have great banter. It's funny to listen to."

"The only thing that's going to be funny to listen to is the sound of your stifled moans while I lick the droplets of sweat off your skin."

My eyes widen, and Blaine actually gasps.

"Got a problem?" Caleb raises his brow at Blaine right as we pass through the gates.

"You sure are confident you'll ever get a chance, considering Ares nearly ended my life yesterday just for kissing her."

"You kissed her?" Caleb growls, his grip on my waist growing stronger with every passing second.

"Yes," Blaine says, narrowing his eyes. "It was delicate. Sweet. Delectable."

Now I can't control the blush anymore.

"And if you must know …. she actually enjoyed kissing *me*."

Caleb stops halfway across the path to the door and releases me, then grabs Blaine's shirt. "What the fuck do you want to say with that, huh? You insinuating something?"

Oh God.

"She kissed *me* back," Blaine says with a smug smile.

Caleb raises a fist, but Blaine's stern gaze makes him pause midair.

"Hit me then, darling. Try if you dare. I'll cut off those fingers you used to fuck her with before you even get a chance," he hisses.

Well shit, I didn't ever think I'd find overly possessive men sexy, but here we are.

"Guys," I mutter. "Don't fight over me. Please."

It's not like I have a choice in the matter. They've collectively decided to make me their plaything, and I'm just along for the ride.

Caleb slowly lowers his fist. "Fine. But only because she asked me to leave your pretty fucking face whole."

"Mm-hmm." Blaine snorts. "Glad you finally recognize I'm prettier than you."

"Oh fuck off, Blaine," Caleb says, flipping him off. "Don't forget what Ares told you."

"What?" Blaine muses. "The same thing he told you?" He raises a brow, making Caleb fume even more.

A guard at the front of the door stops us in our tracks. "No weapons allowed inside. I will need to do a check."

Grumbling to myself, I pull my only knife out of my boot and hand it to him.

"Wow … you brought that here, darling?" Blaine muses. "I'm impressed."

"I don't leave the sorority without it," I tell him.

The guard holds out a box, and I place it inside. "This is special to me. If it isn't here when I get back, someone will pay," I warn him.

He swallows uncomfortably.

"Hold up your arms."

The guy pats me for any leftover weapons, but that was the only one I brought.

"You're good," he says. "Next."

"I didn't bring any weapons, darling," Blaine muses. "Except the one in my pants if you want to cop a feel."

The guard groans, annoyed. "Blaine. Turn around." The guy frisks him too. "You're good."

"I know, darling, no need to tell me."

Caleb rolls his eyes as he gets inspected too. "Can't you just shut up for a second? Please?"

"Beg some more," Blaine retorts. "I might be incentivized to try."

Caleb's nostrils flare, and he looks away.

"You're good too," the guard says. "No entry for any of you without a mask, though."

He holds out a new box filled with masks.

It's the same kind of demonic-looking golden masks that Ares and Caleb wore when they chased me through the maze, and the sight of them makes goose bumps scatter on my skin.

"Put this on," the guy at the front door says.

He holds out a version without the demonic features. Instead, it's a completely glossy golden mask.

"For the women," Caleb whispers into my ear as he grabs a demonic one.

When he puts it on, my heart rate jumps.

He looks just like I remember, and when he throws me a glance, I can feel my pussy thump like it responds to the memory of his dominance alone.

Blaine steals my mask and lifts it over my head, putting it on. "There you go. Perfect." He grabs my shoulders. "Ready?"

I shake my head. "Will I ever be?"

He snorts. "No one ever is. But once they're in, they never want to leave either."

"C'mon," Caleb says, leading the way. "The party awaits."

The hall in this house still overwhelms me, but the majority of the party seems to be taking place in the big common room to the left because that's where all the music comes from.

"Oh, Blaine, I'm so happy you're back." A guy wearing nothing but a fishnet and leather pants along with an actual collar and chain around his neck approaches and kisses him on the cheek. "Just a couple minutes and I already miss you."

He releases my arm to hug the guy. "Here for the rest of the night, don't worry."

A girl approaches and kisses him on the other cheek. "Are you up for some fun again?"

"Fun?" I mutter.

Caleb snorts. "You don't want to know, trust me."

Blaine rubs his lips. "Not tonight, sorry."

"Aw ..." The woman blows him a kiss. "Another time, then."

Caleb clears his throat. "Anyway, I'm gonna go grab some booze. Wanna come?"

I shake my head, but I'm too occupied by the music in the other room, luring me in.

"I'll give her a small tour," Blaine says, winking at him.

"Suit yourself." Caleb shrugs and leaves.

Blaine pulls me into the common room, but I come to a full stop when I realize what kind of party this really is.

The common room and dining room have been connected, and all the chairs and tables have been shoved aside to make room for a dance floor on one side ... and a sex room on the other, complete with benches, crosses, kinky beds, cages, flagellation devices, and more.

Couples are fucking all over the place—men with women, women with women, men with men, foursomes, threesomes, five people, all sorts of combinations and in all sorts of positions. Right in front of a crowd.

"What ... is this?" I mutter to myself.

My whole face turns red as I almost feel like I'm intruding, but not everyone watches them. A crowd of people just dance and kiss in a sultry manner like they don't even care what's happening.

"*This* is a true Tartarus party," Blaine murmurs in my ear. "The one you previously experienced was the one outside, meant for the paupers. But inside is where the real fun begins."

So this is what they were doing inside the house when they stood on that balcony?

"There's a good reason we're called the Tartarus House, darling," he muses.

I swallow as he leans in. "I thought it meant hell ... right?"

"Hell is pain to those who live by rules ... to us, it's an everlasting hedonistic lifestyle." He places a soft peck underneath my ear, and I nearly melt away.

Next to me, the lady who just spoke with Blaine drags a guy on an actual chain out of the room while the guy seems smitten with her and is practically drooling.

"Where are they going?" I ask.

"To a more private room," Blaine says. "Where they can live out their filthiest fantasies." Blaine grabs my hand and kisses the top. "Come."

He pulls me up the stairs, following in the couple's footsteps, and we head into a hallway to the right with many bedroom doors labeled with some sort of color.

"What do those colors mean?"

"The kind of kinks people are interested in."

Kinks? I gulp.

We pause near a door marked with purple and gray. "Purple means they like to be watched," Blaine whispers into my ear as he opens the door slightly. "And that there's soft BDSM involved."

He nudges me forward, and I can't help but peek at the couple. Two women, one bound to the bed, the other pouring champagne all over her tits before tickling her with a feather so it runs off her body, and her tongue follows to lick it off.

Blaine tugs me toward a different room with purple and black. Inside the room, loud thwacks accompanied by cries of pain reverberate through the door.

"Someone's in pain," I say.

"They're being flogged," Blaine responds. "Willingly, of course. Black is heavy sadism. Not for the fainthearted. Everyone knows what they're getting into when they come to these rooms. That's the fun part."

I swallow, but Blaine pulls me away toward another door marked with purple and green. "Green means it's open for multiple people, and they love it when you watch."

We take a glimpse inside the room, where two men are fucking a woman in the ass and mouth while there's a couple in the back on a couch watching them, kissing and groping each other.

I can't believe I'm watching this, but at the same time, I can't look away, the lust slowly building in my body.

"Tartarus parties are famous," Blaine mumbles behind me.

"I can see why," I reply.

The door slowly opens farther, and the people in the back glance at us without stopping their fondling. It's like they want me to watch and enjoy the sight of me salivating over their scene.

Blaine's hands wrap around my body, one hand curling around my breast while the other dips between my legs, and I'm helpless against the onslaught of lust coursing through my veins.

"I told you I enjoy a lot of things, and that includes a lot of people," he murmurs. "But my only wish is to experience it with you."

My breathing comes in short, ragged gasps as he begins to rub my pussy.

"No underwear …" He groans with excitement.

The thrusts and moans in front of me make it hard to focus.

I'm no match for his strength, but even if I could run, would I?

"This could get us both in trouble," I whimper as he doesn't stop circling my clit. It's only getting harder and harder not to succumb to his expert strokes. "Ares will kill you."

"I don't care," he whispers. "I need you. And if feeling you come on my fingers will be the death of me, then so be it."

My head tilts back against his shoulder as I watch the scene in front of me unfold, the two men thrusting into the woman wildly, her moans filling the room. My moans come out in short gasps as I let go in the moment, my sounds mingling with the lady being fucked, but it only seems to drive the people fucking her to go faster, harder, deeper.

I can almost picture myself in that very same position … only with Ares, Blaine, and Caleb instead.

I swallow away the lump in my throat as Blaine rolls his fingers around my pussy and dips inside. "Fuck, you're so tight, darling. No wonder they enjoy you so much," he murmurs. "Do you enjoy watching these people fuck?"

I nod, and he pushes me up against his hard-on. I'm nearly gyrating against him, desperate to get closer to that little piece of nirvana he's offering me.

Could I let myself go in front of all these people?

Could I give myself to Blaine, knowing it will cost him his head?

"I want you so badly, Crystal," he whispers. "Will you show me what you look like when you fall apart from watching these people?"

His fingers dip in and out of me, and he swirls them around until my pussy begins to throb with need, and it slowly begins to dawn on me that it's too late.

Too late for me to deny him what he wants.

"Do you fantasize about being the girl in the middle?" he moans. "Or do you wish to be the one holding the reins?"

I gasp. "The reins?"

"There are plenty of ways to fuck, and it doesn't always need to end with you on your knees," he murmurs, slipping his fingers through my slit, making me feel greedy. "You could make Ares and Caleb bend for you."

My eyes open wide.

No. They would never.

"You don't know what they're capable of. What they'd do for each other. What they'd do for you if you'd let them," he says, groaning. "What I'm willing to do for you."

He releases me from his grip and dances around me, and with a filthy smile on his face, he grabs my hand, kisses the top … and goes to his knees.

***

Blaine

I throw off the mask, grip her thighs, and dive in. I lap her up, the taste as divine as Caleb told me. No fucking wonder he got addicted so fast. She tastes like a literal goddess I need to worship.

My tongue drives into her, desperate for more, every taste not nearly enough to satiate my desire for her. I already knew I wouldn't be able to resist her the moment I met her, but I never thought she'd make me this greedy this fast.

My tongue circles her clit, and the way she moans makes my cock nearly tear my pants in half. She's looking down at me, a blush spreading on her face as I eat her out in front of these people. But that apprehension she feels will be lost soon as I swirl my tongue around and kiss her pussy lips, waiting for her to give it all to me.

"God, you taste so good," I murmur into her skin, and her moan brings me so much fucking delight.

I didn't just bring her here to watch. I brought her here to loosen up and release that inner vixen she's been hiding from all of us.

I could sense it from the moment I first saw her. She has so much to offer if only she'd let that part of her reign. But I will be here to coax out the goddess hiding inside her.

My fucking beautiful diamond deserves to be worshipped, and I am here to be her first disciple.

Her hand finds its way to my hair, and she fumbles with it, so I push down and make her grip me tightly.

"That's it. Make me choke on it."

When my tongue presses against her clit, she stops trying to resist and actually pushes her fingers into my head, forcing me closer, and damn, am I a sucker for the way she's taking control.

"Yes, make my tongue your whore," I groan into her pussy. "Chain down my fleshly desires and make them yours."

She moans with desperation, her entire body shivering as I clutch her ass tight and dig in.

The other people in this room moan along with her, but it only makes it more erotic as I thrust my tongue into her pussy, wetness dripping all over my face.

"God, yes," she moans, licking her lips as her knees begin to quake.

"Come all over my face," I murmur, rolling my tongue around her clit. "Please. Please, give it to me, darling. I need it."

She shivers in place, her toes curling, fingers digging into my skull, smashing me into her pussy, and I can feel her clit throb as she lets out a choked but deepening moan. Wetness gushes into my mouth, and I gobble it all up with glee.

I lick my lips and lean back to look at her satisfied face, her fingers unraveling from my hair like it's slowly dawned on her what we just did.

The people on the couch in the back bite their lips and wink at her, and the blush on her cheeks grows redder and redder.

"I can bring anyone to their knees with ease, yet you make me want to drop to mine," I murmur, grasping her fingers so I can peck those too. "Do you see now the power you hold?"

Suddenly, furious hazel eyes hiding behind a mask appear behind her shoulder, and I peer up, feeling the pressure of that judgmental gaze.

Oh dear.

THIRTY ONE

ARES

I grab the glass of wine off the table in front of me and swirl the contents, but neither this wine nor the entire party will ever remotely offer me the pleasure or release I'm looking for.

I take a reluctant sip as I watch the people I invited dance and fuck around in the common room. There are couples everywhere—threesomes, foursomes, men, women, anything and every combination fucking with each other, spurting dicks and sloshing wet pussies across the entire room—and not an inkling of lust courses through my veins.

I've never once not enjoyed the parties we threw until today.

Until … that fucking girl.

I clench the glass tighter and take another sip, angered that not even a Tartarus party filled with debauchery and indulging in all the seven fucking sins can sway me.

But the two things I know could are the two men missing in action right now.

I tilt my head and look at Arlo sitting next to me, being kissed by a random girl on his lap while he feeds her chocolates and liquor.

"Arlo," I say.

He looks up despite the girl still having her lips all over his neck. "Where are Caleb and Blaine?"

"Last I saw them, they went upstairs."

My eyes narrow.

To the private sex rooms?

"With who?"

He shrugs. "There's talk in the crowd that Blaine's sticking his tongue inside Crystal Murphy."

The glass shatters into a million pieces in my hand, blood dripping down onto the floor.

The girl stops kissing Arlo and looks at me, fear in her eyes. She jumps off his lap and flees into the crowd of partygoers before all hell breaks loose.

I guess my reputation precedes me.

"Get them for me," I say, narrowing my eyes at him. "All of them, including the girl."

***

Blaine

I get up, only to narrowly avoid being pummeled right in the face by Caleb's fist.

Caleb's seething, and he tears off his mask to yell at me. "Keep your filthy tongue out of my fucking gir—"

"Your what?" Crystal interjects swiftly, turning around and tucking down her dress in the process.

I get up and nudge her aside, settling my gaze on Caleb. "I can do what I want. Last I checked, you weren't my boss, darling, nor are you hers."

"You know what she is to me, what my father is to her mother," he grits, getting up in my face. "And then you go around and eat her out in front of all these people?"

He points at the people in the back, and they've actually stopped their scene to gape at us.

"Darling, you're just jealous she actually let me eat her out."

"You have no fucking clue what she wants or what she needs," he growls, pointing a finger at my chest.

"Excuse me, what is this even?" Crystal mutters. "Are you really trying to defend my honor?"

"Yes, Caleb, what is this?" I parrot.

"I didn't ask you to," Crystal says, trying to intervene.

"You don't have to," Caleb says without even looking at her. "Not against this slime."

"Slime?"

Okay, now I am offended.

"Yes, you're a skeeze who slithers his way into people's lives," he hisses, and I slap away his finger. "Ares and I already claimed her. She isn't yours to take," he growls.

"Yet she willingly gave me her orgasm. Can you say the same?" I taunt.

He leans his forehead against mine, pushing me forward. "Say what you're implying. Go on then, I fucking dare you."

Crystal grimaces. "Wait … Are you guys actually fighting over *me*?"

"Ares fucking warned you not to touch her," Caleb growls, ignoring me. "And then you did it anyway."

"Just like you," I retort.

"Fuck you."

"I'm prepared for the consequences. Don't worry, darling. Were you, though?"

"Could you guys take this outside, please?" the people in the back ask.

A sudden knock on the door makes us all stop and stare.

It's a Tartarus guy, one of our own, but even with his mask on, I recognize him as one of Ares's close confidants. Arlo.

"Sorry for the intrusion," he says. "Ares requested that you three come downstairs."

"Requested? Or demanded?" she asks.

He tilts his head as he glares at her. "Is there a difference?"

I take in a deep breath, and Caleb puts on his mask again.

Arlo's jaw tightens. "Whatever you're doing up here in this room … it's over."

Crystal grabs my hand and squeezes.

"Now," Arlo adds in a low tone.

"Fine," I say, releasing her fingers.

I know I have it coming for me. News here travels like fire. He

238

must know by now what I've done with her. But I still don't regret it, even if I know it'll probably cost me my life.

I pick up my mask off the floor and put it back on. "I'm ready to face him."

***

Crystal

"Let's go," Arlo says.

We all stroll through the hallway under Arlo's watchful eye and the gun in his pocket itching to shoot its load.

All while I'm still glowing from Blaine making me feel so damn good, I almost forgot where I was and with who. I let myself go in the moment, and lust won over common sense. Blaine so easily swayed me to part my legs that I almost feel guilty.

But then he glances at me over his shoulder, and I instantly forget why I was regretful to begin with. He really knows how to toy with people's hearts.

We make our way downstairs and through the crowd to the common room.

On top of the raised plateau in the back, behind a giant table, sits a guy with a golden demonic mask on his face, a shiny black and gold jacket on top of a black shirt and black pants, his legs leisurely thrown over the armrests. He watches us enter the room like a king on a throne.

When his bright gray eyes settle on mine, I gulp down the ball forming in my throat.

Slowly, he begins to clap his hands, and within a minute, everyone around us has stopped dancing and fucking around to focus solely on us.

"I'm impressed," Ares says from his seat on top of the plateau, looking down on us with disdain. "I was almost convinced by both of your false promises." His eyes darken. "But now the charade is over."

He snaps his fingers, and Arlo shoves me to my knees.

Blaine grabs his hand and twists it. "Do *not* touch her without my permission."

"Please," Arlo groans, rolling his eyes.

"I may have let you escort us downstairs, but you are still my lesser. Do not forget," Blaine warns.

Ares snaps his fingers, and Blaine releases him. Arlo backs away, but I'm still on my knees.

"You took her upstairs to the sex rooms," Ares says.

"I won't deny that I did," Blaine says.

Ares's face is hidden behind the demon mask, but I can still see those eyes burn with rage as they bore a hole into my chest.

"I gave you both a chance, and you threw it in my face. Why?"

"I can't stay away," Blaine says, swallowing. "I won't."

"And what about you?" He turns his attention to Caleb. "Hmm?"

"They were fighting over her when I found them," Arlo says, outing them both.

Fighting over me like I'm some kind of prize to win, tsk.

"Fighting ... over her ..." Ares repeats, clenching his teeth before he steals a rose from the vase on the table and takes a deep whiff. "Fine, then. Show me what it is worth to you. Show me what you're willing to do to get your hands on our little rose over here." He tilts his head. "Strip her."

What?

My eyes land on both boys as they approach me.

"Wait," I mutter in shock.

Ares throws his black and gold boots back over the armrest until he's seated on his ass and then leans back, legs spread wide, settling into the chair like a king. "Do you wish to offer up someone else?" he asks. "Because tonight we will *take* and leave nothing but scraps of you." His tongue darts out to wet his lips. "So choose wisely, little rose."

Fuck. Offering up someone else can only mean one thing in his world ... my mother.

And I'm not about to risk losing her too after I already lost my body.

So I swallow and nod. "Fine. Take me, then."

Caleb stands beside me and hooks his finger underneath my straps while Blaine grips my hand and places another kiss on it. "We'll be gentle, darling."

"Speak for yourself," Caleb growls, tearing down my straps. "I've been dreaming of nothing but ravaging her." And he places a wicked kiss on top of my shoulder as he pulls down my dress.

I let out a soft moan when Blaine covers my nipples with his hands and squeezes. Caleb goes to his knees as he pulls off the last inch of my dress, leaving nothing to the imagination.

My body is on full display in front of all of these people I don't know.

The only thing protecting my identity is this golden mask concealing my face.

"You want her so badly?" Ares says, sporting a wicked grin beneath the demon mask. "Then use her. Kiss her lips. Lick her tits. Make her pussy come so hard she squeals with delight. And when you're done ..." He leans in. "You bring her to me."

THIRTY TWO

Crystal

Blaine's lips land on my skin, and I close my eyes and drift away into their madness.

Caleb grips my breast and pinches my nipple, groaning into my ear before kissing my neck with greed. All while Blaine's kissing my shoulder and arm and fondling my other nipple, making it hard to concentrate.

But everyone's watching us as these boys ravage me.

"Don't look at them," Blaine whispers. "Focus on me."

"On *us*," Caleb interjects, whispering into my other ear. "Or do you honestly think you can choose?"

His hand slowly dives down between my breasts, all the way to my pussy, where he dips a finger inside. I gasp as he adds another one in me in front of all these people.

"Not once have I stopped thinking about you," Caleb murmurs. "Not since that fucking night in my car."

"But you almost killed us," I say, my voice fluctuating in tone as I try to resist, but I still glance his way. "Why?"

He narrows his eyes and glares up to where Ares is seated. "Him."

I swallow as he leans in from the side, tipping up my chin. "Now

242

give him what he wants before it ruins us both."

He plants his lips right onto mine, and I don't fight him off. Not this time. Despite the fact that his ravenous, coarse lips are like a starving animal devouring its prey.

"F-fuck," he murmurs when our lips briefly unlatch before he dives right back in, his fingers still swirling around inside me.

"I want you," Blaine whispers into my ear on the other side, and he steals me away from Caleb mid-kiss, only to smash his mouth onto mine, mixing their tastes into one.

And my God, I didn't think I could get any wetter than I already was.

Blaine's fingers toy with my nipples while his other hand dives between my legs too.

"What's the point in having fun if we can't share?" Blaine says as he dips a finger inside me.

Two different hands play with my pussy, driving me insane with lust, and I can barely keep my eyes open, but Ares's demanding gaze forces me to keep them homed in on him.

It's like he wants me to know he's watching.

Ever yearning.

"Fuck, she's so tight," Caleb groans, pulling out only to flick my clit instead, making me all hot and bothered.

All the people around us gaze at us with hungry eyes, some toying with their partners, others licking their lips like they're waiting for the feast to begin.

But the meal is me.

I gulp, glancing at the man who calls himself a god, sitting on his throne like a king almighty, his eyes fixated on me.

Waiting for me to crack and beg.

"Show me, then. Show me what you did to her up in those rooms," Ares says.

Blaine goes down on his knees in front of me and pulls me down with him, dragging me over his face. "Sit on my face and let me spoil this pretty pussy with my tongue," he groans.

His hands splay against my ass as he holds me down, but the second his tongue spears my pussy, I gasp and slap my hand in front of my mouth to prevent the moan from spilling out.

Caleb immediately grips my throat and tilts me back to press an upside-down kiss on top of my lips. And I'm smothered by their uncontrollable need for me.

A need that ends with my damnation ... and my body being given to the devil himself.

***

CALEB

Not once tonight have I stopped thinking about kissing those lips. So I kiss them as hard as I can, wishing I could claim this mouth and make it mine forever. Her taste is fucking divine, and it makes my cock rock-hard from the mere seconds her tongue rolls around mine.

But I know why we're doing this.

Ares's greed looms over my shoulder, forcing me to obey.

The only reason Ares allows us to do this is to make us bend to his will and his will alone.

And this girl ... this girl is getting in his way.

He'll kill her.

I tear my lips away and gaze at her, wondering how I'll save her from his wrath.

It's too late.

He knows how much I want her ... how much we both need her.

And it makes him want to ruin her.

I smash my mouth back onto hers, tasting sweet oblivion on her lips, desperate to forget about all the implications.

"Fuck," I groan, squeezing that throat even harder as I kiss her, wondering if I should kill her myself out of mercy. But the more I press my thumbs down on her veins, the harder it becomes to kiss her, knowing I'm the one stealing her breath away.

I can't. I fucking can't.

My fingers untighten a little, and she lets out a stifled moan from both the lack of oxygen and Blaine's tongue spearing her.

She doesn't just belong to me. She belongs to all of us, and that includes Ares. And I know he'll claim her, no matter what. No matter if it ends me.

"I need you," I grit. "I need you to do exactly what he wants. Do you understand?"

She nods, and I slowly release my grip on her throat further so she can breathe.

"Be a slut," I whisper. "Be his good girl, and maybe you'll survive."

"Don't listen to him," Blaine murmurs from underneath him. "I'll protect you and give you everything you need at the same time."

I pinch her nipples so hard she's forced to tilt her head forward and look at Ares. "He can't protect you from *him*."

"But you can, right?" she mutters.

"Wrong," I growl, and I move to her side so I can take one of her nipples into my mouth and suck hard.

She's so goddamn beautiful. Even with that mask on, it's hard not to want to take every inch of her.

But I have to control myself because he's watching, and I know it's a goddamn test of loyalty. He's letting us feel what we could have before he takes it away again.

But dammit, my cock's growing rock-hard just from licking these taut nipples.

She moans, suffocating on the need to let go as Blaine rolls his tongue around her needy little clit.

Despite the fact that I could kill Blaine too for even daring to swipe his tongue across her pussy, a part of me is obsessed with watching her come undone for him.

"I'm so goddamn hard for you," I groan against her mouth. "Are you ready?"

She nods as I step over Blaine and unzip to release my hard cock from its confined space. Her mouth begins to salivate when I tip up her chin and say, "Open wide, my little slut."

She does what I say, and I push in, sliding my cock across that delicious little tongue. The feel of her swallowing me down compares to virtually nothing, and I moan with impatience as I sink in deeper and deeper, watching her struggle.

"Ticktock, boys," Ares says, gloating from the chair. "Make her come, or I will."

When Blaine moans and swirls his tongue around, she moans along too, and it makes me thrust inside to the base so she'll think of me instead of him.

He shouldn't have taken her to those rooms, should've kept his fingers and tongue out of her, but it's too late. She knows what it feels like now ... what it feels like to be owned by us.

I pull out and say, "Good girl. Now roll your tongue around my cock. Show me how he's licking you."

Her tongue flicks around my shaft, and I groan as my head tilts back and the sensations take over. My cock begins to throb inside her throat, but then she suddenly stops.

"Don't get too greedy there, Caleb," Blaine muses.

"Goddammit, lick her like you own that fucking clit," I growl at him.

He chuckles, but I know exactly when he proceeds because she does too, and the feeling is insane.

Maybe I should let him lick me sometime.

Fuck.

"Enough," Ares growls.

I pull out, still hard, and look at Ares, annoyed he'd intervene.

He snaps his fingers. "Switch."

I frown and look at him. "What?"

The annoyance on his face is far worse than mine despite the fact he's clutching his rigid cock that he pulled out of his pants somewhere along the way. "Do you really want me to repeat myself?"

I swallow and step away even though I was dying to claim that throat as mine and fill it to the brim with my cum.

Blaine crawls out from underneath her. "I could eat you all day and still not have enough."

She blushes, so I drag him up to his feet. "Enough, slimeball. Move."

He narrows his eyes at me as I sink to my knees in front of her and kiss her thighs. But she's still looking at him instead of me.

"Can you handle it?" he asks, tipping up her chin. "All these eyes watching you come undone."

She nods. "I'm okay."

"I'll kill them all for you if you want, darling," he adds with a wink.

She blushes. "I don't want that on my conscience."

I'm done with them talking, so I bury my face between her thighs and taste her pussy, instantly shutting both of them up as soon as she begins to moan.

"Oh fuck," she groans, grasping for my hair as I dive in and lick her raw.

And I drag her down on top of me and lap her up like there's no tomorrow because there might not be one for either of us.

246

But at least I'll die knowing I was the last to taste this pussy and make it come.

***

Blaine

I step over Caleb and look at her eyes hidden behind that damn mask. I would give anything to see her rosy cheeks right now, but I know it would reveal her identity to the crowd. Her identity is the last thing she has left. The last semblance of humanity as it's slowly stripped away from her inch by inch by the Tartarus devils.

I tip up her chin to make her look at me. "I'll be gentle with my goddess if it pleases her."

She swallows, her whole body exploding into goose bumps as I plant a soft kiss beneath her ear.

"But I need you to take my cock like a good girl now. Can you do that for me?"

She nods, a hampered moan leaving her mouth as I suckle on her skin and create a mark on her neck.

Even if she belongs to all of us, this one part … it belongs to me.

I push down my zipper and pull out my cock as her hungry eyes lay eyes on me for the very first time, another swallow following.

"J-Jesus …" she stutters at my tattooed thickness.

I don't have many tattoos because I don't want to taint my flawless skin, but this rose on my shaft I'm very proud of.

"All of it will fit inside that beautiful mouth of yours," I say, slowly parting her lips. "You'll make it fit, won't you?" I push the tip across her. "I'll be gentle with you."

The way she looks up at me with those doe-like eyes makes me weak in the knees as I slowly push inside her mouth. The feel of her tongue wrapping around my cock is heavenly, and I let out a long and heavy moan.

"Oh God, why does it feel like you know exactly what you're doing?" I mewl, pulling out to allow her to answer.

She eyes Ares and moans when Caleb flicks her clit with his tongue. "They made me swallow them."

"You're so good at it," I murmur as I slowly drive back in again.

247

"It almost makes me want to thrust into your throat, good God." My eyes almost roll into the back of my head. That's how good it feels.

I've had men and women suck me off before, but it never mattered who it was … until now.

This girl has captured my attention and refuses to let it go.

I can't stop gripping her face and pushing in deeper and deeper until my balls hit her chin and my cock begins to throb.

I admit, I'm a bastard for even wanting this, for enjoying it as much as I am, but fuck me, has she gotten me wrapped tightly around her finger … or should I say tongue?

"F-fuck yes, keep licking just like that. You make me want to worship this tongue."

***

Crystal

His filthy words make my clit throb with need, and I find it so hard to contain my moans.

Especially with Caleb thrusting his tongue into my pussy … all while Ares watches us.

My tongue rolls around Blaine's thick shaft while I struggle not to choke on his size. He's not as long as the others but definitely much thicker, so he barely fits in my mouth.

"Time's running out," Ares groans. "Yet you still haven't made her come. Pathetic."

Caleb sucks even harder on my clit, and my knees begin to quake against his body, but his firm palms around my thighs keep me steady.

"Oh God, yes, take me deep," Blaine moans, pushing in so deep tears stain my eyes. "You undo me, darling. I want so badly to come inside that pretty mouth of yours." He tips up my chin and makes me look at him while he's still inside me. "May I?"

How could I possibly say no to those deep, dark eyes begging me to let him use me?

So I nod when he pulls out and rolls his tip around my mouth.

"Her first," Caleb growls from beneath me, and he swirls his tongue around my clit so well that I can't even think straight.

I'm getting so close I can almost taste the high.

Even with all these people watching us, I'm heading for that cliff, and I won't even mind that everyone will see me fall.

"Come with his dick inside your mouth," Caleb groans, suckling and nibbling at my clit, driving me insane with lust to the point that I begin to gyrate on top of his face. "That's it, slut, rub this pussy all over my face and come for me."

His filthy words push me over the edge, and my eyes roll into the back of my head as the biggest orgasm washes over me.

Blaine arches his back, grips my face, and spurts his hot seed out onto my tongue before shoving himself deep inside me, coating the back of my throat.

"Oh, fuck me, yes," he groans, the sound setting my body ablaze.

I actually moan as I gulp it all down, desperate for more of whatever kind of fucked-up drug this is they've injected me with. Their cocks and tongues are like spears coated in delicious venom, poisoning my soul with lust and greed. And for a second, I was almost ready to beg them to do it.

"Enough."

Ares's commanding voice makes them both stop, and the hedonistic pleasure we experienced comes to a grinding halt.

"Come here. Now."

Blaine pulls out of me and steps away, his cock still hard, still needy, while I'm dripping with cum, saliva, and wetness. Caleb crawls out from underneath me and lifts me from the floor, but I can barely stay put without leaning against him.

When they try to walk with me up to the stage, Ares growls, "Her alone."

Caleb releases me, and I walk up farther under the invasive stares from the crowd around us. Though the music still blasts through the room, and some people continue to dance, most have fixated their gazes on us. The only thing protecting me right now is this flimsy mask on my face, shielding my identity.

Ares sits on his throne-like chair, his hand gripping his sizable cock, which still makes my eyes bulge when I look at it, wondering how it ever fit inside my throat, especially with those piercings glistening from his precum.

I swallow away the lump in my throat and walk toward him. When I stop, he arches his finger, beckoning me until I'm right in front of him.

"You thought you could come into my domain and subdue my men?" he asks, stroking his own hard-on right in front of me.

I gulp when he reaches the tip and spreads the precum all over.

"Answer me."

"You invited me to come here," I reply.

"I *commanded* you to come here," he retorts. "Or have you forgotten the deal you made?"

I shake my head, but my hand still balls into a fist.

"You belong to us."

I hate the way he continuously wants to remind me that my body is his to barter now … to use and gift as he sees fit.

"But I don't appreciate you going behind my back to indulge my men in their fantasies."

He swipes a single finger up and down my slit, coaxing out the wetness, dipping his finger in before he brings it to his mouth and licks. And I'd be lying if I said it didn't make my pussy thump.

"They made you so wet … I wonder how often they've been thinking of fucking you … of sticking their tongues inside that sweet, aching pussy of yours." He licks his lips as he looks up at me from underneath those dark eyelashes. "Well, they got their wish." His eyes darken. "And now I will *make* them fucking wish they never even looked at you."

The wicked glimmer in his eyes makes me wish I never relinquished my knife to that guard out front. Dammit.

"Do you remember what I told you the first time I thrust my fingers into your pussy?" he says, and he grips my arm and pulls me toward him. "Tell me."

Oh, I remember all right.

The warning was seared into my mind.

"The next time you penetrate me…"

"It will be the cock of a god thrusting into your wet, aching pussy," he finishes, making me blush.

Suddenly, he grips my waist and pulls me right on top of him, then sinks me down onto the tip of his dripping, hard cock. I gasp as one by one, each piercing enters me, the metal cold and hard against my softness, while the stare behind his mask is even colder and harsher.

"One," he says, and he pushes me down.

I can feel each of his piercings scraping against my insides, coaxing out more delicious shock waves.

"Two."

Digging his nails into my waist, he pushes me down farther.

"Three."

Is he … counting the inches?!

"Four."

I groan from how good it feels. "Fu—"

"We're not even halfway there."

"What?!" I gasp as he forces me down onto his ample length.

"Five."

He forces me to sink even deeper, and I can barely hold on tight as I sit down on his lap slowly. My entire body shivers from the mere size of him.

"Six."

I can feel him go even deeper, my pussy stretching to the limit, clit already thumping from the sheer feel of him inside me.

"Seven."

The piercings add so many sensations deep inside that my pussy begins to contract.

"Eight."

I can barely take it. It's that huge and that filling, as though my pussy is finally filled with the one thing it has always wanted but never received.

"Nine."

"It's so full," I mutter, trying to adjust.

"No. You will take all of me." His fingers dig into my skin as he holds on tight while sinking even deeper into me.

My eyes nearly roll into the back of my head from how full it feels and how blissfully unaware I was before of just how much I craved this. I've never felt anything like this before. It's as if my pussy is being completed, like a sheath perfectly fitting around a sword.

"Oh God," I mutter as my clit thrums from a need I didn't know I had.

And the farther he gets to the base, the less I actually care about people watching … and the more I begin to realize I didn't just sell my body … I sold my goddamn soul.

THIRTY THREE

ARES

The way she whimpers on my lap as I sink deeper and deeper into that filthy wet pussy of hers, the more I want to claim her.

"Yes, I am your fucking god," I say through gritted teeth. "Now beg, little rose. Beg because you will never feel anything closer to paradise than coming all over this cock."

She moans out loud.

"Ten."

Filling her to the base is nothing short of pure ecstasy, and I revel in the way my cock fits so neatly into her tight little pussy. I wonder how many have come before me. Because her apprehension and complete shock over how I'd feel inside her tells me she doesn't have much experience.

But I'll teach her to be a good little slut for me.

We have all the time in the world now that she's finally found her way to me.

I pull out to allow her a few seconds without me, her pussy dripping over my shaft. But within seconds, I push right back in, much less slowly, but still allowing her time to adjust to my ample size.

"You may have had sex before, but you have never been properly fucked by a cock like mine," I growl. "Now sit on your god's lap and show me how badly you want to come, and maybe I'll give it to you."

When I'm fully inside her, she lets out a little whimper, her cheeks and lips all puffed up and rosy. "P-please …"

Fuck.

"That's it, little rose. Beg for my mercy now that you've felt what it's like to be owned by a goddamn god."

"Please … I already came twice. I can't do it again."

"You will come for me as many times as I damn well demand, slut," I growl, pulling out of her, only to thrust back in so hard she sees stars.

And I grip her chin and smash my lips onto hers, the kiss greedy, possessive to the point she actually holds her breath, afraid I might steal that too if she lets go.

My little rose may pretend she was never afraid of me, but I know the truth.

I know she feared one thing …

Not to be killed … but to fall.

And I will be there to fucking catch her when she does.

"You belong to me now," I murmur against her mouth. "And it's about time they fucking know that too."

I lift her off my lap, only to twist her around with my cock still inside her. Facing the room, she can now see all the guests to my party and all the people staring at us with flushed cheeks and hard cocks in their pants, her pussy on full display.

They all came to experience ecstatic pleasure and complete and utter debased debauchery. What kind of host would I be if I didn't give them the most captivating show they could ever see?

I smirk as I watch Blaine's and Caleb's gazes turn into sheer regret.

My fingers find their way to her nipples, and I squeeze them until they're deliciously taut, and her pussy begins to throb from the sizzling pain.

"Look at them. Look at how much they yearn for what I have, for what I own," I whisper into her ear as I slowly sink her down on my cock again. She gasps, her mouth falling wide open as she struggles to keep the moans at bay. "Show Caleb and Blaine just how much you crave to be impaled by the cock of a god. Show them how wet you

253

became for them … and how easily you gave it all up to *me*."

I hook my arms underneath her thighs and lift them up until her knees hit her shoulders and her pussy is on full display.

And in front of everyone in this room, I spear her onto my cock.

Caleb and Blaine are helpless as she's lowered onto my shaft farther and farther until she hits the base, and her eyes roll into the back of her head.

She can't even gasp.

Can't even utter a single syllable.

All that tumbles from her mouth is a stifled, needy moan.

"Look at her," I tell Caleb and Blaine, whose cocks keep bouncing up and down from watching me fuck her. "Look at the girl you thought belonged to you. Does it feel good to watch her be railed by me?"

Caleb swallows and nods, while Blaine just bites his lip, but his bobbing dick reveals the truth.

I thrust in and out of her, not giving a shit that everyone's watching her wet pussy fit neatly around my pulsating cock.

"Is this what you want?" I ask Caleb, looking him directly in the eyes. "Her?"

He sucks in a breath and nods.

"Even when you know what she's going to be?"

He nods again.

"Show me then how much you'd do for it," I challenge him. "Come here."

He steps up onto the plateau.

"On your knees."

He sinks to his knees in front of me while I bury myself to the hilt inside this pussy.

When I pull out again, she moans, and I know he can hear it too. I can see it from the way he looks up at her with those needy eyes. The same kind of needy eyes he gives me. "Lick her while I give her the greatest orgasm she could ever feel."

He falls onto both his hands and begins circling her clit with his tongue while I plow into her, making her moans long and heavy.

"Oh God," she murmurs between thrusts.

"That's it. Make her come all over my cock," I say.

He digs in like a madman, devouring her as though he hasn't had a decent meal in years.

And a part of me is thoroughly pissed off he enjoys her as much as he does ... but another is so vehemently turned on by it all that I don't fucking know whether to love it or hate it.

But there is one thing I'm sure I hate ... and that's the fact that both of these fuckers decided to touch what belonged to me without my presence or permission.

I beckon Blaine with a nod. "You, come here." When he steps up and approaches the chair, I hold up my hand. "That's close enough. You haven't deserved her yet. First, you will learn to fucking appreciate what you already have."

I look at both of them as a wicked grin spreads on my face. "Take his ass."

***

Crystal

Did Ares just tell Blaine to ... fuck Caleb?

"What?" Blaine rasps.

But all I can hear is the sloshing of my own wetness as Ares rips into me.

Caleb looks up at Ares. "But I hate him."

"Good. Hate every inch of his cock as it bores through you, then, because then you might feel even an inkling of the hatred I've felt because you two fucked her without my approval." I snap my fingers, and Blaine moves into position, kneeling behind Caleb.

"Do it. Punish him with a cock up his ass."

Blaine lowers his eyes as he says, "As you wish."

RIP!

He tears Caleb's pants open while Caleb looks back at him and grits, "Fine."

Ares squeezes his legs until Caleb's neck is choked out, and he's forced to face us. "Keep your mouth on her pussy."

Caleb's piercing rolls around my clit so deliciously, but my eyes still home in on Blaine who puts the tip of his dick against Caleb's ass, and ...

Is he really going to do it?

Caleb's mewl as Blaine thrusts into him makes goose bumps

255

scatter on my skin.

Fuck, he really did it.

"Do you really have to go that hard on me?" Caleb growls at Blaine.

"It displeasures me greatly I have to taint my beautiful cock in your ass. But I will enjoy your cries as I fit myself inside you," Blaine grits back.

"Fuck you," Caleb growls.

Blaine smirks. "With pleasure."

Blaine sinks deeper into Caleb's ass, the look on his face anything but pleased. Still, Blaine grabs his thighs and plunges fully, eyes fixated on mine like he wants to tell me he's imagining he's fucking me instead.

And something about that makes me gulp.

"Fuck, it's so goddamn thick," Caleb groans.

"And you will take it all like a good fucking slut, just like her," Ares groans, thrusting into me, no-holds-barred.

I'm shocked at how filthy he talks to Caleb, but I'm even more shocked at Caleb's capitulation with his dominance, as though he's used to it.

Caleb moans while being fucked, as though he enjoys being debased by Ares, and it confuses me.

He was never this submissive with me. What's changed?

But I can't even focus because of the way Ares spears me onto his length to dizzying depths. He's making me wish I never stepped foot in this place ... because his cock is incomparable to anything I've ever felt before. It's like I'm floating in his arms, on my way to nirvana, and with Caleb's pierced tongue rubbing my clit, I'm helpless to stop the inevitable drop into oblivion.

Why does it feel like my soul will be ripped apart by this looming orgasm?

"You feel it, don't you?" Ares whispers into my ear. "The desire to let go as the orgasm slowly builds inside you."

"Fuck ... you," I mutter between thrusts.

"So brazen ..." He chuckles. *THRUST.* "Now whimper."

I can't even stop the sounds from leaving my mouth. That's how much of a hold he has over me.

"That's it, break for me," Ares groans.

As I reach that cliff, he sinks his teeth into my shoulders, and I

256

gasp with shock. Even though I hate him with every fiber of my being, I still fall apart. Not because I want to but because my body forces me to as it undulates on his lap. My pussy contracts around his giant cock so hard I nearly faint from the ensuing orgasm.

But it's Ares's whisper after he lapped up my blood that truly pushes me over the edge, "*Mine.*"

THIRTY FOUR

CALEB

I can feel her clit thump against my tongue, and judging from the loud moan that just rolled off her tongue, she enjoyed herself on his length tearing her goddamn soul from her body.

I lap up the wetness that flows out of her, casually licking Ares's cock too. I can't help myself. I want them both so much it's destroying me from the inside out.

How could I possibly fucking choose?

He's forcing me to, but I can't. I can't fucking pick between these two delights.

I need both, alone, at the same time. I don't care as long as I can have it all.

And he knows this more than anyone else in this room.

He knows I'm so fucking desperate for more that he's using it against me.

She's my nemesis, a vixen I can't get rid of, and instead of pulling me away from her, he only drives me further into her grasp just to make me hate her even more, turning my needs against me by using Blaine as the instrument.

Fuck, his cock is so goddamn thick inside me. It's not as long as Ares but definitely more girthy, and I can barely handle it. All Blaine added was some spit, just to make it easier on me, but I doubt he cares as he thrusts in deep.

"Oh God, I can't keep licking her like this," I groan.

"If you remove your tongue from her clit, I'll have it removed from your goddamn mouth," Ares growls. "Now lick."

God, I wish his threats didn't turn me on, but they do.

Ares's thrusts bounce her against his lap, making it difficult to concentrate. A part of me fantasizes about being the one to bounce on his lap like that … while another desperately wants to be the one in control of her pleasure.

Still, I eat her out like I haven't had a meal in years. "Fuck, she tastes so good," I murmur against her pussy. "Almost makes me forget who's fucking me right now."

"Oh, don't you fucking forget," Blaine seethes, thrusting even harder.

Goddammit, I didn't know he could fuck like that.

Ares laughs. "That's it, boys. It's time to bury those hatchets and fuck for the crowd. You don't want to disappoint them, do you?"

I mewl as Blaine buries himself inside to the hilt while Ares does the same to her, and my mouth completely covers her clit as I'm forced into her.

"Are you imagining it's her you're fucking right now?" Ares asks Blaine as his fingers dig into her thighs. "Tell me the fucking truth."

"Yes," he groans.

Her pussy thumps against my tongue.

"Fuck him so hard he has no choice but to lick her until she comes again," Ares growls. *THRUST.* "And again." *THRUST.* "And again." *THRUST.*

"Oh God." She's moaning out loud now, her clit swollen and needy for more, so I keep licking despite being railed so hard I can barely focus.

"Yes, beg to your fucking God."

I look up at both her and him, and I can see Ares straining for control.

But even he is no match for how good her pussy feels.

"Feel the heaven inside the hellscape we've created," Ares whispers. "Do you need my cock so badly you can't breathe?"

She's not the only one who can't breathe. Blaine's cock rips through me relentlessly, and my whole body begins to quake while I continue licking her.

"I hate you," she hisses, making him laugh.

"Keep saying that. It only makes me harder."

"Oh fuck," I groan as Blaine touches my prostate. "I'm about to—"

I can't even finish my sentence as I look up into both their eyes with complete and utter lust, and I moan out loud as the cum spurts out of me and onto the floor.

I couldn't contain myself.

Couldn't keep myself from releasing all of that pent-up desire as I watched them fuck.

And fuck me, I would do it again if it meant I could see her come undone from him.

***

Blaine

I fuck his ass hard and fast because I want him to suffer for interrupting me while I was spoiling her. For ruining her when she wasn't his to take. I want to punish him for destroying whatever chance I had with her.

If that makes me just as devilish as Ares, then so be it.

If this is the only way I can be close to her, it's worth it.

So I ram my cock into his ass and keep my eyes fixated on the pretty girl languishing in Ares's arms, her body limp from all the orgasms she's already endured tonight.

One. Two. Three. Will it ever be enough for him?

I warned her not to get closer, but she couldn't help herself, couldn't stop wandering into their path, and look where it brought us now ... to the brink of destruction.

He thrusts into her with no remorse at the same pace I am, watching me with keen intent, almost as if he savors the way I'm letting out all my anger on Caleb.

He wants to punish us both for even daring to touch her, but he doesn't realize this only makes me that much more determined to have her. And if I have to fuck my way through this guy to get to her, then I will do it.

260

"Fuck, not so fast," Caleb groans. "I already spilled all my fucking juice."

"And you will do it again," Ares groans at him. "You wanted to come so badly? You have your wish."

I bore into him while my eyes bore into her instead, and I lick my lips when Ares momentarily pulls out only to thrust right back in again, the sight of her face as she's speared on top of him a sight to behold.

Lust courses through my veins as wildly as I can see it ripple on her flushed face, and it makes me so goddamn hard that my balls squeeze together.

Caleb gasps. "Holy shit, you'd better not—"

Too fucking late.

I arch my back and yield to the orgasm, unloading myself inside him, cum spilling out on the edges.

I didn't think I could come again after that last one was inside her delicious mouth, but I guess I was wrong.

"God!" Caleb groans as more cum spurts out of him uncontrollably while his mouth is still on her pussy.

"Yes, beg to me and me alone," Ares says. "All of you."

When it's over, I pull out of him and tuck my cock back into my pants so I can watch the scene in front of me.

"I can't ... I can't take it anymore," Crystal whimpers while Caleb's tongue rolls around her swollen clit.

"Yes, you can. Another," Ares commands. "Come. Now."

She mewls, shaking in his arms as he lifts her from his cock and plows back in right at the peak, and I can literally see her eyes roll into the back of her head.

And that alone makes my flaccid cock almost spring back to life again.

This girl is going to be the death of me.

***

Crystal

"Good girl," Ares whispers into my ear, and I can hear him bite his lip behind me before his balls tighten and release, filling me with warm cum.

Oh God. It's happening.

He strains and thrusts in a few more times, filling me to the brim.

When he finally lifts me, we're both covered in his juices. His tip slowly sinks out of me, releasing a tsunami of wetness and cum, and Caleb is there to catch it all.

"Now fucking lick it all off like a good slut," Ares tells Caleb, whose tongue slides across Ares's length and dips into my pussy, sucking it all out.

And I have honestly never felt anything better than all of this. It almost makes me want to grab his hair and shove him in farther.

What is wrong with me?

Have these boys corrupted me so badly?

Ares plants a sultry kiss beneath my ear, creating goose bumps all over my skin. "You wanted to dance with the devil, little rose ... and I've granted your goddamn wish."

He lowers my legs, which feel like limp noodles as he puts me back on his lap. But I can't maintain my own posture, let alone keep my body from flopping down.

Blaine immediately rushes toward me, shoving Caleb out of the way to catch me.

My head and hand land on his muscular chest while he picks up my legs and lifts me from the floor.

"I've got you, goddess."

I look up into his starstruck eyes, wondering what he was thinking while he was fucking Caleb. If he wished it would've been me instead.

"*Goddess ...*" Ares parrots.

My head turns at his indignation, but his thunderous eyes strike me the most.

His teeth grind together. "Take her to the guest room."

"What?" I frown. "But I did what you asked."

He leans forward and tips up my chin to meet his gaze. "And you will continue doing what I demand from you ... in a prison of your own making."

My breath hitches in my throat.

"Because *that* is the deal you made with us ... little rose." The wicked smile that follows makes my blood boil. "Regret won't save you now."

He flicks his other fingers, and Blaine stands, sighing deeply. "Yes, Sir."

"Caleb. Go with him."

Caleb gets up too and tucks his dick back into his pants before he follows us through the crowd that parts for us.

But my gaze still lands on the king of these devils of Tartarus, perpetually sitting on his throne with his smug grin, never wavering, never showing even an inkling of emotion except the one that has poisoned his heart—hate.

The same poison he injected into my veins the moment he said those words.

A prison of your own making.

A prisoner to his every whim.

And I begged him for it.

Hate doesn't even begin to describe what I feel for this man, this self-proclaimed god who wants me to worship the ground he walks on out of fear.

But even if his cock was godlike ...

I will never, ever give him what he wants.

And as Blaine waltzes out the door with me in his arms, I leave Ares with that same smile I gave him when we first met.

Let the hatred fucking flow.

THIRTY FIVE

CALEB

I walk back into the room, straightening my posture as everyone looks at me.

In front of me, Ares still sits at that table, taking a big whiff from his vape and blowing out the smoke in my direction. The crowd has already continued dancing and fucking around, and the music blasts through the house like nothing ever happened.

But we stripped Crystal bare and used her in front of everyone.

And all he does is smirk.

"Did you have to go that hard on her?" I ask as I step up on the stage.

His left brow rises. "Back so soon?"

I avert my eyes. "She didn't want to talk to me."

Fuck knows, I tried.

But when Blaine and I put her in her room, she lay down on the bed and refused to open her mouth, let alone allow us a simple look. It's like we no longer existed to her.

And for some reason, that stung more than having Blaine's dick up my ass.

Ares smiles at me. "Of course not. She hates you."

Fuck.

264

Does she really hate me?

Did I want her to?

I sigh out loud and grab the chair beside him.

"What? Are you regretting your choice now?" he asks.

"No. I still don't want her mother with my father …" I mumble. "But it doesn't feel right either."

He snorts. "Since when do you have a conscience?" He slides his vape my way across the table. "Take it. You need it more than I do."

I grab it and take a big whiff before sitting down in the chair, but fuck me, my ass feels like it's on fire. "Fuck, my ass hurts."

"Good," Ares says. "If it didn't, it wouldn't be a good lesson, would it?"

My nostrils flare as I look his way, but I can't say the multitude of unspoken words between us out loud.

I know what he's insinuating.

What I've been wondering about all this time too …

But if I were to admit to the truth, what would happen to me? To us?

The way he looks at me makes my skin crawl. He always sees right through my veil of lies.

My lips curl around the vape, and he blows out a circle of smoke in my direction with raised eyebrows, taunting me.

"You don't just want to get rid of her mother for the sake of your dad, do you?"

Fuck.

I pull the vape from my mouth and put it back on the table, keeping my hand there.

"I've seen the way you look at her," he says.

"Stop," I growl.

His wicked smile makes me want to chuck this vape into the bin.

"Admit it," he says, leaning in to whisper. "You desire her."

"Shut up," I hiss through gritted teeth.

He leans back, laughing. "You can't even face the truth."

"I enjoy fucking her mouth and sucking those tits, but that does not make me in lo—"

I cut myself off before I say something I'll definitely regret.

"Hmm?" Ares muses.

I know he heard.

Fuck.

"Forget it. I'm done with this conversation." I shove the vape

265

back in his direction. "You know, I'm not the only one who can't face his own feelings."

He clutches the vape too tightly with his fist. "I'm more than just rage."

I get up. "Then why are you so angry with both me and her? I'm not the only one who won't say the truth out loud either."

Something in his amused face breaks, leaving space for silence and disgust, but I still walk off. I have enough on my plate as it is. I can't carry his emotions for him too.

***

Blaine

I stay in her room and wait until she opens her eyes again before I approach to put the blanket over her body.

"I'm so ... tired ..." she murmurs.

"I know. You need to sleep," I say, shushing her when she tries to get up. "Rest now, darling. You'll need the energy."

I fish into her pocket and take out her phone when she isn't looking, then back away slowly as her eyes start to close.

Even though the music continues to blast downstairs, it doesn't wake her, as it barely penetrates these walls.

I swallow and grab the door handle, looking at her blink one last time before I close the door and swipe the card along the lock, sealing her in, along with my own damn heart.

***

Crystal

The next day

When my eyes burst open, I panic and sit up straight.

I don't know how much time has passed or how long I've been asleep.

It feels as though I simply passed out and woke up here in this room.

All I remember is Blaine carrying me upstairs, his gentle hum lulling me into a deep trance.

And then I was here.

I throw the blanket off me and make my way to the door, but when I jiggle it, it doesn't budge. It's locked.

Fuck.

I'm trapped.

"Let me out!" I yell. "Hello? Can anyone hear me?"

When there's no response, I slam the door with my fists.

"Let me out, goddammit!"

After a while, I hear footsteps and stop moving.

They're getting closer.

I back away from the door.

Thud. Thud. Thud.

I crawl back onto the bed as the handle opens, and a hand slowly pushes open the door.

My heart is racing in my throat.

Long black hair followed by a familiar handsome face peeks inside.

"Are you awake, darling?"

***

Blaine

I bring a bowl filled with strawberries and whipped cream inside. I'm not a great cook, but it'll be a nice treat for her. She's huddled up on the bed like a scared animal hiding in plain sight.

"What do you want?"

I put down the bowl and say, "Brought you some strawberries."

She swallows. "Not interested."

I make a face. "But you haven't eaten since you arrived here."

"I'm not hungry."

"Don't lie to me, please," I say. I approach the bed, but she backs away so much that I stop. "I know you're mad at me."

"Don't."

I frown. Her eyes are laced with fear, and it makes me apprehensive. She glances at the locked door, and I step back, guarding it.

"Where is my phone?" she grits.

"I took it," I say. "But it's safe. I promise."

"Lies," she spits back.

"You won't get it back. Ares's orders."

She rolls her eyes like she knew I was going to say that.

But I cannot let her out of this house. No matter how badly she wants to.

Ares's wishes are my commands. That's how it's always been. That's how it'll be.

But perhaps …

I clear my throat and place something down on the cabinet, setting the strawberries on top. "I'm not here to hurt you."

She ignores me completely, wistfully staring out the window like I mean nothing to her. And it hurts.

I throw her a glance and watch her sparkling green eyes with keen interest as they home in on my hand diving into my pocket. "I can't kill him for you, if that's what you want …" I take out her knife and place it on the cabinet next to the door, knowing the weight of the burden I'm placing on her. But I know she can take it. After all, she's the one who's slowly been wrapping three demons around that cute little finger of hers.

"Now be a good girl, darling, and eat those strawberries."

THIRTY SIX

ARES

"Glad we could do proper business again," my father says, shaking the hand of the man in front of us.

"I'm happy to be able to sell my goods to your customers again," the man says with a gleeful grin, his mouth full of gold teeth. "I'm sure they've been ravenous waiting for it."

My father chuckles awkwardly.

"I'm sure," I say, rolling my eyes.

"Excuse me, I don't think we've been properly introduced," the man says, holding out his hand to me. "Wayne Ferry."

I glance at his hand and then his face.

"No, thanks. I don't shake the hands of murderers."

His face contorts into complete and utter shock, and to my delight, I find myself laughing.

"Ares!" my father barks.

"Are we done here?" I ask as I get up from my seat. "I have things to do."

"Yes, I am," Wayne says, shaking his head. "I'm done here. I'll see myself out."

"Apologies, Wayne," Father says as he follows him out the door. "I am trying to involve my son in the business side of things. It's not going as smoothly as I'd hoped. I do hope you'll forgive his brazenness."

"I'll think about it," Wayne says, throwing me a snooty look.

"You've done it now," Kai whispers to me.

"Shut the fuck up," I growl back.

He shrugs as Dad closes the door again.

"Ares ... That was uncalled for."

"I don't know why you keep wanting me at these meetings when you have him," I say, nodding at Kai.

"Because you're my son, and I'm the man who owns this company that provides the wealth you indulge yourself in," he says, still holding the doorknob. "You'd do well to remember that."

"You should try not to piss off his clients," Kai whispers. "Even the fucked-up ones."

"They aren't fucking clients. They're drug-dealing murderers who are using Dad's customers to earn blood money."

"Ares," my father hisses.

"No, I'm not gonna sit here and pretend they're esteemed businessmen when all they are is petty criminals."

My father slams the light switch. "ARES! How many times do I have to tell you to fucking behave?" His nostrils flare. "One fucking day in the week. You couldn't give me one day of your obedience."

"I am not your fucking pet," I growl back.

"You're my fucking son, and I expect you to act like it."

"Right ..." I scoff. "The same way you've been behaving as a proper dad, you mean?"

"Fuck," Kai grits. "For fuck's sake, just apologize and be done with it."

"No."

I'm not going to sit here and pretend we're holy when we're not.

"You already made up your mind," I tell my dad. "You don't need me here."

When I get up, he growls, "Sit. Down."

I slowly back down again even though I hate listening to anyone, let alone him. But if I don't ... he'll make me.

"Our family was built on trust," he says.

"Lies."

"And I will not have you disobey me."

"They're drug-dealing murderers."

"So are we!" Kai interrupts. "Don't you understand? This is why he picked me and not you. Killing is part of the deal. That's the price we pay for the life we live."

"For you," I say, folding my arms. "And if that's the price you want to pay, you can keep all of it. I don't fucking want it."

My father sucks in a breath.

"Kai. Leave. I want to talk to Ares alone."

***

Two years ago

"Slit his throat."

I stare at the man between my feet, cowering in fear and murmuring the words of God.

My father's powerful gaze bares my soul.

"Mi niño, we don't have all night. He needs to die. Now."

I push the knife into his neck.

"Please. Don't do this," the man begs. "I have a wife. A child. Please."

A few roses from the bushel he was carrying on his way out of the building scatter across the pavement, one releasing a petal which flies off in the wind.

"Ares …" My father's voice echoes through the streets. "Time is running out."

"Why him?" I ask.

"He ruined a great evening with poor customer service for one of my associates," my father replies. "They were not happy, and neither am I because now I'm the one who disappointed my associate … and *he* will pay the price."

Right.

One bad review from the wrong person will be the death of the man beneath me.

"Please, don't kill me," the man begs, tugging at the conscience I didn't think I'd still have. "I haven't done anything."

He's right.

He's an innocent man who chose the wrong day to cross our path.

Is this the fate he deserves?

"Do it," my father rasps.

"Told you he couldn't do it," Kai says.

"Shut up," I quip.

"You know what's at stake here, Ares," my father says. "My legacy could be yours ... all you have to do is take it by taking his life."

A life in exchange for power.

But all I hear are the whimpers of the man beneath me. "Please ..."

His begging is as sharp as the knife in my hand.

"Ares! Do you want the position or not?" my father growls. "¡Hazlo ya!"

I lift the knife and hold it above my head, watching the man's last piteous gaze fall upon me.

And I break.

***

Present

Kai glances at me. "Stop going against him," he whispers to me.

"You have your Phantoms. You have your future. Go get it, then," I tell him.

"Kai," my father says sternly.

Kai sighs out loud and gets up, glancing once more at me before he leaves the room.

CLICK.

My father locks the door to his office.

"I'm going to give you one more chance," he says. "Apologize to Mr. Ferry."

And I look him dead in the eye, knowing full well what the consequences will be, as I say, "No."

I've killed men for this. I have killed for the privilege to look my father in the eyes and deny him the one thing he wants.

Obedience.

To be a trafficker, a drug dealer, a killer without a conscience.

But I will never, ever give him what he wants.

Even if it costs me my goddamn sanity.

THIRTY SEVEN

Crystal

I've been checking all the windows in my room, but there's no way to break out of them. The door is locked, and the bathroom leads nowhere. I've been trying to find a way to escape all day without any luck. Not even my knife helped to crack open the windows or the door.

Being cooped up in here all by myself has driven me insane to the point where I push my ear against the door every time someone walks by, hoping to catch something important.

I already dressed myself in a simple pair of leggings and a gray tee on the off chance that someone might enter my room, and to my surprise, all the clothes fit. It's almost as if Ares prepared for my arrival.

I've seen the sun rise and the sun set through the same window, which means I've already been here a whole day, missing out on class. I have no clue what time it is, as my room doesn't have a clock, but it's definitely dark outside.

The strawberries only eased my hunger a little bit, but I'm too stubborn to ask for more even though my stomach is growling. I've been drinking water from the tap to make sure I feel full enough not

273

to start begging because that sure as hell is lowest on my to-do list.

I'm so angry, I could scream.

Fuck Ares.

How dare he do this to me?

I pick up the leftover bowl and throw it at the wall out of frustration, shattering it into a million pieces.

But my screams and ragged breath stop as my eyes fall on something lying underneath the bowl.

A key card?

I grab it and swipe the door, and it opens.

Holy shit.

I tuck the key card and my knife into my pocket and swiftly open the door to look around and see if anyone waits to pummel me down, but luckily, I'm all alone. I peer downstairs over the banister and see no trace of the party I was dragged out of after they fucked me in front of a whole damn crowd.

My cheeks flush from the memory, so I swiftly walk away through the hallways of this old, poorly lit mansion. I swipe my card along all the doors, but none of them open, and I wonder why.

Odd. Does this key only open my door?

I sneak downstairs and look around to make sure I'm alone before I rush to the front door and swipe it, but of course that won't work either.

I back away, but when I hear voices in the kitchen, I panic and run back upstairs.

I hide behind a sensual woman's statue as two Tartarus boys walk past me, clutching a bag of chips and drinks as they make their way to a room in the back of the middle hallway, where there's a theater room complete with red seats and an actual movie screen.

Damn. If I wasn't being kept as a prisoner, I'd almost want to check it out.

I sneak away, but when I hear more ruckus from both ends of the hallway, I panic and head into the first open room I find, locking myself inside.

The room is completely covered in royal green, and I gawk my eyes out at all the priceless artwork in this room. Blaine sure has expensive taste, that's for sure. I touch a statue, and it almost seems too perfect to be real, so beautifully sculpted it's as if I'm touching the hand of God himself.

Suddenly, two hands land on my shoulders, and a cold draft hits my face.

"Don't be scared. It's me." Blaine's soothing voice almost lulls me into a relaxed state.

Almost.

"I promise I won't hurt you," he whispers into my ear.

My hand slowly dips down into my pocket to clutch my knife. "I can't promise the same."

I swiftly pull it out, spin around on my heels, and point it at his neck. But I pause near his vein as he swallows, unwavering in his stance as he hovers over me.

He's a born fighter, an expert at the katana, so he should've dodged that perfectly.

Why doesn't he move?

"You gave me that key card, didn't you?" I ask, my eyes trailing down his naked pecs all the way down his thick red robes.

"To find me," he says.

"Why?" That's the only thing I manage to whisper before my throat clamps up.

"I know you won't hurt me," he says, his voice cracking too. "Even though you want to."

"You let them use me," I grit.

His eyes are hard to look at, but he doesn't look away. "I warned you they would come for you."

"You made me believe you'd protect me," I say. "But when it came to it, you bent to his will and did exactly what he wanted. I trusted you." The anger twists my voice.

"Darling—"

"No. Don't *darling* me. You're the one who taught me how to fight. Why? Why wouldn't you fight back against him?"

"I tried to warn you ... I am bound to Ares," he says, cupping my face. "If I could, I would take your place in an instant if it would ease the burden."

"You were there too, licking me ... fucking Caleb." A blush creeps onto my cheeks from the mere memory, and I can't shake it off. "I didn't think you'd actually do it."

"Ares's punishments are always debasing. It's one of the few things he actually enjoys."

I wince. "That's messed up."

He chuckles even though I have a literal knife to his throat right

275

now. "You could put it like that ... But aren't we all?"

"You all, not me," I say.

A coy smile tips up his lips. "Oh, is that why you were so wet for all of us? Because you weren't just as messed up?"

My eyes widen, and rage takes over as I push the knife farther into his neck, making him bleed, and I lick my lips at the sight of his blood dripping down.

I haven't come this close to death since my father ...

This close to losing control.

And something about that scares me so much that my hand begins to shake.

Because I don't want to hurt *him*.

"Is this all I am to you all now? A prisoner?"

He sighs. "That's what *he* wants, yes."

I shake my head. "After I already gave him what he wants, he still takes more and more."

"Ares will never have enough of you now that he has you."

"Why?"

"Well, your mother started dating Caleb's father, and he doesn't like that, so Ares—"

"I know that. I know he doesn't want me to become family. But why does Ares care? All he seems to want to do is punish Caleb for touching me."

He swallows, almost as if he has to restrain himself not to say too much. "Ares ... has anger and trust issues. Caleb is the only one he confides in. And now that you've beguiled them ..."

"I'm a threat," I mutter, thinking it through. "You're bound to Ares. So then why did you give me this knife?"

"Because you deserve to be in control of your own fate despite his villainous ways," he says. His tongue darts out to wet his lips. "But it changes nothing about my feelings for you. I crave you. Madly. Deeply. Beyond any doubt."

I swallow away the lump in my throat and turn around so I don't have to look him in the eyes.

But the mirror in front of me forces me to face my own demise.

Those same familiar hands wrap around my shoulders again, making me want to lean into him.

"You are so beautiful, Crystal," he says. "Like a goddess of vengeance."

276

He leans in to plant the softest of kisses on my neck, stealing my breath.

"Would it be so wrong to be loved by someone like me?" he mutters. "To be ours?"

"Do you think I could ever be more than a toy?"

He chuckles softly. "I wouldn't mind it if you stayed our filthy plaything forever." His eyes connect with mine through the mirror. "You would have us all on our knees."

He slowly hovers his hands over my face, and I'm apprehensive.

"You fear me," he whispers.

"How could I not, knowing what you're capable of?"

He groans. "I will do anything to regain your trust."

Am I that important to him?

"How?"

He backs away slowly. "Close your eyes."

Even though my brain tells me not to, my heart screams to listen, so I do.

"Stay there."

My breathing is ragged as I'm left alone in the dark.

After a few shuffles, I hear something slide.

CLICK! CLICK!

"Now open your eyes and look at me."

When I turn around, he's on the bed, the robe draped by his side, leaving only his boxers, his wrists bound to the poles at each edge with metal cuffs. Around his neck is a thick leather band with a metal chain dangling from the ring.

THIRTY EIGHT

Blaine

"Every inch of me is built to kill, whether it's hearts or bodies … but your fear is the last thing I crave," I rasp. "If I cannot take your fear … then I will offer myself to you out of my own free will. Use me to your heart's content like we have used you. Hurt me. Choke me. Fuck me. Kill me. Whatever your desire, I will surrender to it." I suck in a breath as she gasps. "I have chained my life to Ares, but my heart belongs to you."

I've tried so hard to play by the rules, but I can no longer resist her.

She's been used, degraded, completely crushed, and still smiled through it all.

There has never been someone I've so deeply wished to take my soul than for her to make it her own. And if this will be my undoing, then so be it.

She thinks she is the weak one, but I am defenseless when it comes to her.

Her nostrils flare, and she turns around to look at my room, wandering about, before she sits on my bed and stares at me.

My cock bobs up and down from the sheer amount of lust in her

278

eyes.

"You want to be mine?" she asks.

She crawls farther onto the bed, onto me.

"Make me your pawn," I reply.

"You won't kill him for me," she says, still clutching that knife of hers as she reaches me. "But you trained me and guided me to make it happen?"

When she's finally hovering over my face, my boxers strain from my hardened cock. "Use me as your angel of vengeance, darling."

The smirk that slowly forms on her face is something else.

My God.

She lifts herself and sits down on my package, and my eyes nearly roll into the back of my head from the way she feels on top of me. "Fine, then. Beg."

Oh fuck me.

There's never been anything sexier than a girl as innocent as her saying those words to me.

I have no qualms about doing whatever she wants. "Please …"

She slowly gyrates on top of my dick, and it gets me insane within no time.

"F-fuck …" I groan.

"You want this?" she asks, rolling her hips on top of me.

"Yes, please, give it to me," I whimper.

She grips the pillow underneath my head and throws it over my face.

"You want *this*?" she reiterates.

"Yes," I repeat through the fabric even though I can't breathe.

Oxygen escapes me, and I feel myself drifting away into the madness of my own lust and desires as she continues to gyrate on top of me until my boxers are wet with precum.

When she finally removes the pillow, I gasp for air, only for her lips to smother me instead. I moan against her mouth, kissing her back, but she lifts her lips and hovers so closely above them that I want to inch closer.

"You are insane," she mutters.

I chuckle. "Aren't we all?"

"I'm not," she says.

"Aren't you?" I reply as she gyrates around. "Yet you were so wet for us when we toyed with you during that party."

Her eyes narrow, and she leans up to grasp the chain. She yanks it until the leather straps are tightened into my skin, partially cutting off my breathing again.

"F-fuck," I grit when the chain finally stops choking me. "All this to convince me of a lie. You can just admit you enjoyed it."

She swallows. "It's wrong."

"Yes …" I say, sucking in the oxygen like I won't have another chance. "But wrong can also feel so goddamn good. And what I felt in there, licking you out, even if it was in front of all those people, was nothing short of amazing."

She inches away from me and sits down on my knees, only to rip down my boxers and free my hard-on, which bounces up and down.

She pulls her shirt over her head, and I gawk at those beautiful, perky tits of hers. My wrists strain against the shackles, desperate to touch her.

"You licked me, made me suck your cock …" she murmurs. "And then you fucked Caleb because he told you to."

I snort. "Risk of the trade. Besides, I swing all the ways. And I quite liked fucking him and putting him in his place."

The filthy smirk that slowly trickles onto her face makes my heart throb.

A devil exists underneath that angelic mask of hers.

I just have to coax it out.

She rubs her lips together to hide a giggle. "He did deserve it."

"Getting a little vindictive there, darling?" I wink. "The wish for violence looks good on you."

She grabs the pillow again and shoves it over my face.

"Are you ready to beg for mercy?"

I mumble, "Yes!"

"You really are easy," she says, pulling it away again.

"I told you I wasn't a threat to you."

"Yet you're friends with those who are." She huffs, and she tickles my shaft to the point where it bobs up and down. "You obey their commands when they tell you to fuck me raw."

"I would obey you too if you'd let me," I mutter, moaning when the top of her finger flicks against the tip of my length.

"You're that desperate for me?" she murmurs.

"You don't even wanna know how badly … But I held myself back for you."

"Why me?" she asks.

"Because …" I strain against my restraints, almost wishing I hadn't tied myself up just so I could caress her. "You might not believe it, but you hold power over people with your smile alone."

"And now you're tied up in your own bed, subjected to my every whim," she muses.

A smile forms on my face.

She leans up, pushing out her tits as her hand dips between her thighs to touch herself.

"This is what you want so badly?" she asks.

"Fuck yes," I beg, salivating at the mouth when she puts her hands down her leggings and starts rubbing herself right in front of me. She pulls down her leggings slowly, creating a kind of angst in me I never thought I could feel.

She toys with my shaft with her other hand, amused by how easily I can be manipulated. But she doesn't realize the kind of power she holds … and the fact that I don't let just anyone do this to me.

"What do you want from me, then?" she asks. "And what are you willing to give to me in return?"

"I want to fuck you so badly," I groan when she reaches the tip. "I'll do anything. Whatever you want, it's yours."

"*Anything?*" She licks her lips and pulls her hands away, then lifts her hips to hover over my dick, but without settling down, and my God, is it pure torture.

"Anything you desire."

"Give me the key card to the entire house."

I groan with frustration. "Ares will kill me."

"He already will if he finds out you fucked me without him present."

She's got me there.

But fuck, I can't even concentrate because her pussy lips are right there near the tip, and I'm so damn eager, but she keeps leaning away just out of reach.

"Please …" I whimper, my cock bobbing up and down.

Her finger trails down my chest, wet pussy dripping all over me. "You will give me the key card when we're done?"

"Fine, yes, I will give you the key. Now please, darling. Give it to me."

When she finally dips her hips down, my head tilts back, and I let out a moan I've never even heard before.

"Oh …" She moans too, sinking deeper and deeper down my shaft. "You're so … thick."

My dick throbs inside her, not just from the way she feels but also from the words she just said.

"Your pussy can handle it," I reply with a wicked grin on my face.

She smirks and grabs the pillow, smothering me again.

I splutter and cough, sucking in the air, but the thrill of losing my breath is exhilarating. And when she pushes down to the base, I nearly lose myself in the moment.

She tears the pillow away again, and my nostrils suck in the oxygen like they're addicted. And you know what? Maybe I fucking am.

"Don't get cocky now," she says, lifting her hips.

"How could I not when I have you on my lap?" I respond.

Another blush forms on her cheeks, and she grips the pillow again, but she's not just using it to choke me. She's using it to hide her own feelings.

"Wait," I say.

"What?" She holds up the pillow. "Thought you wanted this?"

"I do, but …" I sigh. "God, I wish I could touch you right now."

Her eyes narrow. "Then why did you tie yourself up?"

I swallow, gazing at my own dripping dick, which is begging to be fucked. But I know if I lie now to get it over with, she'll never give herself to me. "I tied myself up because you looked at me with such fear in your eyes … and I finally realized why."

She frowns.

"You like me. And it scares you."

Her eyes widen in shock, and my heart skips a beat.

"It's okay to admit it," I say, whimpering when she slides over my tip with her pussy. "It's only natural to fall for someone as handsome as me."

Her jaw drops. "Why you—" She smothers me with the pillow again, shoving it into my face so hard I truly can't breathe, and fuck me, is it making me want to spurt my load all over this room.

When she pulls it away again, I feel like I'm sucking in a breath for years. "Have you always been this arrogant?"

"Darling, what else do I have to offer but my looks and charm?"

"Do you really think that's the only thing?" she says, tilting her head.

"My dick," I groan. "I can offer you that."

She rolls her eyes. "You can fight. You're honest. You're reliable. Or you were ..."

"Reliable when you know how to twist me around your finger," I respond, raising a brow. "Now let me feel you, darling," I groan, twisting around. "Before I rip through these chains."

She giggles and settles back down on the tip, sliding in deeper and deeper, each time faster than before, the feeling heavenly and beyond this world. When I first met her, I wondered why those boys were obsessed with her, but I get it now.

"F-fuck, just like that," I groan.

She rolls her hips around, and her hand dips between her thighs. She touches herself while riding me, and my wrists strain against the metal that holds me down.

Why did I think this was a good idea? God, I want to run my fingers down her body so badly.

"Hmm ... you like when I touch myself, don't you?" she murmurs, circling her clit.

"Oh, fuck yes," I reply, biting my lip but not too harsh because I don't want to break the skin and destroy my pretty lips.

"More than you like touching me?"

She pulls the chain around my neck, and it tightens the noose.

I gulp. "I have no choice."

"Right ... because you wanted to tie yourself up to protect me," she says, abruptly stopping to lean in and hover over my lips so dangerously close I can almost taste her. "But haven't I told you ..." Her lips brush mine, and I'm nearly close enough to kiss her. Just barely, and she knows. She's purposely drawing out my hunger, and fuck me, am I famished for those beautiful lips.

Her eyes burst open just to watch me suffer. "I'm not scared of anyone."

She grabs the pillow and stuffs it into my face, but I can still feel her ride me, still feel her pussy contract, still hear her fingers flick that wet clit.

Her moans reverberate through the room and my ears, and my breathing grows rapid while she uses me to her heart's content. I can't breathe, can't even think, as her pussy begins to contract around my shaft, and her body begins to shake on top of me.

But I am unable to see the beauty of her last moan as she comes all over my cock.

My dick pulsates inside her, cum shooting out along with my stifled moans, and I almost faint from sheer exhaustion.

She pulls the pillow away just in time, and my eyelids rapidly blink like a wild animal after it's been hunted in the dark. She's already lifted herself off me, but I can't focus on anything as the only thing I see are tits right up in my face. I tilt my head, desperate to lick her nipples, but she's just out of reach as she leans over to grab something off my nightstand ... and out of the first drawer.

My eyes widen.

Her phone.

Fuck, I forgot it was there.

She leans back and hovers near my ear, her breath sending goose bumps down my spine all over, as she whispers, "I hope you enjoyed the nonexistent show."

My eyes narrow, but she still gets off me, and I'm left utterly confused.

"Wait, what? That was it?" I gasp.

She flaunts the key card between two fingers, and my heart shatters into tiny pieces.

"You tricked me," I say, feeling wounded.

"I gave you what you gave me," she muses, winking. "A betrayal for a betrayal."

I let out an audible gasp.

When she waltzes off, I put all my weight into tearing at the metal around my wrists. "Wait. You're not just going to leave me here, are you?"

She pauses, staring at the door, the aura surrounding her suddenly shifting into an arctic ice, scaring even me. "Are you going to help me kill Ares?" Even her voice has changed.

"I *cannot*. You know why."

"Then you're just as much of a prisoner in this house as I am," she says, marching out the door.

Holy shit, have I underestimated her.

Good God. What a girl.

Now I'm definitely rooting for her to kill him ...

Before he kills me when he finds me like this.

But damn, it was worth every second.

THIRTY NINE

CALEB

I take in a deep breath and knock on her door. "Crystal?"

There's no response, and I didn't expect her to welcome me in with open arms either, but the silence beyond this door is telling.

"Crystal, I want to talk," I say.

I knock a few more times.

I would've half expected her to have thrown the furniture by now, but it's completely quiet.

Suspicious.

I fish my key card from my pocket and open the door, peeking inside with my foot jammed against the door in case she tries to ambush me.

But there's not a movement in sight.

I push the door open farther and check her room. "Crystal? Where are you?"

Her blanket has been thrown over and her bed is empty, the closet raided. Her bathroom door is unlocked, and there doesn't appear to be anyone inside.

My heart begins to race.

She's gone.

Fuck!

If I tell Ares, he'll destroy the goddamn campus just to find her.

I bust out the door and storm toward Blaine's room down the hallway. Maybe he took her for his own selfish interests despite the warnings Ares gave.

"Blaine!" I yell before I burst into his room unannounced, but I come to a screeching halt the moment I spot him lying in his bed with a chain around his neck, both wrists locked to his bed, and a deflated cock clearly covered in cum.

My jaw drops.

"A little help, darling?"

Fucking hell.

"What the f—Did you do this yourself? How?" I ask, confused as fuck by the scene in front of me.

I always thought he was the dominant one when it came to his flings, but maybe I was wrong.

"It's easy to unlock them. The key is on the nightstand," Blaine says, nodding at it.

There's no way he would let just anyone tie him up and leave him here.

My jaw tenses. "She was here, wasn't she?"

He smirks. "Should I lie or tell you the truth? Either way, it seems like I'll be dead."

Damn right, he is.

My fist balls. "Where is she?"

"She took my master key card and her phone," he replies, shrugging. "Sorry."

My eyes widen.

She's escaped.

I turn around and run off.

"Hey, aren't you going to help me get out of here?" Blaine yells, but I pay no attention to it as I rush downstairs.

Ares will deal with him later. First, I gotta find her and get her back before he realizes she's gone.

I grasp my car keys and storm out the door, headed straight for my car. I press a button to open the gates to the property before I hop inside and hit the gas. The tires screech as I dial her number and wait until she picks up, but of course she won't.

"Pick up, goddammit! Don't you know what's at stake here?" I growl after the beep. "Where are you?"

My car veers around the corner, barely avoiding the cliff near the school's gates, and I race down the mountain while I smash my fingers onto my phone. Lucky for me, I was fucking prepared for when she'd escape my grasp. I had Blaine install a tracking app on her phone, and it'd better be his saving grace, or I swear to God I will go in there and strangle him with his own cock.

I tap the app and wait until it does its work, impatiently hitting the gas until it finally finds her location. The street outside her mom's house.

Got her.

I race down the mountain, not giving a shit about oncoming traffic as I speed through a red light. All this fighting death only gets me hard.

Does she really not understand what she's messing with here?

She can't save her mother from us just as much as she can't save herself.

My car swerves through the streets as I turn a corner and head for her mother's home. Time is ticking, and there's no time to waste. If she so much as even speaks a single syllable to her mother about what we've done …

Fuck. If only Blaine hadn't been a goddamn weak link.

I slam my hands onto the steering wheel in anger. The image of him lying there in his own cum is really seared into my mind.

What the fuck did he do with her?

Did she mess with his head and then chain him to his bed?

And why was he the one who was tied up?

I swallow away the lump in my throat, pushing the thoughts away. There's no answer to them anyway, not until I find her, and I fucking will.

When I finally get to the street her mother's house is on, the rage takes hold of my heart. Crystal's right there, a mere two houses away.

I push the pedal and race until I finally catch up with her, swerving across the lawn until the car comes to a full stop in a sideways position, blocking her path.

"What the f—" She jumps back and gawks at the car. "Caleb?"

I push open the passenger's door and bark, "Get in."

Her face contorts, and she clutches the same little bag she brought to the party. "No."

"Do I look like I'm up for bargaining?" I growl. "You took our fucking deal. You do what we say."

"I don't fucking care."

She tries to pass by my car, so I open my door and jump out to block her way. "No. You're not going to her house. You're not going to talk to her. You're not going to do anything except sit your ass down in my car, or so help me God … I will fucking end it all myself."

Her pupils dilate. "What?"

I point at the passenger seat, allowing her one last chance to make the right choice. "Get in the car. Now."

She shudders in place, glancing briefly at her mother's door before lowering her gaze.

"I needed to know she was okay," she says, tears welling up in her eyes. "That she could be safe regardless of my choices."

I bite my tongue, but the strain to control my emotions is too much even for me as she unravels in front of me.

Even after escaping from hell, she first chooses to save the one person she wants to save at all costs, even if she has to risk her life doing so.

And something about that breaks the resolve inside my heart.

As the tears begin to flow down her cheeks, I let out a sigh before I wrap my arms around her and pull her into my embrace.

***

Crystal

Caleb's hug comes so out of the blue, I don't know what to do as his arms envelop me. I just stand there with eyes wide open and tears rolling down my face.

Why would he hug me? I thought he didn't care?

His embrace feels so warm that I sink into it, not giving a shit that it's the guy who's been on my ass since day one.

"You have to forget about her. Forget she exists, for both your sake and hers."

For a moment there, I almost believed something other than resentment could exist.

My brain finally finds its sanity again, and I push him away from

288

me. "No. You're insane. She's my mother. I love her."

"If you love her enough, you'll leave with me. Right now."

I frown, glaring at him and the Aston Martin he recklessly drove across her lawn just to stop me. "You came all this way to stop me from talking to her. Are you scared I'll reveal your dirty secret?" I look up at him with disdain. "Don't want your dad to know all about the filthy shit you've been up to with his step—"

He shoves his hand against my mouth, calloused, tattooed fingers pinching my cheeks.

"Don't. Don't say that fucking word out loud."

I bite his finger, and he swiftly retracts, shaking his hand. "Goddammit, woman."

"I'm not your fucking woman. And I can say whatever the hell I want to whoever the hell I want."

"You're not the shy girl I once pegged you as, are you?" he rebukes.

"I never said I was," I retort.

"You just make people believe you are."

I slam my lips shut while his tip up into a lukewarm smile. "Guess I'm not the only one keeping secrets."

"Listen here, asshole." I point my finger at his chest. "I didn't go through all that effort to escape just to have you casually pick me up at my mom's front door and put me back in that prison you call a room."

"And when the fuck did I say I was going to do that?" he says, tilting his head before gripping my finger, his warm hand making me all too aware of just how comforting that hug he just gave me felt. And how badly I want to crush his skull underneath the tires of his own car for making me feel like I needed it.

"Then why did you come?"

"Because I can't let you do this. I can't let you blow it all up. Your life is not the only one at stake here."

"You're the one who's been threatening her," I grit.

"You think I'm the one you should be scared of?" he retorts.

I frown, but slowly, it begins to dawn on me. "Ares ..."

Caleb's face darkens, confirming my suspicions, and my jaw drops.

"Ares? Why would Ares want to keep me away from my mom? Why would he care?"

"Because he *wants* you."

My whole body suddenly feels cold as ice. "He's using my mom as leverage to keep me as a prisoner."

Caleb slowly nods. "I told you I wasn't the worst thing that could happen to you."

I jerk my finger free from Caleb's grip. "Why? Just because your father wanted to marry my mother, I deserve to be treated like a toy?"

When he doesn't say a word, I slap him. Hard. And he doesn't even flinch.

He just stands there and takes it … like it does nothing to him.

Or maybe the exact opposite, I can't tell at this point.

I slap him again. "You asshole!" When he doesn't respond, I add, "Fucking say something, dammit! Why would it matter if your father fell in love with someone? My mother isn't trying to steal your goddamn fortune. She just wants to be happy." More tears sting my eyes, but I slap him once more until his cheeks are red. "My mother deserves to be happy. My father would've wanted her to be."

I sniff and push back more tears, but the way Caleb gazes at me completely catches me off guard. The complete and utter distraught look in his eyes undoes me.

"Your father?" he mutters, his face contorting.

"He's dead," I growl, ignoring the shock riddling his face. I've seen that look of surprise and pity so many times before that it does nothing to me anymore. "My mother is all I have left. I wished for so long she'd smile again. Why are you so desperate to destroy their relationship that you'd try to ruin my life over it?"

His teeth grind together, but then his hand rises, and I almost expect a slap back.

Instead, he picks up one of my leftover tears on his thumb, caressing my cheek so softly my breath falters.

Suddenly, he grips my arm and shoves me into the car.

"Stay," he growls before he opens the driver's side and gets in, locking both doors.

"What are you doing?" I ask.

"You want to know why? I'll fucking show you why." He starts the car and veers across the street, plowing through my mother's freshly mowed lawn, destroying it in the process as slices of dirt and grass are chucked in the air.

"My mom's going to be pissed when she finds her front yard in the morning," I say.

"Trust me, she'd be much more pissed if she found a gun in her face instead," he replies.

I stare at him in shock as he continues to drive. "You'd actually kill her?"

"What makes you think I was talking about me?"

I slam my lips shut and look out the window, angry that he'd found me in the first place. I didn't tell anyone, not even Blaine.

"How the hell did you find me anyway?" I ask after a while.

"I had Blaine install a tracker on your phone."

I snort, shaking my head. "Of course, you did."

"You think that's funny?"

"Of course. Everything's a fucking game to you guys."

"This ain't no fucking game, Crystal," he growls. "I'm trying to keep you alive."

"Yeah, well you're doing a damn bad job at it," I say, pointing at the red light he just ignored. When a truck shoots right past our rear while honking, I scream, "Look out!"

The car veers sideways to avoid another oncoming car, and I look at him, wondering if he's gone insane or if he has a death wish. Maybe both.

He bites his lip and swerves from left to right, headed for a direction unknown to me, and that's what scares me the most. The only thing I know for sure is that we're not going back up the hill to Spine Ridge U, which means he won't put me back in that room like a bird in a cage. At least for now.

"Where are you taking me?" I ask.

He races around the curves of the road, narrowly escaping a bin.

"You'll see."

But every time I glance at him, I can't help but trail my eyes down his body, remembering just how good it felt when he licked me while Ares fucked me. And something tells me he's thinking about it too, judging from how his bulge just grew.

He's glancing at me with his provocative eyes, and I swiftly look away.

A vehicle approaches us from the side, and he makes no attempt to avoid it, making me scream once more. "Caleb!"

He swerves just in time, but his cock twitches again, and he groans

291

in frustration … or is it excitement?

"You're getting hard," I say. "Because you're putting me in danger?"

He shakes his head, gripping the steering wheel tightly. "Because I'm putting myself in danger. It makes me feel alive."

My lips part to let out a gasp, but nothing escapes because the shock is too great.

Putting himself in danger? As in … the thought of getting killed turns him on?

The car slips on the streets as we make our way downtown toward a tall skyscraper. But when it finally comes to a stop, I feel like I've been tumbled through a washer because my hair is definitely sticking to my sweaty body.

"Jesus," I mutter.

He gets out and taps on the hood. "We're here."

He walks toward a building and looks at me over his shoulder as though he's waiting for me to follow him, so I open the door and hop out too.

The building looks intimidating from up close. I wonder what's inside.

"C'mon," he says, opening the door.

Downstairs is a lobby, and a woman at the front desk greets him. "Hello, Mr. Preston. Back for the usual check-in with—"

"Tell the staff to leave. I need twenty minutes undisturbed," he interjects, waltzing to the elevator.

Undisturbed … with who?

I get inside too even though his penetrative stare makes me feel anything but comfortable while stuck together in an elevator. He pulls out a very peculiar key card and holds it in front of a pad, then presses a button. The doors close, and the silence is overwhelming as we go up and up and up, seemingly unending. And all I can do is listen to his breathing grow more rapid with every level we pass, as though he's mentally preparing himself for what's to come.

"What's up there?" I ask, but he doesn't answer until the elevator comes to a stop.

He clears his throat. "You asked me why I didn't want my father dating your mother. I'll show you."

There's a long hallway up ahead filled with doors, each leading to a numbered room, and I follow him inside.

"What is this place?"

"One of my father's many properties," he says. "He rents out the rooms. Except this floor."

"What's on this floor?" I ask, gulping when he glances at me over his shoulder without answering my question.

He stops in front of a door at the end of the hallway and holds the key card in front of another pad. Something beeps, and a lock springs loose. He pushes down the handle and heads inside.

It's a two-part home, one bathroom, one bedroom, and a small kitchen barely large enough to make a coffee or a snack. To my right is a round beige leather chair, and to my left, a small table with two seats. But what draws in my eyes is the big bed in the middle of the room and all the machinery beside it beeping and churning away.

In the bed lies a woman with skin so pale it nearly turns translucent, her thin, brittle hair lying on top of her shoulders as her hands rest beside her lifeless body. Tubes go in her veins, and another one is connected to her mouth, pushing oxygen in and out to her lungs.

"Who ... who is that?" I mutter.

My breathing falters as Caleb sits on the bed and grabs her hand. "My mom."

CALEB

I squeeze my mom's hand tightly even though it's cold to the touch. Some part of me feels like maybe if I squeeze hard enough, she might feel it.

I stare at her lifeless body in the bed. Every day, her skin sheds more and more, like the bark on a tree flaking off as it's slowly deprived of nutrients. A shell of a once magnificent tree that crowned the forest and gave so much to so many.

A tear wells up in my eyes, but I push it away.

I've already given up on the idea that she'll ever remember me.

That time has long since passed.

All that remains now is a wake. Day in, day out. Until she slowly withers away.

I lift my head and look at the girl standing in the door opening. The girl who forced her way into my life … the girl who invaded every corner of my mind until there was no escaping her.

Her eyes are filled with so much compassion it's sickening, and it makes me want to scream.

But that would only push her further away from me.

And the thought of losing her too would drive me insane.

All this time, I've been hanging on by a thread.

And her seeing my world for what it truly is ... will unravel me.

***

I stare at him, heart struck with so many emotions I can't utter a single syllable.

Tears well up in my eyes, but I push them away.

It wouldn't be right to cry, but damn, it has never been harder to keep them at bay.

"This is why I didn't want your mother to be with my dad," he says, his voice fluctuating in tone from all the pent-up emotions. "Somewhere in there, inside that fainting husk, is a living, breathing human being." He pauses, the weight of his emotions sinking into each word like a stone in the pond of my soul, leaving ripples in its wake. "Waiting for her family that no longer exists."

I swallow.

What words would do justice to this kind of pain? There are none.

This is the visceral suffering of those who have experienced grief. And even though his mother is still alive by a hair, she's more a ghost than a person. Death has already claimed her just like it claimed my father—whether it's yesterday, today, or tomorrow, a future for them in our lives no longer exists.

No wonder Caleb broke the second I told him about my father.

This is what he's been hiding. This is the secret that's torn him apart at the seam.

And even though I once believed I hated him, the idea that I ever could seems so cruel right now.

All of his anger, all of the revulsions, the fights ... all of it was because of this.

His mother, lying motionless in a bed, more dead than living, the last remnant he has of the woman who once called him her baby.

How could my heart not ache for him?

"What ... what happened to her?"

His eyes trail off to her face. "A few years ago, she had a stroke." He swallows. "She never recovered. Even though a part of her may still be in there ... her mind has long since left this world. All that remains is her body." He pushes away the hair off her face so gently it cracks what little resistance I had left. "But I can't say goodbye. Not yet."

He touches the ring on her finger.

"My father swore he wouldn't abandon her," he says, his voice darkening. "He *swore*."

"They're still ... married?" I mutter.

He nods, the silence that follows deafening.

He gets up, slowly walking toward me with a hazy look on his face, stopping mere inches in front of me. "My father hid her in this building to conceal what happened to her from the outside world. Couldn't face his own damn CFO and tell him the truth. He's been pretending she's sick and unable to show her face, but we both know better," he says, swallowing. "But even he couldn't pull the plug. Not while there was still some hope." His brows draw together as his eyes slowly leer up and bore into mine. "Until my father saw your mother and decided he would forget. Forget my mother ever existed."

"No," I say, shaking my head. "He wouldn't forget her."

"He's still fucking married, and he doesn't even care," he spits. "He's soiled her memory. My mother. She's in there." He points at the body being ventilated. "She's waiting on him, and he abandoned her."

"You're angry," I say, trying to reason with him.

"Of course, I fucking am!" He grabs the vase filled with fresh flowers standing on a pedestal near the door and chucks it at the wall, shattering it into a million pieces. "There is nothing left for me to fight for! *Nothing!*"

"Nothing?" My brows furrow together.

Even if he can't think of anything, there must be something ...

"All I have ... all I want, so desperately," he says, suddenly gripping my face with both hands. "Doesn't want me back."

My lips part in shock.

He ... wants me?

As more than just a plaything?

He releases me and saunters away, staring out the window wistfully.

"You actually ... *want* me?"

He makes a tsk sound. "Didn't you hear Ares?"

"I thought you were just playing games, that it was just my body, but ... it isn't, is it?"

He tilts his head, the forlorn look in his eyes so striking it makes me want to run over to him and kiss him.

But something about the violence in his eyes stops me.

"I thought I had to hate you," he says, snorting before shaking his head. "That it would make it easier to shut you out."

"But you said it was because Ares—"

"Ares has always been there for me. *Always*," he interjects. "And then he set his eyes on you. How was I supposed to feel?"

It feels like stone upon stone is thrown. "Wait, you ... were jealous of him?"

"Of *you*." He pauses.

That's why he was so aggressive with me even though I hadn't done anything to him?

"And then eventually him ..."

Both of us?

Caleb's Adam's apple rises and falls. "But Ares always gets what he wants. That is a fact."

I shake my head. "He hasn't gotten me."

"Hasn't he?"

I swallow, trying to keep my mind from spinning.

"When he plays with you, doesn't it make your heart throb and your head dizzy?" he says, biting his bottom lip, drawing in his piercing. "When you hate so deeply, doesn't it make you loathe the very thought of loving someone?"

"Yes, but—" I choke on my own words.

Because I understand what he's trying to tell me now ...

That my own feelings for Ares mirror Caleb's for me.

Oh God.

I can't breathe.

"Your mother got in the way. So I did what I did best. Destroy," he says, his voice gritty, unhinged. "Destroy every happy thought, every good emotion, every inch of your goddamn angelic soul just so I could tell myself I didn't desire it more than anything. Because how could I possibly desire someone who's supposed to become my step—"

"Don't." I interrupt. "Don't say that word."

He leans away from the window, the sunlight casting a beam of light on half his face, like an angel shot an arrow straight from heaven, and it strips me bare of everything I thought I knew.

"Why?" he asks. "Does the thought scare you as much as it scares me?" His tongue darts out. "After all the filthy, fucked-up, delicious fucking shit we did, does the thought of losing what we have ruin you?"

I swallow down the lump in my throat, wondering if there was ever a world out there where we could've been lovers instead.

Still, he turns and steps closer and closer while I back away into the door, leaving no place left to go as he traps me between his arms.

"Deny it all you want, but we can both feel the electric current between us," he says, inching so close I can almost taste his futile rage. "Can you even resist?"

"I should've …" I mutter.

A devilish smirk forms on his face. "You should've run when you had the chance."

"I don't want to run anymore," I murmur.

His lips graze mine. "But you make it feel so damn good to chase you."

When his lips finally connect, it doesn't even register with me anymore that I'm supposed to hate him, that he's made me his toy, that he's tried to destroy my life all for the sake of needing me. Because I can't resist the way he kisses me with so much raw passion that it takes my breath away.

His mouth encloses mine, his sultry tongue prying open my lips until it twists around mine, and he moans into me, causing goose bumps to spread all over. He pushes me against the door, pressing his hard-on into me while licking the roof of my mouth with that pierced tongue.

And a part of me almost wants to give in. Give in to the moment, fuck all my worries away.

But I don't want to use him.

I push him off me and look him in the eyes, searching for answers I no longer have.

I thought I understood myself, that I knew exactly what I wanted and needed in this world to survive, but slowly, that steadfast part of me realizes I may have been wrong.

"Kiss me," he says. "Kiss me, Crystal. Do you even want it as much as I do?"

When I lean in, he leans back, tempting, twisting the narrative until I'm chasing his lips instead, and the smile that cracks on his face makes me want to slap him.

Suddenly, he grips my wrists and shoves me up against the door, his half-mast hazel eyes so striking it's hard to look away. "Make me believe it."

With a taunting gaze, he hovers close again, and I slam my lips right back on his.

He kisses me back with just as much fervor, claiming my mouth like it's the only thing keeping him from jumping off a goddamn cliff, and it feels powerful. Daunting. Wrecking.

To the point where I claw my way out of his grip and wrap my arms around his neck, pulling him closer into me so our two broken souls meld into one.

***

CALEB

I could no longer stop myself. I had to kiss those beautiful perky lips even though I know I'm sucking the life out of her like a goddamn soul-stealing demon from hell.

But I don't care anymore.

I need that spark, that little ounce of happiness I siphon out of her every time our lips collide.

It's the only thing that's keeping me breathing.

Keeping me sane.

The thought of her ruins me.

Destroys every inch of my sanity until I can no longer think straight, and I hate her for it.

I hate how much she's weaved her way into my life without a thought as to how easily she makes everyone around her fall for her. How easily she makes us all crave to poison her innocence.

But I hate most of all that it's driven a wedge between Ares and me. The only man who's ever understood me. The only man who's ever cared enough to be there for me.

I wanted him, and then he wanted her, so I had to make her pay.

But along the way, I fell.

I fell so hard my lungs began to crack, and the only way I could suck in the oxygen was when I was with her.

God …

God can't help me now.

I kiss her so hard it makes the tears in my soul dry up as I pour every ounce of my sadness into her. She can take it. She knows what it feels like to need something so desperately you feel like you can't live without it. What it is to grieve without grieving, to live like a shadow of oneself, to haunt the world, searching for your own goddamn soul.

She's seen death with her own damn eyes.

She knows. I can feel it in the way she kisses me back with equal desperation.

And the second she told me the truth about her father, the last ounce of hostility I was holding on to vanished.

"We have to stop," she murmurs, but I can't take my lips off hers.

I refuse. If I do, the dream will shatter, and so will I.

"No."

"Caleb."

I groan into her mouth, kissing her one last time with everything I have to give before I have to return to reality.

"Your phone."

My eyes burst open, and I tear my lips away from hers, still heady from the way she kissed me back.

But then I hear my ringtone.

I clear my throat and fish it out of my pocket, the name on the screen making chills run up and down my spine.

"Ares?" I say as I pick up.

"Open the door."

I hold my breath and look at Crystal, who definitely heard too.

She pushes down the handle and slowly cracks open the door.

Ares stands there with a phone against his ear just like me, staring us both down.

Oh fuck.

FORTY ONE

ARES

I'm surprised.

Not just him … but her too?

Did they sneak out without my knowledge?

Or is something more nefarious going on here?

I home in on her face, her round lips swollen, pink, and freshly kissed.

Fuck.

"What is she doing here?"

Crystal's pupils dilate, and Caleb steps in front of her to save her from my ire. "I brought her with me."

I never thought he'd actually have the balls to show her the truth.

But I guess he would eventually crack.

I grip the door. "So … you brought her here out of all places," I mutter. "For a second there I almost believed you let her escape."

Caleb swallows. "I was going to take her back straight away."

Crystal gawks at him.

"Right," I reply.

I stare at them both until they get the message.

"Let's go," Caleb says.

Crystal nods and follows him outside under my watchful gaze.

"How did he find us?" Crystal whispers to Caleb.

"He's not the only one who knows how to put trackers on phones," I reply.

She seems spooked I responded, throwing glances at me over her shoulder every so often as we walk down the hallway.

It's almost cute.

If it wasn't for the fact that she most definitely tried to fucking escape.

When we get downstairs, Crystal pauses. "How did you get here? There's no car."

"I had a taxi drop me off. We're traveling together," I reply, holding out my hand. "Caleb. Keys."

He sighs out loud and chucks them my way. But he knows better than to make a fuss right now. And there's no way in hell I'll let him behind the wheel in his condition.

The drive all the way home is quiet. Too quiet. And the two of them are sitting in vastly different corners, pushed against the windows, like they're desperately trying to avoid touching each other ...

For fear of what might happen?

Or for fear of what I might say?

My eyes narrow on them in the rearview mirror. Something happened between those two, something more than just a kiss, and I want to know exactly what that is.

I park the car in front of the Tartarus building, and Caleb jumps out first, causing us both to be at her door, simultaneously trying to open it up.

My eyes connect with his, visceral anger firing me up.

He backs away, and I pull the handle without saying a word.

Crystal's eyes bore a hole into my head as she steps out, close enough for me to take a whiff of her scent. My cock twitches as she steps away and waltzes toward the front door with a snooty look on her face.

We all go inside, and I take a deep breath when the door finally closes behind me. "Caleb."

"I'm fine," he grits, hands in his pockets.

"Caleb. Pockets."

His nostrils flare, and he pulls out his knives and places them on the table.

"The others too."

He rolls his eyes and takes out more from his inner pockets and boots, chucking them all onto the floor. "Happy now?"

"Good boy," I say, my lip tipping up into a brief smile.

A blush creeps onto his cheeks. "I'll be in my room."

"Don't stay alone in there too long," I say. "I'll have Blaine check on you."

"Blaine?" Crystal mutters.

"Yes. The guy you chained to the bed and stole the key card from."

Her eyes widen while I hold out my hand.

"I can hear you, you know," Blaine yells from atop the banister. "And if you wanna know, Ares was the one to free me."

"You're welcome," I tell him.

Crystal leers up at him. "Yeah, sorry for leaving you hanging. Literally."

"Ahh, it's fine, I loved it," he muses, sauntering off. "But do tell me the next time you plan on leaving me butt-naked, darling."

She blushes and rubs her lips uncomfortably, like she's trying to hide the fact that she's had sex with him. But I know everything that goes on in this house.

"Aren't you mad?" she asks.

I narrow my eyes. "You think I didn't know what you two were up to?" I eye one of the cameras in the corner, pointed directly at her guest room door.

She shivers. "You were watching me."

A smile tips up my lips. "There has never been a time when I haven't, little rose."

I hold out my hand.

Finally, she surrenders the card along with the phone.

"Good girl."

Her face contorts with both a hint of pleasure and hostility. "You're a menace."

I corner her against the wall, planting my hands beside her head so she can't escape me again. "Try to run away again, and I will break every bone in your mother's body."

She grimaces. "You're a monster."

"Call me what you want. It doesn't change anything." I turn

around and waltz off.

"You had no right to take us away from there."

I pause without looking at her. I fucking can't.

"Caleb needed to see his mother," she adds. "And you forced him to leave."

My teeth grind together, and I ball my fists.

"Why?" she asks.

"You have no idea what I do for that boy …" I growl. "No idea what it's been like to have to watch the one person you need fall slowly into death's claws."

I can hear her gulp. "What?"

I turn to face her. "If I hadn't told him to drop those knives, he would've ended himself up there in his room."

Her pupils dilate. "No."

"Don't you understand? He's in agony. And you almost pushed him over that edge again."

She shakes her head, tears welling up. "I didn't. It wasn't on purpose."

"There's a reason he doesn't fucking tell people the truth. Every time he revisits the trauma, he gets worse."

"Wait, we shouldn't leave him alone then," she mutters.

"Blaine will watch over him."

"That's not enough."

"He won't allow either of us in his room, trust me," I grit. "Why do you even care?"

"Am I not allowed?" she growls back.

My jaw tenses. I don't understand how she went from hating his guts to wanting to console him … unless …

"Grief. It's a fickle thing, isn't it?" I say. "So volatile …" I step closer to her again and grab a strand of her hair, curling it around my finger. "So vivid it controls your every waking thought."

My eyes home in on her from under my lashes, and her green irises are barely able to rip away from mine. "It almost makes you believe you'd want to die too."

She shudders when I tuck her hair behind her ear.

"Come with me," I say.

"Why would I?"

I throw her a warning with just my eyes, and good thing it's enough to make her move from her corner.

304

"Let's choose a better outfit," I say, walking upstairs with her following suit.

"Why? Where are we going?"

I open her guest room door. "You'll see."

I open the closet and pull out a fancy, sparkling dress with golden chains instead of straps, as well as a pair of metallic high heels. Perfect. She'll blend in well.

"Put these on," I say, chucking them her way.

She barely catches them. "Turn around."

I snort, amused she'd still try to hide. "I've already seen and touched every inch of your body, and you're still afraid to show a little skin?"

Her whole face turns red, and I sigh out loud.

"Fine." I turn, but there's a small mirror next to her closet, through which I can still watch her pull off those tight leggings, and I lick my lips at the sight of those wet pussy lips. She pulls her top over her head, her perky nipples screaming to be licked.

I don't think she understands what she does to us ... what she does to me.

But she will.

When she finally has the dress on, I turn around. "Perfect."

***

Crystal

"You still haven't told me where we're going," I say as he grabs my hand and drags me out the door.

"You'll know when we get there," he replies, pulling me to his Lambo. He opens the doors and pushes me inside before he jumps behind the wheel and closes the doors, sealing us inside.

Good God, what a luxurious way to die.

The car begins to drive, and every second feels like an hour stuck in here with him.

I don't dare to look. His frame alone is intimidating enough, let alone that penetrative gray-eyed stare. Something about his aura gives me the freaks. It's like his whole body is on fire, and if I dared to touch him now, I'm afraid I'd get burned.

305

But there is one thing I didn't forget.

The knife still in my pocket.

The knife he didn't know I got back from Blaine.

I managed to pull it from the pocket of my leggings while he was picking out clothes from the closet and snuck it into the lining of my dress near my tits. He didn't even notice what I was doing. He was too busy looking at my pussy and boobs through the mirror to care.

I swallow away the lump in my throat, viscerally aware of the blade settled beneath my dress.

He parks the car outside a grimy-looking parking lot enclosed with a broken wire fence. There are not a whole lot of streetlights in this area of Crescent Vale City, and the place looks eerie this late at night.

Ares opens the doors, but I hesitate to get out. He walks to the other side of the car and holds out his hand, waiting until I grab it, but I'm not prepared for how warm he feels and just how snugly my hand fits into his.

But the moment I exit the vehicle, I spot a rat running across the parking lot, and I squeal out loud. "A rat!"

Ares pulls me to him, my back pressed against him as his arm envelops me, and he slaps a hand in front of my mouth. "Shh ... Don't scream. Don't shout. Don't let anyone know we're here."

I frown, confused.

When he finally pulls away his hand, I whisper, "Why?"

He tilts my head toward the building we're in front of. On the door is a symbol with bones on it ... And my whole body feels like it's going numb.

"Where we're going, people disappear without a trace," he whispers into my ear. "Once you're in there, you don't exist until you come out safely. Do you understand?"

I nod, my feet wishing I could turn around and flee, but my head telling me to waltz right in there.

That symbol ... I remember it as vividly as the day my father died.

"Don't let go," Ares says as he hooks his arm through mine, and we walk up to the door.

He knocks a couple of times in a strange pattern, after which a slide is opened. Someone peers at both him and me, and my heart begins to race.

The door opens, and the guy steps aside. "Welcome to The Tomb."

"The Tomb?" I whisper as we head down the stairs. "What is that?"

"Part of a network of underground dealers and hustlers."

"Wait ... Mafia?" I mutter.

He nods, and we enter a main area where a ton of people dance to music blasting through the square basement. There are many doors and more hallways, most blocked off by scary-looking guards.

"Come with me," Ares says, hauling me through the crowd.

"What are we doing here?"

"I have a rendezvous with a particularly hard-to-find regular," he says, swooping me across the dance floor until we're in the middle, where he wraps his hands around my waist and sways me around.

Ares pulls me close, too close for comfort, as I can hear his heartbeat through his chest. "Pretend we're dancing."

He spins me around and pushes my ass against his hips so I'm forced to sway along with him, his hand on my waist, guiding my body to move to the rhythm. One hand grabs my hand and lifts it to drape around his neck, fingers slowly sliding down the back of my arm, causing goose bumps in their wake.

"Make them believe it," he whispers into my ear.

"Who?" I murmur, having trouble focusing.

I can hear him smirk. "Everyone."

I try my best to move to the music, but my heart races in my throat because of where I am right now ... and with who.

This place is a gateway to hell, and I'm dancing with the devil coaxing me to lick its flames.

His hand slides down my chest, and I suck in a breath as it dips between my legs, only to narrowly avoid my pussy. On purpose, of course.

He spins me around again and pulls me close to his chest, rubbing his hand over my ass. And I don't think I've ever hated something as much as being turned on by dancing with my enemy.

"Do you see that hallway behind me?" he whispers in my ear.

I nod while trying my best to ignore his hand as it rolls around my ass.

"Tell me when you see a chubby man with a yellow bow tie enter."

That's oddly specific.

"Keep dancing," he says, swirling me around, only to end up in

307

the same spot while I keep my eyes fixated on the hallway.

But his hands ... God those hands of his make it hard to concentrate.

"Having trouble focusing?" he asks.

"Shut up," I retort.

He smirks and spins us around until we're both facing the hallway, and his hands are all over my waist and hips again. "Can't be as hard as my dick."

My cheeks glow red in the dark, and I'm so glad these strobe lights hide most of it from the people in front of me.

Good God.

He rubs himself up against me, and my pussy begins to thump in response to the way he so expertly sways me around. It's almost like he does this daily. The thought of him dancing with other people really doesn't sit right with me, but I keep my mouth shut.

"Are we here to dance or to find someone?" I hiss.

"Both," he muses, swirling me around so we're face-to-face again. Every time I look at his sharp features followed by those beaming gray eyes, I nearly melt away in the heat.

My eyes widen when the man in the yellow bow tie glances at the party before heading into the hallway. "He's there. Saw him enter."

The guard follows him inside, and the hallway is left unattended.

"C'mon." Ares grabs my hand and pulls me into the same hallway as that man.

We pass room after room with only curtains separating us from them ... the people having sex behind each of them. The kind of sex that's probably not allowed, with weapons and blood and pain, and I swear I could see someone beg with their eyes.

I swallow as Ares wraps his arm around my shoulders and tugs me along. "Focus on my voice. This way."

We turn a corner where there are more curtains with couples behind them, but at the end of the hallway is a room with a door. In front, a guard stands waiting.

"Pretend you're drunk," he whispers.

I giggle at him and slap him on the chest as we approach the guard, my heels a perfect height to accidentally fall into him. "Sorry!"

"Private area. Move back," the guard growls at me.

"Excuse us," Ares mutters before pulling out a gun with a silencer and shooting him point-blank between the eyes.

Poof.

Just like that. Gone.

The man sinks to his knees, and Ares catches him before slowly dropping him to the floor and releasing him.

He snatches the key card from his pocket while blood stains the floor. I stare in shock as Ares holds the key card over the lock and pushes open the door, pulling me inside before shutting it behind him.

A man sits in a circular booth, watching a woman behind a glass windowpane dance against a pole. He's oblivious to the fact that we've entered the room, sipping his drink while rubbing himself.

Ares approaches him with the gun pointed at the back of his head and slowly pushes it into his skull.

Only then does the man stop drinking and rubbing himself, his hand still down his pants.

"Don't move an inch. Don't speak a word unless I tell you," Ares says as he guides me forward until we're both in front of the man instead of behind him.

"You ..." the man mutters.

BANG!

Ares shoots the couch right beside his head.

"Last warning," Ares growls. "Tell the woman to leave."

The man slowly bends over to press a button on his table and talk into a tiny speaker. "Leave."

The woman stops dancing and glances at the window in a frustrated way before exiting the room.

Ares glances at me. "Sit on the table."

I swallow but still do what he says, sitting on the table with my legs crossed, as far away from the man as possible.

"Have you ever seen her?" he asks.

The man vigorously shakes his head. "Never."

Ares sits down on the couch behind me, opposite the man, and I'm acutely aware of his presence as he places the gun on the table, his hands slowly finding their way to my waist as he grips me tight.

"Are you sure about that?"

The man gulps and glances at the gun.

"Who ... who is he?" I mutter, glancing at Ares over my shoulder.

"Wayne Ferry. A man who works for the people who own this establishment," Ares says, keeping his gaze fixated on the man. "The man who was directly responsible for your father's death."

All the oxygen instantly evaporates from my lungs.

Because I never told him about my father ...

Or that he was murdered.

FORTY TWO

ARES

Her whole body begins to shake against the tips of my fingers, and I revel in the emotions building inside her, my cock growing harder and harder as the fear begins to build.

Yes, little rose.

Fear. Me.

"Your father owned a flower shop, didn't he?" I say, leaning forward so I can take a whiff of the fear she exudes. "Ferry is the man who denied the order because it wasn't to his liking, who refused to pay him, who made him walk ... only to be killed right in front of the very fucking doorstep of The Tomb."

She gasps, and I watch the single tear running down her cheeks with peak interest like it's a droplet of Ambrosía itself.

Fuck.

I never imagined the truth would be so intoxicating.

Or that I would get so hard at the thought of her finding out. Guess I really am as sadistic as she thinks.

"You've been searching, haven't you?" I murmur as I drag her closer to me across the table until she's seated right in front of me, legs on both sides of my hips. "For the one to blame." I lean in to whisper into her ear. "To kill."

Her eyes find the gun on the table as sweat drops run down her neck, and then they find mine.

"Just like you've been wondering if you should kill me."

Is she going to do it?

Will she attempt to murder me in cold blood?

In an instant, she reaches into her dress at the top and pulls out a knife, swinging it at my neck, but I grasp her wrist and pin her down against the table, knocking the knife out of her hand. It clatters onto the floor.

"You didn't think killing me would be this easy, did you?"

"You asshole!" she grits.

I spin her around so her ass faces me, and I push her up against the table and drag up her dress until her pussy is exposed. "You want me to die by your hand? Earn the privilege."

The man in front of us tries to slip out of the couch, so I home in on him and growl, "Sit. Down."

With my hand still clasping her wrist, I sit down behind her and bring my mouth to her pussy, dipping out my tongue to take a lick. I can taste her rage on my tongue, the taste divine, like nectar for the fucking gods, and I'm about to dine like it's my last meal on this godforsaken earth.

"What the f—" she moans when I spear her with my tongue, rolling it around inside her.

"Doesn't it feel good, the need to kill?" I groan as I lick her out. "Like an aphrodisiac for the mind … nothing compares."

"F-fuck," she murmurs, unable to keep the moans at bay.

Ferry's lips part. "I don't want to interrupt something. Whatever it is you two h—"

"You'll stay and watch me make her come …" I interject, flicking her clit until she mewls. "And it will be the last fucking moment of bliss you'll witness before you die."

"What?" she gasps.

"That gun in front of you has only one bullet left," I say as I lap her up. "So make your choice wisely."

I drive my tongue into her, tasting her sweet revenge before it happens. She's my addiction, my one vice I can't seem to quit, and it will be the end of me.

But at least it'll be a death worth dying, knowing the last thing I felt was her pussy writhing from my tongue as I lap her up.

I press kisses against her mound and grip her ass tight while I dig in, spreading her wetness all over while she struggles on the table. I take one last swipe before I stand and zip down.

She immediately reaches for the gun, but my fingers shoving inside her pussy make her stop midway there. Because the first thing I do when I pull them out is spread her wetness all over her ass.

"What are you doing?" she gasps, turning her head.

"You want to take a life? Then I will take the last inch of your body that has yet to be corrupted."

Her pupils dilate as I push my index finger into her ass, and she moans as it fills her up knuckle deep.

"Another," I groan, pushing the next one inside, stretching her to the limit.

"Oh my God!" she groans.

"Look at her, Ferry. Look at the woman who will be your end," I growl. "Doesn't death look pretty writhing from my fingers?"

"You're fucked up," Ferry says, shaking his head.

"You wish you never crossed paths with me," I grit back.

I pull my fingers out of her, only to push my tip against her ass.

"Wait, I've never done that, you're not going to—" She yelps when I push in.

And fuck me, the feeling is out of this world—so tight, so perfect, so utterly untouched that it almost makes me come instantly at the thought that I'm the first.

"You can take it. Just like you took me up your pussy, you'll take my cock up your ass like the good girl you are ..." I groan, and I grip a fistful of her hair and tilt her head back to make her look at me. "Because you are *my* good girl, whether you want to be or not, and I will own every inch of this goddamn perfect body and make it mine."

I push in farther and farther, allowing her to feel the size of me, and I dribble down spit to lube her up some more.

She moans with every inch, but I've not nearly even begun.

"That's my good girl. Now try to reach for the gun."

"I can't," she yelps. "It's too much."

"Yes, you can," I growl, fisting her hair tighter. "Grab the gun, little rose."

Her fingers stretch out before her as far as I'm stretching her ass, pushing in farther and farther until she can barely take it anymore, but I know it'll fit. She'll make it fit because she is my fucking Ambrosía, and she was fucking made for me.

"Take the gun. Make it yours," I growl.

Her fingers scratch at the table, desperate to cling to hope.

Hope that she may be able to avenge her father, and I will watch her every move with eager eyes, waiting for the moment when she finally cracks.

When fear and despair finally win.

And that goddamn wretched smile finally disappears off her face.

"F-fuck ... it's so tight," she moans as I push her up against the table while I drive inside her.

I place a flat hand on her back and dip in deeper. "More. I need more. Give me fucking more, everything you have."

She mewls when I thrust in fully, but as her nails dig into the wood, she finally makes the leap toward the gun.

And my heart nearly jumps out of my chest with excitement.

"That's it, little rose. Take it. Take what belongs to you like I'm taking what belongs to me."

She holds it like someone who's never held a gun before, and I'm almost certain that's the case. But I know this little vixen can do it.

Violence lives and breathes in her veins just like mine, like a monster scratching at the walls, and all I need to do is coax it out of her until it seeps from her pores.

"You ... you ..." she grits, lifting the gun as I thrust into her, deeper each time, stretching her to the limit.

"Yes. Feed me your fucking hate, little rose, because I cannot survive without it."

Slowly but surely, she points the gun at his face.

"Don't do this," Ferry says. "Please."

"Do you see the monster behind the man?" I groan, pushing in until I'm balls deep and groaning with delight. "Do you feel the thrill of the kill before it happens?"

I lean over her, caressing her back as I slowly close in on her ear. "Shoot. Kill him. Right between the eyes. Show him the murderous demon that hides beneath your skin."

With sweat drops rolling down her neck, she points it at his eyes, her hands shaking as her fingers curl around the trigger.

"Please, let me go," Ferry begs. "Please. Kill him instead. He's the one making you do this."

Ferry points at me, and I grin from his blatant attempt to change her fixation.

But he doesn't understand how deeply I've infested her brain, her mind, her heart.

The gun is still in her hands, still the one focal point as if she's thought of nothing but murder since she laid eyes on it.

"You can listen to him … kill me then … you don't have the heart," I whisper, burying myself to the hilt while I moan along with her. "Or you can listen to me … and end his miserable little life like he deserves."

She shudders in place, torn between her wish to kill and her inability to.

Because I know what's been bothering her all this time now.

The desire is so strong she can barely contain it, yet that fucking smile prevents her from going all the way.

But I will make her lose that innocence.

"If it wasn't for him, your father would still be alive today," I whisper into her ear. "You want to kill me? Show me you can do it."

I pull back, leaning up to grip her ass as I thrust in deeply, coaxing out another moan.

My hand dives between her legs, and I roll my fingers around her clit, applying ample pressure with each thrust. Her hand begins to shake more vigorously with every thrust.

"I can't," she mutters.

"Yes, you can," I retort, circling her clit faster and faster.

"Now come, little rose," I say. "Come and you will find the relief you so badly crave."

She mewls along with every pounding, every fleshly connection between our souls, until our sweat mingles and our hearts beat in sync to our darkest desires.

And as I pull her off the table to meet me in my deranged fantasies, I bite down into her shoulder while pushing her over the edge.

BANG!

The moment her clit thumps, the gun goes off, and a loud moan escapes her mouth.

Blood sprays from his face, onto the table, onto her, and I lick up the mixture of blood, sweat, and tears right off her skin as my own climax begins. Howling, I cover her mouth with one hand to prevent

315

the squeal from rolling off her tongue while I grip her hip with the other and thrust in deeply, coming inside her.

One. Two. Three more thrusts and I'm spent.

But my God …

"Death becomes you," I whisper.

FORTY THREE

Crystal

I stare at my bloodied hands and the weapon that fits so neatly between my fingers like it was made for me and me alone.

But it isn't. This is *his* weapon I'm holding. His gun that I shot that man with.

I look up at the body in front of me. The man once named Ferry, now a hollow corpse, blood spraying from his forehead, eyes dull and lifeless.

I killed a man.

I ended someone's life.

And I can't. Fucking. Breathe.

Ares spins me around and places me down on the table, my ass still hurting from the way he just invaded it.

"Look at me."

His voice sounds distant, like a jumbled mess.

"Crystal. Look at me." He grips my face with equally bloodied hands, but it's his lips pressed onto mine that finally manage to pull me out of this shock.

I tear away from him and stare up into those soulless eyes, which suddenly don't look as demonic as I remember them being, and for a second, it's almost as if there's something else behind them; pride.

But the moment vanishes when I slap him. Hard.

A vicious smirk spreads on his cheeks as he refuses to let go of me.

And fuck me, the way he just tore his way through my ass makes me feel like I want to tear him a new one too. He was too huge and thick for me, but I still did it.

He leans his forehead against mine. "Didn't it feel good?"

I suck in a breath, the red droplets of blood slowly rolling down his skin drawing my attention, like raindrops pitter-pattering on a wet canvas, slowly revealing a new painting.

And for some reason, I feel the need to kiss him back, so I lean in and plant my lips onto his. He doesn't pull away, doesn't fight as I kiss him and let go of the anger and violence that just coursed through my veins the moment I shot that man.

Absolute power.

Bottomless lust.

All melding into one as my tongue twists around his and my arms wrap around his neck, desperate for another hit of whatever kind of hellfire I've walked into. But the flames no longer burn as they lick at my skin, coaxing me to turn into something else … a monster of his making.

His groans send electrical currents down my spine, and his fingers digging into my skin almost make me forget I just took a man's life. But those fiery eyes of his … that's what ultimately made me crack.

I pull away and look at him, wondering how I let it get this far. How I slipped down into this hellhole so effortlessly … how I let this vile boy destroy me so easily.

My eyes travel down his face as my hands unravel from behind his neck, my fingers slowly sliding down his chest, but I stop the moment I spot something hiding behind his unbuttoned white shirt. An obvious scar, like something carved into his skin.

I touch the mark, attempting to push away the fabric of his shirt to see more, but he immediately grabs my wrist, eyes darkening insanely fast. And I feel like I just got caught looking at something I shouldn't have.

He pulls me off the table and sets me down, then opens the door with the key card while I bend over and pick up my knife.

But the longer I stare at it, the more I realize how futile my attempt was.

I didn't even come close to killing him.

"What now?" I ask, slipping the knife back in my dress.

He grabs his gun and tucks it away. "We leave."

He grabs my hand and pulls me through, then we run back through the hallway.

"What about the body?"

"When they find it, we'll be long gone," he says as we head through the crowd toward the exit.

But the moment fresh air hits my lungs, it only truly dawns on me what happened in there.

During the whole ride back home, I sit in silence, constantly aware of the knife poking into my breasts.

He didn't even blink an eye at me picking it up again. Like he didn't even care that I could still try to kill him.

Or maybe he's waiting for me to try again … now that I've finally had a taste of death.

I swallow away the lump in my throat and keep quiet, following him as we make our way back inside the Tartarus House.

But as I walk in his shadows, my thoughts keep tapering off to that moment of me shooting that man … the sound it made when the bullet penetrated his skull … and just how good it felt to have Ares there filling me to the brim as I came so hard I saw nirvana.

It's wrong for something to have felt so right, yet …

"You're back."

Blaine's chirpy voice pulls me from my thoughts.

Ares closes the door behind me, and I feel like I just floated inside without any recollection of walking here.

"Holy shit …" Blaine's eyes widen as he sees me, and I look down at my dress, realizing I'm caked in blood. "You guys had some fun without me, I see."

"How is he?" Ares asks.

"Every time I check on him, he keeps throwing shit at the door to make me leave."

"At least he's alive," Ares says, clearing his throat.

"Where is he?" I ask.

"Upstairs, to the left of the balcony. The door is painted black. You can't miss it," Blaine answers.

I nod a few times, then look at my own hands which don't look like mine at all. Someone else's blood is on me. "I … want to take a shower now."

Ares's eyes narrow. "Fine. Go on, then." He nods at the stairs. "I'll be right there."

He'll be right there?

"What did you do to her?" Blaine whispers behind me.

"Someone got what they deserved …" Ares responds. "And now I need a fucking drink and a smoke."

I head upstairs, still feeling like my own feet aren't mine. I don't want to go back to the guest room. It doesn't feel like mine. Doesn't feel right.

So I knock on Caleb's door, hoping he'll be my salvation.

I can't be alone right now.

I can't be with my own thoughts, or I'll go mad.

Ares left me with such a destructive wantonness that I don't want anything anymore except more blood and cum. Death and desire have been forever interlaced.

And all I want right now is to lay down my head and forget.

***

CALEB

"Leave me alone …" I groan.

I don't want to eat more of Blaine's awful cooking. Besides, I'm not in the mood to listen to his endless stories either.

"It's me."

Crystal's squeaky voice instantly makes me jump out of bed. I run to the door to open it up, but my whole body freezes to the ground at the sight of her covered in blood.

What happened to her?

"Can I come in?" she asks.

I pull open the door farther and let her step inside, but I can't take my eyes off her. She's covered in splatters of blood, and judging from the shell-shocked look on her face, I'm pretty sure she didn't just witness a murder … she took part in one.

She steps inside my room, looking around at my decorations and furniture, all in black and red with as little light as possible as I like to keep the windows shut and the curtains closed.

She picks up a skull lying on the cabinet and stares into its eyes.

"He made you kill, didn't he?" I ask, swallowing.

She places the skull back and sits on the bed, staring at the floor like she's seen ghosts talk.

I sit beside her and softly caress her hand, but she pulls it away.

"I'm sorry," she murmurs.

"What are you sorry for?"

Tears well up in her eyes, and she leans into me, swallowing them away, refusing to let them fall. And I'm torn between loving her and hating him. Even though I was the one who wanted him to ruin her, destroy her … I never realized it was only because I wanted her so badly I couldn't stand her.

But now all I feel is regret.

"I'm the one who should say sorry," I mutter, gently caressing her back. "I was blinded by my own rage."

"Everyone in this house is."

I'd disagree, but I know she's right.

Even she's been corrupted, her heart poisoned with hatred.

All because of us.

***

Crystal

A noise downstairs makes me look up, and I immediately run to the door before Caleb can stop me.

"Crystal, wait!" Caleb says, but I've already opened it up, and I peek through the gap.

A guy with flowy dark brown hair downstairs is yelling at Ares.

"What the fuck have you done, Ares?"

I clutch the door to get a better look at the guy. Something about him feels so familiar.

"Hello to you too," Ares grits.

"Are you insane? That's fucking Bonesmen territory you just barged into."

Bonesmen?

"Why do you fucking care what I do?" Ares quips, casually drinking alcohol from a glass. "When have you ever cared?"

"I've always fucking cared, dammit." The guy slams his fist onto the table next to the door. "This ain't no fucking game, Ares. You murdered one of their men in cold fucking blood."

Ares narrows his eyes. "And you know this … how?"

"Who the fuck do you think told me?" the guy replies, running his fingers through his dark hair. "You know he does business with the Bones Brotherhood."

"Bones Brotherhood …" I mutter.

"Traffickers and drug dealers," Caleb answers, scaring me a little because I didn't even realize he'd creeped up on me.

The symbol of bones flashes across my mind again, and my stomach instantly squeezes together.

Only when I take a closer look at the guy yelling at Ares do I realize why he looks so familiar.

"Wait … is that Kai?" I whisper. "That's Nathan's friend from the Phantom Society."

"Yes." There's a hint of disappointment in Caleb's voice.

"You know both of them?" I ask.

Caleb sighs out loud. "Unfortunately."

"I don't fucking care," Ares tells Kai, stoically drinking more alcohol.

"I don't understand you," Kai replies. "All this time, you've been fighting him, and now you just go around murdering anyone you set your eyes on."

Ares sets down his glass before eyeing him. "I murder those who fucking deserve it. And don't fucking pretend you don't kill whoever you want to kill. I've seen you sneaking off with your friends."

Kai's jaw tightens. "Whatever. He wants you to come to the casino."

Ares snorts. "Of course, he does. That's what you came to tell me, busboy?" He grunts. "Get out of my fucking house."

"Ares …" Kai growls.

"GET. OUT." Ares points at the door.

"Fine," Kai says through gritted teeth as he walks back to the front door. "Don't say I didn't fucking try."

Before he pushes down the handle, he looks up, and when his dark eyes settle on mine, I panic and pull away, hiding behind the door.

"Shit," I mutter. "He saw me."

When I hear the front door close, I peek again. With clenched teeth, Ares picks up the glass and chucks it at the front door, roaring out loud.

I swiftly move back into Caleb's room, and he follows me inside, shutting the door.

"Someone's not happy Ares and I killed that Ferry guy ..." I say.

"That would be Mr. Torres," Caleb replies. "His father."

My eyes widen as I look up at Caleb. "Wait ... Torres? But that would make Kai his—"

"Younger brother."

FORTY FOUR

CALEB

When she shivers, I pull her back toward the bed. "Forget about it. C'mon. Lie with me. You must be tired."

She's way too frazzled by the murder to be thinking about any of Ares's personal issues with his family.

I hold out my hands until she takes them, and I guide her back onto my bed and throw the covers on us. She tentatively lies down, her body rigid as I snuggle up against her and warm her with my body. She feels cold as ice, so I wrap my arms around her and blow hot air on her neck.

"Kai Torres ... his brother?" she mutters, like she's confused as hell. "But they looked like they hated each other."

"Ares does what Ares always does, push people away. It's what he's good at."

"But with his own family?"

"*Especially* his own family," I reply.

She shivers again, so I pull her tighter.

"I don't want to feel anything anymore," she murmurs. "And it's all because of him."

I sigh, wishing I could take it all away, but I can't. I got so caught up in my own need to punish her for my growing desire that I didn't take into account how it would irrevocably change her.

"Why do you look up to him?" she asks.

"Ares loves me as I am."

"But he enjoys hurting people," she says through gritted teeth. "He hurts you too, doesn't he?"

"I live on the edge, always dancing with death for as long as I can remember. Ares was there, picking me up from that ledge, stepping on it together with me without fear." I curl my fingers through her hair. "He's not afraid of those dark parts inside me. He owns them and turns them into strength. Desire. Hope."

"Hope?" she repeats.

"Hope for a better life. One where we can both live without prejudice over who we are and what we like."

"But who would judge him?" she says. "He thinks he's a god. No one can touch him."

"There is someone …"

Shit. I really shouldn't say that.

I shake my head. "Never mind. Doesn't matter."

She yawns. "I'm so tired. I know I should shower, but …"

"Sleep first," I say, placing a kiss against the back of her neck when she slowly starts to doze off. "I'll watch over you."

***

My eyes burst open, and I sit up straight in a bed that isn't mine.

I don't even remember falling asleep. How long was I out for? It must've been hours.

I check the bed, but it's empty apart from me, while I could've sworn Caleb was right beside me.

Where has he gone off to?

I crawl out of bed, ignoring the fact I'm still wearing that same bloodied dress and my skin is still caked in someone else's blood. I'm too preoccupied with finding Caleb. He wouldn't just leave me all by myself in his room without cause.

I open the door and look out across the hallway, but all I see is other students walking about. Nothing particularly alarming is going on. Some take a swift glance at me before walking farther, as though they don't even want to acknowledge I exist for fear of Ares's wrath.

I make my way across the hall to Ares's room. The light is on, and the noise inside draws me closer.

My heart beats in my throat as I push open the door slightly and peer inside.

He's bent over on a wooden chair, and Caleb pushes a wet sponge underneath his black shirt, revealing a small part of his skin. My breath hitches in my throat at the sight of all the blood. The bottom half of his muscular back is covered in cuts and slices. Fresh ones.

I take a step back in shock, bumping into something soft and harsh at the same time … something oddly familiar.

"I wouldn't go farther if I were you."

Blaine's familiar voice makes my whole body erupt into goose bumps.

"What happened to him?" I mutter, my eyes glued on Ares's back as Caleb dabs the sponge against his wounds. Ares hisses in pain but remains seated.

Blaine sighs. "I don't know. Ares refuses to tell us. But for your own sake, don't ask him." He places a hand on my shoulder. "It's best if you go back to Caleb's room."

I briefly glance at him in his red bathrobe, then nod and slowly turn away from him, walking all the way back to Caleb's room before I shut the door to take deep breaths.

Those wounds were fresh, and they looked so damn painful … it's hard not to feel sorry for him. But the thought of feeling not pity but actual compassion for a guy who literally locked me up in his house and uses me as a personal slut is hard to accept.

I hate him with every fiber of my being, yet …

Seeing him all wrangled up like that made it feel like someone carved my flesh too.

My heart hurts just as much as my mind.

I sink to the floor near the bed and bury my face in my hands, hoping that if I sit here long enough, I'll forget what I saw.

***

CALEB

"Leave me."

Ares's stern voice wounds me, but I don't hesitate to listen.

"If you need me—"

"I know," he interjects, but he can't even bear to look at me, let alone himself.

I swallow down the pride and walk out of the room.

"How's he doing?" Blaine asks.

"Not good," I reply, shutting the door.

"*She* saw him."

My eyes narrow. *Fuck.* "I'm gonna go check on her."

I march across the hallway and head into my room. She's sitting against the bed, but she looks up at me the second she hears the door close.

There's not a single tear on her flushed cheeks yet ...

She looks pained.

Wounded.

Not physically, but emotionally.

And it's eating me up alive.

Why does all this have to be so fucking difficult? I don't want to have to choose between the two of them.

She crawls up from the floor, her eyes completely glazed over and emotionless. Like she's shut them all off. And I watch her walk to my bathroom to turn on the rain shower. She grabs the metallic straps on her shoulders and slowly pulls them down, exposing her skin, and I can't take my eyes off her as it drops to the floor, leaving nothing to the imagination.

Her blond hair is still caked with blood from yesterday, and when she glances at me over her shoulder, I swear she's like a fallen angel. So much beauty, corrupted with a single death.

And it's all because of him.

My door is opened, and someone steps inside, but I pay no attention. I can hear the door close, but my eyes remain fixated on her as she steps under the shower and lets the water wash over her.

Blaine stands beside me, his long black hair falling over his red robe as he tilts his head and folds his arms.

"Gorgeous ..." Blaine murmurs, licking his lips. "Even more so with all the blood."

Rivulets of water mixed with blood roll down her neck, across her nipples which peak under our gazes, and my cock nearly bursts out of my sweatpants.

She's seen death with her own damn eyes and survived while I'm here waning because of a death that hasn't happened yet. She's the epitome of strength and all that I wish I could have.

I swallow away the lump in my throat as her presence coaxes me to come closer and closer, not giving a shit about the water splashing onto my pants.

She's a siren luring me in with just her eyes, beckoning me to obey, and I am more than willing to yield.

I grab the sponge off my shelf and run it across her shoulders while I step under too. My clothes are soaked, but all I care about is being close to her. She's the girl I should've stayed away from, the girl who's wormed her way into our lives and made our dark minds her home.

I help her wash off the blood, but a part of me wants to revel in the pain she's caused.

So I tip up her chin and make her look at me, show her that I'm not a threat ... that I would kill for her if she'd ask.

And I plant my lips on hers, claiming that darkness spreading inside her like an infection from a single bite Ares left on her shoulder. He's turned her into a mirror of his own image, a creature of ruin and revenge, and I want nothing more than to bask in their fucking glory.

Blaine steps under the shower too, dropping his red robe on the floor as he plucks her face away from me, only to kiss her right on those very same lips, stealing her away from me.

And I'd be lying if I said it didn't make me jealous ... but fuck, looking at the way they kiss is something else entirely.

"She's mine," I grit, stealing her from him again so I can smash my lips onto hers.

"Sharing is caring, darling," Blaine murmurs, draping his arms over her as he stands behind her.

Fuck, I don't want to share, but if I have to ... then I will. I've shared her with Ares ... what's one more?

I roll my tongue around hers in a desperate attempt to get closer, tasting the murder on her lips. Kissing her is like kissing the fucking sun before it sets, and I don't want to be the one to witness the last bit of light behind those eyes being snuffed out.

"Are you ready to tell me what Ares made you do?" I whisper against her lips.

"I shot someone," she whispers back, coaxing out more kisses, and it's too hard to say no to her.

But I'm not at all surprised by her admission.

"He fucked you too, didn't he?" Blaine asks, pecking her neck from behind while his hand snakes around her waist. "Before, after, or during?"

"During," she says in a single breath.

I cup Crystal's cheeks and kiss her harder, hoping my need for her will drown out the hatred he's instilled in her. I've never hated Ares, but the more he's got his claws in her, the more I want to rebel.

"He may have fucked with your mind... but I can fuck your body and make it all feel better," I groan against her mouth.

"That's awfully bold of you," Blaine murmurs, planting kisses all over her neck. "And awfully sexy too."

"Shut up," I groan.

Her kisses are too good to pass up, and I'm too hungry to step away despite knowing we're all supposed to hate each other.

"F-fuck," I murmur against Crystal's lips. "I want you so badly I can't breathe."

"You want me?" she murmurs between kisses. "Then make me yours."

And fuck me.

There's nothing left of me because she's stolen my goddamn soul already.

***

Blaine

I watch them kiss, and a great need to steal her away from him settles deep within my stomach. I've been watching her play with both of them for so long it's slowly been withering away my resilience, and now I've had enough.

I don't want to just watch from the sidelines anymore.

I want to be the one who owns her heart, and if I can't make it mine entirely, then I will slice it into pieces and divide it among us all.

My hand slowly snakes around her body as I cover her skin with kisses while the water washes away her sins. I don't want to know who she killed or where. I don't need any information to know that I want her, wholly, in whatever state she may come to me.

Her body melts into me as the rivulets of water connect between us, and when Caleb's lips unlatch from hers, I tip her head my way and kiss her too.

I can taste him on her mouth, the added spice only making my dick throb harder as I push her up against me.

Caleb leans in and kisses her chest while I circle my tongue around hers, licking the roof of her mouth. She tastes like a sinful slice of heaven cast down to be with us demons, and I almost want to thank the gods for allowing me a bite.

His mouth covers her nipple, flicking past the tip, making her moan right into my mouth, and I harden from the sound. Who knew playing with her together could be so much fun?

"You make me want to do bad, dirty things to you, darling," I groan when our lips briefly unlatch. "Will you let me please you?"

She nods gently, and I take the opportunity to smother her with more kisses underneath her ear and neck while Caleb licks her nipples until they're peaked, tugging them with his teeth to elicit more moans from her.

Her hands find their way to his sweatpants and fumble to push them down over the head of his swollen cock.

Suddenly, he grips her hips and lifts her from the floor, wrapping her legs around himself.

"You are my slut. *Mine.* Do you hear me?" Caleb growls, smashing his lips onto hers.

I didn't think I'd ever find it sexy he'd debase her like that, but damn, the way she purrs for him is quite something.

He positions her on his tip. "I will only share you with him if you want me to," Caleb murmurs, licking her lips.

"Yes," she whimpers. "Don't make me choose. Not today. Not now. I need you both."

"Fuck," I groan, stepping closer too so I can push between her legs. "That's what I wanted to hear, darling."

He spears her on his cock, and the resounding moan makes me rock hard. I've never wanted to go fully for just one person, but this girl … this girl has made me ravenous for something more than lust, more than sex. I want to be hers, and I want her to be mine. And if that means I'll have to share her, then so be it.

"You're so wet for me," Caleb groans, kissing her on the chin.

"Come here," I groan, gripping her thighs so I can push my cock up against her pussy too.

Caleb's eyes widen. "You're not thinking of—"

Her wild moan interrupts him as I slowly bury myself inside her pussy too. "She begged for two cocks, then she'll have two cocks."

I push inside, feeling his cock next to mine as we both enter her together. And my God, Ares wasn't lying. Those piercings are something else. The pleasure is insurmountable.

"God, your pussy feels amazing around my cock, so tight," I murmur into her ear, my tongue dipping out to draw a line down her neck, suckling along the way.

"It's so full," she mewls. "Fuck!"

She slams her lips onto Caleb's, drowning out his anger with desire until he practically melts into a puddle.

And I must admit, I don't hate the sight. In fact, it's only adding to the pleasure.

Maybe I don't despise him as much as I thought I did.

We're so close to each other I can feel his breath on my chin as I kiss her earlobe and he kisses her cheek, all while we're both fucking her to our heart's content. Our cocks are rubbing up against each other deep inside her, our needs colliding into one. And when I feel him pulsate against me, I let my appetite take over and kiss him too.

FORTY FIVE

CALEB

I pull away in shock, stopping the kinky fuckery even though I was about ready to burst.

Blaine actually ... kissed me?

Crystal giggles, but I can't even focus on her as all I can see are those lips of his still pursed, still waiting for a reaction.

"I was just taken away by the moment," Blaine mutters. "I didn't mean to—"

I grip his face and kiss him right back, not giving a shit that he's the one guy I thought I fucking hated until death and beyond. That kiss just unlocked a hidden desire I didn't even know I had until now.

Maybe it's not so bad after all, maybe I could want all of them and finally have enough.

"Fuck," Blaine groans against my mouth, and his tongue dips out to swirl around mine. He's much less arrogant and controlling than Ares, but much greedier too, as his tongue goes wild inside my mouth, but I like it.

Crystal's moans make me pull away, and I blink a couple of times as we slowly begin to drive into her again. And fuck me, could there ever be anything more perfect than fucking the one girl we love together?

"God, this fucking pussy is going to be the death of me," Blaine murmurs while I press my lips onto hers for more greedy kisses.

Blaine's cock rubs up against mine, creating so much pleasure I can't even begin to describe it without moaning like a madman.

"You're such a good little slut for us," I groan, biting her lip. "I can't get enough."

"Fuck me," she mewls, running her hands through my hair.

My length swells inside her as I get closer and closer to the edge, balls slapping against her inner thighs while Blaine and I alternate kissing her with kissing each other. The hot water doesn't even come close to the heat between us as we give her everything we have and more.

"Fuck, you're so tight," Blaine groans. "I could do this every day for the rest of my life and still not have enough of you. I'm addicted."

"But what about my mother, what about Ares, what about—"

I silence her with a kiss. "I don't fucking care anymore. None of it matters as long as we're with you."

"Yes," she says in a heady trance. "Make me believe it. Just for a day."

"It won't ever be enough," I murmur against her lips.

"We want more. Please let us have you," Blaine begs, thrusting into her. "Let us have you for the rest of your life. Let us fuck you every day until you're satisfied. Will you do that for us?"

She moans out loud when my pubic piercing rubs against her clit, and I just know she loves it as much as I do.

"Admit that you like being my slut," I groan against her earlobe. "You love writhing on our cocks if only to forget about everything else."

"Yes," she moans when I hit that spot. "Harder, please!"

Blaine obliges too, running his hands over her tits while I hold her hips tightly. "So perky, so fucking beautiful."

My fingers dig into her hips as we thrust in and out simultaneously, as the pressure slowly begins to build.

"I know how you feel. You want me to fuck the rage out of you," I whisper into her ear. "So let me give you what you need, little slut." I bury myself to the hilt inside her, making her gasp. "Now moan for me."

The moan that follows is drawn-out and heavy, as though she's releasing all her inner demons and letting them all drain away with the water, and I'll be right fucking here to fuck her until she collapses in my arms, ready to catch her when she fucking falls down from that heavenly peak.

"Shit, I'm so close," she murmurs as the piercings at my base keep rubbing her clit. "Please, please don't stop."

Her begging makes my dick pulsate. "Come for me. Fall apart on our cocks like a good fucking slut would."

I bang her so hard I can see the lights in her eyes go out, and she drops her head on Blaine's shoulder, allowing me to lick the droplets of sweat and water off her throat while her pussy begins to contract from the orgasm rolling through her entire body.

"Fuck, I can feel her coming," Blaine mewls. "It's too much, I'm going to come too."

"Yes, fill her up," I groan. "Let me feel it."

The long-drawn-out groan that follows sets me off too as his cum jets out into her. His warm seed glides down my cock, and I grip his face and kiss him as I shoot my own load into her too, filling her up to the brim.

Suddenly, the door in the back opens up, and I unlatch from Blaine's lips when I realize whose eyes are boring a hole into my chest.

"Ares," I mutter.

Fuck.

***

Crystal

Caleb and Blaine pull out of me, leaving me feeling empty. I swiftly grasp my dress off the floor and clutch it tightly, but Caleb pushes me to the back of the shower and blocks me from Ares's view.

Is he ... protecting me?

"You want to be mad? Be mad at me," he growls. "I seduced her."

My face glows red, but I still can't help but step sideways to watch Ares approach like a demon in all black, his gray eyes forcing me to keep my gaze locked on his.

334

"I wanted this," I say.

"Let us do the talking, darling," Blaine insists, blocking my view too.

Goddammit. Now they choose to protect me from him?

They fold their arms and stare down Ares, so I peek through the gap between Blaine's arm and his well-trained body.

"You're still injured and healing. Shouldn't you lie down?" Caleb asks him.

"I'm fine," Ares says, straightening his back.

Why does it sound like a lie?

"She's had enough of your obsession," Blaine says.

"Really now?" Ares mocks. "I beg to differ."

My eyes are transfixed on his, and they find mine through their bodies with ease.

"I know you're hungry for more ..." Ares murmurs, stopping right in front of them. "No wonder you went to them instead."

"You traumatized her," Blaine says.

Ares tilts his head. "She pulled the trigger out of her own free will. Didn't you, Crystal?"

They all look at me now.

"Didn't it feel good to watch the blood drain from his face?" he asks me directly.

I can't help but nod.

It's true. Even if I wanted to deny it, it felt so fucking good to destroy the man who let my father walk straight into his death.

A wicked smile forms on Ares's face. "See?"

"Do you want her to become like me?" Caleb asks, his voice cracking under the weight of his emotions.

Ares grips his face. "I would never want either of you to die. I need you to stay with me."

"I can't lose her too," Caleb says, breaking my heart. "Even if you want me to stay away from her, I can't. I fucking can't. But we're ruining her."

Ares pulls him against his chest, easily dragging him into his embrace despite getting his own clothes wet too now. "I know."

"I won't deny that you two have a claim on her," Blaine says, swallowing. "But I would die for a girl like her."

"You'd die for me?" I mutter, looking up at him.

No one's ever said that to me.

He immediately grabs my hand and kisses the top just like he always does. "You're my goddess. It would be a fucking honor."

"A goddess?" Ares repeats with great interest. "Yet you were kissing *him*." He looks down upon Caleb with jealousy lacing his eyes. "The one you loathe so much."

Blaine gulps. "I got carried away."

"It didn't mean anyth—"

"Yes, it did," I say.

Now everyone's looking at me, and it makes me blush.

"You like each other," I say.

Blaine's jaw drops. "I do not," he scoffs.

"In his dreams," Caleb says, turning his head. "It just happened, no big deal."

"What he said," Blaine says, but they're both flushing at the cheeks.

"Liars," I mumble.

Ares seems amused by it all even though I'd assumed he'd be red hot with rage by now because he caught them having sex with me while he was writhing in pain in his room.

"Caleb. Blaine," he says through gritted teeth. "On. Your. Knees."

The boys stare him down for a moment, before they both slowly sink to their knees. Caleb first, then Blaine, and with the water rushing down on their heads it almost looks like they've been defeated just by the sheer dominance in Ares's glare.

I thought they'd finally be on my side, fighting for me. But even they can't resist his commanding presence.

"Lick her out."

What?

"Who? Me?" Blaine points at himself.

The devilish glint in Ares's eyes make me gulp. "Both of you."

Both boys turn around to look at me as I brace myself against the wall, but nothing prepares me for when their tongues both land on my pussy, providing so much pleasure I nearly melt into the wall.

Good God, who knew two tongues could feel so much better than just one?

"Suck out that fucking cum," Ares commands. "You want to be hers so badly? Then be the fucking sluts you are."

"Oh fuck," Blaine moans. "You never talked to me like that." He winks. "I quite like it."

Ares grips his head and shoves him right back between my thighs. "Shut your damn mouth and lick."

"F-fuck," I murmur, unable to keep the moans at bay. I'm having so much trouble holding the dress, but I must. The knife is my only failsafe.

"You wanted them … then have them," Ares says through gritted teeth as he steps closer, apparently not giving a shit either that the shower is pouring down on him, and he grabs my chin. "Take all of us like a fucking good girl."

And he slams his lips onto mine, greedily taking my mouth like he already took ownership of it long ago.

The kiss catches me so off guard that I feel numb as he roams my mouth with his tongue, licking the roof of my mouth while those boys lick my pussy raw. My hand wraps around his neck and my fingers crawl through his hair, desperate for more. I'm already quaking with need, my body still reeling from the previous orgasm, but it will never be enough for them.

And it might never be enough for me either now that I know what it feels like to have them all three to myself.

Ares groans into my mouth, making goose bumps scatter on my skin. "So delicious for something so fucking forbidden." He smiles against my lips, droplets of water rolling down his sharp nose and chin. "Now tell me why you refuse to fear me."

Even though our lips are still connected, I look him dead in the eyes. "You *know* why."

A deadly smirk forms on his face, and a low, rumbling laugh fills the room. After a while he says, "Always smiling through the pain. How do you do it?"

I'm instantly reminded of the wounds on his back and how much it must hurt to stand under the scorching hot shower, yet it doesn't seem to faze him in the slightest.

"You know, I hated the very thought of you. Your existence was a nuisance, an unforeseen circumstance I hadn't anticipated … but that smile, I can't get it out of my fucking mind. It's consumed me to the point where I couldn't think, couldn't eat, couldn't sleep without seeing that damn fucking smile of yours." He grips my chin, his thumb running across my bottom lip. "You want *me* to fear it."

A wicked glimmer in his eyes makes me gulp.

Maybe he's right.

Maybe that's why I could never give in, never falter, never stop fighting him.

Even when my heart is slowly unraveling and wrapping around his.

***

ARES

I grip her throat, squeezing so tightly she can't breathe. I can feel her heart pulsate underneath my thumb, the throbbing of life, naked in my very hands. "You've made me so obsessed with you that I can't even fucking think of someone else touching you without wanting to put a bullet through their heads preemptively. You've made me blind with jealousy to the point where the only person I ever cared about nearly slipped away from me because I couldn't stop trying to claim you all for myself."

I grip Caleb's hair with my free hand and tilt his head up to look at both of us. I want her to see the unraveling in his eyes. She has no fucking idea of the power she holds over these boys who once belonged to me.

She stole their obedience from me … and I can't even fucking stay mad at her.

"I need him, and he needs me …" I grit. "But we need you more."

"Fuck, I need her so fucking much," Caleb groans.

I shove him back into her pussy. "Then fucking dine on her like the addicted little slut you are."

"Yes, fuck yes," Caleb groans.

"God, I love it when you guys talk dirty," Blaine murmurs, lapping her up and making it hard for her to focus. I can see it in her eyes, the way they almost roll back into her skull.

So easily persuaded to submit to them …

Yet she still refuses to do it for me.

"You've beguiled all of us, so let me return the favor by turning you into our favorite obsession, our aphrodisiac… my fucking Ambrosía," I say.

My mouth slams back onto hers, claiming what little breath she

338

had left before I finally release her throat and allow her to suck in the air she so desperately needs. Air I share with her as I relentlessly kiss her over and over again until she can feel nothing but our lips on her body and our desire between her own goddamn legs.

"Yield," I groan into her mouth. "Yield, goddammit, and I will fucking give you my soul."

But no matter how hard I kiss her, she won't let go of that one sliver of rage. Her eyes travel toward the dress on the floor and the knife she hides, forever luring her in.

"No," she murmurs. "I can't. I won't."

"Fuck," I growl, still kissing her, and I bite her lip and tug at it. "You are mine, little rose, mine to do with as I please, no matter how much you hate me, how much you'd wish for me to die. Kill me, and I'd only haunt you in your nightmares because you'll never know how much I sacrificed to be able to kiss these lips and make that fucking smile mine."

***

Crystal

My eyes open wide, and I want to ask what he means, but I'm not sure I want to know.

Do I want to know the reason behind all of my own misery?

Could I really relinquish myself of anger that's been coursing through my veins, keeping me alive up to this day?

I swallow as my hands travel down his wet shoulders, my eyes searching his face for answers to questions I don't dare ask. But his bloodied shirt peeling away at the top makes me hunger for more, so I gently pull away the wet fabric, revealing the markings underneath.

Letters ... carved into his flesh.

But there's no time to look at what it says as he pulls me away from the wall.

"Fuck, I want to taste more of her," Blaine mutters. "Please, don't spoil the fun now that we're finally having some."

"Hush," Ares growls, and he picks me up and carries me away in his arms while I desperately hold on to the dress in which I keep the knife. "Follow."

339

I'm completely taken aback when he carries me out of Caleb's room and waltzes across the hallway. I'm completely nude, but he does so without a care in the world that anyone might see me. Because his gaze is completely transfixed on me, and I'm suddenly struck by how beautiful this devil is from this angle, or maybe it's the light cast from above that makes me wonder if I'm staring at a literal fallen angel.

But that doesn't make sense. He's someone who steals life without qualm, who laughs in the face of death itself. A murderer.

So are you.

My breath catches in my throat right as he steps into his own room. Caleb and Blaine follow suit like puppy dogs obeying his every command.

I peer around, surprised by the amount of gray painting on the walls. There's no color of any kind, not even a flower, and it's filled with furniture in muted tones, except for one thing—the bright red cabinet in the back of the room.

I gulp when he puts me on the soft, square chair behind a big glass table.

"Stay," he tells me.

I don't know what'll happen if I don't listen, but judging from the boys' reaction, it's not wise to disobey.

"You two were so happily kissing each other under the shower …" Ares says as he walks to the red cabinet. He glances at them over his shoulder. "I feel fucking left out."

"Sorry," Caleb mutters. "I didn't mean to—"

"Shh," Ares silences him with ease.

"What do you want us to do? Beg?" Blaine asks. "I want her, and I'll do anything to be able to call her mine."

My cheeks flush from his admission.

"Anything?" Ares's brow rises. "Good."

He grabs some stuff, but I can't see, and curiosity is really getting the better of me as I drop the dress on the floor.

But that curiosity is quickly replaced with despair as he places a whole bunch of ribbed dildos on the table, lined up from small to large, with suction cups to secure them tightly.

He adds lube to all of them before sitting down in the gray chair opposite of me, eagerly biting his lip while gazing at me intently.

This … he put all this down for me.

"You want to be freed of my obsession? To be let go of the deal you made?" he growls, tilting his head to the side while rubbing his chin. "Fine. I will ... If you can take all of these in your ass one at a time until you reach the end ... then kiss me." He leans forward with a smug smile. "So come and get your freedom, little rose."

FORTY SIX

ARES

"Boys." I snap my fingers and unzip, freeing my cock from its prison. "On your fucking knees and lick."

Crystal's eyes widen as Caleb and Blaine come to stand before me, slowly kneeling like the obedient sluts they are.

Caleb's the first to stick out his tongue, then Blaine, but within seconds, they're licking me off, and fuck me, the feeling is overwhelmingly powerful.

I groan with excitement, and I can see her shift in her chair, as though the horniness they've made her feel is becoming a bit too much to take.

"You like watching them, don't you?" I ask, gripping the chair. "Answer me."

"Yes," she murmurs, biting her lip when Caleb begins sucking at the tip.

"You want them as much as they want you," I say.

She nods.

I grip Blaine's head and shove him in farther, forcing him to lick the head. "They're all mine."

She swallows.

"But I'm willing to share … as long as you are mine," I groan while the boys go to town. "Now make your choice, little rose. What's it going to be? Your freedom? Or a hedonistic life filled with ecstasy?"

She glances at the dildos that I've placed closer and closer to me, ranging from small to huge. The sheer size of them are intimidating enough to make her second-guess.

But still she stands up from her chair and approaches the table.

I hold my breath, licking my lips the moment she steps over it and hovers above one of the dildos.

Is she going to—?

Slowly but surely she sinks her ass down onto the first one, and my cock swells from the sight.

"How far?" she asks.

I tilt my head and watch her fall apart from each of my words. "To. The. Base."

I can feel Caleb's piercing leave my shaft as he attempts to speak, "She can't, she'll never make it—"

"Keep fucking licking." I interrupt, throwing him a glare. "Make it nice and wet."

"Yes, Sir," he says, wrapping his delicious tongue around my length again.

"You wanted to share with him, then fucking share," I growl.

"Jesus, you're so fucking huge," Blaine murmurs, licking the tip.

"Focus," I say, gripping his hair so I can force him down my shaft. "Lick my cock like you just licked her pussy, and maybe I won't fucking punish you both for daring to go against me."

"Oh God," she mewls as she's taken the first one completely.

"Go on, then," I say, curious how far she thinks she can take it.

She lifts herself off the first, only to lower herself onto the second without holding back, lube dripping down her thighs as she takes it deep.

I lean back in my chair, enjoying the feel of two tongues wrapped around my shaft while she puts on a show for me and me alone.

She takes the third, her face straining, but her body never inching away to stop.

"Next," I groan with excitement at her tenacity.

She keeps going, taking each one of the dildos deeper and deeper into her ass despite the fact that we've already reached my own thickness.

"You can do it, little rose," I murmur, leaning forward to see how far she's willing to go for her precious freedom.

She lifts herself off number five and hovers over to the next. Sweat drops roll down her forehead as she pushes down on the sixth, the size so ample it's making her moan out loud.

"That's it. Feel them penetrate your ass just like my cock when you made your first kill. Doesn't it feel so fucking good?" I say, reveling in her rage.

She sucks in her pride and goes onto the next, hovering over the tip with a dripping pussy that makes my mouth water.

"Take it," I say as she goes down with difficulty. "Take it deep like a good fucking girl."

"How many more?" she asks, grinding her teeth.

My eyes narrow as they settle on her. "All. Of. Them."

Her pupils dilate, and the look on her face shifts to complete despair. And that's the fucking one. The one that'll make me come so hard I'll make her see the fucking afterlife.

But first …

"Continue," I growl.

She pulls herself off the seventh and moves onto the eighth with so much trouble I wonder when she'll give up.

"Ready to stop?" I muse. "You can call it off whenever you want … I'm right here."

"No." She pushes on, taking each ribbed edge like a good girl.

"I can wait for as long as you need," I say, watching her intently as she sinks down to the base, letting out a whimper.

She takes it so well, without any complaints. I'm in awe.

Sweat drops roll down her cheeks as she takes the ninth one, moaning loudly as it enters her and fills her to the brim.

"Fuck …" she murmurs, her whole body quaking with need.

She's right in front of me, just out of grasp, but so very goddamn appeasing that I push the boys away and lean forward to meet her as she lifts herself and hovers above the tenth and final dildo.

"You took all of them," Caleb says as he looks up at her with desire lacing his entire face.

"My God, what a woman," Blaine mutters, licking his lips.

I tip up her chin and make her look at me while she dips down to make the final plunge. "Last one." The mewl that emanates from her mouth sets my fucking soul on fire. "Yes, that's it. Break for me."

She writhes on the dildo as she goes all the way down to the base, hovering so close to my face I could almost kiss her. But I want her to yearn for it, to be desperate for these lips that could end her anguish and bring her complete and utter bliss. All she has to do is choose.

"Fuck ..." she murmurs when she's finally there.

"Good girl," I whisper against her lips. "Now stay there."

"It's so tight," she groans. "It hurts."

"Good. Then you might know an inkling of the pain I've felt for you for all of these fucking years," I growl as I stand from the chair to look at her up close.

Her eyes widen. "Years?"

I grip her thighs and spread her legs. "As long as I've waited for you to come to me and become mine completely. Now let me feel how wet this pussy is for me."

"What?" she gasps.

I grip my cock and slowly enter her pussy, watching the look on her face change into complete and utter destruction.

"Oh my fucking God!" she yelps as I thrust in.

"Yes, my little rose, I am your one and only fucking God, now submit."

I grip her throat and force her to take me deep, unloading all of my anger over desiring something so volatile, so poisonous for me.

But she ... she's clawed her way through my mind and nestled there like a goddamn venomous bug, constantly reminding me of what I lost. What I craved. What I needed so desperately that I ended up just taking it without a fucking care in the world.

Death unites us, and death will be our fucking end.

"I want this pussy to be the last thing I feel before you kill me," I groan, thrusting in and out of her, filling her to the brim. "And you will grant me that final fucking wish like the good girl you are."

***

Crystal

He wants my body to be the last thing he feels before he dies?

I can't believe my ears, but at the same time, I can't concentrate either because of how hard he thrusts into me.

All I hear is *good girl*, and I'm lost.

"Fuck," I murmur, completely lost in his depravity.

Good God, I'm taking two, not one, but two huge cocks up my ass and pussy … and I have never been more turned on in my life.

I'm only doing this to be free of him. To relinquish myself of all of this hatred, but fuck, he makes it so hard.

"Boys, lick those tits. Rub that clit until she comes so hard she'll want for nothing but more cocks up her every goddamn hole."

"Good God, yes," Blaine murmurs. "I thought you'd never ask."

He approaches me and covers my nipple with his mouth, suckling until I'm mewling with delight. Caleb flicks my clit with one hand while rolling his tongue around my other nipple, driving me wild with lust.

"You take my cock so well," Ares groans, thrusting in until the base. "There is not a thing in the world that fits you better than me."

"Fuck, I hate you so damn much," I hiss.

"Yes, little rose, wither away for me," he says. "Take my fucking seed."

He buries inside me again and again until I'm heady with lust and can't control myself any longer. "Fuck!"

"Fuck, she looks so good when you thrust into her like that," Caleb mewls.

And he turns his head away from my nipples, only to kiss Ares on the neck while he drives into me. It's too much, too much seduction, too much indulgence for me not to be turned on so badly I can barely breathe.

"I'm so goddamn hard again," Caleb groans.

"Good," Ares groans. "I'm going to need that cock of yours."

When Caleb takes his lips off Ares, he immediately kisses me instead, sticking his tongue into my mouth under Ares's watchful gaze as though they enjoy looking at each other while playing with me.

"Blaine," I whisper, trying to find a light at the end of the tunnel.

"Kiss me."

Blaine leans up and presses his lips onto mine while Caleb moves right back to my nipples, overloading me with sensations. Both boys are kissing me while my pussy and ass are filled completely, turning me into a puddle of ecstasy.

When Blaine moves away, Ares grips my chin. "Look at me. Look at me while you fall apart on your god's cock and bow to me."

My eyes can't help but find his in all this debauchery, wishing he would end us both just so I wouldn't have to deal with these conflicting emotions. As those boys lick and suck, I fall apart on top of him, my pussy contracting around his shaft.

"Yes, that's it. Give yourself to me. Give me everything and more," he grunts before roaring out loud.

I can feel the warmth of his cum as it fills me up and then some.

His voice is so dark it nearly lulls me into a deep state of carelessness. "Now thank me for it."

"Thank ... you," I whisper.

In my delirium, my eyes scour his, trying to find an inch of love out of desperation, and when they finally connect with his, I'm done for. My kisses are needy, frenzied, like a succubus fighting for a sliver of attention from its master.

But I made it.

I kissed him.

Just like he told me to.

He pulls out of me, almost leaving me feeling like I lost something forever. And he steps back and sinks down onto the chair, watching me intently as he says, "Now fuck both her holes while I watch."

FORTY SEVEN

Blaine

Caleb steps in front of the table and lifts her off the dildo, pushing her over his hard cock with ease. She mewls when he enters her, his rigid piercings intensifying the already overwhelming orgasm that still ripples through her.

I crawl onto the table and sit down behind her.

"I need you to feel what I felt," Crystal whispers to me.

"Of course, my goddess," I answer as I slowly sink down on top of one of the dildos, gasping with both pain and pleasure. "Oh fuck." My cock instantly hardens from the thickness inside my ass, and I pull her back over me. "Come here, darling, let me fill you up."

"Fuck," she moans when I slowly settle her over my cock.

"You can take them both," Ares says, grinning from his chair, his dick still bouncing up and down with need. "Because you're a needy little slut, aren't you?"

"Yes, take us both deep," Caleb groans. "I want to know what every inch of your body feels like."

She feels like I'm thrusting straight into heaven. I couldn't ever possibly have enough.

"I need more. Take me deeper," I groan, sinking farther onto the dildo too.

"Fuck, I could come again just from feeling you inside her too," Caleb groans.

"It's quite something, isn't it?" I muse, bouncing up and down on the dildo while simultaneously pounding into her.

Right when my dick begins to pulsate inside her ass, Ares gets up from his seat and marches to the table, stepping onto it so he can tower over her and force her to look up at him.

"Open your mouth."

When he pinches her nose, she has no choice, and he thrusts in deep.

"Fuck, not two but three cocks inside her," Caleb growls. "Such a good fucking slut, taking us all."

"Yes, swallow me whole," Ares groans, filling up her throat until her eyes water.

And I can no longer stop myself from getting wildly turned on by watching her writhe from all three of us.

"Fuck, I'm going to come again," Blaine says, whimpering as his head tilts back, and his balls empty inside her. "It's so good. You feel so good around my cock. You're a goddamn goddess for taking us all."

If only things were different ... we could've been so fucking good together.

**

CALEB

"Keep pounding into her. Don't stop," I beg Blaine as my whole body tightens before I roar out loud and come too.

"Fuck!" Her moans are immediately silenced by Ares's dick plowing into her, forcing her to take him into her mouth until he hits the base.

"Now gulp down the second load of cum like a good girl," he says, arching his back as he grips her face tight and roars.

It's so much, it explodes out of her mouth and dribbles onto me.

"Don't waste a fucking drop," Ares growls.

So I lean in and lick it off her chest and lips, kissing her immediately after he pulls out of her.

She's covered in cum and sweat, and I suck it all up and spit it out into her mouth, swirling my tongue around hers until she's as satiated as we are.

Blaine pulls out first. "Fuck, that dildo felt good."

Ares jumps off the table to sit back on the chair again and tuck back his spent cock. He watches her with a devilish smirk on his face as she slowly comes down from the high.

I place one last kiss on the side of her lips before I pull out. She falls into me, and I catch her just in time. "You did good, little slut."

I hold her close to me and listen to the sound of her breaths as her heart rate slows. Her body close to mine lulls my mind into a calm state, one I've only ever experienced when Ares hugs me.

I throw him a glance, the intrigue on his face making me question everything I thought I knew. About myself. About us. About her.

Is there a way I could love them both without being torn at the seams?

I push her away and look at her face, searching for the answers, but the look in her eyes is restless. As though her mind has already wandered off somewhere else.

Her eyes, glazed over, deeply connected with Ares's, the air thick with poison.

A cloud has been hanging over us since we first saw her.

One that's about to split open and rain down hell.

***

Crystal

I've given my body to the devil and stepped through the dark gates of hell with him. I did all he asked and more. And now I want what he promised me.

I push Caleb aside so I can focus on Ares. "It's done. I did what you asked … I won."

Ares tilts his head, the smug grin on his face growing deeper and deeper. "You won, little rose … And now you want to be relinquished of your deal with us."

I swallow away all the feelings of lust I had seconds ago as Ares leans forward in his chair until he's a mere inch away from my face just to say, "What would you do if I said I lied?"

"What?" I mutter in disbelief.

Ares's hand supports his face as he leans down with his elbow on the armrest. "There was no deal. I wasn't ever going to kill your mother to begin with. I never kill innocent people."

Innocent people?

"Never?" I parrot as the darkness begins to take hold.

I steady myself against the table as my world shifts on its axis.

Break.

Break.

Break.

It's all he's wanted me to do ... break me.

Break the glass that surrounds my heart.

Shatter the facade.

Show them what truly hides underneath.

Fine.

I'll give him what he fucking wishes for.

***

ARES

The small smile instantly evaporates from her face like it was never even real.

That's it.

That's the face I was looking for.

Suddenly, she jumps off the table and rushes at her dress, fishing out the knife she's so desperately clung to all this time, and within two steps, she lunges at me.

"Crystal, no!" Caleb growls, grasping her arm.

Right before the knife punctures my neck.

"What the—" Caleb mutters, shock riddling his face. "What the fuck are you doing?"

But all I can do is look up at the face of the girl who's haunted my nightmares for years.

"She's finally doing what she's wanted to do since the first time she saw me." I lean into the blade. "Kill me."

"You fucking liar!" she spews.

Caleb wraps his arm around her flailing body to keep her away

351

from me. "Crystal, stop!"

"Let go of me," she grits at him, thrashing around. "He's a fucking liar! Not killing innocents? Bullshit! What about the men who tried to enter the Tartarus property?" she rebukes.

Those men were anything but innocent.

"They were from the Bones Brotherhood. The same underground organization Wayne Ferry belonged to," I reply, staying still against her blade. "And they were going to try to drug girls at my party to capture them."

She winces, confused. "What?"

"You think shady shit doesn't happen on this campus?" I laugh. "You don't even know the half of it."

"Fuck that. You're still a goddamn liar," she retorts, shoving the blade into my skin.

"Why do you suddenly want to kill him?" Caleb asks. "Just because of this deal we made?"

I tap my fingers against the chair. "No. It was never about that, was it, Crystal? But we both knew that already."

"What is he talking about, Crystal?" Blaine asks.

I laugh. "I'm surprised she hasn't told you. After all the training you gave her."

His eyes widen.

"Didn't think you sneaking off wouldn't alert me?" I growl at him. "You've been teaching her how to fight behind my back."

"I did what she asked me to do," Blaine responds. "You were hunting her, and I couldn't say no." He turns his attention to Crystal. "I taught her how to defend herself."

Crystal slowly begins to laugh, the menacing sound behind it catching everyone off guard.

"Don't you see the truth?" I tell him. "She was manipulating both of you."

"What?" Caleb mutters, his grip on her slowly waning. "What does he mean, Crystal? Tell me."

"Your mother dating his father wasn't by accident." My eyes narrow as hers lose every hint of happiness. "You orchestrated it."

She's laughing uncontrollably now. "That's right, I did. I fucking did. I dropped my fucking drink so she would get some tissues and talk to your dad and butter him up."

Caleb lets go of her and steps back, bumping into the table. "You

352

told me you had nothing to do with it ..."

"You call me a liar, but you're the only one who's lied," I say, eyeing her before I focus on Caleb. "It wasn't about you or your father," I tell him, leaning back against the chair as she aims the knife at me. "She needed to find a way to get closer to *me*."

Blaine steps in the second she tries to stab me, grasping her wrist midair. "Don't. Don't do it."

"You should've thought of that before you taught me how to wield a weapon," she growls. "Now let go of me before I hurt you too," she grits.

"Hurt me?" Blaine scoffs. "Darling, I'm already hurt."

"This isn't about you," she says, pointing her knife at me. "*He* deserves to die."

"And now all your secrets are out in the open," I say, licking my lips. "The facade of the sweet, beautiful girl finally broken into pieces."

"You fucking murderer!" she screeches, punching Blaine to get rid of him.

"Crystal!" Blaine yells, trying to hold her down.

"If you can't kill him, I will!" she yells back.

"Release her," I say.

Both boys look at me like I've lost my mind.

But I knew what I signed up for when I made that deal with her and locked her up in the place I call home.

Fate has been chasing me all this time ... and now it's finally caught up with me.

She immediately thrusts the knife underneath my chin, the blade carving another line into my skin. The pain doesn't faze me, it never did. But what I didn't expect was the way my heart beats slower and slower as her ruthless gaze settles onto me.

Caleb struggles to hold himself back as he lifts a hand, desperate to intervene in my inevitable demise. "Why?"

She swallows, staring into my soul as though she's waiting for me to give him the answers that belong to her.

"Because he's the one who killed my father."

FORTY EIGHT

Crystal

Two years ago

The shadow on the other end of the street near a building with a symbol of bones makes me pause in my tracks. Even though it's dark outside, I can still make out the silhouettes of a man huddled over another. The shadowy figure wears a suit and a long coat, his face hidden. On his shoes a fiery emblem of horns.

Beneath him lies a body in a pool of blood.

I gasp and drop my bag on the ground, swiftly covering my hand so the man won't hear me.

Why did Dad want to meet here after he was done with his flower delivery?

I knew it was a bad idea. This neighborhood is dangerous.

My eyes are glued to the shadow as he rips a knife out of the man's body and tucks it into his pocket before he turns around and suddenly locks eyes with me.

Cold gray eyes peer straight into my soul, stealing my breath.

He swiftly runs off to a car in the distance and jumps in, racing off.

But all I can focus on is the dead body lying on the cold, harsh street in the middle of the night, bleeding out slowly.

I suck in a breath and pick up my bag, then step closer, and closer, and closer, until I can no longer stop my feet from running straight to him.

My own father.

"DAD!" I shriek, falling to his side to hold him up.

But the blood streams out of him, coating the pavement in crimson.

"No, no, no!" I shriek, tears welling up in my eyes. "Don't go. Don't leave me. Please!"

His eyes have already turned into themselves, lifeless, his body limp in my arms. I pull my hands back only to see blood caking my skin, and I shiver and shake in place as the tears begin to tumble.

My eyes rise to the streets where the killer just disappeared in a car.

A murderer who doesn't know what's coming for him.

My hands ball into fists. I will never, ever fucking stop until I find him … And slice his throat.

***

Present

"I saw you pull this knife from his body." My lip twitches with anger as I seethe. "You're a coldhearted murderer."

"How?" Blaine mutters, completely caught off guard.

But I've been planning this for so long that it feels like I can finally lift the veil on my own ruse.

"I searched day and night for my father's murderer, scouring the internet for a connection between that Bones symbol and a man with piercing gray eyes," I grit, lost in my own memories. "Finally, I found a picture online of that gray-eyed monster with that horn emblem on his boots."

I push the knife farther into Ares's neck, and a droplet of blood rolls down his skin.

"And then I discovered you were going to the same university I was enrolled in. It was fate beckoning me."

"You planned all of this?" Caleb asks, shivering in place.

And even though it hurts to hear the shock in his voice, I refuse to let it get to me.

I knew it would cost me my soul, heart, and body to avenge my father.

"I promised my father I wouldn't rest until I'd done what I came here to do," I say, watching the blood roll down his neck.

God, I feel so fucking powerful watching the one man who's the cause of all my misery bleed out slowly just like my father did.

When Blaine flinches, Ares warns him, "Don't intervene."

"I made a vow," Blaine responds.

"Crystal ..." Caleb growls. "Don't. Don't do it."

"He deserves it," I grit.

Caleb's voice cracks. "Even if he does, what does that make you?"

"I already am a killer thanks to him," I say, staring Ares in the eyes.

"I wanted you to feel what it was like to take a life before I gave you mine," he replies, suddenly grasping the handle only to push it farther into his skin. "So go on ... take it. Take my life. It belonged to you the second you saw me there on that street, huddled over your father's dead body."

So he admits it.

My teeth clench together as the blade etches into his skin deeper and deeper.

I can barely form words. "Why? Why did he have to die?"

A vicious smile makes his lips tip upward. "Because that's the price that needs to be paid to be part of the Torres family. One single death in exchange for a vast empire. All of us have killed ..."

I wince in disgust. "My father's life was taken just so you could inherit the family company? He was innocent!"

"This is how it's always been. Twisted, don't you think?"

"You motherf—" I grip his shirt and pull him forward, sinking the blade into his flesh until more blood begins to roll.

"Where's that smile gone, little rose? The one you so desperately carried on your face even when you wanted to tear out my heart with your bare hands?" he taunts. "Is it finally gone?"

"Smiling was the only way I could keep you from taking the last shred of dignity and hope I had left," I retort.

"So that's the reason ..." He sighs and smiles almost like a forlorn lover, and it shakes me. "You were the only one who ever smiled at me after watching me kill."

Why is he talking like he's reminiscing?

"Now do it. Kill me."

My face contorts. "Why are you so eager to die?"

No matter how much the blade pushes into his skin, the smug smile on his face refuses to fade.

"All of the pain I've endured, all of the sacrifices I've made ... all of it was for nothing because I knew in the end you would still come for me," he says.

I frown.

Sacrifices he made?

"What the fuck are you talking about?" I respond. "You've sacrificed nothing but other people for your own gain!"

"Do you want to kill me without regret? Then do it now," Ares says, licking his bottom lip. "Look at me," Ares says. "Look at the man you wish to kill."

I push the knife farther into his Adam's apple until he swallows. "You can't do it, can you?"

My lips begin to quiver.

"This is what you fear," he says.

My fear. That's what he wanted from the beginning. The one thing I vowed not to give to him.

***

ARES

"Shut up," she growls, desperate to block out my voice.

"You hate me so badly, yet you can't help but wonder if there's another choice."

"Stop." She forces herself to steady the weapon in her hands now that she's finally so close to taking what she's wanted all this time.

My life.

"Even if you so desperately want to kill me to get revenge, you can't bring yourself to actually take my life and put an end to your suffering just like I haven't been able to put an end to mine. Because I didn't just take your sanity ... I stole your fucking heart too, and there is nothing in this world I wouldn't do to keep it, little rose.

357

Whether you kill me now or years from now, it doesn't change the fact that your soul already belongs to me." My hand slowly curls around hers as it begins to shake. "And my soul has never been anything but yours."

She pulls away, desperate to unlatch from whatever feelings have just grasped her heart.

Suddenly, she snatches the key card out of my pocket and backs away from all of us, still clutching the knife like it's her only lifeline.

"Crystal ..." Caleb mutters, holding out his hand, hoping she'll take it.

"Don't," she says, shaking her head, her jaws clenched. "This, whatever we had ... It's over."

She fishes her dress off the floor and swiftly puts it on before she marches out the door.

I take a deep breath.

In the end, she still couldn't do it.

***

Crystal

"Darling, wait, please!" Blaine yells after me. "Don't leave us."

"Leave me alone," I yell back as I storm toward the stairs.

"Crystal, don't do this. We can talk this out," Caleb calls out.

"It's too late," Ares says, his voice making me want to scream. "It was always too late. She made up her mind long ago."

He's right. I did.

And if I could, I would thrust this knife into my own goddamn heart to stop it from getting in the way of killing my father's murderer.

But that would mean the end of me too.

And he knows.

He always knew I would come for him, so he set me up to fall ...

Because I quite literally fell for him.

I fell for my father's murderer.

I open the front door and run out, slamming it shut behind me, determined never to return to the Tartarus House ...

A hellhole of my own making.

FORTY NINE

Blaine

I watch her storm out the front door, shattering my heart into a million pieces.

I thought I could be there for her through thick and thin, but even I can't force her to stay around someone she wants to kill so badly.

Now more than ever, I wish I wasn't bound to Ares's life.

I was almost ready to stab him with that knife myself.

I close the door and hang my head in defeat. "We lost her because of you."

"Why? Why didn't you tell us the truth?" Caleb growls at Ares.

"You think I'm proud of lying?" Ares says, slumping in his chair.

"You knew this would happen and chose not to tell us."

"What should I have said, then? Crystal, the tiny innocent-looking blonde, wants to kill me? You think you would've believed me?"

"You could've at least tried," Caleb says.

Ares snorts. "Stop lying to yourself. You were smitten with her."

"I thought we'd made a deal with her, not that you were secretly scheming behind our backs to make her fall for us." Caleb grabs the chair and flings it across the room. "You fucking used us!"

"No," Ares retorts. "I didn't force you to do anything. You both

359

did it all on your own."

Caleb marches up to him and slaps him in the face. Hard.

"I fucking loved you. And you betrayed me."

Ares's face contorts. "I know you don't believe me, but I loved you too. I still do." He grabs Caleb's hand and caresses his own cheek with it, pressing soft kisses on the top, and I can see Caleb melt to his charms. "I can't do this without you. Don't leave me too. Please."

"You wanted to die for her," Caleb says, frowning.

"I knew she'd be my end. I always did," Ares says. "Nothing will change that." He pulls Caleb closer. "But I would die for both of you. Believe me."

He grabs Caleb's face and kisses him so passionately I feel like I'm intruding on something, so I leave the room to go grab my clothes.

But before I close the door, his voice looms in the background.

"Don't try to convince her to stay. It won't work," Ares warns.

"I'm not," I reply, clearing my throat. "But you should know I was ready to kill you for her if she needed me to. The only thing that stopped me was my life debt."

There's a pause. "I know."

And I close the door behind me and walk off, wishing I could chase her while knowing deep down she'll never forgive me for intervening and stopping her from taking his life.

My fist balls.

Ares has ruined us all.

***

She's perched over The Edge near Priory Forest at the top of the hill, which overlooks Crescent Vale City and the sea beyond.

I step closer, but a twig underneath my feet gives me away.

"Don't come closer."

"I just want to talk."

"I'm not going back to that house," she says staunchly without even looking at me.

"I won't ask you to," I reply. "And I don't think Caleb or Ares will either."

"So … I'm free of the deal that never existed in the first place." She scoffs with disdain. "How did you find me?"

"I followed you the minute you walked out the door," I reply.

She snorts. "Figured. Stalker."

"I couldn't let you walk away without letting you know someone still cares," I say, swallowing the lump in my throat.

"Right. Even after I admitted that I used you two to get closer to Ares so I could kill him?"

I chuckle. "Even then. Besides, I kind of already knew you wanted him dead, darling."

I approach her even though she said I shouldn't. I can't stay away.

"I know you still want to kill him," I reply.

"I should have." Her fist balls, collecting grass in the palm of her hand. "He deserved nothing more than a painful death for what he did to my father." She crushes the grass in her hand and lets it blow away in the wind. "Yet I couldn't do it."

"Killing isn't so easy when it involves your heart," I say.

"How would you know?"

"Darling, I've seen the way you two kiss. You need him as much as you hate the very air he breathes." I take another step.

"Look at what he's done to me." She turns her head, tears rolling down her cheeks. "All I ever wanted was to see him suffer and make him pay for his crime. And I couldn't."

I feel for her.

"All the training in the world couldn't prepare you for what you had to do …" I whisper as I approach her slowly. "I'm sorry."

I go to my knees in front of her and place a hand on her shoulder, after which she slowly caves into me, crying her eyes out against my chest, and it strips me bare of everything I thought I knew. About myself, about her, about us.

All my life, I have only ever chased fleeting desires, getting drunk on sex and the hedonistic lifestyle we enjoyed. All temporary, waning … until her.

She's made me fall in love with her by simply existing.

"You stormed into our lives, and I haven't been able to let you go. Even if you want to push me away right now, I don't want to leave you when I know you're hurting," I say, holding her tight. "I just wish I could make it all go away."

"Why? Why are you even here when you belong with *them*?" she asks, wiping away her tears as she looks up into my eyes.

"I belong to the Tartarus House because I gave my word to Ares

361

after he saved my life … but my heart … I've given that to you."

A brief smile adorns her face.

A smile so pure it takes my breath away.

She's taken my soul, and I can no longer call it mine.

That honor belongs to her.

"But I understand if you can no longer be with me," I say, shattering my own heart for her.

She nods and looks away at the horizon. "I just … want to be alone for now."

I nod too despite the fact that I feel like my heart is being ripped to shreds.

I know this is for the best.

After all … how could she be with any of us when we've enabled a monster?

"Will he still come after me?" she asks.

I shake my head. "He's made his point."

"Right. He won."

"What will you do now? Leave Spine Ridge?" I ask.

She stares out at Crescent Vale City, admiring the twinkling lights. "No. My father always wanted me to complete my studies here. So I will. For him. But I will do it on my own."

I swallow. "I will always wait for you." I pull another rose from my pocket, one I plucked on my way here, and I place it down on the grass before her. "When you're ready, I'll be there to mend your heart."

And I turn around, leaving The Edge without a heart to call my own.

***

CALEB

That night

I climb up to her room at her sorority and peer inside. I'm surprised she's already made her way back here.

Has she spoken with them and told them about our dirty secrets?

Did she tell anyone what we've made her do?

I stare at her as she's curled up in her bed, clutching her pillow tightly.

Her soft whimpers break my heart.

I place a hand against the window, contemplating whether to break through just so I can hold her tight.

But I know she'd only drive that knife of hers straight through my heart just for touching her.

She hates us now …

Not because of my actions but because I can't let her kill him.

When I first met her, I thought I wanted her to hate me. Because I was terrified of Ares's obsession with her, of losing him to her. But I slowly came to realize he wasn't the only one obsessed.

All I ever wanted was for her to be mine.

And when her mother came between us, I felt lost, confused, angry that she'd let it happen. I blamed her for my feelings when my heart was the one that had chained itself to her.

The one constant between us is Ares.

I love him, and he loves me …

But I love her too.

And he ruined that for me.

My hand slowly twists into a fist against the window, but I can't bring myself to act.

She wouldn't want me to. She made that very clear.

So I swallow away the frustration and slowly back away despite the burning flame inside my body, realizing she was destroyed by the one I love.

And with it, he destroyed me too.

FIFTY

I'm studying in the library, determined to make sure I at least succeed in my studies despite not being present for any of the classes these past couple of days.

I'm already glad the girls at Alpha Psi didn't continue asking questions after I told them I'd been gone for a few days to camp in the woods with my mother.

It was only a half lie, but I felt bad about lying nonetheless.

Not to mention the fact that those Tartarus guys kept me from so much schoolwork.

Too much is at stake here. I promised my dad I would succeed. I've already disappointed my father in one aspect. I can't risk this too.

But damn, those assholes really got the best of me.

I'm trying to keep my mind focused on the books because I really need to ace these tests that I have coming up, but it's really hard when I know one of those boys, Caleb, is also in this very same room.

And I don't want to turn around and see if he's staring at me.

I grumble to myself and read the same sentence over and over. But every time I try to home in on some paragraphs, I hear his voice, and it makes me turn my head.

I really shouldn't be listening, shouldn't even remotely be interested in what he does.

But I can't help myself. Every time I hear his voice, my heart skips a beat.

He's talking with Nathan, but Nathan doesn't seem at all interested in what he has to say.

I sigh out loud, disappointed in myself, and I flip the page to see if that part of the book is any easier, but I'm out of luck. This whole section is like trying to read a language you've never seen before. Ugh.

I reach for another book in my bag when my hands suddenly find something prickly instead, and I pull out a rose. The rose Blaine placed on the grass when he left me to my thoughts at The Edge.

My heart warms to the point that I can't help but pull it out of my bag and stare at it.

He was so gentle and kind with me. I can still feel his kisses on the palm of my hand and his warm hugs enveloping me, and it makes me smile. Maybe I made a mistake by denying him.

Would it hurt if I allowed just one of those Tartarus boys to show me affection?

I tuck the rose behind my ear, my cheeks flushing with heat knowing this is the one he plucked for me.

Suddenly, Nathan's phone rings and distracts me. "Fuck," he grits.

I can clearly hear them both from where I'm sitting.

"Who is it?" Caleb asks.

Nathan scoots back his chair and gets up. "I gotta take this one. Watch my stuff."

Caleb throws him a grimace and sighs out loud before he gets up and waltzes off through the opposite exit, leaving Nathan's laptop out in the open. And my book, with all its complexity, stares at me, practically begging me to seek help.

Goddammit.

I close my book and shove it into my bag, then make my way over to his laptop.

Nathan wouldn't mind if I used it to look something up, would he? He gave me the password for a reason last year. He always said I could help myself if I needed it.

Besides, it would only take a few seconds, and then I can move on to the next chapter. I really need the extra information, and I know he'd give it to me if I asked, but he's busy with that phone call, and I don't want to bother him.

So I sit down at his desk and type in the password, then press enter. It's an Apple, and I have no idea how to use these things. Mom never had the money to afford these products. We only had an ancient computer that barely turned on after like thirty minutes.

What the hell do I do?

I press some buttons, but it doesn't bring up a browser. Instead, some kind of file browsing thing has been opened, and I begin to panic a little. But when I see a particularly racy photo, my breathing pauses.

Is that... Lana?

When I open it up, my eyes widen.

It's her all right, bound to a chair in some kind of grimy-looking shack, with three masked guys standing around her, doing all sorts of nasty, vulgar things with their cocks and her body.

Oh my God.

Kai, Nathan, and Milo.

I close the image and look around to make sure no one else here saw.

My heart races in my throat.

Does Lana know Nathan has this?

I don't want to look at it again. I can't.

But I have to do something. I can't just let that image sit there on his laptop without Lana knowing about it. I mean, Nathan's my friend, but I don't stand for literal revenge porn if that's what this is. She told me once she was seeing all three, but I didn't expect it to go this far.

Maybe she already knows about him having this picture ... maybe they're into some kinky stuff.

But what if she doesn't know he has this in his possession?

I have to tell her.

I gather my courage and grab the file, clicking on some stuff in the hopes of bringing up some type of email I can use to send it to her. But all of a sudden, the file is opened up in a multitude of screens, and I'm at a loss of what to do.

"No, no, no," I mutter as email after email is loaded.

I try to exit, to no avail, so I keep pressing the buttons.

And that's when it happens. The email disappears ... In the outbox.

And when I see the recipients ... my heart stops beating.

Oh God.

I jolt up from the chair, staring at the laptop.

What have I done?

Panic washes over me.

The image is still there, sent not to only Lana Rivera herself ... but the entire fucking school.

I can't. I can't. I can't. Can't breathe.

I shut the laptop and run straight for the bathroom, where I lock myself inside a stall as my panic seizes control. Heat rushes over my entire body, my lungs constricted by my own breath stuck between my ribs. But no matter how hard I gulp, I still can't freaking breathe.

I take a moment to calm my racing heart, then grab some toilet paper and dab my face, cleaning myself up before I exit the stall again and pretend nothing happened.

But the first thing I do is run straight back to my dorm and lock myself inside my room in order to scream into the void.

***

After a few hours, my phone rings. Brooke's calling me, and I don't know whether I should pick up because we rarely talk. But I can't go AWOL for a week either. It would be too suspicious.

"Hey, Brooke," I say with a fake chirpy voice when I finally gather the courage to answer.

"Crystal, you gotta help."

"What's going on?" I ask.

"A lewd picture of Lana has been shared all over the university. There was a fight between some Phantom Society boys and Lana out in public, and now she's locked herself up in her room and refuses to talk to me."

Oh God.

It's happening.

My stomach almost turns over, but I manage to hold it all down as I sit up straight.

"I thought maybe you could try talking to her?"

I swallow. "Umm ..."

"I'm worried about her. Maybe she'll talk to you instead of me."

I sigh out loud. "Okay. I can try."

Oh man, how am I going to do this?

"Thank you," she says. "And please let me know how it goes!"

"I'm on my way," I say as I grab my stuff.

Briefly looking in the mirror, I pull the red rose from behind my ear and tuck it into my pocket. I don't want Lana to ask any questions I'm not ready to answer.

I exit my room and head out, but my courage wanes with every step I take.

I know exactly why she doesn't want to talk and why she had that fight.

It's all my fault, but could I say those words out loud?

When I finally make it to the building she lives in, it feels like I practically floated there. I don't remember walking. Or knocking on her door.

All I know is that I'm here.

"Lana? Brooke called and said you wouldn't let anyone into your room so I thought I'd come over. Are you okay in there?"

It takes her a while to respond.

"Yeah, I'm fine."

I open the door and slowly peek inside. She's sitting on her bed with puffy eyes, pretending she didn't just cry. It's the same face I put up after bawling my eyes out.

"She told you about the picture?" She pushes her pillow into her chest like she's looking for a hug.

I swallow and nod.

Brooke didn't just tell me. I was the one who sent it. But I can't get the words across my lips.

"I saw it. I'm sorry. Can I sit down next to you?"

When she nods, I walk over and gently sit down beside her, wrapping my arms around her so I can at least offer her some comfort. I owe her that and so much more.

"It's okay," I mutter.

How do I ever go about fixing this?

It's too late. Everyone already saw the picture.

"I'm mortified," Lana says, her voice fluctuating in tone.

"It's not your fault," I swiftly say.

The last thing I want is for her to blame herself.

She turns to gaze at me. "Please promise me you won't tell my dad or my brother."

That's what she's worried about? Her brother?

I place a hand on her knee. "I won't. I promise, but I can't guarantee other people won't." I can barely look at her. "Most of the students at school already saw it."

She grimaces. "I hope the one who spread it dies a miserable death."

Oh God.

I don't want to die.

But after what happened ... I probably deserve it. And knowing Lana and just how fiery she is, she'd probably kill me herself if she knew the truth.

I shiver in place at the thought. "You know what? I think you need some ice cream to cheer you up."

Anything to take her mind off this.

"Ice cream?" she repeats.

I get up and drag her to the door. "Yeah, let's go. Before you turn into a pile of mush."

***

The ice cream we get is delicious, and I bought her the flavors she loves the most.

I want to make it up to her, but I don't know how.

I don't even know how to come clean. How to say the words.

So I just chat and eat the ice cream, searching for the right words to bring her the news. But after a while, Lana's eyes drift to a van near the park we're having our little treat in. Something about the way her hawk eyes settle on it makes me pause.

"Hi, ladies," someone behind us says.

We both turn our heads, but the sound of something clicking makes my heart stop.

"Don't turn. Don't make a sound."

A man hiding his face behind a hoodie and a mask has pointed a gun at her head.

But I definitely recognize the symbol on his mask.

The Bones Brotherhood.

"Lana ..." I whisper, ice cream dripping down my hand.

She shushes me.

"That's right, you're gonna be real quiet, and you're gonna get up and walk to that van," the guy behind her growls.

"And what if I don't?" she says.

We can't win from a gun ... and especially not one owned by a Bones Brotherhood guy.

Slowly, the man hovers the gun to my head instead, and I quake in place. "You really wanna try me out?"

Tears form in my eyes, and one of them trickles down my face at the thought of facing death again.

"Move," the man says.

Have they come for me?

We get up, and Lana immediately grabs my hand. "It's gonna be okay."

It won't be.

They know I killed Wayne Ferry with Ares, and now they want revenge.

The ice cream drops from my hand as we slowly make our way to the gate toward the approaching van. Two guys wearing a hat and fake hair grab us by the arms and drag us inside.

And I nearly choke on my own saliva as the shadows swallow me whole.

I'm terrified.

"Please, don't kill us," I yelp.

"Shut up," one of the men says, and he directs his attention toward the guy in front of the wheel. "Drive."

The van races off so fast I can barely hold on, but something in the dark finds its way to my fingers, curling around in a warm embrace ...

Lana's hand.

The one thing I don't deserve.

My only lifeline as we're headed toward hell.

FIFTY ONE

Crystal

My whole body shakes as the van veers from left to right to whatever destination these guys are taking us. We're chained to the van like cattle, and I'm deathly terrified.

But when Lana squeezes my hand, I break under the weight of what I've done.

"I'm sorry," I mutter. "I'm so sorry."

"It's not your fault—"

"Yes, it is," I say, my voice cracking. "I took you to the park for some ice cream."

"Oh, girl ..." Lana leans into me. "You don't need to apologize."

"Yes, I do." My whole body erupts into goose bumps from knowing the truth she's about to learn. "When I heard about the fight from Brooke, I got too scared to tell you the truth. I was afraid you never wanted to talk to me again."

I swallow away the lump in my throat. "That picture that got shared around ... it's my fault."

She looks startled.

"Nathan gave me his passcode once, so when I saw he left his laptop at the library, I figured he wouldn't mind if I used it to look something up for my course. But then I saw that picture of you and them. I thought he'd taken that picture without your permission and wanted to send it to you so you'd know about it. But I didn't understand how his email worked and accidentally sent it to the entire school." Tears roll down my cheeks. "It was too late to un-send it. The damage was already done."

When she doesn't respond at all, I continue. "I'm sorry, Lana. I'm so sorry," I say. "I didn't mean to. It was an accident. Please, don't be mad at me."

"Shut it!" the driver growls at us.

Lana looks at me like she doesn't even know who I am, and I don't blame her for it.

When the van finally comes to a stop, my whole body feels like it's about to get crushed. The van doors open, and some guy steps inside to unlock the chains around our wrists.

Lana immediately throws a punch at a guy's face, teeth flying left and right before she punches him in the abdomen. He nearly vomits while she kicks him to the side, fighting her way through the men while they try to hold her back.

But all I can do is shiver in the dark.

Lana turns to me, compassion riddling her eyes.

"Jump! Now!" she yells at me.

My eyes widen in shock.

She actually wants me to be safe?

I jump out of the van and run off as fast as I can, but one of the men swiftly grasps my arms and flings me to the ground, pinning me down.

"No! Let her go!" Lana screams.

And it hurts my fucking soul.

"Give it to her," one of the guys holding her down says.

Another one brings out a needle and shoves it into her neck, making her go limp.

"Bring them inside," he growls.

I try to shriek, but the man holding me stuffs a dirty rag into my mouth, and then the needle hits my skin.

The pain and subsequent energy loss are almost instant, as though something drains me of my life until I can no longer keep my eyes open, and everything goes dark.

***

When I come to again, I don't know how much time has passed.
Or where I am.

And I can't feel my legs.

Everything is fuzzy—not just my head but my sight too.

"What … what's happening?" I mutter, but my speech slurs.

A man laughs. "Enjoying the little trip, princess?"

Who is that?

And what does he mean by trip?

Memories of a gun flash through my mind, followed by hands
shoving me into a van, the darkness surrounding me, the images all
blurring into one jumbled mess. But the one thing I remember is the
sharp object piercing my skin near my neck.

"What did you do to me?" I ask with a raspy voice.

"Gave you a li'l something so you'd stop fighting," he replies.
"Don't worry, it'll wear off soon enough." He grips my cheeks and
smushes them together. "And then you'll be able to fully enjoy all
your fucking cell has to offer."

My … cell?

I can hear footsteps along with a door squeaking before being
shuttered, metal against metal, and my eyes open wide.

The room I'm in is large enough to fit maybe one or two people,
the walls and ceiling encased with tiles that look bloated.
Soundproofing.

Oh God.

I jerk my hands, but they're tied to the wall with a chain, just like
my ankles.

Oh no, no, no!

"Let me out!" I shriek. "Please, let me out!"

Panic bubbles to the surface as I fight the chains, to no avail.

Every sound I make falls on deaf ears.

Every inch I try to move, I'm blocked.

Nothing works.

Nothing at all.

And slowly but surely, I'm starting to lose my mind.

Like a prisoner inside my own body, I cease to exist.

***

373

I don't know how much time has passed since the door last opened.

I barely hear anything beyond these walls.

My mind spins in circles, drifting in and out of consciousness as time slips away.

Seconds. Minutes. Hours.

It's all blending into one giant scream.

But no matter how much I exert my voice, no one comes to save me.

My cell is not just a prison of the body but also a prison of the mind.

There is nothing except my own thoughts to keep me company, and I am lost within them.

When the doors finally open again, I scream for help.

"Please, let me out. I didn't do anything," I say.

"Unlock her," someone beyond the doors says.

A woman?

I hold my breath and wait until the man steps forward and shoves a key into the locks. My ankles are released, and the weight of the metal around them lifts, but I can barely stand.

He unhooks the metal around my wrists, and I nearly fall, but he grabs my waist and chucks me over his shoulder.

"Take her to the main hall. I'm not going to give this one to the Bones Brotherhood. This one could fetch a far bigger prize."

Prize?

"Wait!" I shriek. "Where are we going?"

There are no answers to my questions.

Nothing but laughter and smug smiles as men force me through a bunch of grimy-looking hallways. But each door we pass strikes fear into my heart.

There are cells just like mine, all lined up, one after the other. Fifty, maybe a hundred.

And the more shrieks I hear, the less I feel like I can breathe.

"Put her with the others," the woman says.

"Who?" I ask. "Please, just let me go. I promise, I won't tell anyone."

"Shut your damn mouth," the man carrying me barks.

He throws me down in a bigger room with five other people, girls, boys, most my age. But I don't recognize any of them.

"Don't make a sound," the guard warns before closing the door.

Behind it, gunfire erupts.

I immediately crawl to the door to listen while the others huddle in the back of the room.

What is going on?

What's going to happen to me?

Panic fills my veins as I slam my fists onto the door, desperate to get out. "Let us go!"

"It won't work," a girl in the back says.

I turn my head to look at her, her face hiding behind a curtain of messy hair.

"Neither of us is getting out. Once you're in here, you're in here until you're sold to the highest bidder."

My skin begins to crawl.

This place … it's a human auction.

And I'm going to be sold.

FIFTY TWO

Several guards step into the cell, and I crawl back against the wall, their guns pointed at our faces.

"Out. All of you."

I can't let them do this to us.

I have to fight, just like how Blaine taught me. Even if you don't have a knife, use whatever you can find.

One by one, we move to the door, but when I pass the guard, I lunge at his weapon.

Everyone shrieks as I grasp it.

BANG!

A shot is fired into the floor, making me tiptoe, but I refuse to let go.

"Motherf—"

SLAP!

I'm knocked to the floor, a harsh handprint on my face, and I touch my skin where he hit me.

"You fucking bitch," the guard growls as he grabs me by the hair and drags me off the floor.

The others cower near the wall in fear of being shot by the other guards.

"You think you can just take my gun?"

"Let. Me. Go," I say through gritted teeth with the little bit of courage I have.

He laughs in my face. "You're about to pay a hefty price for that." He shoves me toward a hallway. "Get up. You go first."

I only walk because he makes me.

Behind me, the others follow suit, their heads bowed between their shoulders, courage waning with every step.

When we get to the exit, I feel frozen to the floor.

Twenty, if not more, men all stare at me from their chairs in the back of the room. All hiding behind masks, as though they're afraid I might tell someone what they looked like.

And they're right.

"The rest of you, wait here," the guard growls at the people behind me, waiting in line for their turn.

Then he focuses his attention on me. "Don't speak. Don't fucking utter a single syllable. Just stand there and listen to what the seller tells you to do." The guard pushes me toward the stage. "Now get up there."

I stumble up the stairs and onto the stage, my heart thrumming as their gazes all fixate on me. I don't know who these men are, but I know they want my flesh as they lick their lips at me like I'm minced meat to devour. The tension is palpable as I walk toward the center and stand still, while the seller, a woman, approaches the microphone in the front.

To both my left and my right are two guards, their guns aimed toward me. Should I run, they'd put bullets through my legs.

If I tried to grasp the mic, they'd gun that down too along with me.

There's no point in resisting.

"This one right here is fresh off the streets. Blonde, around twenty years, voluptuous, and her skin is flawless, not a scar in sight." The woman swings her finger in a circle. "Turn around for us."

I awkwardly spin around, and the oohs and aahs make me gag.

"See? A perfect specimen. So let's start the bidding at eighty thousand."

"Hundred," someone in the back calls out.

I can't believe I'm up here. That I can even stand without passing out from pure shock.

"Hundred and twenty."

Is that the worth of a human life?

"Hundred and fifty," the next one calls out.

All of it feels like a blur, like I no longer exist and am merely floating around in a vessel. Maybe that's for the best.

Suddenly, loud bangs make my ears perk up.

"What was that?" the woman on the stage asks the guards, who shrug in response.

More bangs follow, and all the men in the seats start to chat with each other.

The woman on stage claps her hands. "Now, gentlemen, there's no need to—"

BANG!

The loudest gunshot makes them duck for cover.

"Get the girls out of here. Don't lose our precious cargo. Bring them to the other compound," the woman on the stage commands.

The guard swiftly steps up the stage and grabs me. "Come. Now."

"Gentlemen, please follow the van to our new location. We've got some unforeseen circumstances that are being taken care of. For now, let's move to our new auction location, shall we?" the woman on the stage says, and she clears her throat. "No need to panic, our men will take swift care of any uprising."

"Is it safe?" one of the men asks.

"Of course!" the woman on the stage says. "But just to be sure, follow me to the side exit."

"Move!" the guard growls at me, shoving me back into the hallway with all the other girls and boys. "Line them up. Check them. Make sure they're ready for transport."

The guards swiftly take care of any cries for help, punching and kicking those who appear too scared to move. I stand next to the girl that talked to me. A gun pokes into my back, a reminder not to try to rebel. Wherever we're going can't be any better than this.

BANG! BANG! BANG!

Screams from the hallways behind us make us turn our heads.

What is going on out there that has even these grimy men antsy?

"Walk!" the guard growls in my ear.

I swallow away the lump in my throat and follow the rest back out, my heart beating so fast I feel like it's about to jump out of my chest.

My clammy hands shake uncontrollably, and I put them in my pocket to find relief.

Instead, I find a half-crumpled rose with missing petals.

And the thought of this tiny semblance of hope puts a small smile on my face.

"What the fuck do you have there?" the guard growls, snatching it away from me. "A rose?" He laughs and chucks it onto the dirty floor covered in blood stains, then stomps on it. "Pathetic."

Tears well up in my eyes as I glance at the rose.

My last connection to the outside world.

Gone.

**

CALEB

"Where the fuck is Caleb?"

Who the hell is that?

I hear some ruckus downstairs, so I pick up my bag and head down to see what's going on. Arlo is being dragged off the floor near the door.

"What the fuck do you want from Caleb?" he yells.

I gaze at the Phantoms—Nathan, Kai, and Milo—as I rush toward the door. "No worries, I'm here."

What the fuck do they want?

"You ..." Nathan turns his attention toward me. "You motherfucking asshole!" He grabs me by the collar. "You stole my pictures, didn't you?"

What the—

"I didn't steal shit," I bark. "Are you accusing me?"

Nathan stares at me like he's about to rip the skin off my body.

"Nathan," Kai warns him. "Don't."

But he's here punching my fellow Tartarus guys for a reason, so let him fucking talk. I'd like to fucking know the reason.

"Go on. Ask me what you wanna ask," I say.

"Did you send my picture of Lana to everyone's email?" he grits.

"No."

He balls his fist. "Don't. Fucking. Lie."

"It wasn't me," I say. "I already tried to tell you that, but you won't believe me."

"No shit!" he retorts, fuming. "You were the only one in the library with me."

Aha. So this is about the laptop.

"There were a ton of other people," I say.

"Yet you were the one watching my laptop."

"Was I?" I tilt my head and raise a brow. "Or did you just tell me to?"

I'm not his lapdog he can just order around.

"We weren't the only ones there," I say.

"You're the only one to hate me enough to send that picture to the whole goddamn school." Nathan raises his fist at me. "You motherf—"

"Enough."

Blaine's voice makes even Nathan back off.

Good.

I'm not about to get pummeled in the face for his mistakes.

"I won't allow you to soil this ground with blood," Blaine says with a sly smile. "You're all better than that. C'mon. You were lovers once, right?"

A long time ago, maybe. And I really tried to be friends with him, but he wouldn't let me.

"True," Milo muses.

"Shut up," Nathan quips.

"Your boy Caleb over here decided to put some very private pictures of Lana and us on the group chat," Kai says to Blaine.

What? That's bullshit!

"I did not," I say. "And I keep telling them that, but they refuse to believe me."

Blaine steps out of the house too.

"Interesting." He stops right in front of Nathan even though he's still got his hands on my collar. "Caleb, you'll fix this."

My jaw drops. "What? But I didn't do shi—"

Blaine lifts his finger. "Just do it."

"How is he gonna fix this?" Nathan barks. "Everyone's already seen the picture. Fuck knows the entire internet by now."

"Turn it into a story." Blaine waves his hand around. "Make her look like a victim."

"What … you mean turn us into predators?" Kai narrows his eyes and folds his arms. "You think I'm going to agree to that?"

"Your girlfriend must hate you right now, no?" Blaine retorts.

"Then I guess this is the only chance you've got to make it right."

"Um … is everyone forgetting the dead body in the picture?"

Milo pulls out his phone to show us the lewd picture they took of her. It is not something I wanted to see today, but I guess I won't be able to get that out of my retina.

Great.

Kai snatches the phone out of his hand. "Great job, Milo. Now even more people saw it."

Milo shrugs. "They already did."

"Yes, I'm aware of the dead body," Blaine says. "I've seen the picture."

Who gives a shit about any of this? We're not responsible for whatever the fuck they're doing in their free time, and I don't give a fuck about who they kill.

"People will assume she's a killer now," Kai says.

Blaine smirks. "Not if we make people believe the three masked men in the photo were responsible."

Kai seems intrigued. "Go on."

"Take your guy off Caleb first."

Finally, Nathan lets me out of his death grip, and I pat down my shirt. "Asshole."

"You'll probably have to pose for another kill with those masks on for it to work, though," Blaine says.

"Caleb can help with that," Nathan says, glaring at me. "I can turn you into a corpse in no time."

"Fine. I don't care how. Just make it happen," Kai says. "We have to make the school believe she's innocent."

Suddenly, Nathan's distracted by his phone, and he pulls it out. Hopefully, this'll get those boys off our fucking property. Though, I'm not looking forward to helping any of them.

But then he sinks to the ground, eyes nearly bulging out of his head, and part of me really wants to know what he just saw.

"What the fuck happened?" Milo asks him.

"Nathan?" Kai tries to touch him, but Nathan grabs him and yells, "Romeo took Lana!"

Oh boy.

One minute, I'm nearly being pummeled into the ground by Nathan Reed, and then those Phantom fuckers force me to come help them save their precious Lana from Romeo's claws, who is apparently in the fucking Bones Brotherhood.

They even brought Felix, Dylan, Alistair from the Skull & Serpent Society, as well as their fucking girlfriend Penelope to help save her.

I really don't want to be on any of these fuckers' bad sides, so I'll play along nicely. Even though they accused me of something I didn't even fucking do.

Man, the things a guy does for a friendship that's already sailed long ago.

When the car finally stops, we're near a grimy looking building downtown. I'm surprised these Skull & Serpent Society fuckers know exactly where one of their hangouts is. But whatever.

I just want to get in, get out, and stay alive.

We fetch our weapons and prepare, and I can already feel myself getting fired up because I'm about to put some bullets in Bonesmen heads. When it's finally time to move inside the compound, I grin and pull out my gun, taking off the safety. "Okay, guess it's time for our little showdown."

***

Present

I pull out my knife and stab one of the fuckers in the chest, pulling it out before I move on to the next. It's a game of cat and mouse with these Bonesmen and a delicious way to let go of all the rage I've kept bottled up.

I take a glance at Nathan while we knife down these fuckers left and right, trying to see who has the biggest body count. Halfway through the compound, we get separated from the main group, but at least I have Nathan. He might be an ass for making me his enemy, but at least he knows how to kill.

"I'm gonna go back to Kai and Milo and see if they found Lana yet," Nathan yells at me after we've taken down a dozen more men.

"Fine, I'll secure the entrance," I reply.

"Felix and the others are there too," Nathan replies before leaving.

The Skull & Serpent Society guys are with me, shooting Bonesmen left and right to clear a path for everyone so we can make our way out again after they've found Lana.

What's taking them so long?

"I'm going back in," I tell them. "Guard the exit."

I run back into the hallway where Kai, Milo, and Nathan are, and lock eyes with a girl with long, black hair, covered in blood.

One of the Bonesmen comes out of nowhere, aiming at Kai, so I shoot him down. "I have you covered. Don't worry."

"Who is that?" the girl with the long black hair asks.

"Caleb. Long story," Milo says. "We should run."

Suddenly, more shots go off, and Nathan jumps in front of Lana, shielding her from the fire, and the bullet lodges in his body.

"Nathan!" she screams.

Kai and I fight off the Bonesmen with everything we have, and I chuck around knives like a madman while Milo and Lana focus on stopping Nathan's wounds from bleeding out.

Suddenly, the girl with the long black hair pulls out her own knives and starts chopping up all the men in front of us like a butcher, cutting away at them with expert slices like she's never done anything but kill since she was pushed out of her mother's womb, and for a moment, I'm too flabbergasted to even fight.

My God, that woman's got skills.

She kills the Bonesmen one by one, until only their leader, Romeo, is left and on his knees, blood pouring from a wound in his abdomen. He whimpers as she pushes a knife straight into his eye, and I wince from how disgusting it looks.

Jesus.

In the big open space behind Romeo, rows and rows of chairs are all thrown about as though the people who were here left in a hurry, and I look beyond at a stage.

What the ... was this an auction?

To the left of the stage is a big door that's wide open.

And two burly guards manhandle people into the van. Boys. Girls.

But one particular blond-haired girl with pink lips and rosy cheeks makes all the hairs on the back of my neck stand up.

"Crystal?" I yell in disbelief.

FIFTY THREE

CALEB

She turns to look at Lana and then me.

What the fuck is going on?

How is she here?

But then she's shoved into the van.

I storm past Lana, headed straight for the door … right when the van races off.

"FUCK!" I scream, losing my goddamn fucking soul along with it as the van's gone before I even manage to step one foot outside.

I try to run after it, but it's no use.

I won't ever catch up on foot.

"No, no, no!" I mutter, sinking to the ground outside, still clutching my knives, my only tether to this world before I tear it all to shreds.

These fucking Bonesmen have the only girl I ever loved, and now I'll never fucking see her again.

How could this happen?

How dare they steal her away from me?

"You, you're one of them." The voice behind me makes me turn around.

Anger gets the best of me, and I roar out loud as I kill a guard, ramming the knife straight into his neck before I cut it off entirely and let the head roll across the street.

I feel feral, completely unhinged, as though there isn't enough blood in the world to satisfy my craving for murder.

I head back inside, determined to get revenge and get her back. The guys from Skull & Serpent Society and Phantom Society have managed to make the guards fear them, as there's a standoff near the hallway. I physically have to swallow away my rage to make sure I don't lose it and throw myself at them.

I need to get back to the Tartarus House ASAP and tell the boys so we can fucking track Crystal down and free her.

If I let these guys here know just how badly it affects me that they took Crystal, I'll never get out of here in time to rescue her. I have to keep my cool, play it off like it's no big deal, so they don't suspect me. None of those fuckers, not even Kai, knows what she means to us, to his own fucking brother who doesn't even know she's been taken. Taken by the Bones Brotherhood … the underground Mafia his own dad works with.

My hand clutches tightly around the knife as I make my way back through the hallway, eyeing those guards with suspicion, before I approach the group. "We should go." I clear my throat. "This truce won't last long."

God, it's so fucking hard to maintain this facade when all I want to do is scream.

We head back out of the compound through the way we came in and run to the two cars where we split up.

"I'll take our car back with Nathan and Milo," Kai says, then he turns to Lana. "You go with your brother. Caleb, you go with her too."

I jump into Dylan's car, and we race off before those guards change their mind and decide to chase us. But fuck, it feels so bad to leave the scene of the crime knowing Crystal is out there somewhere, probably wondering if she'll ever get out.

My fingers dig into my thighs as I clench my teeth together.

"What's wrong?" Penelope asks Lana, who begins to cry.

"Crystal got taken with me."

Fuck. So they were together at one point.

"She was here too?" Penelope grabs Lana's shoulders. "Why didn't you tell me?"

385

"I thought there was still time to save her," she says. "But when I finally found her, she was getting shoved into a van, and it raced off before I could get to her. I couldn't see the license plate. And now they've taken her to God knows where."

Fuck. I can't say anything.

My lips part. "I'll ask the Tartarus boys to check with their connections and see if they can find her whereabouts."

***

ARES

I clutch the banister of the balcony overlooking the maze and breathe out a sigh. The sun is setting, and it's been days since I've last felt alive.

My soul is waning along with the petals on those goddamn roses beneath me.

Was there ever a different way this could go?

No.

She would've never believed a word of my story.

I grab my drink off the table and take a much-needed sip, the heat as it slides down my throat barely enough to cause a sizzle. I feel nothing. Anger has long ago taken ahold of my heart and shriveled it up into dust.

But when her fingers thrummed my chest and touched the most hated part of me it's almost as if she collected the specks of dust with her bare hands just to see if my heart could ever beat again.

And for a moment, I almost believed it could … for her.

I sigh out loud, but a loud slam of the doors pulls me out of my thoughts, and I turn my head toward the noise.

Caleb barges out onto the balcony. "Crystal's been taken."

My eyes twitch, and I turn around to listen, praying I misheard.

"The Skull & Serpents and Phantoms forced me to come with them to save one of their own, Lana—"

"You went into a Bones Brotherhood compound alone?" I grit.

"Are you even listening to me?" Caleb says. "Crystal was there."

My eyes widen, and my lips part in shock.

Bones Brotherhood? But how?

"Lana and Crystal were snatched off the streets together, and we managed to save Lana, but we couldn't fucking find Crystal until it was too late." His voice fluctuates in tone, emotions taking hold. "I couldn't get to her. But I *saw* her." His eyes tear up. "Right when they drove her off in a van."

The glass in my hand cracks.

My little rose ... taken by those wretched monsters?

"None of them even knew she was taken too. I had to pretend I didn't know her. I had to leave and couldn't save her ..." He nearly collapses, so I chuck the glass away and catch him in my arms, holding him tight.

This isn't just going to kill him.

It's going to kill me too.

"She'll be sold," he murmurs, the desperation in his voice making me want to scream.

My teeth grind together tightly. "No. I won't fucking allow it."

"But they'll know it was you, and your father will never—"

"To hell with him," I whisper into his ear. "I didn't let her go so she could get taken and sold. She belongs to us, and we *will* track her down and take her from their fucking claws."

A smile slowly spreads on his cheeks. "Are you thinking what I'm thinking?"

"What's this?" Blaine's standing in the door opening, clutching the banister as he sways his hips sideways. "Concocting evil plans to rescue a certain damsel in distress?" He holds up his hand and looks at his nails. "And to think I just got my nails done. Such a pity I'm going to have to stain them with the blood of our enemies." A filthy grin spreads on his cheeks. "I'm so ready. When are we going?"

I grip Caleb's shoulder and look at them both, licking my teeth. "Grab your guns and knives. Let's show them the demons of Tartarus. Tonight, we feast on their fucking bones."

387

FIFTY FOUR

ARES

It was easy to find the location they took her to. My father has a whole host of contacts at his disposal, contacts I could easily swipe from his laptop at the casino. Just a quick five minutes in and out of his office while he was too busy chatting up new clients at the blackjack table, and I know exactly where they're keeping her.

These Bones Brotherhood have so many different locations all over the country, but only a couple of them actively sell humans, and two near Crescent Vale City. One of which just got raided by the Skull & Serpents and Phantoms to find Lana Rivera.

And of course, my father has a contact at the nearest location, so I've already called them and asked if they sell petite blond-haired girls, posing as one of his clients.

No names.

Just the description is enough for them to offer me and my two friends a seat at the auction.

I shift in my seat and look around the room to try to gauge just how many I need to kill in order to succeed. Fifteen guards at the very least, just for this room. There must be far more beyond the doors where they keep the prisoners, as well as in the multitude of offices, and multiple standing guard near each exit.

Caleb leans sideways to whisper. "How much longer do we have to wait?"

"I want her to be safe first," I whisper. "After, you're free to kill whoever you want."

He licks his lips, antsy at the prospect of unleashing his violence on these poor souls.

I smile. They won't even know what's coming for them until it's too late.

And I will happily take my last shower in a spray of their blood.

***

Crystal

My whole body shakes as I huddle in a corner, just like the others.

I have no clue where I am or how long I'll remain.

The moment I was shoved into that van, all my senses went into overdrive, but the blindfold they put around our heads made it impossible to know where they took us. They only let us take it off once we were in this cell, where we've remained.

I promised my father I would never fear the life I was given, but I can't stop the terror from slowly eating me alive. I wasn't scared of the Tartarus boys, but the prospect of being sold to someone I don't even know, someone of any age, of any type, makes all the hairs on the back of my neck stand up.

When the door opens up again, I hide into a pillar, hoping they don't pick me as one of them steps inside the cell.

"You." The guard's stern voice isn't what makes me look.

It's the gun pushed into my skin.

"It's your turn. Get up."

With my heart beating in my throat, I crawl up from the floor and the guard grabs my arm and shoves me toward the door. I take one more glance back at the other people in the cell before the door is shut.

"Where are we going?" I mutter under my breath, already regretting having asked a question.

He pushes the barrel into my back, and I'm very conscious of the fact that I could be taking my last breath at any moment. That this could be my last few steps before I'm sold to the highest bidder. Before my body no longer belongs to me.

We walk into a long hallway and go left, toward a crooked, wooden staircase in the back.

"Up the stairs," the guard growls, shoving me forward.

Above me is a bright light shining down onto a stage.

"Don't speak unless you're spoken to."

Oh God. It's happening again.

"Do as you're told or you will feel pain. Understood?"

I nod, but I don't feel physically present as I slowly turn into myself, desperate for this to stop.

Still, my feet move up, each step slowly pulling my mind into oblivion until I get to the top.

The guard nudges me toward the stage. In the middle, the same woman I recognize from before stands at a microphone and clears her throat.

"Our next girl has been on the stage previously, you may recognize her from when we had to move to this location. As you can tell, she is still well behaved, well trained."

She swirls her finger around, and I spin again, just like I was told to do last time. "A perfect girl for whatever cravings you may have."

She holds up her hand, and I stop. "Bidding starts at a hundred and eighty thousand."

A guy in the back raises a paddle. "Hundred and ninety."

"Two hundred," another guy calls out.

I shiver in place, trying to remember the voices and imprint them in my brain so I can recognize whoever tried to buy me if I ever meet them again.

"Two twenty," the next one says.

I feel like cattle being sold on the market for breeding.

My eyes find the guard in the back, his gun fixated on my legs to make sure I get the message: If you fight, we will shoot.

My eyes flutter back and forth between the stage and the exits around the room, trying to search for a way out. Maybe I can overpower whoever buys me and run like hell the second they try to transport me into his car.

I look around at all the men beyond the stage holding up their hands one by one to try to get their hands on me like I'm some prized jewel, but the second I spot two feverishly gray eyes I stop.

Even though he's wearing a mask, his veiny hands and slick, combed-over black hair make my heart stop.

Could it be … ?

No, don't trust your tired mind. It's making you see things.

"Any more bidders?" the woman calls out.

The guy with the black hair raises his hand, and his lips part, a hint of a smile at each edge. "Five million."

Audible gasps erupt from the audience, and even I can't believe what I'm hearing.

"Five million, going once," the woman says. "Going twice."

No one says a single word.

"Sold to the gentleman in black."

The guard comes up the stage and grabs my wrist, dragging me away, but the last thing my gaze finds are gray eyes piercing through the dark like a beam of light, taking ahold of my soul.

Could it be …?

"Walk," the guard growls, shoving me down the stairs and into a separate chamber, away from the other girls. "Sit."

He closes the door, and I'm left alone in the darkness with nothing to hold except the clothes on my back.

I sit down on the floor and close my eyes.

There's no point in looking when there's nothing to see. From what others have told me, this is where they make the girls that are sold wait for their buyer to come pick them up.

After a while, the door cracks open, and I take a deep breath, expecting the worst of whoever wanted me so badly they'd put down five million for me.

"In here. Do whatever you want. You've got twenty minutes," the guard growls. "Then you gotta pay up."

I look up right as the guard steps away and in walk three men with masks on their faces, one with an umbrella, two others in suits, their figures casting shadows on the concrete floor.

One of them steps closer, and I crawl away, backing into the cold, hard wall. But he still gets closer and goes to his knees in front of me. He leans in, his hand caressing my cheek so softly I hold my breath. "Your face is far too pretty to be poisoned by so much fear."

That voice…

He pulls off his mask, casting it aside, and I gasp in shock at the chiseled face appearing underneath, the one I've loathed for so long … the one I could kiss just by seeing.

"Ares," I mutter in disbelief, a brief smile forming on my face. *How is he here?*

Blaine

Ares cups her face. "I missed that wretched smile of yours, little rose."

Her jaw nearly hits the floor, but then she does a double take, almost like she remembers the last time she saw him she wanted him dead.

"Don't kill him just yet, darling." My voice makes her look up at me, and I tear off my mask too. "We still need him to pay up so we can get you out of here."

"What?" she mutters, shell-shocked.

Caleb takes off his mask too, chucking it to the ground before running his fingers through his blond hair. "Miss me, slut?"

Tears well up in her eyes, and a grin spreads on her cheeks. "You came for me."

"Of course we did. Couldn't let you rot away in a place like this, now could we?" I say, flicking my hair to the side. "I'm going to need to bathe with a million different soaps to get the stench of this disgusting place out of my skin."

Ares offers his hand, and she makes a distrustful glance. "Trust me."

And for some reason, despite all the things he's done, she still takes his hand and lets him pull her up.

Caleb approaches, and it takes her a second to adjust to the situation before she jumps into his arms and hugs him tight. "Thank you."

"Don't thank me yet. We haven't made it out yet," he says, chuckling.

"What about me?" I pout from the corner. "Don't I get a hug?"

She snorts and releases Caleb only to run into my strong arms instead, and I hug her as tightly as I can. She buries her face into my ample chest like I'm a teddy bear.

"I missed you too, darling," I say, and I grab her hand and place a kiss on top again just like always. Her smile alone makes me want to ravage her here and now. Would it be so terrible? I mean, they gave us twenty minutes alone in this cell, might as well make use of it.

"Wait, where's Lana?" she suddenly asks, turning around to look at both guys. "We have to save her."

"The Phantom Society boys have her, don't worry," Caleb replies, throwing his knives in the air. "Helped them get her out myself. Thankless job."

"Good, I was so worried about her when they split us up. I don't even know why they took us."

"I do," Caleb replies. "The Phantoms have beef with the Bonesmen Brotherhood, and Lana was in the middle of it all."

"Enough small talk," Ares says, clearing his throat. "Tell the guards we want to take her outside for fresh air."

"Yes, Sir," Caleb says, and he turns around and marches off to get the guard. "We're taking her outside."

"Fine. Pay up first, and you can take her," the guard growls.

"We require her phone too," I say.

"Why?" the guard snaps.

I just slip him more money. "If you don't ask questions, you get paid. Now bring the phone."

The guard rolls his eyes and pulls it out of his own damn pocket. That slime was keeping it for himself all this time. I wonder if his supervisor even knew what he was trying to steal.

When he's handed it over to me, I say, "Good boy." He seethes with rage.

Ares grabs her hand and pulls her along with him. She cowers as we pass the guard, but Ares fishes a paper from his pocket and smashes it into his chest.

The guard eyeballs the paper and steadies himself so he doesn't fall from sheer surprise that someone would lay down that amount of money for a girl like her.

"Let's go," Ares says, and we all follow him through the long hallway, past a bunch of doors, and up a set of stairs that lead to another door. Behind it, the auction room makes her pause and stare like a deer looking into the headlights.

"They're not looking at you," I whisper into her ear, and she nods. "Keep walking. The exit is right in front of you."

The guards near the exit stop us, but the guard behind us holds up the paper Ares gave him, and they finally move out of our way.

Caleb grabs her shoulder and helps her push through the fear of passing them while Ares opens the door.

When we're outside, Caleb and Ares release her, and I marvel at the way she gently strolls around the open road while looking up at the sky as raindrops pitter-patter down on her. It doesn't seem to faze her. In fact, it almost seems as though the rain gives her life.

She spins around in the fresh air, sucking in lungfuls of oxygen like she was terrified she might never have the opportunity again. It even makes me blink away a few tears.

"Are you crying?" Caleb asks.

"It's the rain," I reply.

He pats me on the back with a snort. "Sure it is."

But I can't stop looking at her.

No wonder Ares calls her his little rose.

She truly looks like a flower spreading its leaves under the pouring rain to catch all the droplets. And all we ever did was tear off her petals one by one.

***

ARES

She stands in the rain with her arms opened wide, gorging on the freedom of the outside world.

And I think, out of us three watching her, I'm the only one who truly understands.

I take in a breath and revel in her beauty under the pouring rain, letting her soak it all in for a moment longer. Then I walk up to her and place a hand on her shoulder, whispering into her ear, "I will kill them all for you. All you have to do is say yes, and I will be your vessel for slaughter."

Her body freezes under my touch.

"But when I'm done ... you will be mine."

She takes a short breath, still gazing into nothingness as she says, "Yes."

Such a simple word for such a significant choice.

Even now, after everything I've done, she'd still let me be her justice.

I smile against her ear. "That's my girl."

***

He wants to risk his life by going back in there and kill them ... for me?

Even though I longed so much for him to die, the prospect of it actually happening makes it hard to continue breathing.

His, forever more, if he survives. My father's slayer, a tool for revenge.

And I just said yes.

When I turn around, he throws off his jacket to reveal a godly amount of guns and knives all tucked away neatly, and the second he pulls them out, Caleb's eyes begin to twinkle.

"Fuck, I'm so goddamn ready to split them open," Caleb grits, and he pulls out his pocket knives. "Let's go butcher some animals."

The guard watching us does a double take, but Blaine pulls his katana out of his umbrella and, with one fell swoop, cuts the head off his body.

My eyes widen at the sight of the blood spraying around.

They run inside and screams erupt from the auction room.

BANG!

BANG!

Shots are fired left and right, and I peer in through the door opening to see what they're doing, too curious to back away. Caleb and Blaine are killing guards that pour in from all sides, thrusting their weapons into their abdomens like they've done it a million times before, while Ares guts the men bidding on me one by one, slicing them open from their abdomens to their necks.

Suddenly, one of the guards comes out of a room near the exit, blocking my only way out. I make a fist and punch him in the face, but it doesn't seem to faze him.

His eyes look murderous. "You bitch!"

Shit, I don't have anything to defend myself.

I run into the main chamber where bullets ricochet against the walls.

The guard grabs my arm, and I shriek. "You're not going anywhere, bitch!"

Ares's gaze fixates on me, the rage on his face nothing I've ever seen before as he aims and shoots.

BANG!

The guard who grabbed me drops to the floor, blood pouring from his forehead.

Ares rushes over to me, despite the fact that the auctiongoers are bolting all over the area. He pulls out one of his guns and pushes it into my hand. "Use it. You know how, little rose."

I gulp and nod, and he softly pecks me on the forehead before he walks off like it was nothing … even though I can still feel the kiss searing into my skin.

One. Two. Three. One after the other is put down with a knife to the throat or a shot in the head like he's crushing ants under his boots. All while Caleb and Blaine are counting which one of them killed more guards.

"Fifteen!" Blaine yells.

"Liar, I threw that knife at him!" Caleb says. "Fourteen."

Blaine cuts through a guard coming up behind Caleb and says,

"Fifteen now, darling. Better catch up."

"You motherf—" Caleb growls and he chucks his knife at one of the men at the auction attempting to flee through the exit. "Happy now?"

From the corner of my eye, I spot three guards together with the woman who sold me sneak off into a hidden door behind a cabinet, along with several of the people I was in a cell with, all forced to walk with a gun aimed at their backs.

Oh God. I have to save them.

"The others! We have to save them!" I shriek, trying to get the boys' attention.

But they're far too busy murdering the men who have tried to keep us chained.

I rush to the cabinet, desperate to take the life she wanted to take from me, but when I open the hidden door, she's gone.

There's a secondary exit from the building at the end of a long hallway.

A secret route.

And the woman along with all the girls are nowhere to be seen.

Fuck.

I'm too late.

"You little shit—" A guard comes up behind me, and I turn around and shoot. The bullet enters his stomach and goes out the other end, and I step back as he groans and nearly falls on top of me.

With bloodied hands, he pulls out a gun and aims at me, but before he can shoot, I hold the gun over his head and finish him off. Blood sprays everywhere, but I don't give a shit anymore as I stand on top of the corpse of the man who has kept me a prisoner in a cold, harsh cell.

His death is on my hands, and my God … does it feel good.

Ares was right; death does become me.

Even if I can't save the others, at least I can make these fuckers pay for putting their hands on us.

I turn around and head out with the gun still firmly in my hand, but the second I step out of the room, I come face-to-face with Ares. "There you are. I wondered if you'd run off."

His eyes briefly swipe over my gun, the barrel directed at him, before he turns around and blocks my body with his.

BANG!

A bullet hits the wall right behind me.

Ares tries to shoot, but his gun's gone empty, so he tucks it away and pulls out a knife instead. He chucks it right at the man who shot us, without a single inch of fear in his eyes. And it makes me wonder if he's ever felt what it's like to be afraid at all?

Despite the fact that I could easily cripple him for life or take him out for good with this gun in my hands ... he's still standing with his back turned against me.

As if it doesn't bother him that I could end it all.

Or maybe he doesn't care if I did.

Trust me.

I hear his voice in my head again, whispering to me, begging me to follow.

And when I look up, there he is, glancing at me over his shoulder before aiming to shoot at a man fleeing for his life.

He takes life like it means nothing, yet he's keeping mine safe like it's sacred to him.

And for some reason I can feel the little bits of hatred slowly unfurl from around my heart.

Suddenly, he spins on his heels and pulls me down. "Duck."

He shields me with his body, hands firmly planted against the wall.

A knife is thrown right at us, and I blink once only to hear Ares groan as it pierces his back.

"Ares!" I shriek, unable to keep the terror at bay.

He peers down at me, the pain clearly visible in his eyes, but it still doesn't make him break. Grinding his teeth, he tears the knife from his own back and throws it right back at his attacker, hitting him in the heart. An instant death sentence.

"Hey! That was my kill!" Caleb yells.

"Then fucking kill him before he kills me, goddammit," Ares growls back.

"Twenty-five!" Blaine yells as he pulls his katana out of the guard's body. "Who's next? Don't all beg at the same time, please."

Caleb chucks his knife at the last guy's head and plucks it out, licking up the blood. "Delicious. Twenty-five."

"It's safe now," Ares tells me. "Let's go."

He grabs my hand and pulls me away from the wall, but I pause to look at all the dead bodies littering the floor. It's insane the amount of people they managed to kill in such a short amount of time.

There's a river of blood in front of me. Chilling.

Ares grabs the check off the guard he just murdered, blood staining the paper as he holds it up. Five million dollars. All for me.

He pulls out a lighter and sets the paper ablaze, throwing it back onto the corpse.

"No amount of money is worth a single drop of her blood," he murmurs at the guard before he looks my way, making me blush again.

My blood invaluable?

He tasted it on his tongue, licked my wounds like I was a delectable dessert. All while calling me his Ambrosía ...

He tucks the lighter back into his pocket, grabs my hand again, and pulls me along with him, but I can't stop looking at the wound in his back, wondering why it doesn't seem to bother him.

We make our way back to the exit, and Blaine wipes his katana on the last guard lying on the floor in the middle of the hallway. "You look a little pale. You guys were so much fun, but we have to run now. Toodles, darlings."

I chuckle a little from his comments, then follow Ares back outside, and we run through the rain to his car. He sits down behind the wheel, while Caleb sits down in the passenger's seat, and Blaine in the back with me. But all of them are looking at me.

"Are you okay?"

I nod a few times. "I'm not injured."

Ares narrows his eyes. "Did any of them touch you?"

I shake my head, a blush creeping onto my cheeks because he'd even think to ask about my well-being.

"Good. He puts the car into reverse and slams the gas pedal. "I would've hated myself for ending their lives without cutting off their dicks and balls first."

FIFTY SIX

CALEB

I breathe a sigh of relief when we're finally back at Tartarus House.

We were so close to losing Crystal forever that I still can't believe it.

I glance at her, but her gaze evades me, almost as if she can't bear to look at me without questioning her own heart and why it so easily gave itself away to me. To us.

But maybe we were all lying to ourselves when we believed this could just be flesh against flesh.

Suddenly, her fingers touch mine while my hand rests on my lap, and I look her way again. She gently smiles, interlacing her fingers through mine, and it makes me feel so damn fucking good I want to smash my lips onto hers.

But it's too soon. Too early. Too fresh after all that killing.

She used me for her own gain, pushed her mother into my father's arms just to get closer to Ares ...

I unfurl my fingers from hers and look away, but the soft, breathy sigh leaving her lips doesn't go unnoticed.

Ares parks the car and opens the door, but the second he steps out he nearly collapses. I immediately jump out and run to him to

401

support him under my shoulder.

"I'm fine," he says.

"Stop lying," I say. "Let me help you."

He snorts. "You're one to talk."

"Guess we're both perfect liars then," I murmur with a grin. "Let's get you inside."

I tug him with me, but not before glancing over my shoulder at Blaine and Crystal who just stepped out of the car. Even though she stomped on my heart by admitting to her lies, it still aches for her. And I don't think anything will ever change that fact.

I've fallen in love with not just one but two liars.

***

Blaine

Crystal looks as pale as snow, and I offer her a hand when she steps out of the car.

"I can walk," she says, nearly falling over, but I catch her just in time, my palm fitting neatly into the small of her back.

Perfect.

"I ... I ..." she murmurs, a blush creeping onto her cheek.

I place a finger on her lips. "You don't have to say anything. I know how you feel." I smile. "Even though you only wanted me to teach you so you could kill Ares, I knew what I was getting myself into."

Her eyes flash with surprise. "But Ares didn't tell you why." She pauses. "Or did he?"

I swallow and nod. "Ares tells me almost everything, except for the blood on his back, but he doesn't speak about that to Caleb either. Not to anyone, I think." I clear my throat. "Regardless, even if I did know, it's not up to me to tell someone else's story. It would've only fueled the hatred. Something I wish didn't exist between us."

She sighs and looks down. "I just ... wish I knew what to do."

I tip up her chin. "Whatever choice you make, I'll be there with you every step of the way."

"So you're not mad?"

"I don't know, are you mad at me?" I raise a brow. "We both kept information from each other."

She snorts. "I guess we're all liars here."

"That's what Tartarus is known for," I muse, hooking my arm through hers. "Liars, deceivers, killers, gamblers, all the riffraff of society living under the same roof. I feel so lucky."

She hides her laughter under her hand.

"Glad I could make you smile a little," I say, winking.

"I'm surprised you almost let me kill him, though, that was very unlike you," she says.

"Believe me, it took every ounce of my restraint." I shrug as I add, "But you heard him warn us not to intervene."

She frowns and looks up at the staircase where Caleb is helping Ares get back to his room. "It almost felt like he … *wanted* me to kill him."

"Maybe …" I mutter. "He's been dancing on that edge with Caleb for quite some time. Both of them keep each other alive when the other was about to fall."

"They really have a complicated relationship," she mutters.

"Yes. But when you came into the mix, it was like chucking a fire at a concoction of gasoline and alcohol."

She swallows as though it falls hard on her, especially when Caleb glances at her over his shoulder. Even I can feel their palpable connection from this distance, like lightning zapping across the room, the same lightning I feel whenever I touch and kiss her.

I sigh out loud. "I'm sorry, darling. I don't want you to think it's all your fault. Those boys have been toxic for a very long time, believe me."

"It's fine. I know what I've done." Her resolve strengthens, I can see it in her eyes. "I'm not finished yet. I just need to figure out …" Her words taper off as though she's still trying to decide on the words to say. But no words will ever suffice for the complicated feelings we have.

I grab her hand and press another kiss to the top. "Whatever you choose, you know I'll always be here waiting for you."

***

CALEB

When she approaches Ares's room, I immediately walk to the door and stop her from entering. I don't want to get between them, but if she still intends on ending his life, this would be the perfect opportunity.

She peers at him over my shoulder at his blood staining his shirt, so I block the view with my body and fold my arms while I peer down at her.

"I can't let you see him when he's at his weakest," I say.

Her gaze sweeps across all the blood caking my skin, a hint of shock riddling her face. Still, she doesn't back away despite the horrors she just watched us inflict on our enemies, and it surprises me.

"I just … wanted to say thank you. For saving me."

I want to believe her. I really do. But I know she'd kill him in a heartbeat too.

"Why? You still want to kill him."

Her face darkens. "You know *why*."

"Yes. I do." The look in her eyes has definitely changed into something less vicious than before. But I'd be lying if I said I didn't feel hurt. "But Ares and I need each other, and I won't let you take that away from me too."

Her round lips part. "I … I'm sorry for lying to you."

Her apology catches me off guard.

She averts her eyes. "I did mean to tell you about my struggle with him at some point, but I needed to prove first why I did what I did so you could understand."

I can feel myself softening up, and I bite my lip piercing, torn between her and him. Because I know exactly why she wants to kill him. A fire has been churning inside her for so long that it was bound to burn out. "I know you want to avenge your father." I pause. "But you have it all wrong. I just know it. And this thing? It's breaking him, just like it broke me when I found out your mother was dating my father."

Her eyes tear up slowly. "I …"

"Let her in."

Ares's voice rips through me, and she blinks away a few tears in a hurry.

"I can't let her kill you," I growl at him, rubbing my forehead in despair as I turn to her again. "I won't." I grab her shirt and pull her close. "Don't you understand? I need you both alive. I need you, and I need him. You're both my salvation and my downfall. I fucking need you both so much I can't stand to live without. How am I supposed to survive when it feels like I can't fucking breathe?" I say, desperation poisoning my voice. "How am I supposed to survive knowing you two will be each other's end?"

Guilt riddles her blood-caked face. "But—"

"Don't make me choose. Please," I murmur, slowly releasing her from my grip. "I'm begging you."

Surprise flashes across her face.

"I … love him," I whisper, letting my hand travel down her chest as my own tightens with desire. "But I've also fallen in love with you."

FIFTY SEVEN

Crystal

"What?"

He ... loves me?

I don't even know what else to say.

I'm too stunned.

I almost can't believe my ears, but something about the way he looks at me with those anguish-laced hazel eyes makes me trust him.

I never knew how much it would hurt to watch him suffer.

To watch him literally bleed for me.

My hand instinctively rises to touch the gash on his chin from the fight. A small wound compared to the festering hole in his heart eating away at him. And I am the one to blame. All this time, all he wanted was to protect his mother, for his father to stay, for his family not to break apart.

And it's been killing him to the point where he's equated his own death with pleasure.

I swallow away the lump in my throat, realizing what a complicated individual he is, even though I initially believed he was nothing more than a rampant bully.

And just how much I've begun to feel for him.

My finger slowly travels up to his lip as my defiance slowly unravels from the last hanging thread.

"Show me what it's like when you love."

Within an instant, his lips smash on mine, practically making my heart sing. His tongue sweeps around my mouth and the roof of my mouth, desperately circling around my tongue as though he wants to mesh our hearts together just so I can feel the kind of love he feels for Ares.

He kisses me like he's torn between loving me and hating me for making him fall in love. And I can't blame him. He's made me feel the same way as my fingers curl around his hair and hold on tight.

But my God, do these forbidden kisses feel so damn good.

"I can't. I can't choose," he murmurs between kissing me. "I want both of you to be mine."

His kisses are feverish, and for a second, I almost forget to breathe. "Yes."

He slowly tears away from my lips. "Is it possible?"

I bite my lip and shudder in place. "Let me talk with him."

He takes a deep breath and averts his eyes before he finally steps aside and allows me to pass.

"Thank you," I say as my hand lingers on his, and I squeeze softly.

He nods as I step inside the room, where Ares is still partially hunched over in a seat, his fingers in his coal-black hair caked in blood, like he's overthinking his sins.

I swallow away the lump in my throat and step closer to the devil himself, desperate to know whether all I ever believed was the truth … or a lie.

"I wanted to thank—"

"Don't." He interjects. "Don't thank me for doing what's right. I know you still hate me because I made you hate me."

He stands, clearly in pain, but still turns to face me, and I'm not prepared for how my heart feels severed in two.

"You asked me why I was so eager to die …" he says, slowly unbuttoning his bloodied shirt, making me gulp as the letters begin to appear underneath. "Why your father was killed …" It's hard to take my eyes off him as he's never taken off his shirt before, and the abs beneath it are a sight to behold. "But all this time, you've been asking the wrong man."

He turns around as his shirt slowly drops to the floor, and my jaw drops at the sight of all the scars on his muscular back, more than I could ever imagine, one slice after the other, searing red marks engraved into his skin. Some newer than others, almost as if they were welts chiseled into his skin mere days ago.

And in the top left corner, the wound caused by the knife that impaled him when he protected me from harm.

His thick, muscular arm lifts over his head, and his fingertips graze across the wound.

"Go ahead … feel it."

I shudder as I step toward him and touch his back, the scars clearly as old as years yet as fresh as can be, as though it's been done to him again and again.

They're coarse, rough on all edges, like the careless strikes of a whip.

My eyes widen.

After we killed Ferry, Ares was dragged back into the Tartarus House with blood seeping through his shirt.

Did someone hurt him because of what we did?

"This. This is what your father's death cost me."

Oh God.

His sacrifice.

My lip trembles. "This … this was done to you because you killed my father?"

Slowly, he turns to grab my hand, his piercing gray eyes haunting my very soul. "No. I was punished because I refused."

***

ARES

Two years ago

"Please. Don't do this. I have a wife. A daughter," the man begs.

My eyes travel across my victim's face and down his chest, where a little patch is sutured onto his jacket with the name "Murphy's Flowers." But it's the man's pleading green eyes that make me drop the knife onto the ground.

"No."

I get up and walk away from the man who was supposed to be my victim, knowing full well what it will cost me.

My God-given right as firstborn son, the vast empire of the Torres family, all the companies my father has under his belt … and his undying devotion.

All of it gone with one simple word.

But I have made my choice now. There's no going back from here.

"Ares," my father grits. "Come. Here."

"Didn't you hear me?" I say, glancing at him over my shoulder. "I said no."

Kai makes a tsk sound. "Ares, c'mon. It's not that hard."

"Just because you have no shame who you kill doesn't mean I don't."

"If you don't do this," my father warns, pausing midsentence, "If you won't kill for me … That's it. That's the end of it. Of *everything*."

I know what's at stake here.

But I've already made my decision, and I'm sticking to it.

"Jesus, Ares. It's just one kill," Kai scoffs.

I refuse to become the monster he wants me to be, and if this is what it takes to be the man *I* want to be, then so be it.

"The killing of an innocent man. I don't murder innocent people."

"Fine. You want to betray your family? Have the moral high ground? Then stay there."

My father snatches the knife off the ground, and my eyes widen.

I rush toward the man. "Wait! No—"

Too late.

My father jams it straight into the man's heart, and I stop halfway there.

Fuck. I didn't think he'd actually do it.

The man howls in pain … and then nothing.

"This is what happens when you don't do your duty to your family." My father marches at me and grips my shirt. "You just lost *everything*. My trust. My love. My fucking company. All of it."

The look in his eyes is murderous as he shoves me away.

"Kai. Get in the fucking car. We're going."

Kai throws me a worried glance, but I brush it off as I waltz toward the man and hover over him, watching the light slowly dim in his eyes. I push my index finger against his neck and feel. No pulse.

Fuck.

I should've let him run when I had the chance. Maybe then he could've escaped this fate.

"Your death is on my hands," I say as my fingers curl around the blade.

I tug it out, but the man is already lost, his heart no longer pumping blood.

This fucking man … didn't deserve to die. But I know the cost of his life will be great.

I glare at the car being started in the distance, the car lights like a cop's flashlight beaming onto my crime.

"Ares. Come," Kai beckons me from the window.

Sighing, I get up and tuck the knife into my pocket while my eyes happen to connect with a pair of green eyes in the distance that strike me so much I stop breathing for a moment. They're hauntingly beautiful and riddled with death.

Goose bumps scatter on my skin before I pull up my coat and run off to the car, jumping into the back seat as my father hits the gas.

But I still can't help but look out the back window at the girl hovering over the man's corpse, bawling her eyes out before a visceral scream can be heard.

It's the kind of pain one can only feel once in a lifetime.

The kind of pain that haunts not just one but two souls.

***

Present

"There is nothing I wouldn't do to turn back time …" I say, "So I could've saved him."

I turn around so she can look at my chest. Her eyes gawk at the scars etched into my skin, a name which quite literally chains me to her.

Murphy.

Her last name.

"I carved this into my own flesh that night to remind me of what I've sacrificed. What it cost me. What I have to live with for the rest of eternity."

She sucks in a breath, and tears well up in her eyes.

She looks completely shell-shocked.

But this is the naked truth.

"Why didn't you tell her about the letters?" Caleb mutters from the doorway.

"Did you know?" Crystal asks him.

Caleb shakes his head. "I never saw much of the scars. I was only allowed to dab them, but he didn't want me to look. And the letters ... I only saw partially." Caleb swallows, like he's realizing for the first time how much Ares kept hidden from all of us.

"Because I didn't want anyone to know what he's done to me," I say. "But I realize now I should've shown this long ago."

I lick my lips and fish a knife out of my pocket. "This is the knife my father gave me to prove my worth to him. Instead, he used it to punish me by slicing my back open that very same night."

I don't hesitate to step closer, closer to the edge of oblivion, closer to the fringes where we both belong. I push the knife into her bloodstained hand as she begins to tremble.

"Every time I killed to oppose him, he would whip me raw. Every time I went against his rules, he would slice me open. Every time I tried to save those who didn't deserve it in his eyes, he would hurt me."

I grab her free hand and place it on the letters I carved into my skin.

"But this pain? This is my own. This is the pain I chose to endure."

Her lip quivers. "Your father hurt you every time you disobeyed?"

I nod.

"This Ferry guy we killed," she mutters, tears welling up in her eyes. "You knew your father would come after you, didn't you?"

I nod. "No amount of his rage will stop me from punishing the people directly responsible for destroying my life ..." I look into her eyes. "And yours."

She shudders in place as her fingers slowly traipse over the scars on my chest.

"Your father punished you ... because of my father and me," she whispers.

"The moment I met you, I wanted nothing more than for you to fear me so all my suffering would've made sense," I murmur, grabbing a loose strand of her hair so I can tuck it behind her ear.

411

"Instead, you smiled at me. *Smiled.* At the man you thought was your father's killer." My jaw tenses. "And it broke me."

A tear rolls down her cheeks, and I pick it up with my index finger.

When I first met her, I wanted nothing more than to see her cry. To witness the hatred that I deserved just so I could make peace with all the pain I endured. Fear was the only feeling I knew, the only feeling I trusted.

Fear was what I was owed.

But she … she wouldn't fear me, no matter what I or any of us did, and it twisted my heart.

My fingertips slide down her cheek, spreading my own blood across her skin, which comes alive under my touch. Electricity sparks between us, and a decrepit smile slowly sneaks onto my face.

I guess there's no escaping now.

"I wanted to hate you, little rose," I murmur. "So badly. But the more I watched you suffer as much as I had, the more it made me bleed." My finger slides down her neck, spreading the bloody line to her chest. "This heart I longed so hard to crumble with my bare hands just so I could die in peace. What kind of a soul-crushing monster would fall for the one girl who wanted him dead?"

Her eyes widen, but I have to push through.

This is it.

"I've only known cruelty. But in the end, I was the cruel one to take away your smile. The one thing that kept me alive. Breathing. Yearning. Hoping. When that smile vanished …" She sucks in a breath when I inch closer. "My soul vanished too."

She shudders in place. "Ares …"

I look into those sparkling eyes, wondering if I could ever earn back that smile that has haunted me so.

I grab her hand, the one that holds the knife, and push it into my own abdomen. "You've taken ahold of my soul. Stolen it right out of my chest along with my heart. All that's left of me is an empty vessel. I'm nothing but a ghost wandering through life, but I'm not the one who haunts. It is *you.* You have haunted me since the very first day I saw you, and I don't want to let go until I've killed everyone who even so much as breathes in your direction." I pause and watch her breathing pick up. "I am a man possessed. Possessed by the fantasy of owning this heart …" I push my fingertip into her chest, blood connecting with blood. "This heart that never wanted to be mine because of the pain I've put it through. This heart poisoned by my hatred. And no amount of pain my father inflicts on me compares to that kind of suffering."

I sink to my knees in front of her, holding her wrist tightly so the knife is pushed into my neck. "So take your revenge, little rose, and end my suffering," I murmur. "Please."

"Ares, no!" Caleb shouts, and I throw him a glance.

"Don't," Blaine says, grabbing his arm. "Let him do this. I know it's hard for you, but you have to let it happen."

Caleb's face contorts, but he finally gives up fighting the inevitable.

Crystal averts her gaze, but I want her to see me, the real me. "Look at me," I say, forcing our eyes to find each other in our darkest moment. "He named me Ares because he wanted to raise a god. I was made to rule his fucking empire, and there is nothing in this world I would bend for, not even him ... But I will for you."

FIFTY EIGHT

Crystal

I try to breathe, but my lungs have never felt more constricted than they do now.

Ares is on his knees ... for me ... begging *me* to end his life, all because he's made me hate him.

I can't.

I can't even move a muscle, let alone drive this knife farther into his skin.

Even though I've so desperately wanted to kill him all this time.

Ares didn't murder my father. He took the blame and went through so much pain because of his death. Knowing what it would cost him, he still refused.

All those scars, layers upon layers, every decision he made, led him to anguish ... Led him to me.

Knowing what I know now ... How could I ever kill him?

"Blaine was right. You've managed to bring a god to his knees, little rose," Ares says. "What does that make of you?"

He doesn't release my wrist as he pushes it farther and farther into his neck.

His lip tips up into a cold smile. "A goddess."

My whole body begins to shake as the knife pushes into his neck. The neck of the man I once thought I wanted to murder in cold blood. The man I swore would never break me.

But it's too late.

The knife drops to the floor.

I grip Ares's bloodied face with both hands and kiss him harder than I have ever kissed a man before, pouring out all my love into this soul that's been crushed again and again until nothing was left of his heart but broken shards and dust. And with every kiss I can feel his heart rebuild itself piece by piece, his lips siphoning the life straight out of my mouth.

All this pain and suffering will end with me and with these kisses, chaining our hearts until eternity. Because this … this admission of him sacrificing his goddamn soul for my father has instantly unraveled every inch of my hatred and replaced it with adoration.

When my lips unlatch from his, there's a moment of disbelief churning in his gray eyes, and I stare at him with equal bewilderment at my own desires finally coming to their right.

Suddenly, he grips my waist with both hands, smashing his lips onto mine as he comes to a stand while kissing me with such deliciously cruel lips I'm swept away. He lifts me up in his arms, our tongues still entangled, and he sets me down on his desk, swiping aside every important paper to kiss me so deeply I nearly melt away in his arms.

He's never claimed me like this before, so impassioned, filled with unchained need and desire.

"Fuck," he groans into my mouth. "Should've killed me when you had the chance, little rose, because I won't be able to hold back now."

"Don't. Don't hold back," I murmur between his feverish kisses.

"You don't fucking know what you're asking for," he grumbles. "I'm not capable of restraint. All I know is how to make people submit and use them."

My eyes connect with his as they sparkle with a kind of greed that's almost too heavy to contain. "Then make me submit and use me."

***

415

ARES

One second. One fucking second.

That's how long I could stop myself before I completely devour her.

I smash my lips onto hers and taste my own damn desire on her, the sweet taste of fucking victory over my own damn decrepit mind. Her lips undo me. Every kiss of hers is like morphine, sweet, sweet relief injected straight into my veins.

Every cell in my body comes alive when our mouths connect.

Her kiss unraveled everything I thought I knew about myself and every inch of resistance I still had left in my brokenhearted body.

There is nothing I have left to give. I've already offered her my life and my soul, and I don't want either of them back if it means having to release her heart from the cage I put it in.

Her heart belongs to me.

She belongs to *me*.

"Mine," I growl, and I slide my lips across her neck and bury my teeth into her shoulder. Her whimpers and cries are like music to my ears as I suck up the blood off her delectable skin.

All the purity she once held has been tainted by me, and I don't regret it, not for one single second.

I gave her a way out.

I gave her my fucking death on a silver platter.

Instead, she ensnared my heart just like I've roped in hers.

And fuck me, nothing could give this damaged soul more life than her offering herself to me.

"*Ours*," Caleb says, wringing himself loose from Blaine's grip, only to march right at us. "And if you want her ... you share with us."

Caleb grips her arm and turns her around, away from me, only to smash his lips onto hers, and I realize at that moment we've both been fighting our deepest desires ...

It's about time we surrendered.

I lick her skin and run my tongue along her neck until I find his mouth against hers and kiss them both at the same time, rolling my tongue around his and her mouth until our tongues are entwined and our moans meld into each other.

"Fuck, this is too hot," Blaine says from the back, and he marches into the room too. "I love watching you all finally getting it on like you should have from the beginning."

"Shut up," I growl at him.

He chuckles as he sits down in the chair to the side of the desk and pushes his hand into his pants. "Don't mind me enjoying the show."

Blaine can do whatever the fuck he wants. Nothing's going to stop me from claiming Crystal and Caleb now.

"I want you," I murmur into her mouth, pulling Caleb closer so we can both kiss her. "I want you both."

"Fuck, yes, I need you two so desperately," he murmurs back, and we both trail kisses along her neck, meeting at the base of her chest where we both kiss each other before we rip down her shirt and take her nipples into our mouths and listen to her squeals.

I push her down onto the desk until her head falls over the edge, and I rip apart what those monsters left of her pants, tearing it all away for quick access. With splayed fingers, I circle her clit, while I slowly push two inside.

She moans, and I take her mouth while Caleb sucks on her nipple, and I am in love with her sounds.

"Yes, that's it, little rose, show me how badly you want this. Let me hear you unravel for us."

"Fuck," she groans as I thrust in with my fingers.

Caleb leans up, his cock obviously hard, and I tear down his zipper and pull out his cock with ease, jerking him off in front of her.

"You want both of us so desperately, don't you?" I groan, toying with them both. "Then you will have us both."

"Us three," Blaine interjects as he gets up from the seat with his cock already out and fully erect. "I don't intend to let you two have all the fun."

He moves to her face and places his hands flat on the desk before leaning over to say, "Hello, darling. Miss me?"

And he smiles before kissing her lips upside down.

So I pull my fingers out of her and replace them with my tongue to watch her writhe on the desk. "You're so fucking wet already."

I spread her pussy lips and dive in until I hear her moan out loud. But I don't stop circling her clit with my tongue until she's dripping and can barely kiss Blaine back.

"Go on then. Give me the first one," I say. "Give me your fucking orgasm while you give him your mouth."

I press my tongue against her clit and swirl it around until I can feel it thump against my tip.

"F-fuck," she murmurs when Blaine unlatches his lips from hers.

He grins against her face and continues to press kisses all over her neck and shoulders.

"One," I say, looking up at her when she lifts her head.

"Are you going to count my orgasms?" she mutters in surprise.

"I warned you what would happen if you didn't kill me. Now you face the consequences of your choice. I will never, ever be satisfied with just one of your orgasms, little rose."

I lean up and spread her legs wide, placing my pierced dick against her entrance before I slowly push inside. "Count the inches for me, little rose."

"Fuck. One," she moans.

When the piercings disappear inside her, she adds, "Two."

"Good girl," I murmur.

"Oh fuck, this is so goddamn sexy," Caleb groans while I jerk him off.

"Don't come just yet," I growl at him, thrusting deeper and deeper into her.

"Fuck," she murmurs. "Three."

I'm not nearly there yet.

"Four."

"Keep going," I say, pushing in even farther.

Blaine's kisses onto her neck and mouth distract her enough for me to bury myself inside her.

"Five," she mewls between breathy moans.

"That's it, little rose," I coax her, my fingers digging into her thighs while my other hand curls around Caleb's dick.

"Six."

She feels so fucking good, I could nearly come just from feeling her fit neatly around me, but I want to savor this moment of pure submission for as long as it lasts.

Because that fire inside her cannot be fucking doused, and I love watching it burn in her eyes.

"Seven."

"You'll take all of me," I grit, burying in even deeper. "You've done it before. You can do it again. And again. And again."

"Eight," she mewls.

Blaine squeezes her nipples, making her squeal. "Fuck!"

"Focus, little rose."

"It's my fault for making it so hard on her," Blaine muses, rubbing his dick up against her body.

"Nine!" she yelps.

"Show Caleb how badly you want him," I groan.

Caleb's already thrusting into her hand from sheer pleasure, and my hand finds him too in the heat of it as we both toy with his length and watch him suffer with unending need.

"Almost there. You can take it," I groan. "I know you can because this body was fucking made for me."

I thrust in to the base, until my balls slap against her ass, and a long-drawn-out groan leaves my body. Good God, nothing sweeter than taming a goddess with my cock alone.

"Ten!"

"Good girl," I say, as her pussy envelops my dick.

"Fuck!" she moans when I begin thrusting in and out.

But nothing will stop me from claiming what belongs to me.

I lean over to grip her throat and squeeze until I feel her pussy contract around me. "You like this. You like being dominated. To be used. To be marked and tainted. You're my little slut, just like he is, and you both deserve nothing more, nothing less than complete and utter subjugation to my cock."

"Yes," she murmurs, and I squeeze even tighter until her eyes nearly roll into her head.

"Call me by my name."

"Ares," she mewls as I thrust in again and again.

"What." *THRUST.* "Am." *THRUST.* "I?"

"My god."

Fuck.

Those are the words I wanted to hear from her lips.

I thrust so deep into her that she can't help but let go of Caleb, too consumed by lust. "And what are you?"

"Your goddess?"

"You are food for the fucking gods, *my* fucking ambrosia, made to be devoured."

I lean over to lick around her navel and jerk off Caleb until he reaches the edge, that edge he loves so damn much, and then I release him and listen to him whimper in agony while his length bounces upside down.

And I bury myself inside her to the hilt and watch the lights go out in her eyes before I come together with her, filling her to the brim with my fucking seed while her pussy contracts around my shaft, dragging out my orgasm, making me howl with delight.

"Two," I growl as I pull out of her and watch my cum drip out.

Caleb swirls his fingers around her pussy and shoves the cum right back in, thrusting his fingers back and forth into her wetness. "God, this pussy feels so good. It's almost like I'm fucking and being fucked at the same time."

A smirk grows on my face. "Well then … let me give you what you want."

I pull him toward me and step aside, guiding him toward her pussy by pointing his dick at her entrance, and I shove him forward until he sinks in while I watch both their faces come undone.

And fuck me, the pleasure in their eyes is unmatched.

Until I position myself behind him, spit on my dick, and enter his ass.

FIFTY NINE

CALEB

"Oh fuck!" My teeth clench together when I feel him slip into me slowly, spitting on his dick with every passing inch.

"You wanted to fuck her and be fucked ... then be a fucking good slut and do as you're told," he groans.

Every time he enters me, it feels like I'm on cloud nine. I can never get enough of how good it feels to have those piercings rub against my insides. The more he pushes, the more I'm forced into her pussy, and it feels divine to have my cock enveloped by the only girl I've ever loved.

But good God, he's so fucking hard and huge to take, but with every inch I begin to moan louder and louder.

Crystal whimpers as I thrust in fully, burying myself to the hilt inside her sweet, delectable pussy while Ares forces his way into my ass.

"Fuck, I need it, I need you so desperately, I can't fucking take it anymore." And I pull her up by her shirt so I can kiss her while I drive into her. She moans into my mouth, her lips so delicious they drive me insane with lust.

Blaine kisses the back of her neck, whispering, "You belong to us now. No going back."

"Yes," she murmurs, and fuck me, never has that word ever sounded so good.

Ares's lips cover my neck and spread sweet kisses all over just like Blaine is doing to Crystal. He licks and sucks at my neck before biting down and making me bleed.

I whimper and kiss her the way he kissed me, feverishly chaining our toxic love into one addicting affair.

"Kiss him too," Crystal murmurs, eyeing Blaine. "Please."

How could I say no to her?

So I grab Blaine's shirt and tear him to my lips, kissing him right over her shoulder while my dick is buried inches deep inside her. And fuck me, even his lips make my dick throb inside her.

"Oh fuck, I could get used to this," Blaine murmurs when our lips unlatch. "You're so rough."

"Not nearly as rough as he is with me," I grit.

Ares grips my hair and tilts my head back, forcing me to look at him while he plows into me.

"Be a good little slut and thrust into this needy little pussy for me," he says.

"Yes, Sir," I moan, gripping her legs as I collide with him.

"Good boy," Ares says, pounding into my ass. "You two were made for me."

Blaine pulls back her head by her hair and smashes his lips onto hers, slowly bringing her back down again where her head is bent over the desk. "I want to feel these lips wrap around my cock," he murmurs as he pushes the tip against her mouth. "Sweet fucking mercy, give it to me."

He sinks into her mouth with ease, drowning out the moans with splashing thrusts, drool dribbling out of her and onto the floor.

And my eyes nearly roll into the back of my head from the way Ares plows into me, and I thrust into her.

"Fuck, I'm gonna come," I groan as Ares buries himself inside me.

"That's it, slut. Come for me." He bites down into my skin, and I jet my seed into her pussy, howling like an animal.

But it was fucking worth it because I have never felt anything more satisfying than getting fucked at both ends.

***

Blaine

I push into her mouth slowly, taking my time to enjoy just how good it feels for her to finally belong to us without any objections. Her tongue wraps around my shaft so well I groan with desire, and I lean over to suck her nipples, desperate for her to feel the same pleasure I'm feeling.

"God, you lick me so well," I murmur against her nipples, suckling at them as I bury myself deeper and deeper into her mouth. "Darling, you make me want to do bad things."

"Do it, then," Ares eggs me on. "Give her what she begged for."

On his command, I thrust in to the base, listening to her gulp and gag for me.

And fuck, the sound really makes me hungry for more.

"That's it, little rose, take his cock into your throat like it's a goddamn pussy too."

Ares pulls out of Caleb and grips his shoulders, forcing him to go to his knees. "Now lick her out."

Caleb's pierced tongue rolls around her pussy, and I can feel her moans reverberate against my dick.

"Oh fuck, that feels good. Do it again, Caleb. Lick that clitty raw," I muse.

"The only one who can order me around is Ares, so shut your damn mouth and enjoy that fucking throat while you still can," Caleb growls back.

"That's the spirit," I retort.

I grab her nipples and squeeze tightly as I thrust in and out of her mouth. I pause to allow her a breath and push right back in again, overcome by sheer lust.

But the way Ares jerks himself off to the way we're licking and thrusting into her is making me quite greedy for more too. He's looking at both Caleb and me, our eyes finding each other in our most depraved moment, all of us realizing we've gone off the deep end.

And none of us care even the slightest.

We want her, and she wants us, and everything else ceases to matter in the equation.

"Lick my tip, darling," I groan at her, and I lick my lips as I watch Ares and Caleb toy with her. "God, you do it so well. When I'm done with you, I want you to smother me just like I'm smothering you now."

Caleb snorts. "I can fucking smother you if you want."

Ares shoves his face back down into her pussy. "Suck out your goddamn cum first, whore."

"Fuck," Caleb groans as his tongue is forced into her, and he laps up all her juices.

"Oh fuck, I'm gonna—" She mewls, her toes curling as her body begins to convulse.

I moan with delight when her tongue wraps around my cock, and her throat squeezes as she comes undone.

"Three," Ares says with a smug smile on his face.

He pulls Caleb away, spinning him around before shoving him face-first onto his own dick.

"Clean my fucking dick, slut," Ares growls, choking him on his length.

God, it's so hot watching him subdue Caleb.

As I kiss her nipples with my dick buried deep inside her mouth, her hands suddenly find their way to my throat.

"Yes, God yes, suffocate me," I groan, and her fingers begin to squeeze.

Harder. Tighter.

Just like that.

Thrust. Thrust. Thrust.

"Oh God," I moan, burying myself inside her while the oxygen slowly evades my brain.

The feeling is so intoxicating I ejaculate inside her, coating her throat with cum.

The second she releases my throat, I pull back and lift her head. "Darling, you don't fucking know just how badly I needed that."

Suddenly, Ares rips her off the table and helps her stand.

"Blaine. Lie down on my couch," he says, pointing at the couch in front of his bed. "It's time we gave her everything we have to give and more."

SIXTY

Crystal

Ares pulls me toward the couch while my insides feel like they've been rearranged. But I can feel from his strong grip around my arm he's not nearly done with me yet.

"Sit on his face," he says.

"What?" I gasp.

I shriek when he lifts me by the waist and easily sets me down right on top of Blaine.

"Ah!"

His tongue piercing my pussy has me gripping the couch armrest.

I look down at him between my legs. "What about oxygen? You won't be able to—"

"Who needs oxygen when we have you?" He interjects, placing both hands on my ass as he digs in.

Ares grabs something off a shelf, then gets onto the couch too behind me, ignoring Blaine's still erect cock as he sits down right on top of it and squashes it underneath his weight.

Blaine groans out of frustration but still continues to lick me, and I'm too lost in lust to care.

I didn't even notice Caleb's standing in front of me until he grips

425

my chin and forces me to look at him before he pushes me down onto his cock.

"Taste me like I've tasted you," he says, pushing in deep right away.

I gag, but the sound only makes him harder.

"Now spread your ass for me, little slut," Ares says. "You wanted me, then take all of me in every hole I demand."

When my hands splay on my butt cheeks, I can feel his piercings poke against my ass.

"Blaine, lick that pussy like your life depends on it," Ares growls.

A couple of squirts of cold gel, and he slowly pushes inside.

I mewl at the feel of his piercings while he enters me, and it feels so good, I begin to writhe against Blaine's tongue.

"Oh, fuck yes, darling. Rub your pussy along my lips," Blaine says.

"But you can't breathe," I murmur.

"He wanted to be suffocated, then take his fucking breath with that goddamn perfect pussy of yours," Ares growls, thrusting in deeper and deeper until I lose all self-control.

I start gyrating on top of Blaine while Caleb takes my mouth and Ares takes my ass.

It's too much for one person, too much arousal, too much lust all boiling over into another orgasm. Everything feels just that good.

"Yes, that's it, come for me," Ares growls, slowly amping up the speed of his thrusts.

"But—"

Caleb buries himself inside my mouth, and I can taste my own sweetness on his shaft, mingling with the salty taste of Blaine's cum. "Don't fucking speak when you're supposed to be coming, slut."

"Good boy," Ares says, and Caleb's eyes find his behind me, egging him on to go even deeper and make me gag even harder.

But instead of hating these boys who ripped my heart out of my chest, I drown in them and let them sweep me away into their hedonistic, heavenly hell.

Caleb pulls out to allow me a short breath before he rams right back inside, the feeling of his cock poking in the back of my throat only making me gyrate harder on top of Blaine, while Ares buries himself deep within me.

And I mewl against his shaft as they both begin to pulsate inside me.

"Yes, fuck yes," Caleb groans. "Eat my fucking cum like a good little slut."

An animalistic groan slips off his tongue as he jets into me, and it makes me wild with lust to the point that my clit begins to throb, and I come undone again.

"Four," Ares says.

When Caleb pulls out, I whimper, "How?"

"You think I can't feel your ass contract around my cock?" he muses, snorting. "I can feel you, just like you will feel every inch of me inside you as I fill you to the brim with my fucking cum."

He buries himself inside me so far, I have to hold the couch.

"Oh God," I say.

"Yes, pray to me, little rose, and your God will fucking come at your beck and call."

One. Two. Three more thrusts of his giant cock inside me, and he spends his load in me, jetting so deep into me I can feel him in my abdomen.

I groan and fall over on the couch, completely wasted.

"Can't. Breathe."

I lift my hips. "Sorry."

"Don't be," he says, sucking in the breaths. "I love being your ride."

My cheeks flush from his comment.

Ares steps off the couch and immediately grips my hair, tilting my head back. "Look at me. Look at these words inscribed on my skin. Whose name is this?"

"Mine," I say.

"Your name, and all that you are, has always belonged to me." A smirk forms on his face as he leans in and presses his mouth on mine, suffocating me with so much greedy love I'd be grateful to die.

God, this man.

When his lips unlatch, I'm still lost on cloud nine as he brings his dick to my lips. "Now open that pretty mouth and let me own these fucking holes of yours."

He pinches my nose and makes me part my lips, thrusting in with no mercy as I struggle to take him.

"Oh fuck, I'm so goddamn horny again," Blaine mewls beneath me.

Caleb climbs on top of the couch behind me. "You whimpering

little simp," he growls. "Fine? You want to be taken care of? Fuck her ass with me, then."

"Wait, two?" I gasp as Blaine lifts me and crawls back further into the armrest of the couch. Ares has to hover over him to claim my mouth.

Caleb then grips Blaine's dick and guides it to my ass, pushing two tips against the entrance. "Yes, you will take both of us like the good little slut you are, won't you?"

He slowly dips in, and my nails dig into the couch from the sheer thickness of them both inside my ass.

"Oh God, her ass is so tight," Blaine murmurs beneath me. "Oh yes, just like that, I can feel your piercings. Fuck her harder, please."

His mouth covers my nipples, and he suckles them like he wants to worship me.

"Fuck, Ares's cum is such good lube," Caleb groans, both of them deepening their strokes.

"Good, stretch her fucking holes," Ares growls at him before returning his attention to me and sinking in farther. "That's it. Take all of us like the good fucking girl you are."

They fill me up on both ends, and I can hear Caleb and Blaine moaning as they fit into me, and it's such a pleasurable ache I nearly fall apart again.

"You going to come from our cocks alone, little rose?" Ares says, bemused by my arousal. "Just like a good, willing slut."

I nod even though he's inside me so far tears stain my eyes. Still, he pushes on until he's balls deep and I'm gagging, struggling to swallow.

"Look into my eyes, Crystal," he says. "Look at your fucking god enjoying your body to the fullest."

I can't help but stare into those gray eyes I once thought soulless, now filled with so much passion I can't look away. I won't. Even though it's like staring into the sun, knowing you'll get burned. The pain is worth every second.

"Darling, you're gonna make me come again if you go on like that," Blaine moans at Caleb.

"Whore," Caleb groans, thrusting in deep, forcing Blaine inside too.

Blaine's tongue rolling around my nipple drives me insane as he howls with desire.

"Fuck, I can feel you throb," Caleb groans, both of them pounding into me with fervor.

"Don't get distracted, little rose," Ares growls. "Eyes on me."

I fixate on his eyes even though I'm being railed on both ends. But that look in Ares's eyes has subdued me. It's nothing like before, all the hatred has somehow vanished and been replaced by adoration. My submission has turned him from a monster into a lover, and I want nothing more than to be theirs.

Blaine's hand finds its way between our bodies, flicking my clit while slathering my nipples in sweet kisses.

A moan escapes my lips, and Ares thrusts into my mouth, making me gurgle. Tears spring into my eyes as he squeezes my throat while fucking me, feeling himself go down my throat, almost like he savors the power he holds over me.

"Caleb. Blaine. You come on my command," Ares growls.

As his dick hits the back of my throat, he remains put. "Hold it."

Fuck. I can't breathe.

But Ares's penetrative stare calms me. "Trust. Me."

Blaine's lips cover my nipple, and he nibbles lightly while his fingers slide up and down my pussy and roll around my clit.

"Now."

Caleb's howl and Blaine's aching moan reverberate through the room, and I can feel them spurt their cum into my ass, pushing me over the edge. I fall apart with them just from the sheer depravity of it all. Right then, Ares arches his back and jets into my throat, forcing me to swallow it all down.

An avalanche of cum has brought me to the highest peak imaginable, and I don't want to take the journey down. Until I hear Ares's voice and all I feel is pride. "Five."

***

ARES

When Caleb finally pulls out, she slumps over the couch, breathing ragged breaths. I was planning on continuing until she had ten orgasms, but maybe we pushed her too far.

I lift her from Blaine's face with an arm around her belly and carry her away.

"What the—I can walk, you know," she says.

"No. You've expended enough energy. After today, it's about time you had a rest," I respond, setting her on my bed. "And I'm not taking no for an answer."

"God, I need a chiropractor now. But it was worth it," Blaine muses as he gets up from the couch.

"It wasn't your butthole that got stretched to the max." Caleb grins.

Blaine folds his arms and throws him back a smirk. "Darling, I'd let both of you stretch mine. All you need to do is ask."

"Really?" Caleb retorts with furrowed brows.

"I'm just saying, my ass is always available, I don't discriminate what enters." Blaine raises a brow. "As long as it's cleaned properly."

Caleb's eyes narrow, his lip twitching as his fist hardens. "Are you telling me I'm filthy?"

"You're a pig, darling," Blaine says, blowing him an air-kiss. "But a cute one. Like a little piglet. Oink. Oink."

Caleb's eyes boil over with rage as he raises his hand, ready to strike. "You motherf—"

"Caleb," I warn. "Blaine." Both of them stop whatever they were doing and focus on Crystal, and I can finally see their tenseness relax. "Enough."

I put Crystal's head down on my pillow and put the blanket over her, before I press my lips to hers, claiming that sweet, sweet aftertaste of hellish hedonistic enjoyment. And when she kisses me back, my heart almost beats out of my chest.

Kissing her makes me feel like the most powerful man on earth.

Like I could scorch the entire planet just to have her.

When I come back to a stand, my wound cracks open again, and I hiss in pain.

Her eyes shoot up to mine in panic, the kind of panic I haven't witnessed in anyone else but Caleb, and it makes me pause.

"You're still hurt," she says.

"I'm fine," I say, raising a brow at her. "Now sleep."

She defiantly crosses her arms on the bed. "I'm fine. I don't need sleep."

Parroting me like a kid?

The filthy half smile on her face makes me tilt my head. This little rose is sharpening her thorns, and I'm not sure I entirely loathe it.

"Crystal …" I mutter.

"No."

"She looks adorable when she thinks she can win this from you," Blaine murmurs, rubbing his own cheek.

"I'll go grab the kit," Caleb says, walking to the cabinet with supplies I keep in my bathroom.

I sigh out loud. "You really don't have to—"

Crystal suddenly grabs my hand, and my mind goes numb. "Let him help you. Please."

The way she looks at me has me momentarily stunned.

Caleb sits down behind me on the bed and says, "Sit down, please. I can't reach the wound if you don't."

Grumbling, I do what they want me to, and Caleb unscrews the bottle, dabbing the cotton into the alcohol before shoving it straight into the wound.

The pain doesn't faze me nearly as much as her warm hand squeezing mine, an unfamiliar feeling rushing to bring life to the shriveled-up heart still miraculously beating behind this rib cage.

"Do you need any help with that, darling?" Blaine asks.

"No, thanks," Caleb growls back.

Blaine lifts his fingers and makes a claw. "Rawr."

Caleb sighs behind me. "Can I kill him?"

Crystal snorts and hides her laughter behind her hand.

"No, you cannot," I reply in all seriousness. "You need him, and he needs you."

"Don't be mad at me, darling," Blaine says, approaching. "I'm just having fun with you."

"There, all done," Caleb says after he places the final suture and pats down the wound with some alcohol.

"Thanks," I say, and I turn around to grab his face and kiss him on the lips.

His kisses are so different from hers, much more needy, but both taste divine. And I'll be damned if I don't have both of them.

"I mean it," I say.

He leans his forehead against mine. "I know."

"God, I'm so fucking tired," Blaine says, yawning wildly.

I crawl onto the bed behind Crystal and drag her to me. "Caleb. Blaine. Lie down."

"What? In your bed?" Blaine asks with widened eyes.

"Is there a problem with my bed?" I retort.

His cheeks redden. "No. But you've never asked me before."

"Don't make me change my mind," I say.

A smile forms on his face before he crawls onto the bed and lies down next to Crystal, with his back turned to her. "I want to be the little spoon."

She wraps her arms around his giant body and laughs.

Caleb rolls his eyes and jumps between us, separating me from my girl.

"Scoot over," he says, squeezing in, rubbing his butt against me.

"Caleb." I sigh. "Fine, come here." And I wrap my arm around both of them, then close my eyes. "Good night."

"If this is going to be our new normal now," Crystal mutters. "Then I'm not a prisoner anymore, and I will be going to school tomorrow."

My whole body jolts up. "What?"

Is she insane?

She just got home after being taken by a bunch of traffickers, and she wants to go to school?

She doesn't even look at me, but that mischievous grin makes me want to stab her with my dick for being such a bad fucking girl. "Good night."

SIXTY ONE

Crystal

"Everyone's staring at us," Caleb says as we walk through the university's hallways.

"I'm enjoying the spotlight," Blaine says, throwing his hair over his shoulder.

"This is such a bad idea," Caleb says, pulling up his hoodie.

"Yes, go and hide your face, then," Blaine jests.

"Shut up," Caleb growls at him.

I snigger.

This day is already going so well. Everyone in the school hallways is staring at us when we walk past, probably wondering why three of the most toxic guys on campus are walking along with me like they're some kind of lap dogs. And the fact that Ares actually snarls at anyone who dares to look too long doesn't help either.

Blaine taps Ares on the shoulder, who grips his finger and squeezes so tightly Blaine whimpers.

"Ow."

"Don't touch me," Ares grits.

"I just wanted to ask if you could please pretend you don't want to kill everyone staring at us."

Ares releases him. "Fine."

Blaine retracts his finger and pouts. "That was my good finger."

"The one you stick up your own ass?" Caleb snorts.

Blaine throws him a glare. "The one I use to unlock my katana from my umbrella, the kind of tech you wouldn't know a thing about, you brute."

Caleb grunts at him, but I stop in the middle of the hallway and they all nearly bump into me.

I spin on my heels and point at them. "Stop."

They all look like they got caught in the act, and Caleb's even blushing underneath that hoodie of his.

"If you want this to work, you guys gotta stop fighting like that."

"He started it," Caleb snarls.

"What?" Blaine scoffs, offended.

"Shut it. Both of you," Ares tells them. "We're just going to school. Act normal."

"Normal?" Blaine laughs in an exaggerated manner. "Good one, darling."

"I'm serious," I say. "I can't have people thinking I've lost my mind walking around with you three. I just want things to go back to normal."

Ares suddenly directs his stern gaze to me, making me gulp. "You will have your normal. But I will not allow you to walk around unguarded." His gentle caress to my cheeks makes me blush too. "So go to your classes and we will be by the door waiting when it's finished to take you to the next."

He places a kiss on my forehead in front of everyone, unafraid to claim me while the school watches. Part of me is mortified, but another glows with pride.

"Now go on. Get to class, little rose."

I blush and give him a kiss on the cheek before I turn around and walk off under their searing gaze, as well as pretty much everyone else in this hallway.

Good God.

I head inside for my first class and nearly faint when I see Penelope sitting there with bruises all over her arms. When she looks up, she drops the pen she was holding, and I can barely breathe.

"Crystal?"

She sounds shocked, and I don't know how to react as I

434

approach.

"Is that you?" She looks like she's seen a ghost, and suddenly gets up and hugs me tight. "Oh my God, it really is you. I was so worried about you. Are you hurt?" She immediately pushes me away and inspects me.

"I'm fine," I mutter. "At least, physically. I'm still a little shaken up from what happened."

"How did you even get out of the Bonesmen grasp?" she asks. "Felix and I looked everywhere for you. We even scoured all the Bones Brotherhood locations we knew about."

"I was taken to a different compound where they tried to sell me again. Luckily, the guys from the Tartarus House found me."

"Caleb?" she asks. "Oh wow, I'm impressed he managed to find you."

I nod. "And Blaine and Ares too."

She hugs me again, and I sink into her chest, breathing out a sigh of relief. "I'm so glad you're okay. We were all worried sick. I didn't even know you were in there. No one did. We went into the first compound to get Lana out together with the Phantom Society boys, but then we lost you, and I couldn't get to the van in time ..." she says, lowering her brows in shame. "I'm sorry. I'm sorry I wasn't there in time to save you."

"It's okay," I say, rubbing her back. "I'm here. I'm safe. I'm not going anywhere. At least not without screaming at the top of my lungs."

She sniggers. "When Caleb said he was going to ask his boys for help, I didn't expect him to actually come through."

I make a face. I don't think she knows the full truth. "Yeah ... about that ..." I squeak. "We're actually kind of, sort of, dating?"

"What?!"

I cover her mouth so no one hears her scream.

"Don't make a scene, please. They already hate that everyone is looking."

Her eyes widen. "*They?*"

Oh God.

"Are you telling me you're dating *multiple* Tartarus boys?"

"Uhh ... I plead the Fifth?"

The blush on my cheeks apparently gives it all away, and she grabs me and shoves me back and forth like a crazy person. "Oh my God,

Crystal! A foursome?"

"Shhh …" I murmur, looking around. "It's hard on them."

"Right, right, I get it," she says, winking. "Is the sex good? They say the boys from Tartarus are like hedonistic fuck toys."

"Don't embarrass me. I'm already mortified."

"But it's so much fun," she jests, and she pulls me in for another hug. "But I'm so glad you're back, girl."

"What did I miss?"

Kayla's voice makes me look up. She just walked into class, which is about to start, and the look on her face immediately goes blank the moment she sees me sitting in one of the benches.

"Oh my … God."

She throws herself into my arms, practically smothering me. "Crystal! You're back! I've missed you so damn much."

"It was only a couple of days," I say.

"Yeah, yeah, I know. Mini family vacation," she says, rolling her eyes, which confuses me. I stare at Penelope, who just shrugs and touches her lips like she doesn't want me to tell Kayla the truth.

I guess Kayla is not aware of all the things that go on around this campus. Maybe it's better this way. Wouldn't want her to get dragged in too.

"It's not the same here without you," she says.

"I missed you too," I say. "But you're killing my back."

She laughs and leans away. "Sorry, girl. You look scrawny, though. Did your mom feed you well?"

I rub my lips together. "No, she was far too busy with her new boyfriend, so I was the one doing most of the cooking," I lie.

"Oh, is it that same guy we saw last time at Fi's Cups and Cakes?" she asks.

I nod. "Yup. Caleb's dad. Awkward."

"Oh wow …" Penelope says with owl-like eyes, and it makes me want to hide underneath the table. "That is messed up."

The teacher begins his class, and we sit and listen, but Penelope still texts me.

Penelope: I want to talk with those guys. Ares, Blaine, Caleb. I just want to make sure they have good intentions with you. Do you have their number?

Me: Please don't ask. I don't want you dead too.

Penelope: They can't kill me that easily. Besides, I've got

436

Felix, Alistair, and Dylan to back me up.

Me: Okay … if you're sure about this. But don't blame me if they end up killing each other.

Penelope: Do you care about them?

It takes me a few seconds to respond.

Me: Yes.

Penelope: A lot?

Me: Like a lot, a lot.

She smiles at me before she continues typing.

Penelope: I don't judge. I remember that feeling from when I first got together with the Skull & Serpent Society guys. I just want you to be safe. You're my friend.

Me: I know. I trust you.

Penelope: Good. Because I think it's already making rounds at school.

She lifts her phone and shows the group chat for our class, which is filled with responses and comments to a picture that was shared. A picture of me kissing Ares while Caleb and Blaine happily stand behind us.

Oh God.

Me: Nathan's going to try to kill them, isn't he?

Penelope: 99/100 chance.

***

Blaine

When she finally gets out of class, my heart begins to race with excitement.

My beautiful, darling Crystal so content to finally make it back to her college education like a normal girl even though she's far from it after what she's endured.

Of all the joys in life, this is what makes her happy?

I snigger to myself.

"How was it?" I ask.

"Good," she replies. "Why are you all acting like you don't go to this school too?"

"We do, but we don't enjoy it like you do," I muse.

"Did you learn anything?" Caleb raises his brow. "I saw a ton of texts flying by in the group chat."

She tucks her hair behind her ear. "A little bit. It's just good that I can finally go back to semi-normal."

"Whatever that is," Caleb growls.

"I'm guessing you guys saw the texts about us?" she asks.

Oh, we all definitely saw, and I don't mind one bit. Let the world know I love her, I don't care, not even the slightest, as long as she's mine.

Ares sighs out loud and turns around, walking off. "Don't want to talk about it."

Party pooper.

"Oh …" She follows him, clutching her bag, but when Ares glances at her over his shoulder, she stops and gazes up at him with doe-like eyes.

"What they say has no influence whatsoever over my feelings for you. None."

Her whole face turns red, and oh my God, I am living for this literal real-life romance novel.

None of the books could ever come close to this.

She gulps and murmurs, "Me too."

"What's that? You have feelings for us?" I lean over her shoulder to look into her eyes, and she nearly squeals like she forgot I was there.

"Jesus, don't scare me like that."

Caleb bursts out into laughter, and it irritates me. "Don't make me pull out my—"

"Sword?" Caleb interjects.

Now he's really ruined my good mood.

"It's a katana, you seventh-century swine," I retort.

Caleb narrows his eyes at me. "Oink, oink, motherfucker." And he sticks up his middle finger.

What the—

"If you don't stop, I'll have you both fucking each other's assholes tonight," Ares growls.

"Fine, fine, although … I wouldn't be opposed to that," I say, winking. "I was just saying, I'm happy she's content. This is what I wanted."

"What *you* wanted?" she parrots like she can't believe it.

"Of course, darling." I grab her hand and kiss the top as I always do, instilling my love for her with my lips. She's like a precious jewel I want to cherish. "I never thought you'd actually fall for these violent boys, but I am glad it led you straight into my arms."

***

Crystal

We head outside to the fountain, where Nathan, Kai, Milo, and Lana all sit on the stone edge, smoking.

"Wait here," I tell my boys.

"Are you sure?" Caleb says, narrowing his eyes at Nathan like he's got a beef.

"Yeah, I'm safe with them. Don't worry," I reply.

"We'll keep an eye on you to make sure," Ares says.

"Good luck, my little diamond in the rough," Blaine says, squeezing my cheek like I'm some kind of chipmunk before I walk toward the fountain.

But every step I take feels more and more unreal.

"Lana?" I mutter when I see her throw her black hair over her shoulder.

Her body freezes at the sound of my voice. Her eyes are as wide as can be when they finally find mine.

"Crystal?" she mutters in disbelief.

She jumps off the fountain, runs across the pebbles, and throws her arms around me. "I can't believe you're here and that you're safe. How did you even get out?"

"Long story, but … the guys from the Tartarus House got me out of that hellhole," I say, sighing because I really don't want to think about my time there. "Ares, Caleb, and Blaine were there to save me," I say. "Anyway, I just wanted to say I'm sorry. It's my fault those pictures—"

"I don't want to hear it." She interjects. "I'm not mad at you. I've made peace with it. I don't blame you, and I don't want you to feel guilty. In fact, I'm the one who should feel guilty for leaving you all alone in that Bonesmen den." She hugs me even tighter. "I'm sorry. They were after me and then took you too as collateral damage."

My eyes tear up, but I swallow them away. "Thank you." I lean away. "But why were they after you in the first place?"

She takes one glance over her shoulders at the three boys standing there, watching us, and Kai's penetrative stare makes me gulp.

"Them?" I whisper.

She nods and smiles.

"So … those fuckers actually managed to find you?" Nathan chucks his smoke into the fountain. "I'm impressed."

I unfurl myself from Lana's embrace and run to him, hugging him tight.

"I'm glad you're safe, Crystal," he says. "I just wish I got there in time to save you too when we got Lana out." He leans away and grabs my shoulders to take a good look at me. "Did they hurt you?"

I shake my head. "One of them hit me, but—"

"Remind me to cut off some extra fingers the next time I come across any of those Bonesmen," Nathan hisses at Milo behind him.

"Oooh … I love it when you get all aggressive," Milo says.

"I'm okay," I say, placing my hand on top of his. "I don't want you to get into more trouble because of me."

"Don't worry about me. So what happened after you got taken away in that van?" he asks.

"The Bones Brotherhood tried to sell me to some rich men, but Ares, Caleb, and Blaine got to me before they succeeded."

"Ares?" Kai raises a brow and chucks his smoke away too. "Interesting."

"Is it that strange?" I say, feeling brave. "You wanted to save Lana too. Brothers think alike."

"Brothers?" Lana's eyes almost bulge out of her skull. "Ares is your brother?"

Kai shrugs.

"Why didn't you tell me?"

Oh boy. I did not realize what I was about to unchain by saying that out loud.

"Didn't think it was necessary. We don't see eye to eye."

"That's an understatement," I say.

Kai and Ares make eye contact, but Ares immediately looks the other way and pulls out a smoke instead.

"We have our issues. Just like any other family," Kai says. "I don't like to talk about mine, however." Kai turns around and yells at Ares,

440

"Ares. Explain to me why you wouldn't help us find Lana, yet you happily assisted in finding Crystal, a girl you don't even know."

Ares, Caleb, and Blaine walk toward us like they finally feel invited to join the conversation.

"Who says he doesn't know her?" Blaine says.

Kai frowns. "How?"

"You think you're the only one who's been fucking around?" Caleb retorts, tilting his head.

Nathan's eyes widen. "You've been fucking Crystal?"

Oh boy.

"What the f—" Lana glances my way. "Seriously?"

"Holy shit," Milo muses.

I hide my face in my hands. "This is not how I imagined this would go."

"Oh my God," Lana says. "So it's true? You're dating Ares?"

My whole face turns red. "Dating is a complicated word."

Ares folds his arms, staring at them all with contempt. "She's mine."

Milo fans himself. "When you put it like that, I understand."

"Really?" Nathan scoffs at him. "She's my friend. She should not be dating any of those guys."

A smug grin spreads on Caleb's face. "Tough luck for you then, because she wants all three of us."

"Jesus Christ," Kai says, rolling his eyes. "You've been busy."

"So a foursome, huh?" Milo says. "Guess we're all banging like crazy."

Nathan smacks him on the head with a packet of cigarettes.

"It's not like that. We just ... stumbled into it," I say, trying to tone it down.

"Uh-huh," Milo responds.

Nathan jumps off the fountain. "I never gave you permission to go ahead and jump in bed with my goddamn friend, Caleb."

"I don't need your permission to fuck who I want," Caleb retorts.

Nathan grabs Caleb by the collar. "Give me one good reason not to punch your teeth out."

"Guys, guys." I shove my way between them. "Please stop."

"And all this time, I thought you just wanted to get back in my pants," Nathan grits.

"I never said that. I said I missed you as a friend," Caleb replies.

"Whatever," Nathan says.

Ares steps up and points a finger at Nathan. "You touch Caleb again, and I'll kill you right here, right now."

"Possessive," Milo hums. "I love it."

"Can we stop fighting, please?" I ask, placing a hand on Ares's chest to calm him down. "I don't want more bloodshed."

His nostrils flare, but he finally backs away. "Only because he is your friend."

"So you three have been doing this behind everyone's backs?" Lana asks, narrowing her eyes like she can't believe what she's hearing.

"I could say the same for you," I retort, smiling.

She rolls her eyes but smiles anyway. "I guess you're right."

"Guess everyone here is lucky," Milo says, grinning like a bastard. "You get a foursome, we get a foursome, everyone gets a foursome!"

I just stare at them for a moment before I burst out into laughter eventually.

It's all so ridiculous that it's starting to make sense in a weird way.

Suddenly, Caleb's phone rings, and he turns away to answer it.

"Yeah, Dad?" His voice begins to tremble. "What?"

He suddenly goes down on both hands and knees, still clutching the phone. A scream unlike anything else decimates all happiness from my heart.

I immediately run to him and place a hand on his shoulder. "What happened?"

Ares marches to him and goes to his knees in front of him, gripping his face to make him look at him. "Tell me."

"My mom ... is dead."

SIXTY TWO

ARES

This is the day I feared would come.

I pull him to me and hold him tight, letting him release all of the pent-up anger and anguish in my arms. He screams and cries, then punches my shoulders.

"It's not. Fucking. Fair." *PUNCH!* "She was supposed to LIVE!"

His wails go through marrow and bone.

When I look up, Crystal is also crying, and she slowly comes to the ground too and wraps her arms around his belly, placing her head on his back.

"Let it all out," she whispers.

His screams become louder and louder until half the people outside have come to check what's going on, but Blaine shoos them away to keep Caleb safe in our arms.

Right now, there is nothing anyone can do for him except be there in the moment and allow him to feel the grief he's been holding on to for so long. The desperate hope we all knew was in vain, suddenly vanishing into thin air.

***

Crystal

Nothing can prepare one for this amount of grief.

At some point in our lives, we will all feel this devastation, this gaping hole we're about to fall into. There is no escaping it, no bargaining, no exceptions. Trying to claw at it will only make it harder to let go.

I understand that all too well.

Grief is releasing all the love you kept inside you and relinquishing it to the void.

What's left is unchangeable memories, fitting inside the little hole in your heart.

And with time, each of them will be able to put a smile on your face again.

I take a deep breath as we walk into Caleb's mom's room, where his dad waits for him. His father holds his mother's hand, gently rubbing it as though he believes she can still feel it somewhere.

I squeeze Caleb's hand, and he looks at Ares and me before releasing us. His movement is unsteady but focused as if the only thing keeping him walking is his undying need to be at his mother's side. She is the last thread of pain holding his family together.

Ares places his hand on my shoulder and whispers, "It's okay if you want to leave. I know it's hard for you. I can take it."

I shake my head. "I want to be here for him. I'm the only one who understands what it's like."

He nods. "I'll respect your wish."

And I whisper back, "Let's just be here for when he needs us."

***

CALEB

I approach my father, who stands from his seat. We stare at each other for a moment while my heart slowly begins to bleed. He releases Mom's hand and holds out his hands to me, and with tears rolling down my face, I run into his arms.

I have never wanted to hug him this hard before, but now it feels like I can't get close enough.

The one thing that connected us is now gone.

There is nothing that could've prepared me for this day. Nothing.

"Mom ..." I mutter into his chest.

"I'm sorry, Caleb," he says, but I can hear him cry too.

He buries his face into my shoulder and bawls just like me, but in each other's arms, we find relief.

Memories flash through my mind of her smile, the way she picked me up when I was a kid, how she cooked the most delicious pancakes, of all the times she made me laugh and rubbed the bottom of my back when I cried, and all the ways we danced whenever I was feeling down. Oh, how she loved to dance.

I miss her so much even though she hasn't been present these past few years. I still talked with her, I still felt her presence, but now?

I turn to look at the body lying in the bed, her skin gone pale gray. She looks like a shell of what was once a living, breathing human being. As if her soul has already vacated long ago, and all that's left is a husk, eyes no longer reflecting any light.

I breathe out a ragged breath and grab her hand, sitting down on her bed, before I lean over to kiss her on the cheeks.

"I'll miss you, Mom. I hope you're able to dance up there."

My father hugs me from behind, and I place my hand on his, the severed connection between us renewed.

I turn my head and look into his tearstained red eyes.

"She's gone," he murmurs.

"This is what you wanted, right?" I ask.

He shakes his head. "No."

"You've already replaced her!" I yell, my frustrations finally out in the open, and it makes his eyes widen.

"I ... Is that how you see my relationship with Crystal's mother?"

"Don't pretend it isn't true," I say. "You were still married to Mom, and then you decided to abandon her."

His brows furrow as pain strikes his face. "I'm sorry. I'm sorry, Caleb. Even though your mother isn't, I'm still here. I always will be with you. I won't abandon you, no matter how much you hate me. I will—"

I fall into his arms and hold him so tightly I can't breathe.

"I have never wanted you to feel like I was replacing her. I was

445

just trying to stop the wound in my heart from growing," he mutters. "I'm sorry, Caleb. I'm sorry."

He hugs me just as tightly, refusing to let me go when I try, and it moves me.

"I love you," he says. "I fucking love you, Caleb. I mean it. With every inch of my soul."

And it breaks me.

Tears roll down my cheeks as I bury my face in his shoulders and let out all of the grief and rage I'd been holding on to until nothing but a vapid shell was left of me, just like my mother.

SIXTY THREE

Blaine

The funeral is the day after Caleb's mother died. He and his father collectively agreed to have it done quickly so she wouldn't have to stay another day on this earth. Something about her soul having already left this place.

If it were up to me, I'd want people to burn my corpse on a pyre and have a dance with some drinks. Make it a big-ass party. All the doom and gloom really isn't for me.

I languish in this black suit.

But today isn't about me, so I won't pity myself.

After all, it's Caleb and his father who are experiencing the biggest hurt.

They throw flowers on top of the casket as it's hoisted down into the hole they dug. Everyone around us is weeping and holding hands.

Crystal's mom grabs Caleb's dad's hand, but he jerks away and turns to his son, and she steps away, out of sight.

I sigh and grab Crystal's hand instead, squeezing it so she'll know I'm here while Ares holds the other. If Caleb needs us, we're here for him, but until then, we'll stand on the sidelines, waiting.

***

Crystal

Ares, Blaine, and I sit at a table, eating badly made sandwiches that taste like cardboard. I'm not that hungry, but eating food helps digest grief, they say.

I place my sandwich down and sigh.

"C'mon, eat," my mom says as she sits down and places a plate of veggies in front of me. "If you won't have the sandwiches, at least eat some cucumbers or something."

She hands some sticks to me, and I hesitantly take a bite.

"What about you?" I ask.

She reluctantly takes a bite out of her own cardboard sandwich. "Yummy."

"Don't lie." I snort.

"Shhh," she hisses. "No need to offend the hosts."

"Funeral food never tastes good," Blaine says while Ares rolls his eyes.

"So you two are her friends?"

Blaine nearly chokes on his sandwich, and he swallows down a whole chunk. "Friends?"

I throw him a look.

"Oh … wait…"

"What?" my mother mutters.

"Nothing," I swiftly say. "Yes, they're my … friends."

Ares glares at me, his arms folded.

"They seem nice," she says, swallowing a big bite.

"Very," Blaine muses.

I shove Ares with my elbow, whispering, "Say something."

"I don't do small talk," Ares grumbles.

He scoots his chair back and walks off, leaving me in a really awkward position.

Goddammit.

"Well, he sure seems like a fun one," Mom says.

"Definitely the fun one," Blaine says, chuckling to his own joke.

In the corner of the room, Caleb and his father are accepting hugs and handshakes for their loss, but the more hands he shakes the more he seems to be disassociating.

"He's not doing too well, is he?" I mutter.

Blaine shakes his head.

I get up and walk up to him from behind, squeezing his hand to signal that I'm there.

"How are you holding up?" I whisper.

He briefly pulls away from the crowd of people to hug me tightly. "Barely surviving." He snorts. "But I'll make it."

"If you need anything, let me know, okay?"

He leans away to look at me. "For a girl who used to hate my guts, you sure are nice to me," he says, smirking at me.

His father throws a single glance at my mother before turning the other direction.

"Has my mother talked with your dad at all?" I ask.

Caleb shakes his head. "I don't know what happened between those two, but they've been cold to each other."

His father clears his throat. "I can hear you."

I blush. "Sorry."

"It's fine," he says and he turns to his son. "I've actually been meaning to tell you this before, but I didn't know how. And now that your mother is gone, it feels like such a bad time, but ..."

"What is it, Dad?" Caleb asks.

"Abigail and I actually broke up."

I'm too stunned to even say a word.

Caleb frowns. "Wait, for real?"

His dad nods. "A few days ago. I realized I may have jumped into an engagement too quickly to pretend everything was fine. I just wanted to heal this broken heart." He throws in a weak smile. "And now that your mother is gone, it truly doesn't feel right to go back to that. I want to take the proper time to grieve."

"But you loved her, right?" Caleb asks.

"I did ... but we weren't as compatible as I thought we were," he says, rubbing his lips together. "I didn't want to string her along." He looks at me. "I'm sorry, was I the first one to tell you this? I apologize, I assumed she'd already spoken to you about it."

Maybe she didn't want to tell me because it hurt too bad. Shit.

"I think I'm gonna go talk to my mom. Will you be okay?" I ask Caleb.

He smiles at me. "I'm fine, go talk to her. I'll see you later."

449

I walk back to my mom who's stirring her coffee a bit too long. I sit down beside her and grab her hand. "Hey. Caleb's dad told me what happened between you and Jonathan."

Her eyes widen. "Oh. Shit. I'm … I'm sorry, I wanted to tell you, but I didn't know how. I feel so bad, this isn't how I had it planned."

"I know, Mom," I say, squeezing her hand. "I'm not mad at you or anything. I just wanted you to know I'm here for you."

She tips her head, smiles at me, and caresses my cheek. "You're always so sweet. What did I ever do to deserve you?"

We hug tightly, her embrace making me feel loved. Death reminds me of what I still have left in this world, and how hard I'll fight to keep it. And I'm sure the Tartarus boys … my boys … would do the same.

***

CALEB

When all the guests have finally left, I breathe a sigh of relief. My mother's picture behind me makes me feel conscious of each thrumming of my heart.

But when Ares's phone rings, I glare up at him. He'd never pick up a phone at a funeral, unless it was important. His face turns darker and darker with each passing second, and he walks outside.

I follow him.

He's been my rock through all this, and even though I'm supposed to be mourning, I still want to know what's happening to him. He won't ever admit that he has any weaknesses, but I know better.

He's outside, loitering around the building, and I step out to approach.

"I'm at a funeral," Ares grits. "What do you want me to do? What, now?" He kicks some rocks. "Do you have any ide—Fine."

He ends the call, but I can hear his phone crack in his hands.

Another screen damaged from pure rage.

"Who was that?" I ask.

His muscles suddenly soften, and when he turns around, all the anger seems to have dissipated. "No one important. Don't worry about it." He walks to me and places his hand on my shoulder. "Are you feeling okay?" I nod and he leans in to kiss me, reminding me of all the good in the world. He leans his forehead against mine and stares me down. "If you feel angry, any bad feelings at all, you call me. Immediately."

"Yes, Sir," I reply.

A smile forms on his lips. "Good boy. I have to go now."

"Where?" I ask.

"Doesn't matter," he replies. "Just focus on your family for now, okay?"

I swallow down the feeling of impending doom as he walks away.

"And don't get any weird ideas, Blaine will be watching you," he says, winking at me, before marching out the front gate.

None of it feels right.

He took that call, despite knowing how important this thing was for me, which means it was something really fucking bad.

Fuck.

I kick the same rock he was kicking and head back inside where Blaine's already waiting for me.

"Don't go hiding on me now," Blaine says.

I narrow my eyes. "Stop fucking babysitting me."

"Nope," Blaine replies. "You know why."

"Jesus Christ." I roll my eyes and sit down on a chair. "Does no one here trust me?"

Crystal chuckles as she sits down too. "I do."

"Yeah, well, you're not exactly the one to stop me from jumping off that cliff, so—"

"Were you going to?" she asks.

"No. Hypothetically."

"Exactly. So hypothetically, I'm just making sure you're still alive," Blaine says before he rubs my hair and turns it all into garbage.

"Goddammit, get your hands off me," I growl at him.

Crystal laughs at us, and her smile makes my heart throb, if even just for a moment of bliss in all of the misery from these past few days.

***

ARES

I blow out my final smoke and chuck the cig on the ground before I exit the gates.

Several cars are already out front, waiting for me. What a welcome party.

A door opens, and out steps not one but two guards with automatic guns, not pointed at me but clearly a threat.

"That won't be necessary," I say.

"Get in the car," one of them growls.

I don't need to ask where we're going.

I already know.

I take a deep breath and walk toward them, getting in without a complaint. If I fought them off now, it wouldn't end well for me anyway since I didn't bring my guns or my knives to a fucking funeral.

Maybe I should have.

They truly waited for the most opportune moment to bring me in so I'd come quietly.

But when the doors close, there is only noise in my head.

***

Crystal

"Where's Caleb?" I ask my mom, hoping she's seen him.

I was just talking with someone and then all the boys suddenly vanished from my sight.

Mom points me into a corner where Blaine is sitting with him, and I immediately get off my seat and approach them.

"Hey," I say as I sit in front of Caleb and grab his hand. "How are you holding up?"

He shrugs. "Fine."

I pull him in for a tight hug.

"Seems you're already getting used to his lies," Blaine says.

"Shut up," Caleb growls.

But instead of throwing out another rebuke, Blaine moves in for a hug from above, wrapping his arms around his neck. "We know you love us."

"Love is a strong word," Caleb mutters, but he still accepts it.

"Lucky for you I have plenty of time to force you to love me back," Blaine says, nearly choking him out.

"Okay, okay, I get it," Caleb says, pushing his arms away. "I won't die from sorrow, but I will from your determination to suffocate me." He rolls his eyes. "Ares sure left me in competent hands."

"I'm just doing exactly what he told me," Blaine says. "Being an annoying pest to keep you safe is my favorite thing in the world."

"Wait, what do you mean 'Ares left you'?" I ask, frowning. "Where did he go?"

Caleb shrugs. "He got some phone call that he didn't want to tell me anything about. I don't know."

My blood suddenly feels icy cold, and I shiver in place.

Caleb continues, "He just seemed antsy. Hasty. Out of it."

"Oh God," I mutter, my eyes widening.

"What?" Blaine looks up at me.

"Caleb, open your phone. Do you have any way of tracking his location?"

"Yeah, why?" he responds, fishing it out of his pocket.

"That phone call ... It was his father."

Blaine frowns. "But why toda—" I can see it click in his eyes. "He's going to punish him for all the murders at the Bonesmen auction."

SIXTY FOUR

ARES

I walk up to the casino and stare up at the lights on the front of the building. Just one of so many buildings, I can't even count all of the riches he owns on two hands. Yet none of them will ever belong to me.

"Move." My father's guard shoves me in the back.

"Keep your hands to yourself." I glance at him over my shoulder. "Unless you'd like to see them bitten off."

His face contorts with horror, and I take pride in being the cause before I step forward into a hell far worse than Tartarus ever will be.

But I have no regrets.

I knew my choices would lead me here, and I would repeat them a thousand times over.

For her.

I swallow and walk through the crowd of people with the guards right behind me. My eyes skid from left to right across each of the hallways we march through, spotting a ton more guards, all of which have earpieces in. There's never been this many.

Are they all here for me?

I smirk to myself as we march into the dark hallways, beyond the

454

scope of where guests are allowed, and head straight toward the door at the end where my father's domain makes my heart throb in my throat.

This is it. There's no way back from here.

I step inside my father's office, and the guard behind me closes the door again.

I'm left in a room with my father and one single guard I could possibly overpower … but at what cost? I'd be killed the second I stepped foot outside this door.

No, he wants me to know I'm outnumbered.

That it's futile to resist.

He clears his throat from behind his desk. "Sit. Down."

With a monotonous look on my face I step forward and grab the chair, scooting it back far enough so I don't have to sit right in front of him. I don't care if it pisses him off.

"Do you know why I've called you here?" he says.

"No."

His eyes twitch. "Take a guess."

"I have no clue."

WHAM!

His fist comes down on the table. "*Don't* play coy with me. You know better than to act like a fool in front of your father."

I fold my arms. "Does it even matter? We both know what you want."

His nostrils flare. "Tell me it wasn't you that went inside that Bones Brotherhood auction. Tell me it wasn't you who murdered all of them." When I don't answer, he screams, "Tell me!"

"What do you want to hear? That I'm sorry?" I ask. "I'm not. I never will be. They deserved every inch of pain I gave them."

The more I speak, the more my father's face contorts. And honestly, that look on his face alone was worth it.

He stands up, planting two hands on the desk as he towers over me. "How fucking dare you?!"

I already knew I was never going to be the perfect son.

But this … his rage over the fact that he can't control me … is what I call true perfection.

He suddenly comes out from behind the desk and grips my chin. "Tell. Me. Why."

My lips are sealed but a wretched smile still forms on my lips, however painful this might get.

SMACK!

The hit of the palm of his hand to my cheek flushes heat into my skin.

"Tell me!"

I look up at him with nothing but disdain. "No."

His lip twitches. "You dare to sit here in my office, look up at me with those remorseless eyes, all while taking money from my hard-earned work, mountains of work you so happily destroy for whatever fucked-up reason," he grits. "Some of those men were personal friends. And you somehow got it in your head you had the right to take their lives."

"They were buying and selling people like cattle."

"I don't fucking care what they did! They spend money at *my* casinos. Money that's now gone because of the likes of you." He taps his finger into my chest. "Do you have any idea the kind of pain the Bones Brotherhood will inflict on my business when they find out it was *my* son who destroyed one of their hubs? They paid for your fucking Tartarus House *and* these fucking clothes you wear so mightily like you're goddamn God's gift from heaven."

I don't respond even though I want to, badly.

"You are nothing. You are not a god nor a gift. You have been insufferable since the day you chose to defy me. And for what? A good conscience?" He scoffs and shakes his head. "You are nothing but a disgrace." He leans back and looks at me, then slowly takes off his jacket. My skin begins to crawl as he places it on the desk. "Take off your fucking shirt."

Here we go.

My nostrils flare, but I still do what he says, eyeing the guard in the corner. His gun flashes in the single light fixture above us, a stark reminder of what little power I hold inside these walls.

I unbutton my shirt and slowly take it off, throwing it to the floor, then kicking it away so it won't get covered in blood.

His eyes glance over the engraved letters on my chest, a single word that will haunt his soul forever. This name caused the rift between us. This name reminds him of his lost son and all the ways I will never be his puppet again.

I ruined that for him.

"Get up," my father says through gritted teeth.

I do what he says, and the guard immediately plucks the chair away from underneath me.

My father marches to his cabinet and takes out a long, black bullwhip on the end of which is a sharp metal point, the sight of which makes my whole body quake.

THWACK!

The sound of it hitting the floor has me blinking rapidly.

My father turns to me. "Turn around. On your knees."

I stare him down, rage boiling over, not giving him an inch of my fear before I turn around. But I won't fucking kneel. Not for him.

THWACK!

When the whip comes down on my back, I hiss from the pain.

"Do as I say," he grits.

I stay put, grinding my teeth together as I hear it flick behind me.

THWACK!

Another painful lash makes my eyes teary, but I stay standing.

"ARES!" my father growls.

But I ignore him.

THWACK!

Each strike is harder than the previous one.

"On." *THWACK.* "Your." *THWACK.* "Fucking." *THWACK.* "Knees!"

I bite my tongue out of sheer pain to keep myself from screaming.

"Are you so eager to hurt? Is that it, boy? Do you enjoy it when I whip you?"

THWACK. THWACK. THWACK.

Droplets of warm blood roll down my back.

I nearly cave. Nearly.

But I will not give him this fucking pleasure. I fucking won't.

His voice makes me want to lash out. "Kneel."

"I don't bend for a coward who can't even face his own fucking son while he mutilates him," I growl back.

He grunts like a beast. "Then you are no longer my son."

THWACK! THWACK! THWACK!

The strikes are so harsh and painful that I can barely take it anymore, but I must. I made my choice. I have to stick with it. For her. For that little bit of good that's been injected into my life, however fucking small, it's worth surviving for.

But at what cost?

THWACK!

The crack on the whip on my back makes me close my eyes, my knees unsteady as I suffer through the pain in both my body and my mind.

But I refuse to fucking fold, and if this is going to be the end of me, then so be it.

"I don't want to be your son," I say through gritted teeth. "You make me wish I was never born."

My father pauses and rasps, "Maybe I should've killed you long ago."

SIXTY FIVE

Crystal

Caleb throws what looks like all the guns and weapons they have in their arsenal into the back of his car.

"Are you sure we need that much?" Blaine asks. "We're only three people."

Crystal gulps. "I think I only count for a half, tops."

"Darling, you have that all wrong," Blaine says, and he chucks me a knife in a way that could've stabbed me, but I manage to catch it. He winks. "See?"

Sighing, I tuck it into my pocket. "Isn't there a side entrance we can take to get in without getting in danger? There has to be an easier way than this."

"Nope," Caleb replies, throwing even more in a box. "Torres has every exit guarded, and he probably knows we're coming because he'll force Ares to talk."

"And then he'll tell those Bonesmen all about us," Blaine adds.

I shiver in place. Ares saved me and then killed those people for me.

I have to save him.

I push Caleb aside and steal more knives from his box, as well as a gun, loading it up. He looks at me like he can't believe his eyes.

"What?"

"You're serious?" he asks.

"Dead serious. He's in there suffering because of me, so I'm gonna be the one to pull him out, and if I have to kill a bunch of people to do it, then so be it."

A grin slowly spreads on his cheeks. "Now you're talking my love-language."

"I'm already in love!" Blaine professes, running up to me to hug me so tightly I can barely breathe. "Oh, I trained you so well, darling. I'm proud."

I physically have to pry my own body out of his hands, and I pull out my phone. "I'm not done yet." I dial the number of one of my best friends. "Penelope, I need your help."

"What's up?"

"Ares got taken by his father who's probably going to kill him."

"What?" She sounds shocked. "Wait, but you and Ares—"

"Exactly. I don't want to ask too much, but since you helped free Lana ... please."

"Don't. I don't need a please. You don't even need to ask. I'm coming. Give me five."

She hangs up before I can even reply. Well, guess that's settled.

"Hey."

I turn around to see Kai Torres from the Phantom Society standing behind us, peering into the car.

What is he doing here?

"Well, hello there," Blaine muses, winking at Kai, who is unimpressed. "What brings you to the Tartarus House?"

"Where's Ares? He's not picking up his phone. I'm worried."

"Ask your goddamn father," Caleb growls back.

"Father?" Kai frowns. "What does he have to do with this?"

"We killed a bunch of those Bonesmen fuckers to free Crystal."

"So what? So have I," Kai responds, shrugging.

"Yeah, well you're not the one getting punished now, are you?" Caleb retorts, grinding his teeth. "Since your father has a favorite son and one he wants to murder."

Kai's eyes widen. "What?"

"Don't pretend you don't know," Caleb growls, clutching a knife, ready to fight.

"Wait," I say, stepping between them. "Maybe he doesn't."

"Bullshit," Caleb quips.

"Calm down, Caleb, we might need him," Blaine says.

"Caleb, please," I say.

Caleb takes in a deep breath through his nose, then retracts his blade. "Fine."

"I don't know what the hell you're talking about," Kai says. "All I know is that my father sometimes summons him after he's done some shit."

"Do you know what his father does to him?" I ask.

"He scolds him," Kai says. "It's not like they're on good standing. Ares hasn't exactly been ... willing to live by the Torres rules."

"Rules," I scoff. "Your father hasn't just been scolding him every time he makes him come to his office." I don't know if I'm the one who should be telling him this, but I feel like I have no choice. "He hurts him. Physically."

Kai's face contorts. "What?"

"He never told you?" Caleb asks, frowning.

"No." Kai shakes his head. "My father woul—"

"Believe me, he would," Caleb responds. "Every fucking time Ares makes a decision that doesn't benefit his screwed-up vision."

Slowly but surely, the anger begins to take over every inch of Kai's face. "No. I don't want to believe it. If that's true, then ..." His fist balls. "I need to see this for myself."

Blaine snorts. "Good luck getting in."

"I'm a Torres," he says.

"You think your father will let you see what he does to Ares?" Blaine asks. "There's no way any of us are getting in there quietly."

Kai's eye twitches. "Who says I'll come quietly?"

He pulls out his phone and walks off to make a call, and I don't know if this is going to go well, but maybe he'll assist us. We can use every bit of help.

"Guess that's it," Caleb growls.

"Can't we bring more Tartarus guys?" I ask Blaine.

He shakes his head. "I don't want their deaths on our hands. We can do this. I have faith."

"Faith won't stop your head from rolling," Caleb growls back.

"You think I'll let them get close to me?" Blaine flashes his katana from the umbrella he always brings with him wherever he goes. "No one touches this delicious body."

"Gag," Caleb says, making me chuckle.

"Hey!" Penelope's voice in the distance makes me turn my head.

"You're here!" I yell, but then my eyes widen when I see three familiar faces behind her; Felix, Dylan, and Alistair have all shown up too.

"Who summoned those sickos?" Blaine asks.

"I did," I say, smirking.

"You rang?" Dylan says as he approaches, throwing a lighter up and down. "It's been too long since our last barbecue."

Caleb furrows his brows. "Barbecue? Are you for real?"

"Of course, I am," he responds. "Caleb *something* ..."

"Preston," Caleb grits, visibly annoyed. "How could you already forget—"

"Because I don't care." Dylan narrows his eyes.

"Well fuck you too," Caleb retorts.

"I just have poor memory, don't take it personal," Dylan mutters.

Alistair waves at me and smiles awkwardly. "So who are we killing?"

"Well, that's one way to say hi," Blaine says, then he focuses on the last of Penelope's boyfriends. "And who are you?"

"Felix," Penelope says.

"I'm only here because of her, so I hope for you it's worth my fucking time," he says, cracking his knuckles. "As long as there's people to kill, I'm happy. Where are we going?"

"That's all I wanted to hear," Blaine muses. "Torres Casino downtown."

Dylan makes a face. "Wait, isn't that Kai's—"

"Yes," I reply. "It is. Is that a problem?"

He shrugs. "Not my problem if Kai hates us all."

"He won't," I say. "He already knows."

"And he'd let us bust up the place without making a fuss?"

"Yes." Kai's voice makes us all turn around.

And I'm not the only one shocked that both Nathan Reed and Milo Fletcher have also joined him.

"This had better be worth it, if I have to join up with those fuckers again," Nathan says, as he approaches me, and I run to hug him.

"You came," I say.

462

"Of course, I did. I told you, you call me when you need help, and I'll be fucking there. I don't fucking care what it is."

"Fuck. Not these guys too," Alistair says, rolling his eyes like he's already tired before the fighting has started.

"Wait, you have some issues with them?" I ask Alistair.

"Duh, they've been fucking around with Felix's sister," Dylan answers.

"Hi, Blaine!" Milo says, waving like he's happy to see him.

When I pull back and see Nathan staring at Felix and Kai at Dylan, I just know this whole thing is going to be awkward as hell. Half of these guys hate each other's guts, and the only thing keeping them from slaughtering each other is us girls.

"Don't start fighting, please," I say.

"I won't," Nathan promises.

"I can't promise I won't," Felix quips.

"Play nice," Penelope tells him.

"You still owe me a finger," Nathan grits back.

Kai throws him a glare, making him back down. "Don't. Not now."

"So who are we killing?" Milo asks, throwing around his nunchucks like he's mentally preparing himself.

"Wait, what about Crystal?" Dylan asks.

"What about me?" I reply, folding my arms.

"Well … isn't this like a little too much for you? I mean, you don't have to come. It must be a shock to see us with all of these weapons," he says, pointing at the weapon's stash.

I shrug. "Nope."

Alistair frowns. "None at all?"

I fish two knives out of the stash and chuck them at both of them, catching them off guard.

Dylan smirks. "Whoa, where'd you learn those moves?"

I point at Blaine who grins smugly and then wriggles his brows.

"I'm impressed," Alistair says.

"Thank you, thank you." Blaine bows.

"Hey now, don't take all the credit," I say, shoving my elbow into his side.

A motorcycle drives up to the Tartarus House, and black hair spills from a helmet as it's pulled off. "Did I hear the word kill?"

Lana commands attention the second she steps off her motorcycle and approaches the group, and I hug her too. "Thank you."

"Don't say thank you yet. I haven't killed anyone." She snorts. "But I'm ready for whoever we're going to murder." She opens up her coat, revealing all the weapons she brought with her.

No wonder those Phantom boys wanted her so badly.

"And I can't wait to watch you do it," Milo says, all swoony.

God, I love my friends.

"We're going into the Torres Casino," I say, and I show everyone a picture of the location in Crescent Vale City on my phone. "There will be a ton of guards at every exit, and they're heavily armed."

"Right. No problem." Dylan says, licking his lips.

"We'll butcher them," Felix adds, chucking his knife up and down.

Butcher? Jesus. Wish Penelope would've warned me about her guys.

"Hello, has no one thought of our disguises?" Lana says.

"Disguise?" Alistair frowns.

Lana gives him a deadpan look. "You think you'll get away with murdering everyone at a casino downtown?"

"Oh shit … I hadn't actually thought about that," Dylan mutters, tapping his lip.

"I had," Caleb says, and he pulls a few masks from the car and chucks them on the ground. "Grab one each."

Penelope picks it up from the ground and stares at it. "Is this what I think it is?"

"This has the Bones Brotherhood emblem on it," Milo says.

"Yes. Exactly the point," Caleb says. "Do I have to spell it out?"

Lana begins to smirk. "You want us to pretend we're Bonesmen to set them up against each other."

"Smart," I mutter.

"Bet you didn't expect that from me," Caleb says with a smug grin.

Blaine holds up the mask with two fingers and sniffs, then winces. "Ew, I'm not wearing this."

"Blaine," Caleb grits.

"It stinks!"

"He's right, it does smell," Milo says, making a face when he smells it again.

"See?" Blaine makes a face. "This is going to ruin my skin."

"Do you have a better idea?" Caleb raises his brow.

Blaine rolls his eyes and sighs out loud. "Fine. But you owe me a new cream."

"Fuck your fucking cream," Nathan growls, putting on the mask. "How does it look?"

"Excuse you, darling," Blaine mutters under his breath.

"Looks good to me," Penelope says.

Dylan, Alistair, Lana, Milo, and Felix all put on their mask as well.

"This had better not take all fucking day," Felix snarls. "Get in, kill people, get out."

"Are we doing a kill count?" Nathan asks everyone, licking his lips.

"Most definitely," Blaine responds.

Dylan's eyes sparkle. "Count me in." He shoves Felix in the side. "What about you? You game?"

"I don't play, I win," Felix growls back, making everyone grin.

"You wish," Lana quips, getting them all hyped.

"Oh, it's on," Caleb says.

"Kill as many as you like, but don't touch my father," Kai growls. "I want to speak with him."

"Why?" Alistair asks.

"Because he's the reason we're there in the first place," I say. "Now let's go get Ares."

***

ARES

Another strike with the bullwhip has my knee caving in on me, and I slowly collapse but crawl up from the floor. I will stand. Each time he hits me, I come back up to my feet despite the searing pain.

THWACK!

Another one has me roaring out loud.

"Get on your knees, Ares, and maybe I will spare you."

Blood rolls down my back in streams.

"Fuck you," I hiss.

THWACK! THWACK! THWACK!

I fall to my knees and crawl right back up again, but the second my feet push up on the ground, I collapse onto the floor.

It's too much.

My body can barely take it anymore.

I've already disassociated long ago, but now I'm on the brink of letting go. Of just drifting off into nothing and surrendering to my end. Even though it didn't come by her hand, at least I know I did the right thing. If he truly intends to kill me, then I hope it's a swift death because I can't stand this pain much longer.

BANG!

I suck in a breath.

That sounded like a … gunshot.

BANG! BANG! BANG!

Multiple.

The sound of screams beyond the door makes me blink rapidly.

I look up at the door and the guard standing in front of it, wondering what's going on behind that door.

"What's going on out there?" my father growls at him.

The guard pulls out his walkie-talkie and says, "Update."

"Shots fired, shots fired, three down! We need backup."

My eyes widen, and I lift my head.

"Who is it?" my father growls.

"Details!" the guard yells into his walkie-talkie.

"Group of fucking young kids, barely twenty, and there's two, no three fucking girls too!"

My heart comes back to life, and I get back up from the floor, invigorated by the mere idea.

It's them.

SIXTY SIX

CALEB

BANG! BANG!

I'm shooting at the guards near the front of the building despite the fact that the rest have already gone inside. I just want every one of these motherfuckers to bleed to death for taking Ares, and I don't care how long it takes. I'm going for the kill.

BANG!

A guard goes down and cries for his mommy as the bullet enters his knee, making him collapse, and I spit on him before I go inside too.

Everywhere I look, guards come pouring out while preparing an attack on all of us, while the casino's guests flock to the emergency exits, screaming their lungs out.

I don't know which one of these fuckers was involved with bringing Ares in, but I'll make sure they'll all regret it.

"Where do we go first?" Milo asks.

Kai points at a giant hallway in the back. "That way."

"There's a ton of guards," Crystal says.

"So?" Blaine shrugs. "The more the merrier."

"Where are your guns, then?" Felix asks him.

Blaine pulls out his umbrella, and Felix and Dylan begin to laugh until he pulls out the katana.

"What the f—really?" Felix says.

"Don't laugh, he'll skewer you," Milo muses.

"I didn't ask you a damn thing," Felix growls at him.

"You want to touch it?" Blaine asks, raising a brow.

Felix's face contorts. "No thanks."

"It'll be gentle with you," Blaine adds.

"Ew, gross," Nathan says.

One of the guards storms at us with his gun pointed right at us, but Milo takes him down with his nunchucks. "Nothing's gross about killing. I'm fucking excited!"

"I'm not," Alistair says, pulling out his knives with a smug smile. "But I'll make it work."

A giant casino floor filled with slot machines is in our way.

"You go that side. We'll take this side," Kai says, directing each group. "Caleb, Crystal, Lana, Nathan, Milo you're with me. Blaine, Felix, Dylan, Penelope, Alistair, you go that way. Meet us at the entry to the hallway in the back."

"Got it." Felix nods, and he pulls out his guns. "Time to get some fucking blood on our hands."

And as I pull out a new magazine and shove it into my gun, I whisper to myself, "Ares, we're coming for you."

***

ARES

"What the fuck is going on out there?" my father growls, and I can hear him place the whip down somewhere and waltz off. The door opens. "Stay here and watch him. Make sure he doesn't move."

The door slams shut again, leaving me alone with a guard holding an automatic rifle.

But if he'd shoot me now, I don't think I'd even care.

The momentary pause from the whipping makes me let out a sigh of relief. Every breath I take hurts like a knife to the lungs, so sharp, but I persist.

If they're here … Blaine, Caleb, Crystal …

I have to see them.

Just one last time so I'll remember their faces before I perish.

But dammit … they shouldn't have come.

It's too dangerous, and if my father comes back to gloat while telling me he saw one of their dead bodies it would be worse than death.

I couldn't take it.

I'd rather die in horrible pain instead of knowing one of my friends, my lovers, got killed trying to save me.

"No …" I whisper to myself, wishing I could tell them instead to stay away.

Leave me to rot.

Leave me and save yourself.

Just … leave.

And let me die in peace.

***

Crystal

Kai and Milo take the lead, knifing down any guard that comes close, while Lana and Nathan provide backup. Milo swings his nunchucks around like a pro, and it honestly makes me wonder how he decided that would be his weapon, but I'm not complaining as none of the guards can get near him.

Caleb's shooting twice and then chucking his knife at someone in the back to make sure no one tries to come at us. He's an expert at spotting them before they even have a chance to get near us, and so far I haven't had to shoot.

The thought of killing people still makes me nauseous, but watching Lana and Penelope shoot like it means nothing gives me strength. I aim at one of the guards headed for us from the side and shoot.

BANG!

It hits him in the foot.

"Whoooo, I didn't know you could shoot like that!" Milo says enthusiastically before nunchucking the dude right in the balls.

"Me neither," I retort, laughing it off.

"Kai, behind you!" Lana yells.

Kai turns around and shoves one of his knives straight into the abdomen of one of the guards who was just about to knife him down, and he tears him open from belly to neck.

Jesus.

Blood sprays from his wound, and he sinks to the floor.

"Five," Kai grits.

"Well, I have six already!" Dylan yells from the other side of the room.

"Fuck him," Nathan grits. "I'm gonna win this shit."

"Focus," Kai tells him.

BANG! BANG!

Lana shoots down two guys who were aiming at Nathan and Kai. "Less talking, more killing."

"I love it when you're all bloodthirsty," Milo muses as we head farther through the casino.

People are still screaming and running for their lives left and right, and it makes it hard to distinguish who is an actual foe and who is an innocent bystander. I don't want someone's life on my hands if they don't deserve to die.

But then I see a guard from behind a pillar, and I point at him. "There!"

Caleb chucks a knife at his face, and it lodges inside the pillar instead because the guy immediately hid again the moment I pointed at him.

"Fuck!" Caleb shouts, and he pulls out even more knives from his coat. "Come here, you little bitch!"

He doesn't notice the guard coming out of the toilet to his right, so I point my gun at him and shoot.

I miss.

Panic swirls through my veins.

"Caleb!"

BANG!

Lana hits him in the head with a knife, and he falls to the floor while Caleb engages in a fistfight with the guard behind the pillar.

Kai runs to him and stabs the guard in the side, allowing Caleb to thrust his knife straight into his throat, causing a gush of blood.

"Stay together!" Kai says.

"There are too many," I say.

"This motherfucker needed to die," Caleb growls.

"Let's go!" Lana yells, signaling them to move.

"Yes, queen!" Milo cheers.

"Out of bullets?" Nathan asks, and he chucks some at Caleb as we keep heading forward. "Here."

Caleb shoves them into his magazine and reloads. "Thanks."

"Is this your way of making up with him?" Milo muses.

"Shut up," Nathan grits.

"You know, I don't mind if you two are friends." Milo swats a guy away with his nunchucks and kicks him to the floor, easily bashing his head in. Covered in blood, he turns to smile. "I don't feel threatened at all."

"Jesus," I mutter to myself.

"Yep, they're something all right," Lana says, laughing.

"Let's go," Kai says. "No time to waste."

"You're the one to talk. You let this fucking happen to him," Caleb growls at him.

"I already told you I didn't fucking know," Kai says. "But the more we talk, the longer it'll take to get to him."

"Enough. No fighting. You guys promised," I say.

On the other side of the room, Felix, Dylan, Penelope, Alistair, and Blaine are fending off the guards streaming in like their lives depend on it, and we've got one extra person in our group.

"They're overwhelmed," I say. "We gotta go help them."

"Nonsense," Milo muses, poking a guard on the floor with his nunchuck to make sure he's actually dead. "Have you seen Blaine?"

I look again, and my eyes nearly bulge out of my skull from the way he swiftly takes care of each one of them with a single slice, thrusting in and out of people's bodies as though he's cutting through butter. One by one, they all fall down in front of him, and all Felix, Dylan, Alistair, and Penelope have to do is provide backup.

"My God …" I mutter.

But then a guard suddenly runs up to him from the side right when he's got one of them on the edge of his knife and stabs him.

I shriek. "BLAINE!"

SIXTY SEVEN

Blaine

Searing pin hits me like lightning, and I turn around and slice through the guy who punctured my precious skin. "NO ONE FUCKING TOUCHES ME. NO ONE."

I stab his eye out with my sword and shove it into his mouth with the same blade, forcing him onto the floor with his last taste being his own entrails.

But fuck, his knife is still stuck inside me.

I yank it out and groan from the pain.

"Don't," Penelope runs to me and rips off a piece of her shirt, then rips up mine to wrap it around my waist. "Gotta stop the bleeding."

BANG! BANG!

Felix takes down the guards shooting at us one by one, alternating bullets with knives, keeping them at bay, while Penelope takes care of my wound.

"Blaine, are you okay?" I can hear Crystal's voice before I see her, and the second she runs up to me and wraps her arm around me, I breathe a sigh of relief.

At least she's still intact.

472

"Look at what that fucker did," I groan. "My beautiful body."

"You're not any less beautiful, my guy," Dylan says, snorting.

"Why thank you," I muse.

Dylan turns around to shoot at one of the guards, then drags his body toward the stack of partially living, groaning guards they've been collecting. One of them tries to crawl out, and Dylan promptly grabs his ankle and drags him right back in. "This place is perfect for a fire, don't you think?" Dylan grabs a few bottles of expensive liquor left on the play tables and chucks them at the pile of guards. Then he fishes out his lighter and sets them on fire. "Burn, bitches, burn!"

"What the …?" Nathan stares at him like Dylan's completely lost his mind.

And maybe he's right because I'm thinking the same thing. These Skull & Serpent Society guys are something else, that's for sure.

Alistair blocks attackers from the side with sneak attacks from behind a pillar, gouging out their eyes and slicing up their Achilles tendons when they run past so they stop running forever.

"Don't think you'll get away," he says as the guards cry in pain.

The cruelty is immeasurable, and I'm loving it.

This is the kind of violence my blade lives for.

So I push Penelope aside as the guards approach and pierce them on my blade one by one, avoiding their bullets with ease. Penelope fires another shot at a guard at our backs, taking one after the other down with a single shot. She's a very good sniper, a perfect rear for me.

"Fuck, this stab wound hurts," I hiss, and I take my anger out on the next one who approaches me, slicing through his balls. "There, that feels better."

"No time to waste on chitchat," Kai says.

"What about my pretty little bonfire?" Dylan mopes. "Now I'm gonna miss seeing it burn."

"Plenty of chances to start fires elsewhere," Felix growls at him.

Dylan sighs out loud. "Fine, fine."

"You're still alive," Milo says in a cheery voice, staring at all of us. "Didn't think you'd make it out. I'm impressed."

"Ha ha." Penelope throws him a glare.

"Where to?" Alistair asks.

Kai points at the back of the hallway. "My father's office is in there. End of the hallway, to the left. It won't be easy getting in. He has a ton of personal guards."

Felix cracks his knuckles. "I love a challenge."

"They won't stand a chance," Nathan says.

"What's your body count?" Caleb asks.

"Twelve," Dylan muses. "Yours?"

Caleb smirks. "Thirteen."

Dylan's nostrils flare, and he pulls out two sets of knives. "No bastard from the Tartarus House is going to beat me."

"Who are you calling a bastard, Phantom bitch?" Caleb retorts.

"Use your anger on them, not us," Kai says.

"Ares is waiting for us," Crystal says.

"Darlings, less talking, more fighting, please. You'll never catch up with me otherwise." I add a wink when they all look incensed.

BANG! BANG!

Shots are fired in our direction.

We move forward as a group, slicing through guards coming at us left and right. No guests are left in the casino, so we can go all out.

Felix and Kai shoot as fast as they can while I cut up anyone who comes too close with a simple flick of my katana. Despite the pain, I push on, determined to reach Ares. It's my duty to protect him, and I will fucking save him, no matter how much it costs me.

I owe him my life.

So I will give it to him.

"Fifteen!" Dylan yells over the fighting after he's gutted someone from lip to lip, carving him a new smile. "I'm on a roll, bitches!"

"Fuck you, I'm just getting started!" Nathan screams.

"Sixteen," Kai says with a snort.

"Twenty," I muse.

"Cheater," Dylan growls at me. "See how you do without your stupid umbrella."

"Katana. If you use your weapon as badly as you use your words, I understand exactly why you'll lose, and I win," I quip.

BANG!

Gunfire to the left has Milo and Nathan going wild on a guard, alternating strikes with gunshots until the guy is on the floor, and the next one too.

Felix and Kai are back to back, shooting at anyone who tries to get too close to them, while Penelope and Lana protect each other by throwing knives around and plucking them from the bodies of their victims with ease.

Only Crystal seems to be having problems killing people, opting to aim for the legs instead to make them go down. So I finish them off and let their heads roll.

I have never intervened with what Ares did here in this casino because he explicitly told me not to. He must've thought there was still a chance to win this without destroying everything. To fight his father on his own and come out as the conqueror. Even if it meant his death.

No. I won't allow it.

"Move!" I yell as everyone's stalling from the guards that keep pouring out from the hallway ahead.

But I can clearly see the door behind them … along with the man standing in front of it, pushing his own guards toward us when he spots us.

"Torres," I growl under my breath.

"There," Kai says, pointing at him. "Fight your way through!"

"Happily," Milo replies, throwing his nunchucks around like a good boy, making me proud.

I taught him well.

Torres backtracks into the hallway and runs back into his office, shutting it tightly.

Caleb's grunt draws my attention. A bullet grazes his cheek, and the rage he exudes is nothing short of magnificent.

"Motherfucker!" He throws a knife at the guy's dick, who cries in pain when it hits him, collapsing on the spot. Caleb marches at him and stabs him through the cheek. "How does it feel, asshole?"

"Fuck, he's wild," Alistair mutters to me.

"Yup," I reply. "That's why Ares keeps him around."

Alistair snorts and aims over my shoulder. "Duck."

BANG!

A guard goes down right behind me.

"Thanks," I say.

"Don't mention it," he replies.

"We're almost there!" Felix yells before he stabs the last two guards in the belly, and Nathan shoots them in the head.

"Felix, Alistair, Dylan, Penelope, Milo, Nathan, Lana," Kai says, "guard the hallway. Don't let anyone through."

"What about you?" Lana asks.

"I'm going in with them," Kai says, looking at Caleb, me, and Crystal. "I want to see the truth for myself."

Penelope and Lana nod. "Good luck," Penelope says.

We pass beyond the hallway while they stay behind and block the way out.

Everyone tears off their masks and throws them onto the floor, as they're useless now that we're here.

"Ready?" Crystal asks.

Caleb doesn't wait and kicks in the door. "TORRES! GET YOUR FUCKING HA—"

We all stand in the door opening, shocked by the pool of blood underneath the carved-up body lying on the floor. Ares.

***

Crystal

Is he ...?

I cover my mouth as I gasp for air, tears forming in my eyes at the sight of the wretched amount of lashes to Ares's skin. It's far beyond anything he's had before. His back is covered in gashes and fresh blood, his body collapsed on the floor out of sheer exhaustion in a puddle of his own blood.

Oh God.

"What the f—This is what you've been doing to him?" Kai screams at his own father. "You told me you were talking to him!"

A guard standing beside the door points an automatic rifle at us. "Don't. Move."

A man in a gray striped suit and a freshly shaved face along with a wavy, gelled-back coup of hair stands close to Ares. Mr. Torres. "You're too late."

Ares lets out a muffled groan and his head tilts, his eyes barely opening to look at us.

But I can still see the hurt on his face, the absolute destruction of his will to live.

His gray eyes reach inside mine, clawing out my soul the moment his fingers scrape down on the floor and begin to claw their way to me in desperation, leaving bloodied streaks on the floor.

The sight haunts me. Destroys the very core of my being and grinds it into dust.

"Still think you have any semblance of power?" his father grits.

THWACK!

He strikes Ares's back with an actual bullwhip right in front of us.

I shriek from the sound it makes, the flick of his wrist as he so easily scars his own son.

"NO!" Kai screams, to no avail.

"Move, and I'll put a bullet in all of you," the guard growls. "And I'll do it far quicker than any of you can ever pull the triggers on those measly guns you have."

But it's the way Ares gazes up at me with a pleading look in his eyes that breaks me as he begs, "Please ... run."

"STOP!" Caleb screams at Mr. Torres. "What the fuck is wrong with you? That's your fucking son!"

"What is wrong with me?" Torres growls. "It's your fault he's behaving this way. You degenerate pieces of shit, breaking into my casino, have destroyed his mind. He's no fucking son of mine."

Despite the pain, Ares manages to curl up and bring his knees forward, leaning on both hands and knees, blood dripping down on both sides.

His father whips him again, causing his body to buckle under its own weight, and tears spring to my eyes. "Stay down and let these friends of yours watch you whimper like the useless animal you are!"

But Ares refuses to lie down, continuously shoving his own knees underneath his body to try to stand, even when his whole body caves in on him.

I can't. I can't watch this.

Not again.

Even if there's an automatic rifle pointed at me, ready to kill me, I can't let Ares suffer. He's suffered enough.

Right before the third strike hits him, I bolt away from the door and wrap my arms around his body, shielding him from the impact right when it strikes. "NO!"

THWACK!

"CRYSTAL!" Blaine's voice rips through me, but not nearly as harshly as this whip.

The sizzling pain is beyond anything I've ever experienced, a crackle to the spine like thunder, heat striking my skin causing a loud shriek to emanate from my lungs.

Just one strike, compared to the hundreds Ares might have received ...

And I am struck in awe at how long he endured.

I thought I *knew* what hatred was as Ares tried to instill it within me with every one of his stares, but now ... now I've *felt* it enter my skin and seep into my bones, twisting my mind into furious knots until all I see is red from blinding rage.

I turn and grip the whip at the edge, holding on as tightly as I can while staring into the eyes of the real monster. "This stops. Now."

"You ... You dare to interfere?" he says, grinding his teeth. "It is my *right* to punish him."

"Your right is nothing but to feel the same pain you inflicted on him!" I scream. "How dare you? How fucking dare you?"

He yanks away the whip and pulls out a gun instead, aiming it at my head. "Move."

"Torres, don't you fucking dare!" Caleb yells.

"Stay out of this," Mr. Torres grits before he focuses his attention back on me. "You ... you ... I recognize you. Why do I recognize you?"

"Because I look like my father ... the innocent man you callously murdered without a care just because you thought you had the right," I growl. "And I watched your son pull the knife out of his body."

His face contorts with utter evilness and a hint of disgusting pride. "You ... you're the reason my son destroyed his chances to be a true Torres."

The barrel is pushed into my forehead.

"No," Ares grumbles from underneath me. "Please. Don't kill her."

His father begins to laugh maniacally. "You all came here to do what? Save him?" He laughs again, even more menacingly than before. "You think I took him against his will? He came on his own accord. He doesn't want to be saved."

"Bullshit!" Caleb yells. "He never asked you to fucking whip him!"

"He needed to be shown the punishment for defying me, for continuously killing the people I work with, for purposely getting in my way every single time just to defy me."

"You broke him," I mutter. "You broke his spirit. His body. His mind. Even his heart."

"Torreses have no conscience. No remorse. We don't need a fucking heart," his father growls, glaring at Ares. "And yours made you weak. Vulnerable. Useless. You couldn't even kill one man to solidify your place as my goddamn heir. You chose his life over your own, for her?" He spits on me. "What a disgrace."

When his hand rises to strike me with the whip, Kai swiftly takes out the momentarily distracted guard with a single shot to the temple while Caleb runs toward Mr. Torres and grips his wrist, twisting it to stop him from hitting me. "Don't you fucking dare!"

I roll away.

Suddenly, Mr. Torres aims his weapon at Ares instead. "HE'S MINE TO FUCKING PUNISH!"

Blaine runs up to us and throws himself between Ares and his father right as he pulls the trigger.

BANG!

SIXTY EIGHT

Crystal

"NO!" I scream, grabbing Blaine as he sinks to the floor.

Blood pours from an open wound in his chest, and he begins to gurgle.

"You motherf—" Caleb smashes his fist into Mr. Torres's face and knocks him to the floor. Kai kicks the gun out of his hand and cracks the bones in his fingers underneath his boot. His screams are the only consolation I have as I wrap my arms around both Ares and Blaine, bleeding out in my lap.

"No, no, no," I murmur at Blaine. "Please, stay with me."

"GUARDS!" his father squeals. "GUARDS!"

"There are no more guards," Kai growls at his father, gripping his collar. "We killed them all."

Mr. Torres's pupils dilate. "What? No, no, that can't be true—"

Kai snatches the whip from his father's hand and starts lashing out, striking him with the whip just as harshly as he did to Ares. "Does it hurt?! Do you think it hurt as much as you hurt Ares?" *THWACK. THWACK. THWACK.* "The pain doesn't even come close to the years of suffering you put him through!" *THWACK. THWACK.* "You motherfucking piece of shit, how dare you hurt my fucking brother!" *THWACK!*

Kai is out of control, completely unhinged by rage as he whips his own father's belly and face while he screams in terror from the blood rolling down his body and neck.

"Kai, please!" his father begs.

"Did you stop when he pleaded with you?" Kai responds, only to strike him even harder. "All these years, I thought you were talking with him, getting him to change his mind, to prepare him. And now I find out you've been torturing him all this time right under my very fucking nose?"

THWACK! THWACK! THWACK! THWACK! THWACK!

He doesn't stop.

Not until Caleb grabs his wrist midair. "Enough."

"He needs to fucking pay!" Kai grits.

"But do you really want to murder your own father?"

Ragged breaths come out of Kai's mouth. "He deserves nothing less."

"Kai …" His father groans.

Kai kicks him in the side. "Even now, you can't even think of Ares instead. You motherfucker, you don't deserve me."

"Guys …" I mutter, looking up at both of them. "Please, help."

I'm cradling two gravely injured men while blood seeps down my back, and I can't hold on much longer.

Kai and Caleb come to us, and while Caleb rips off his own shirt and wraps it around Blaine's bullet wound, Kai lifts his own brother off the floor and carries him on his back.

"Call for help," Kai tells me.

When both boys are off me, I get up and bolt through the door, rushing through the hallway until I get to the others. "Guys! We need help!"

Felix, Alistair, Dylan, Penelope, Lana, Milo, and Nathan run back with me and gawk inside the office. "What happened? Did you save hi—Oh God," Penelope mutters when she sees the pools of blood on the floor.

"Jesus Christ," Dylan says when he peers inside. "What happened?"

"Kai's father tortured Ares and shot Blaine. We need help carrying them out. No time to waste," I say.

But the moment they run past me to assist Kai and Caleb, I'm the

481

only one who looks at Mr. Torres. He's reaching for the gun on the floor and aims it at Ares again.

So I snatch Lana's gun from her belt, aim it at Torres, and shoot. *BANG!*

One bullet and everyone's attention is focused on the body flopping to the floor, the gun still firmly clutched in his stiff hand.

Everyone takes a glance at me, but I can't take my eyes off the body of the man who murdered my father in cold blood. The burden of my vow to him ... has finally been released.

Caleb approaches me and has to pry the weapon out of my hand before he hugs me tight. "It's okay. You did good. It's over now."

I nod a few times and swallow away the tears. "I'm sorry. He was about to kill A—"

Kai interrupts me. "I know." He places a hand on my shoulder. "Thank you."

I'm shocked. Completely and utterly shocked.

But he just walks away like I didn't just kill his father, supporting Ares together with Milo.

I turn around and look at Blaine who's hanging onto Felix and Dylan for dear life. "Will they be okay?"

Caleb wraps his arm around my waist. "I won't allow them to leave us behind. So yes." He briefly smiles at me. "Let's go."

***

CALEB

We race back to school in our cars, ignoring red lights everywhere. Felix, Kai, Dylan, and Nathan help me carry Blaine and Ares haphazardly to the nurse's office even though it's already way past opening hours.

I'm already glad most students are in their dorms fast asleep, so they don't have to witness us dragging in two bloodied people and have their screams fill the campus.

Right as we place both guys down on the bed, the nurse marches in.

"What is going on in here? I—"

She stops in her tracks the second she sees us all scrambling in her office, trying to find something to stop the bleeding.

"Dear God," she mutters. "All of you?"

Dylan smashes his lips together for a quick smile. "Hi again."

Alistair waves awkwardly, and Milo just coyly smiles at her. Meanwhile, Penelope and Lana stand in the corner with their arms folded, while Felix and Nathan just don't give a fuck and simply shrug.

"Are you going to help us or not?" Kai grits.

"Well, what's going on?" The nurse steps in and places her phone down on the table. "I got another warning that someone was in my office, but I didn't think you guys had the balls to come in again after last time. Who got shot up now?"

Nathan points at the bloodied bodies on the beds.

"Please," I mutter as I grab Ares's hand. "We need your help."

Crystal's hovering over his face, checking his temperature. "He's heating up."

Blaine coughs and groans. "Don't worry about me, darlings. I feel fine."

"He's been shot," Crystal says before she unwraps the shirt around his wounds to show her. "Please, you have to help us."

The nurse's eyes widen, and she swiftly grabs her toolkit from her cabinet, puts on gloves, and sits on a stool near Blaine. "Move, girl."

She shoves Crystal aside and rubs some alcohol into his skin. "This is going to hurt."

"Fuck," Blaine growls when she shoots him up with drugs.

"You people are getting on my nerve," the nurse says. "This is the third time now you're just dumping bodies in my office."

"We're still alive," Blaine replies, grinding his teeth through the pain as she digs into his wounds.

"Stay still, boy," she says. "I need to stop the bleed and suture it."

She injects something into him and goes to work on the wound left from the knife, but the blood keeps pouring out of his chest every time he takes in a breath.

"There, I've sutured this one. But you're going to need to go to the hospital for this," she says, pointing at the bullet hole.

"Oh God," Milo mutters, chewing his nails. "Is he going to be okay?"

"That all depends on how fast you can get there," she says.

"What about Ares?" Crystal asks.

The nurse rolls her little stool to his side and says, "Where?"

Kai and Nathan help roll him over, and she gags when she sees the lashes on his back and all the blood seeping into the bed.

"Oh God indeed ..." she says.

"That doesn't sound good," Alistair mutters from the corner.

"Hand me my phone, boy," she yells at Dylan, who throws it at her.

It's impressive she manages to catch it at her age. She swiftly pulls off her gloves and dials a number. "Rivera, it's Daisy Lewis."

"Daisy?" Dylan makes a face and grins, but a simple, stern look from Nurse Daisy shuts him up.

"I need you to call in a code at the clinic. Students brought in two injured, one with a bullet wound and a stab wound that I sutured up quickly, one in the peritoneum, one in the pectoralis major muscle. Another patient with major lashes and ruptured skin, possibly through the dermis and subcutaneous. Uh-huh. Uh-huh. Yeah, got it."

She hangs up the phone and turns to us. "Ambulance is on the way."

"What? No," Felix grits, stepping in. "We all agreed, no hospitals. If we go there, they'll fucking report us to the police, and then we're done for."

"My father's going to kill me," Alistair mutters, staring off into the distance.

"Relax, no one's involving the police," Penelope says. "As long as everyone keeps their mouths shut."

"That's going to be tough," Milo mutters, tapping his fingers together.

"They need help, guys. We can't just sit around and do nothing," Crystal says.

"I'm with her," I say. "I'm not going to let them die. If that means going to the hospital and risking jail time, then so be it."

Dylan sighs, but then his eyes widen the moment he sees who steps through the door.

"No one here is going to jail."

Mr. Rivera, the dean of Spine Ridge University, has us all standing.

"Dad?" Lana mutters. "What are you doing here—" Her eyes skitter around the room. "It's not what it looks like."

Rivera raises a brow. "Two injured students and my kids all covered in blood?"

"It wasn't a fight between us, I swear," Penelope says.

"Felix," his father looks sternly at him. "Tell me the truth."

Felix folds his arms. "We went to the Torres Casino to save Ares, who was being tortured by his father. We shot up maybe a hundred guards to get to him. Torres is dead."

Their father groans in frustration and rubs his eyes, taking a pause. "And the guests?"

"They ran," Milo fills in. "We didn't kill any innocent people if that's what you're asking."

"Did anyone see you?"

"We wore masks," I reply.

"Can we hurry up, please?" Crystal asks. "There's no time for any of this. They're dying."

"What if the doctors there tell the cops?" Kai asks.

Mr. Rivera clears his throat. "They won't because the specialist working there is on the goddamn board."

"Oh …" Dylan mutters. "Well, why didn't you tell us sooner?"

Suddenly, two people knock on the door. "Who called for an ambulance?"

Mr. Rivera steps aside. "You're just in time."

SIXTY NINE

Crystal

It feels like the wait takes ages.

I just sit and chew on my lip while the clock keeps ticking and the doctors are busy trying to save both their lives. I pray they make it out alive.

A nurse here at the clinic kindly looked at my wounds from his father's bullwhip and cleaned it up nicely, and she said I was lucky that I didn't require stitches, only some medical glue.

Ares and Blaine aren't as lucky.

The guys and girls from the Skull & Serpent Society and the Phantom Society have already gone back to their homes, patiently awaiting the news via text. I didn't expect them to stay, of course, but it is rather silent with just the two of us in this waiting room and a clock slowly ticking away at time.

"Here." Caleb pushes a can of Coke into my hands. "Drink."

"I'm not thirsty."

"Gotta keep your fluids up. It's important," he says, opening it for me. "Now drink."

I do what he wants just so he'll stop telling me, but he was right … my throat was dried out. "Thanks." I take another sip. "How long do you think it'll take?"

"I don't know. Could be minutes. Hours. Days."

I nearly choke on my Coke. "Days?"

He smirks. "Knowing both of them, probably hours before they start begging for you."

A blush creeps onto my cheeks.

"How are you feeling?" he asks. "Your back must hurt."

I gently smile. "It's fine. I can take it. Besides, Ares and Blaine have got it way worse than I do."

"True. But ... I don't want you to hurt, so take your medicine." He places it in front of me.

Suddenly, the doc comes in, and I forgot all about what we were talking about and can only focus on him.

"Mr. Navarro has just come out of surgery."

My eyes light up. "How is he?"

"Doing good under the circumstances," the doctor replies, and I breathe a sigh of relief. "We've removed one bullet from his body, and cleaned out both wounds and sutured them. He will need plenty of rest and allow for healing, though."

"Of course," I say. "Can we see him?"

The doctor nods.

"What about Ares?" Caleb asks.

"He's still in recovery. I will let the nurses know to call you when he's awake."

We nod and quickly walk into the corridor that leads to Blaine's room. When I see him reading a book, I nearly burst out into both tears and laughter.

"Don't they have anything better to read here? This is dreadful," he says, flipping through the pages.

I run up to him and hug him tight, and he groans in pain. "Gently, darling, be gentle with me."

"Sorry," I mutter, quickly leaning away, but he cups my face and leans in to kiss me instead, and my heart nearly sings out of joy.

His kisses make me feel light as a feather, like I could float up into the sky, and they take all the destructive emotions swirling inside my mind away until all that's left is his undying love for me.

He smiles against my lips and murmurs, "Now, this is what's worth dying for."

I smile back as he rubs his nose against mine. "I'm glad you're still alive, though."

He snorts. "You're the only one in this room."

"Ha ha," Caleb responds. "Good one."

"How are you feeling?" I ask.

"Like I got run over by a truck, but I'll manage," he says, tucking his own hair behind his ear. "I'm just glad they managed to take out the bullet. But my God, is it painful to take a breath."

"Glad to see you're back to your winging self," Caleb muses, slapping him on the back.

Blaine coughs. "Should I put a bullet hole into your body, see how you take it?"

"Please don't," Caleb retorts, snorting.

"Thought so. Now get your hands off me, piglet."

Caleb narrows his eyes at him. "You what?"

"Okay, enough, enough," I say, laughing it off. "You guys can throw fits at each other when everyone's healthy and back at Spine Ridge."

Caleb rolls his eyes. "You sound just like Ares."

"Maybe you just require a hard hand from time to time," Blaine says, winking.

"Says the guy who enjoys getting choked out by small girls," Caleb retorts.

I scoff. "Who are you calling *small*?"

Blaine laughs out loud, but it swiftly turns into a moan from the pain, and then a sigh. "I really should not be laughing. Stop making all of this so goddamn funny."

"Whoops," I say, hiding my snort.

"How's Ares?" Blaine asks.

"Don't know. He's still in recovery," Caleb answers.

"But he's alive?" Blaine chucks the book aside and sits up straight even though it hurts to watch him struggle.

"Wait a second, what are you doing?" I ask.

"I want to go see him."

"Fuck no, not in your condition," Caleb growls.

Blaine pauses and looks up at him. "Since when do you care about my well-being?"

Caleb just stares him down for a moment, but slowly a clear blush begins to appear on his cheeks, and it makes me giggle. "I don't."

Blaine seems stupefied. "You care about me?"

"No!" Caleb frowns.

"You're blushing," I say.

"No, I'm not." Caleb rubs his cheeks. "It's just fucking hot in here."

I laugh, and Blaine grabs his cheek. "Cute."

Caleb swats him away. "Stop. You're embarrassing me."

"Good," Blaine retorts. "But now you look like a real piglet."

Caleb's face tightens, and his eyes begin to twitch. "I'm going to kill you after you're out of this bed."

I burst out into laughter, and so does Blaine, who immediately regrets it of course.

A knock on the door makes us all pause as a nurse clears her throat. "Mr. Torres is awake now. You can go visit him."

"I'm coming too," Blaine says.

"The fuck you are," Caleb grits.

"Help me, darling." Blaine beckons me and points at the wheelchair in the corner. "Just put me in there."

Caleb folds his arms. "I'm not pushing you."

Blaine scoots off the bed with difficulty. "I didn't ask you to."

"Are you sure about this?" I ask.

"Please ..." he begs. "I want to see him too."

It's too hard to say no, so I grab the wheelchair in the corner of the room and bring it to his bed, then assist him in getting off. It's like trying to lift some lumber, and I can barely take his weight.

"Jesus, a little help here," I ask, and Caleb eventually reluctantly agrees.

"Thanks," Blaine says when he's finally seated. "Hope I didn't rupture any sutures."

"If they didn't, I'll rip them open when you get home just for trying this shit," Caleb growls.

"Oh ... kinky." Blaine winks, getting Caleb all hot and bothered.

"Save the hot talk for later," I say, pushing his wheelchair toward the door.

We head up via the elevator and go down another hallway until we find the room Ares is in. But I can barely push Blaine's wheelchair forward as I see all the dressings around his body and the beeping of the machines monitoring him.

"Ares ..." I murmur.

His eyes and mouth are closed, but the beeping puts me at ease as

I approach. I sit on his bed and place my hand on his, softly caressing it. "I hope you can hear me. But I'm so glad you're still alive."

His lips slowly tip up into a smile, and his raspy voice makes my heart throb in my throat. "Are you now, little rose?"

***

ARES

My skin feels like it's been set on fire, like I've walked through hell on bare feet, trying to find my way back to them ... back to her.

She smiles as tears form in her eyes, and she leans in to wrap her arms around my neck, letting go of all the pent-up fear she was holding back. "I'm so glad you're alive."

The one girl who wanted me dead is happy I'm alive?

What a strange thing to hear, yet ... it warms my heart.

My hand softly curls through her hair, petting her. "I'm sorry you had to witness me in that position."

"No, don't say sorry!" She lifts her pretty little face to look at me. "It's not your fault, it's—"

I place a finger on her lips, silencing her. "It was my choice. Mine. And even if I knew then what kind of pain I would have to go through, I would still make the same choice if it meant I could make you mine."

My spine tingles from the way she looks at me, and I lean in to press a kiss to her lips. She doesn't push me away, doesn't fight me, doesn't fear me anymore, and the smile that appears on her face only makes me greedy for more.

But the pain prevents me from claiming her.

I groan in frustration and lean against the pillow, my back feeling like it had aged twenty years.

When her head softly rests on my chest, I still smile through the pain, knowing she's here with me, even after everything I did, and it eases the aching a little.

My hand slides across her back, and I can feel the wounds through her shirt, making me stop.

I'd recognize this pattern anywhere.

The bullwhip's lash.

And my heart skips a beat.

"You took a lashing for me," I mutter.

"I couldn't watch him hurt you any longer," she replies. "You were bleeding all over. It looked so bad, I thought you were going to die. I've never felt so afraid," she murmurs.

Smugness tugs at my lips. "Finally ... I made the innocent girl fear me."

She glances up at me with those doe-like eyes and snorts, amused by my victory, however small. But this victory pales in comparison to knowing I survived because someone cared enough to come and save me.

"We were all afraid you'd die on us," Blaine says, and I look up to see him sitting in a wheelchair in the corner of the room. I swallow away my pride when the memory of him jumping in front of me to catch a bullet crosses my mind in a flash.

"You ... took that bullet for me," I mutter.

He nods. "I promised you I would guard you with my life, so I did."

I'm moved by how far he'd go for me, all because of one good thing I did a long time ago. "And now you're finally relinquished of your debt," I muse.

"Don't write me off yet, darling. I'm not going anywhere," Blaine replies, winking.

"Thank you." I look up at all of them. "All of you. For saving me."

Caleb folds his arms. "You should've told me." The anger practically flows off his body like lava. "You should've told me your dad summoned you. That he was the one who was hurting you all this time."

I take in a deep breath. "I didn't want you to get hu—"

"I would've taken all of those lashes for you!" Caleb yells.

My eyes widen.

He would've taken all of them ... for me?

"You should've told me." His voice is much more brittle than before.

"I couldn't," I say, my own voice cracking too. "He was my father."

"So?" Caleb grits.

"What he means is ... some part of him still craved his love."

Crystal interjects as she leans up to look at both of us while squeezing my hand. "Right?"

I don't answer. It's too fresh, too rough to deal with.

"You didn't want us to kill him," Blaine says.

I slowly shake my head, but Crystal releases my hand. "I … I …"

"Say it," I tell her.

"I was the one who shot him," she mutters, her gaze drifting away.

I cup her face and make her look at me. "Thank you. You did the one thing I never could," I say. "I couldn't ask anyone to do it for me because it wasn't right. But you … you were the only one who really could. Who had the right." I swipe away a single tear rolling down her cheek. "You want to know why I made you shoot Ferry? To make you feel what it was like to kill a human being so you'd be prepared when the time came to kill him. To take your revenge. And I'm proud of you."

Now even more tears roll down her cheeks, and she falls into my chest, hugging me so tightly I can barely breathe, but it's worth it.

"Caleb," I growl. "Come here."

He reluctantly agrees, grumbling all the way over to me before he too collapses in my arms, and we hug tight.

"I was worried he'd kill you," Caleb mutters.

"I'm sorry I made you worry," I respond.

He leans away and stares at me for a moment. "I don't think you've ever said that word to me."

"Haven't I?" I swipe aside some of his hair. "I'll say it a million times more if it means you'll all stop being mad at me."

He lets out a giant sigh. "You make it really damn hard to stay mad, goddammit."

I chuckle, but immediately regret it because of the pain. "Then I guess you'll just have to forgive me."

"Fine," he grumbles, but I know he means it.

"How did you guys even manage to get inside the casino with all those guards? I'm impressed."

"We had help," Blaine answers. "I know you don't approve, but I asked them anyway."

My eyes narrow. "You asked those Phantom bastards?"

"And the Skull & Serpent Society," he adds, raising a brow. "Never come unprepared is what I always say. And they sure were ready for a good fight."

"So *he* was there too?"

"If you mean Kai, yes," Blaine answers.

I suck in a breath through my nose, annoyed they'd bring him.

"You never told him your father tortured you, did you?" Blaine asks.

I avert my gaze because I don't want them to see the only weakness I have left guarded.

"You thought you couldn't trust him," Blaine adds.

Always prying into my mind like it comes easy to him.

"My father chose him as a successor when I failed to kill the target because Kai had no qualms about killing whoever came in his way. He and I have never seen eye to eye."

"When I tried to stop your father from killing you, Kai snatched the whip and started lashing him with it instead," Caleb says.

My jaw drops because I can't believe what he just said. "Kai did what?"

"He seemed incensed, kept lashing him with zero restraint," Blaine says. "I quite enjoyed the spectacle, to be fair."

Crystal rubs her lips together. "There wasn't much left of your father's body ... or face."

Fuck.

I always thought Kai would be on my father's side regardless, but I never imagined he'd actually go against him and ... fight for me.

"Am I interrupting something?"

Kai's voice pulls me from my thoughts, and I'm shocked to see him standing in the doorway.

"Doctor said you were out of surgery, so I came to check on you," he says.

"We'll be outside," Crystal murmurs, and she drags Caleb away from me and swiftly carts Blaine out the door, leaving me with my brother.

Fucking awkward.

I clear my throat. "I'm fine." I swallow away my pride. "Thanks."

He approaches, frowning. "I'm glad to see you're on the mend."

I don't know what to say.

"Look, I ..." He sighs. "I wanted to apologize to you. For not realizing sooner what Dad—Father—was doing to you."

"He picked you," I say through gritted teeth. "He didn't *want* you to see."

"But the signs were there," he responds. "And I missed them. And I am sorry. I'm sorry I failed you as a brother."

I push the blanket off and take my feet off the bed, steadying myself on the floor.

Kai takes a step forward. "What are you doing?"

I stand, grabbing the IV pole for balance as I take my first step toward him.

"I want to—" My knees cave in on me, and Kai swiftly runs up to me and supports my shoulder to keep me standing, and at the moment, he gazes right at me. "Look my brother in the eye."

His eyes flow with tears that he blinks away as if they never even existed.

"I'm sorry. I should've been there, but I wasn't. And I will take this regret with me for the rest of my life as punishment."

And even though I want nothing more than to push him away so I don't have to feel my own heart trying to suture itself back together, I still place my hand on his back and allow him to hug me.

"Don't shut me out. Let me be a part of your life again," he says.

"I asked you for help so many times," I growl.

"I know, and I'm sorry. Father made me believe all he did was talk with you and reprimand you for rebelling against him." He leans away to look at me. "But I envied you. I envied your ability to refuse him and deny him his own goddamn son's love."

"He took that away from me," I reply. "How could I love the man who beat me when I disobeyed?"

"I understand it now," he says. "Does Mom know?"

I shake my head. "I didn't ever have the heart to tell her, and of course he didn't tell her either."

"Then why didn't you tell me?"

"Because you fucking enjoyed being his chosen heir," I growl back.

Kai shakes his head. "No. I never fucking wanted it to begin with. I wished you'd just told me the truth, but he's the one who put us up against each other. And I *hate* that he did this to you. I hate it so much I couldn't stop myself from giving him all the lashes he gave to you with that same goddamn whip."

His forehead leans against mine as he holds me steady to keep me from falling. "I wanted to kill him for hurting you."

"He's dead now," I reply. "Thanks to my friends who were there for me."

"I know," he says. "And I will forever be grateful they cared enough to tell me the truth so I could help them save you and that Crystal ended Father's miserable life."

I lick my lips. "You're not upset that he's gone?"

"No. I'm upset I almost lost my goddamn brother."

I close my eyes for a moment to let the feelings settle in my bones.

"I love you, goddammit," he says. "You're my big brother, and I don't want to fucking lose you. Ever."

I take in a deep breath as a slow but steady smile begins to form on my face. "I missed you, little brother."

He throws his arms around me and holds me tight, and in the end, I cave and wrap my arms around him too.

"How are we going to tell Mother what happened?"

I smile. "One word at a time."

SEVENTY

Blaine

It's odd reading about your own murder spree in a newspaper as though you're just a casual bystander and not at all the one who caused it, but Crescent Vale City is pretty shocked by the gang violence that suddenly erupted between the Bones Brotherhood and the Torres Casino. Apparently, they had been doing shady deals together for a long time, and somewhere along the way, they snapped and turned on each other. What followed was a violent bloodbath with tons of dead bodies and the Torres patriarch dead.

What a turn of events.

I chuck the newspaper into the bin next to the Tartarus House and take in a deep breath.

"Ahhh, the smell of opulence and hedonism. My two favorite things," I murmur as I follow everyone inside.

I'm happy as can be to see my own place again. I even missed my fellow Tartarus boys that come and greet us at the door.

"Welcome back, boys. Glad to see you're doing well, but I won't ask," Arlo says, winking before giving us all a bro-hug. "Miss us?"

"Not a chance," Caleb retorts, making everyone laugh.

"I did," I reply. "But most of all, my books."

"Wow, more than me?" Arlo adds a wink, and it makes us all snigger. "Just kidding, I know about your addiction."

"Addicted to romance, correct," I reply, smiling.

I can't wait to finish the book I'd started before all of this went down because the reading material in that hospital was beyond pitiful. And a mind like mine needs nurturing, sustenance, and romance.

I take a deep breath and snort the smell of the Tartarus House, then hug the pillar. "Oh, darling, I missed you so."

Everyone's laughing, but I don't care.

"Is he okay? Talking to a house now," Caleb asks Crystal, who bursts into laughter.

"I'm perfect!" I respond, and I wrap my arms around Caleb instead, hugging him as tightly as I just did to the pillar.

"Stop. Crushing. Me."

"See? Perfect," I say.

"Fine, fine, you missed this place," he says. "I get it."

"Missed it? That's an understatement. I could've possibly never seen it again," I quip.

He makes a tsk sound. "Doubt it."

"I almost died, Caleb. DIED. Do you even care?"

"Of course, I do, asshole," he retorts, folding his arms. "I already told you that."

"Did you?" I tilt my head. "But I love hearing you say it."

He rolls his eyes and punches me in the side, and I groan. "Not there."

"Sorry," he replies. "Forgot."

A wretched smile forms on my face. "Of course, you did."

"Okay, enough with the back-and-forth bullying," Ares interrupts. "Caleb, help me unpack upstairs."

"Wait, but ..." Crystal glances at the door. "It's still open."

Ares tilts his head. "It is."

My eyes narrow.

That was intentional.

I turn to Crystal, who stays put near the door that is still wide open, ready for her to close. She's wistfully staring at the two boys walking upstairs, and I just know thoughts are swirling through her head.

So I place a hand on her shoulder and say, "You made it through alive ... and now you're free."

She smiles. "So are you."

My brows draw together. "Yet here we are."

She tilts her head. "He saved your life; you saved his. The debt is gone. So what will you do now?"

I grin and lift my hands, showing off the beauty that is Tartarus. "Darling, I belong here. There isn't anywhere in the world I'd rather be." I place one fingertip against her chest. "Except with you."

A blush creeps onto her cheeks, and I lean in to press a kiss to her lips, tasting her deliciously sweet virtue, making me all hot and bothered once more.

"And if you want to leave, I'll follow," I whisper against her lips.

Her eyes open while our mouths are still connected, and she kisses me back only once before whispering, "I don't think I can."

My fingers entwine with hers as I plant another kiss beneath her ear. "I told you they wouldn't ever let you go." And I smile against her neck when her heart rate picks up. "It's a good thing you made us all fall in love with you, darling. Because you wouldn't have survived otherwise."

I wink as I lean back and watch the smug grin besmudge her pretty little face. "Now go on." I slap her ass in the direction of the stairs. "Get up there and talk to them."

"One more thing," she says, waltzing toward the door to give it a good swivel so it closes on its own.

And I'm so fucking proud of her. No one can slap the beaming smile off my face.

Not even Caleb and his insufferably bad quips.

***

CALEB

I place a box of clothes on the floor and pull out some of his shirts. "Jesus, you needed all this in a hospital?"

"You're the one who packed it," Ares replies, making me snort. "True."

When I hang it in the closet, he wraps his arms around me and sniffs my neck. "I missed you. I missed this." He presses his lips down on my neck, and I tilt my head back. "But I don't want to move too quickly after you just lost your mother."

I turn my head sideways and glance at him. "You and Crystal are what keep me together, keep me sane. Keep me from wanting to die with her."

He turns me around and kisses me on the lips, claiming my mouth in the same way I remember he always used to before we all got destroyed by sorrow. But we will build each other up again and fix what was broken.

When my eyes open, Crystal's staring at us from the doorway, and my lips tear away. Ares turns his head to look at her, and her cheeky blush clearly gives away she enjoyed watching us.

"Sorry, I didn't want to interrupt—"

"You're not," Ares says.

I swallow away the lump in my throat, feeling my heart throb not just for him but for her too. I never thought I could fall for someone, let alone give my heart to two people. But I did. I fucking did.

I waltz right past him and grab her face, kissing her just as hard as he just kissed me, licking the roof of her mouth, rolling my pierced tongue around hers to show her my commitment.

"What you just saw ..." I murmur. "I feel for both of you."

Her reddened lips brush against mine. "I know."

"Do you? Because I don't think you understand how much I crave you ... how badly my heart bleeds when you're not around. And now that my father is no longer dating your mom, I don't have to feel guilty for what I feel." I plant another kiss on her lips. "I fucking fell in love with both of you. And I need you. I need you more than ever. Stay. Please."

**

Crystal

Could we be together? All of us?

"I ..."

"Don't. Don't force her to stay," Ares says, and my eyes find his over Caleb's shoulder. "She needs to make the choice."

Caleb steps back, allowing me room to breathe and think as I stare at the two handsome men standing in front of me.

"She already closed the door," Blaine says behind me, peeking in from the hallway.

Ares's jaw tenses, and I can see the spark of excitement lighting a fire in his eyes. I walk closer and look up into those eyes that could tear a girl's heart out with a simple gaze.

He softly caresses my cheek, and I lean into his hand.

"I was the one who took your smile … but I will do anything to bring it back to this pretty face again."

A mischievous grin forms on my face as his hand lowers. "Anything?"

My hands rise to his shirt, which I begin to unbutton one by one, his strict gaze on me at all times, but he doesn't stop me. Not even when I reach the top and push the fabric slowly off his shoulders.

There's my name, in all its glory, carved into his flesh.

I circle him, my hand still on his muscular body as it slowly slides to his back and across all the fresh scars. I touch the raised skin like the painting on a canvas, ruined by a vandal. All his pain and suffering are out in the opening underneath my fingertips, and he doesn't even flinch. I am in awe.

"There is one more thing I need to do," I say as I circle back to his stern gaze again. "Give me your knife."

His brows furrow as he glares at me for a moment. "Why?"

I hold out my hand. "Trust me."

With narrowed eyes, he studies me.

I gave him the same words he gave me. The only question is whether he will honor them or not.

But if he wants this, and I know he does, he'd better treat me like an equal.

He finally makes the decision to fish the knife from his pocket and tucks it into my hand. The same knife he pulled from my father's body. I stare at it for a moment, swallowing away the lump in my throat as I look up into his haunting and beautiful gray eyes.

"Kneel."

His Adam's apple moves up and down as he looks up at me with desire.

Thud. Thud.

Thick knee muscles slowly collide with the floor, and I lift the knife until it's against his neck, chin tilted up to meet my gaze. And it is the most awe-inspiring sight.

A god on his knees for me.

SEVENTY ONE

ARES

"Darling, wherever this is going, I'm already turned on," Blaine mutters behind her.

She pushes the blade up to my neck.

"Stop," Caleb growls, stepping up.

"Don't," I tell him.

Caleb stops right before he grabs the handle, but my eyes never leave hers.

With ease, she's gotten me to my knees.

She didn't even need to beg. All she had to do was ask, and I was hers.

"Take off my leggings," she says.

And I must say, even though I'm normally not the submissive type, I quite like the way she's ordering me around. My eyes slowly lower to her waist, and I curl my fingers around her leggings underneath that pretty floral dress with roses on it, slowly sliding them down.

"Oh my, I am certainly going to enjoy this show," Blaine murmurs, folding his arms as he leans against the doorpost, watching us.

Her breathing picks up, but it doesn't stop me from dipping my fingers underneath the fabric of her panties and tearing it all down until she's stepped out, and all that's left is her naked pussy, begging to be filled.

"F-fuck," Caleb groans, and he too sinks to his knees in front of her without her even having to ask.

She pushes the tip of the knife into my jaw, forcing me closer. "Tell me what I am to you."

"My goddess," I reply.

Her eyes narrow. "Why?"

"Because you saved my life … and my heart. And I will be in your debt for the rest of my life."

"No," she says, pushing the knife in even farther. "You carry my name on your chest and the scars on your back because of me."

"Hasn't he suffered enough?" Caleb asks.

She briefly glances at him before redirecting her gaze to me. "Tell me you want me."

I suck in a hampered breath. "I don't want you. I *need* you."

"Then show me. Show me how far you're willing to go to make me yours," she says, pulling the knife away. "I want you both to keep your mouths on my pussy until I say so. Don't look up. Don't stop under any circumstance unless I say so."

She grips my hair and shoves me into her pussy, and for a second, I fight the idea, clasping onto her thighs, nails digging into her skin, but the moment I taste her sweetness, I'm sold.

Fuck.

My tongue swirls around her slit, and I run my nose and mouth up and down, taking in the sweet scent of the pussy that belongs to me.

Caleb's face comes closer, and I'm pushed to the side to allow room for his tongue too as we both start to lick her out. I grumble at him taking up too much space, and I nip at him, then swipe my tongue around her clit until it's nice and swollen. "Mine."

His hand finds its way to my dick, catching me off guard as he begins to stroke me right through the fabric of my pants. And in a surprise, he pushes me away and laps her up instead, moaning into her pussy.

"Oh fuck, I'm getting hard," Blaine groans, and I can see him rubbing himself from the corner of my eye. I don't mind him watching us as long as he doesn't try to steal her away.

Crystal has managed to bring us both to our knees, and I'm not even mad. We fight over her like dogs fight over a bone, tongues twisted in a battle over her pussy, circling all along her clit and down inside her, causing her to shudder in place.

"Oh yes, just like that," she murmurs. "Keep your lips and your eyes on my pussy, don't look up."

I don't know why she's so absorbed with not letting me see her orgasmic face, but I suppose I'll allow her this little victory over me and let her think she's got us under her control. For now.

Caleb's hand slowly wriggles into my pants, however, and it distracts me so much I begin to moan against her clit too.

Fuck.

"Oh fuck, I love when you make those sounds," he groans.

"Shut up," I murmur against her pussy before I lick his tongue too, toying with his piercing, pushing it up against her sensitive bits until she moans along too.

I can hear her breathing pick up as I close my eyes and circle my tongue around both of them, kissing him between kissing her pussylips, sharing the fun.

My hand slides across her ass cheeks, finding her entrance, and I dip in to feel her wetness dripping down my fingers. Fuck, her wetness is such a goddamn turn-on I can barely contain myself.

"Guys ..." Blaine says from the door, but I pay no attention to him.

Caleb's fingers quickly join mine, and as we begin alternating thrusts, the desire building inside her causes her to moan out loud. I pull out of her pussy only to enter her ass with both fingers instead.

"Double the tongues, double the fingers. You sure are one lucky girl," Caleb says as he flicks his pierced tongue around her clit, driving her wild.

"Crystal, please ..." Blaine's begging almost makes me stop, but I don't fucking want to.

I want to keep tasting her, keep feeling her writhe against both of our tongues and fingers.

I can feel Caleb's fingers from inside her, pushing up against mine as we pleasure her. Her moans become louder and louder, nearly turning into squeals as she begins to roll her hips around, smothering us with her pussy as she reaches that edge that makes me want to come too. But I hold myself together as she grips my hair and squeezes tightly while her clit begins to thump.

She sucks in a breath and murmurs, "Fuck," in such a breathy manner that the precum bursts out of my cock.

But then something warm rolls down over my tongue and into my mouth, the taste so bitter it makes me pause. I recognize this taste …

Blood.

I pull my fingers out. Caleb's eyes open too, and we both gaze at each other in dismay, as the red tinge of blood is all over our mouths.

"Don't stop, please," Crystal begs, but the fiery protector in me forces me to find whatever is hurting her.

The knife she just stole from me, the same knife I used to carve these letters into my chest, is now in her hands … as she slowly etches letters into her skin right underneath her neck while staring into the mirror behind me.

T. O. R.

My eyes widen, along with Caleb's.

"Crystal, don't!" Caleb screams.

I grip the handle of the knife as I come to a stand, stopping her in the process. "Stop."

"No," she says, tears staining her eyes. "I told you not to look."

"Goddammit, listen to him," Caleb growls, and he looks at Blaine. "Why didn't you fucking stop her?"

"Because she wanted me to stay quiet," Blaine says, putting his finger against his lip, mimicking what she apparently did when we were too busy licking her. "She wants to do this, so who am I to stop her?"

She refuses to let go of the knife. "Let me do this. I can do this. I can take it."

I forcefully open her fingers until she finally relinquishes the knife. "Why? Tell me why you would desecrate this goddamn perfect body of yours!"

"Ares …" Blaine mutters, but I ignore him.

Crystal sucks in a breath through her teeth. "You went through so much pain. I needed to know what it felt like. I needed to know what you went through for me."

Oh God …

"You'll carry my name for the rest of your life, so I want to carry yours."

That's the one.

The one and only thing that's managed to knock the air from my lungs hard enough to make me feel like I've died and gone to heaven.

Fuck.

I grip her face with both hands and kiss her so hard I don't need the breath back that she stole from me. I've never fallen harder for anyone as hard as I have fallen for her, but I am smitten, completely and utterly in love with this woman who has taken my pain and made it her own.

"You shouldn't have done that," I growl against her lips.

"I don't regret it. Not for one second," she says, her mouth arching up to meet mine in desperation for more, but I won't let her have it. Not yet.

"You had one chance, little rose, one chance to escape us. And you chose to stay and mark yourself in my name," I growl.

"She's lost it," Caleb says.

"No. I found myself." She looks at both of us. "Because of you."

My hand slowly drifts down her face and neck to the markings she left, my fingers dipping into the scratches she made in her own damn skin just to watch her shudder in place. And I'd be lying if I said it didn't turn me on more than anything in this entire fucking world to watch my woman bleed *for me*.

"Caleb. Grab the masks."

"What? Why?"

"Do as I say," I grit.

He reluctantly turns and does what I ask, pilfering through the contents of my cabinet until he finds the ones we used during the night we first claimed her together in the rose maze.

"What are you planning to do?" Blaine asks, tilting his head.

"You know what we're going to do," I respond.

A filthy smirk forms on Blaine's face. "*We?*"

My hand slowly circles around Crystal's throat, cutting off her oxygen. "You want me to show you how badly I want you to be mine forever? How badly I wished I could take your breath just so no one else would ever have the privilege of hearing your moans?"

She nods, and I lean in to whisper, "I've stolen all your innocent little petals, little rose. Now go find them in the dark corners of our wicked fantasy."

I grasp the mask from Caleb's hand and put it on, watching her eyes slowly widen in both excitement and fear.

Fear of all the ways I'll make her beg for it.

I release her, and as she steps back, I point the knife at her chest.

"Run. Run as fast as you can. If I catch you … that name you were carving into your skin will be mine to finish."

SEVENTY TWO

Crystal

I stumble out of the room, glancing back at the boys who've all put on the same golden devil masks I remember from the first time Caleb and Ares chased me.

Fear finally makes my heart tremble behind my rib cage.

But this kind of fear ... it's not the kind you want to deny. It's the kind you want to obey.

So I turn around and run while the boys stay behind, collecting God knows what other toys from Ares's cabinet. By the time I've made it out of the Tartarus House, I can already hear them rushing down the stairs.

Fuck.

My heart races as I run through the back exit and come out in the rose maze.

Remember the route. Remember.

God, why can't I remember?

Panicked, I run off to one side and into the maze, left, right, straight, right, right, left, left. I don't know where I'm going, and when I turn a corner and come to a dead end, I can feel my own breathing pick up.

"Little rose … I can smell your perfume luring me."

His low, gravelly voice makes goose bumps scatter on my skin.

I turn around, and a rose's thorns scratch my cheek, but I keep running into the next turn and another one until I'm lost in the maze once more. The roses in this part are unkempt and completely overgrown, and I stumble over the prickly branches, nearly falling into the bushes. I only manage to capture myself on … two strong arms.

"Hello, darling, going somewhere?" Long black hair flows behind the mask, and I take a step back.

"Blaine," I mutter, jerking myself free from his grip, and I bolt off as fast as I can.

"Run, run, my darling! We both know they'll find you eventually. But I do enjoy watching this chase."

I can hear him laugh behind me as I keep running in the opposite direction of wherever the crackling sounds are coming from. Twigs snap in half and make me gasp as I turn around to a ghostly figure wearing nothing but a black pair of pants and shoes appearing from behind the hedge, sparkling gray eyes boring a hole into my chest.

Ares.

My blood runs thick with icy cold fear as I rush in the opposite direction, but then I see another figure emerge from the darkness, blond streaks of hair and tattooed skin peeking out from underneath a hoodie.

Shit. Shit. Shit.

I run to the left, and within seconds, I find myself out of the maze, running across campus grounds, past the Skull & Serpent Society building, and into Priory Forest and beyond. I don't stop running, not even as my lungs grow frigid and my body begins to shiver as painful spasms shoot up my legs.

The adrenaline keeps me going, makes me feel alive. It makes me feel like I could face the world with a smile because no matter what it sends my way, I can take it.

Thanks to them.

***

CALEB

I can see her bolting past the campus grounds from a distance, and I signal Ares to her location, who goes for the pursuit.

A chase like this is all I'll ever crave, and now that Crystal had a taste of us, I just know she can't get enough of it either.

Blaine passes me by. "Gotta run quicker than that."

"I don't see you helping," I rebuke.

"I already had her in my clutches," he muses.

I frown at him. "You *had* her? And you let her go?"

"Of course. Gotta give her a head start against you guys."

I grumble. "What the fuck, Blaine!"

"Where's the fun without a chase?" he says, shrugging. "Now go on, chase her. I'll be waiting."

He runs right past me, headed straight for Priory Forest, and I fucking hate that the sheer length of his legs makes him faster than me.

"Keep running, slut! Doesn't matter where you go; we're going to fucking catch you," I yell at Crystal, letting off some steam before I bolt into the woods she just entered.

I zigzag past the fallen trees, keeping an eye on the others. Ares is to my right, a little in front of me, but when I look ahead, I can clearly see Crystal running up the hills behind the school.

That cheeky little thing thought she could escape us by exiting the rose maze? Not a chance.

We run as fast as our legs will take us, slowly but surely catching up with her.

One glance over her shoulder has me going wild with lust.

"That's it, slut, run for your fucking life because when we catch you, it belongs to us!"

We come up to a giant wall, which she's scaling, and I jump up and make the climb right behind her. To my left, Ares runs around the other side, disappearing from view. But I don't give a damn what he's going to do because I'm nearly there. I can hear her breath and heavy grunts as she drags herself up the slopes toward Priory Lake.

Right before she manages to lift herself at the top, I grab her ankle and hold on tight, adrenaline invigorating my decrepit mind. "Gotcha."

When I look down and see the demonic mask staring back at me, I shriek. Caleb's tattooed hand curls around my ankle, forcing me to stay put when I was just reaching the top.

Shit.

I try to shake him off, to no avail, and then I see the shadowy outline of two feet crackling on the dead leaves in front of me. My gaze tilts upward toward the stars, a familiar set of equally blinding eyes staring right back at me through the devil's mask as the man goes to his knees and takes my chin with a firm grip.

"Mine."

My eyes widen as his hand moves to my wrists, and he lifts me off the cliff with ease. But my mind is at war with my body, wanting two very different things. Have the power, or submit to his every whim. With a swift jerk, I break free of his grasp and run for Priory Lake in the back, but Ares quickly overtakes me, throwing both hands around my body to drag me to the ground. I crawl through the dead leaves, but with a simple, strong grip, he forces me to stop and twists me around underneath him.

"I have you now, little rose. And I *will* give you what I promised you."

Caleb towers over me with a few feet of rope. "You ready, little slut?"

Ares pins my wrists above my head and leans over to smash his lips onto mine briefly before he murmurs, "Tie her up."

Caleb wraps the rope around my wrists and suddenly drags me from underneath Ares. "Wait, where are we—"

I shriek as he hoists me up a fallen log and lays me down with my back flat against the wood, tying my wrists beneath the wood so I have no way to escape as my legs fall to the side.

From the corner of my eye, I spot Blaine approaching.

"This isn't necessary," I say.

"It very much is," Ares answers, pushing my legs up one by one so Caleb can tie them together.

I'm blushing from the hog-tie position they have me in right now.

"My, oh, my, you've got yourself in quite a beautiful position there," Blaine muses, removing his mask, his tongue running along his lips. "Just like the dirty smut books I read."

Caleb snorts. "What kind of racy books do you read?"

"None that would ever tickle your caveman brain," Blaine retorts.

Caleb narrows his eyes at him. "While you were reading about all those things, we were actually doing them to her. Now watch."

"Gladly," Blaine replies as he sits down on a stump and leans back against the tree behind it, pulling out his large cock to play with it.

But when Ares's fingers slide up my thighs, I forget everything I was focusing on.

"Your fear excites me," he murmurs, fingers curling underneath my dress. "But it's no fun when you give it to me willingly."

He pulls the knife from his pocket and slides it up my belly, making all the hairs on my body stand up. He looks damn terrifying with that mask on, but I know what I signed up for when I ran like hell from them.

It's this ... this part, not just the thrill to run but the thrill to be caught that makes me feel alive.

The knife cuts through my dress like butter, splaying it over the wood as my naked body is on full display, and from the corner of my eye, I definitely see a hard-on in Blaine's hands. Ares circles my nipples with the tip, toying with me, teasing me to my limits. The knife reaches my throat, and I can feel my own heartbeat against the metal.

"You like me teasing you ..." he says. "Admit it."

"Yes," I say in a breathy moan.

The knife slides up to my cheeks, where the rosebushes cut me. "You collect scratches like I collect scars, little rose."

"Pain doesn't faze me," I murmur.

He leans over me, a devilish smile appearing behind the equally devilish mask. "Then you won't mind if I carve deep enough to hear you scream."

SEVENTY THREE

ARES

I position myself behind her and zip down, pulling out my already hard cock, glistening at the tip. I place the knife down between her tits, pointed at her neck, and say, "Stay still. Don't let it drop."

Slowly, I enter her pussy while watching her face unravel with pleasure as my piercings flood her with endorphins. I press the palm of my hand on that good spot on top of her belly as I push in deeper and deeper, allowing her a hint of ecstasy before I take her to the next fucking plane.

"Oh fuck," she moans as I thrust in.

"Only halfway there, but you'll take it like a good girl, won't you?" I say.

Caleb pulls out his cock too and spreads the precum all over, using it as lube as he slowly jerks himself off beside her face. And I watch with great delight as he gets harder and harder just from me laying my claim on her.

"Now take a deep breath, little rose," I murmur as I pick up the knife, caressing her hardened nipples with it.

She sucks in a breath, and I thrust in deep, then press the tip of the knife against her chest and push down. She bites on her lip as the blood begins to roll across her chest, and I slowly slide down the knife, pushing my length farther into her as I carve the fourth letter of my name into her chest.

R.

She clenches her jaw as her body tenses up against the blade.

"You can take it, little rose," I murmur, thrusting even deeper into this wet little pussy. "What is the tip of my knife compared to the size of my cock inside you?"

She mewls when I circle around her clit with one hand while I draw the round shape of the R with the other on her chest.

"Fuck!" she hisses.

"That's it," I say, etching in the curve. "You take it so well."

I lean over to pick up a droplet of her blood, rolling down with my tongue right through the mask, rolling it over her nipple so her pain turns into pleasure. I lean back up again and thrust in another inch.

"That's what you want, isn't it? More of me deep in the crevices of your darkest desires," I tease, burying myself deeper and deeper.

I place the knife next to the R I just carved and begin shaping the letter E.

"Take my name and make each letter your own," I say as I carve it into her skin right above her tits. "Own my goddamn soul like yours belongs to me."

While I cut her, I flick her clit under the pad of my thumb so her brain confuses the pain with lust.

She bites down on her tongue but still can't keep the loud moan at bay as I thrust in deeper.

"So wet, even when I hurt you," I say, carving out the final piece of the E. "Good girl. You can take one more, can't you?"

"Oh God, it didn't feel like this when I did the other letters," she murmurs.

"When it isn't your hand applying the pressure, the pain is so much more visceral," I say, coaxing out more blood from her skin. "So much more like you're descending into hell itself." I hover close to her lips and listen to her breathy moans as I fit myself inside her pussy. "But I will be there with you every step of the way."

I tear off the mask, chuck it aside, and press a seductive kiss onto her top lip before I lean up to carve the final letter into her chest. S.

"Now scream for me."

Each curve makes her hiss louder and louder until, finally, she's no longer able to withhold the screams that consume my soul and chain it to hers forever.

And I flick my finger back and forth across her clit until it begins to thump, and her moans fill the forest.

"Yes, just like that," I groan, curling the knife around deep into her skin. "Scream, little rose, scream!"

She shrieks wildly, and my cock swells with excitement inside her, and while I draw the final shape of the S, I bury myself inside her to the hilt, coaxing out the final drawn-out squeal as she comes all over my cock. I stab the knife into the wood right beside her face and lean over to lick every droplet of blood right off her body, then seal it into her mouth with a passionate kiss.

"That is *my* last name. My fucking name engraved on this body. You belong to me now," I whisper against her lips. "Say it."

"I belong to you," she murmurs, her eyes sparkling with devotion, the kind that you could only come across once in a lifetime, the kind that could rebuild even the most broken of hearts and put it back together.

"I love you," I whisper.

Her eyes burst open. "What did you say?"

A smirk forms on my face as I leave a small, enticing peck next to her lips. "You heard me. Now repeat it."

She nips back at me, but I'm just out of reach, teasing her until she finally gives me what I want.

"I love you."

"Good girl," I murmur, and I smash my lips back on hers, enjoying the taste of conquest. "And now my good girl deserves her reward."

***

CALEB

I grip her throat and tilt her head back until her mouth falls open, and my cock slides in with ease. "Fuck," I groan. "Take it deep. Just like that. Swallow me whole; don't leave out a single inch of me."

I tear off my mask and take what belongs to me while Ares plows into her. I match his pace as he flicks her clit and makes her writhe on the wood. Her throat fits so neatly around my cock it's unreal, and the way her tongue wraps around my shaft is nothing short of pure sin. And good fucking God, if this is hell, I don't ever want to leave this purgatory. Let her set fire to my fucking soul.

Blaine gets up too and approaches, throwing his arms around my neck while he watches me take her deep.

"You're so hard for her," he murmurs, pinching my nipples until I can barely focus. "Is it because of how Ares carved his name into her skin?"

"Fuck yes," I groan. "Of course, it is."

"There is nothing more you love than the idea of death, don't you?" Blaine says. Suddenly, he rips the knife out of the wood and holds it up to my neck. "You're not afraid of it. You welcome it. You're aroused by the thought of edging close."

Oh fuck, now I'm getting even harder.

"Yes, make him bleed like I made her bleed," Ares growls, thrusting into her pussy while I stifle her moans.

Blaine pushes the knife into my throat, and droplets of warm blood roll down my neck and onto her face. "Fuck, yes," I groan.

"You bleed like a pig too."

That's it.

I pull out of her throat and pummel him with my fist, but he catches it with a single hand and twists my wrist until I whimper. "Don't even try. You know I'll always win," Blaine says. "But go on, enjoy that pretty little mouth while I watch."

He fucking enjoys watching me rage at him, doesn't he?

"Fucking masochist," I grit at him.

"Only for her," he says.

"Stop," Ares groans, and he pulls out of her. "Take out your anger on her body. Lift her."

Blaine slips the knife away from my throat and cuts through the rope around her wrists, then plants the knife into the earth. "My turn," he growls.

***

515

Blaine

"Straddle me, darling," I tell her, wrapping her arms around my neck, and I lean in to lick her skin where Ares cut her to ease her wounds a bit. "Let me feel how wet you are."

She writhes on top of me, coyly playing with my cock by sliding her pussy back and forth. "Beg."

Oh, I'm not opposed to begging at all. "Please, darling, give me that sweet, perfect pussy."

When she finally sinks down, my mouth falls open wide as a loud moan spills from my lips, and she covers my mouth with hers, kissing me so deeply I fall even harder in love than I already did.

Ares fishes the knife from the soil and stands behind Caleb, putting it to his throat while he grips his cock. He toys with Caleb's dick until it bobs up and down from sheer excitement, dripping precum onto the soil but never letting him reach a climax. And I can see it on his face that he can barely take the fact that she's fucking me instead of him.

"Oh yes, just like that," Crystal moans, riding me.

"Take one step, and your neck will be severed by this blade," Ares groans behind him, but it only makes Caleb's cock bounce harder.

Crystal throws her hair back and rolls her hips around on my length, making it so damn hard for me not to explode all over her. But I want to savor the moment, let her take the reins, and make her feel like the goddess she is.

"Oh fuck," Caleb groans, his hand finding Ares's cock so he can stroke it. But he can barely restrain himself when I begin plowing into Crystal's pussy.

"You want to die so badly for her?" Ares asks him.

Caleb moans loudly, and right then, Ares releases him, edging him until he whimpers. "Please."

"Oh God," she murmurs, clearly turned on by us.

"God, I fucking love you," I whisper against Crystal's lips while she bounces up and down on my cock. "I love this body." I grip her thighs to thrust in farther. "I love these lips." I kiss her gently. "And I love this pure heart that belongs to all of us," I murmur, trailing my lips all the way down her chest, across the scars Ares left on her body, and down to her nipple, taking it into my mouth.

Ares lowers the knife from Caleb's neck and walks toward us. "And I love how she enjoys taking all three of us." He perches himself right behind us. "Now bend over."

With a flat hand, he pushes her down on top of me until her bloodied chest connects with mine. And he slowly pushes into her pussy too.

I gasp when I feel his piercings slide up against my shaft, coaxing out more throbs than I could ever imagine.

"Oh God, it's so good," she mewls as we sink deeper into her.

We move in tandem, one in, the other out, until both of us are inside her together, and her wetness explodes on both of us.

"Fuck!"

I can feel her contracting around my shaft, nearly milking me, and my head tilts back from the sheer amount of pleasure.

"Fuck, I want her too," Caleb groans, and he steps between Ares and Crystal, crawling on top of her back, only to shove his cock inside her pussy too.

SEVENTY FOUR

CALEB

I can't control myself any longer.

Ares made that impossible.

It's exactly what he wants, what he craves; to push people to their edges and watch them fall over.

So I straddle her in front of him and force my way inside until all three of our dicks touch inside her, and our moans meld into one.

And my God, does it fucking feel good to claim this girl as our own.

I can't get enough as I thrust into her and rub my cock up against Blaine's and Ares's shafts. I can feel our piercings collide inside her, pushing against my tip until I throb with a need so great I can't contain myself.

My head tilts back onto his shoulder, and he leans over to kiss me, his dick bouncing against mine when our tongues latch.

But then I feel something poke into my ass, and I mewl with delight.

Three fingers bore into me.

"You want her to take us three, then you'll take three as well," Ares groans against my lips. "Now bend over and fuck her like a good boy."

We all fuck her like madmen, moans filling the forest far and wide. But no one here will hear her scream and beg for mercy.

No one but us.

***

Crystal

I gasp from the mixture of pain and pleasure as all three boys enter my pussy. I can't believe I'm taking three dicks at once and that it could ever feel so fucking good.

The boys slip in and out of me with ease, spreading my wetness all over, moaning to each other's movements.

"Please," I whimper, rolling my hips around. I've never felt more debased, more aroused in my whole life. "I need it."

Caleb grasps my hair and tilts my head back. "Beg. Beg for our cum."

"Please, give me your cum," I murmur.

I have no more shame, no more restraints, no more morals, nothing that could ever hold me back from falling harder and deeper for these devils.

"Good girl," Caleb grits, thrusting into me with no restraint.

He clenches tightly, and I just know Ares toys with his ass because his cock throbs wildly.

"Oh fuck," Caleb moans.

"Go on then. You've wanted to fill her up so badly … so give her all of your fucking cum," Ares groans in Caleb's ear.

His voice and my begging sets him off, and he explodes inside me, all over their dicks.

Caleb grabs my hair and forces me to turn my head, smashing his lips to mine to claim my breath while he fills me up.

"Oh fuck, it's too much," Blaine whimpers, and I can feel him throb too while he jets his seed into me.

The cum is already dripping out by the time Ares buries himself to the hilt against their dicks and empties inside me.

Their orgasms bring me to a new edge I never thought I'd reach, and I fall apart together with them, satiated, filled to the brim with both lust and love.

"Stay with me," Blaine murmurs, gently kissing my lips to keep me from floating off.

But Ares and Caleb pulling out brings me right back to the here and now. My pussy almost feels empty without all three.

Ares cuts through the rope around my legs, and I sink down onto Blaine, who holds me in his arms. "Breathe. I'm not going anywhere."

"None of us are," Ares says.

After Blaine has crawled out from underneath me, I sit up straight, but Ares grips my face and brings it down to his cock. "Taste yourself on my cock."

He thrusts inside with no remorse until I can feel his piercings slip down behind my uvula, and even though the tears spring to my eyes, I wouldn't have it any other way.

"Caleb, Blaine, on your fucking knees," Ares growls while deep inside me.

Blaine and Caleb do what he says, kneeling between his legs.

"Lick her out and taste your own fucking cum," he adds.

Their tongues are on my pussy before I can even blink, and my eyes nearly roll into the back of my head.

"Fuck, she's so goddamn filled," Caleb groans, his tongue piercing fluttering against my opening and my clit, sending sweet shocks of bliss up my spine.

"I love the sweet and salty taste," Blaine murmurs, lapping me up, kissing me so gently I nearly melt.

But this thick cock inside my throat forces me to look up and into those piercing gray eyes. "You take my cock so well, slut of mine. Should this be the second name I mark on your skin?"

My eyes widen. He wouldn't ... right?

"Does the idea terrorize you?" he says, a wicked smirk appearing on his chiseled face.

I nod, eagerly swallowing him deeper and deeper despite how hard it is.

I can take it. I can take all of him.

"Good. Let me see the fear in your eyes, little rose. Nothing turns me on more."

My clit thrums with excitement as the boys lick their way through the cum, bringing me to another peak. When Ares momentarily pulls out, I mutter, "Shit, I'm going to—"

Too late.

A long-drawn-out moan flows out of my mouth, and I nearly faint on the spot.

But then Ares grips both boys by the hair and lifts their heads away from my pussy. "Lick me."

They do as he says, dipping out their tongues to lick him off while he enters me.

"Oh fuck, I can taste us all on your dick," Caleb groans, rolling his tongue around his length.

Blaine presses a kiss to my lips between each lick he gives Ares's length. "Don't make me come all over myself, darlings."

Both boys bring their lips to my mouth and kiss both me and Ares's shaft at the same time.

"Don't fucking stop," Ares groans, enjoying all three of our tongues, which collide near his tip as it thrusts in and out of my mouth.

Ares buries himself to the hilt until I can no longer breathe, and the orgasm ripples through my entire body. He arches his back, his dick swelling up, throbbing as he empties himself inside me once again, coming together with me.

"That's it. Good girl," he groans.

And I swallow it all down just like the good girl he says I am.

The boys stop licking him too, and they both look up at Ares in awe as he pulls out of me.

I drag in a breath.

"Now thank your god for all that fucking cum."

"Thank you …" I whimper, spit and cum dripping down my lips.

He tips my chin up. "Thank you, what?"

"Thank you, god," I say.

He smirks. "You carry my name now, little rose. Even if you beg, I'm not ever going to let you go. Do you understand?"

I nod, still overcome by desire.

He grips my hair and tilts my head back. "You're ours. From now until forever." He smashes his lips onto mine, claiming my mouth, swirling his tongue around until I can no longer separate where he ends and I begin, and a slow but steady smile forces its way onto my face from the endorphins flooding my veins.

A smug grin spreads on his lips. "There it is. That beautiful, bold little smile I missed so much. Welcome back."

EPILOGUE

ARES

I stare at my father's grave as he's hoisted inside. My mother cuddles up to Kai for hugs as she sniffles into a handkerchief. Neither of us says a word.

Not because we have nothing to say but because it wouldn't be positive.

Even if she's crying, she's probably only mourning the idea of the power he had over this city, not the love he dished out occasionally, like one would throw a bone at a dog.

She swiftly tucks the handkerchief into her pocket and blows out a sigh.

Not one of regret but one of relief.

My eyes flutter up to Kai, who just blinks and nods.

Finally, it's over.

This fucker has been laid to rest along with the dirt he belonged to.

And I doubt any of us will ever miss his presence.

When the funeral is finished, my mother is accompanied by family from her side, while Kai stays behind with me.

"Who knew a bastard like him could leave such a stain on this world?" I mutter.

Kai spits on his grave, and I look up in surprise. "Desecrating holy grounds already?"

"He deserves nothing less. Hope he rots in hell."

I smile. "Nah. That's where all the fun people are."

He smirks back at me. "Wherever he is, I never want to follow."

"You sure about that?" I tuck my hands into my pockets. "I mean, the Torres company is left without anyone to lead it now."

"I don't want a legacy built on blood and lies," Kai answers, tilting his head. "Father would've hated for you to take over." A filthy smile forms on his lips. "So how about we give him one final big fuck you?"

Sly little brother.

I shake my head and chuckle. "I knew you'd pull something like this."

"Fuck what Father said. You're the smartest, most reliable one of us." He places a hand on my shoulder. "I mean it. It's yours."

"What about Mother?"

"I'm sure she's just happy her sons are still alive," he says. "Besides, I'm far too busy."

"With what? Sex and murder?"

He shrugs, and a dirty grin spreads on his face. "You, of all people, should know."

Busy with his murderous girlfriend?

We really are a family of devils.

"Love ya." He winks. "See you at school."

"Definitely. And don't think I'll let you off the hook with the Torres company. I'm going to need extra hands to take care of the mess he left."

He lifts both middle fingers in the air. "This enough hands?"

I laugh and shake it off. "Love you too, Kai."

I gaze at the graves and the lonesome, round-faced girl with blond hair and big eyes sitting behind one of them. She didn't want to attend the funeral, but she still wanted to be here for me, even if only from a distance.

I walk toward her, the pebbles beneath my feet giving my presence away.

But she doesn't move.

"I miss you," she mutters at the grave, touching the ground as tears form in her eyes.

I kneel behind her and place a hand on her shoulder.

"You did it," I say.

She turns to look at me, eyes filled with both sadness and hope. Hope for a future beyond the suffering.

"You took your revenge."

The most beautiful, heart-wrenching smile forms on her lips. We both know the duplicitous nature of that smile. How, on the one hand, she's overjoyed to end this chapter of her life, while on the other, the guilt of knowing she killed my father will forever stay etched within her soul. "I did."

But if she hadn't ended his life, mine would have been forfeited.

And I am forever grateful she chose me. Even if it cost my brother and me our own blood.

"If your father was here ... I just know he would tell you how proud he is of you."

She breathes out a sigh of relief. "Thank you."

***

Blaine

Weeks later

Crystal sits beside me on the bench beneath the tree in the rose garden and pats her thighs.

"Do we really have to do this?" Ares grumbles.

"Yes. Stop complaining," I reply.

Caleb sighs out loud and lays his head on Crystal's lap, his legs splayed over my lap and the edge of the bench.

"How long is this going to take?" Ares asks, sitting on the bench's armrest next to Crystal.

I rub my forehead. "Do you guys really have such a short attention span?"

Ares folds his arms. "No one ever asked if I wanted to do this."

"Do it for me, please?" Crystal begs, looking up at him with those sweet eyes of hers.

She knows just how to wrap all of us around her pretty little fingers.

Ares's eye roll makes me chuckle. "Fine."

"Great," I say. "Then let's begin."

"With what?" Ares asks. "What book is this even? What's the genre?"

"Romance, darling."

"Romance?" both boys say in tandem.

Caleb tries to lean up. "Nuh-uh, I ain't reading that shit."

"No one asked you to read. I'm reading it to you," I reply.

When he moves his legs off, I grab them and place them back on top of me where they were before. "Stay."

"Jesus," he grumbles.

"Caleb, just shut up and listen," Ares growls at him.

"What? Like you don't feel the same way."

"She wants us to do this together," Ares says, throwing his hand over her shoulder. "So let's just get it over with."

"Yes. I want us to have more bonding time," she says, melting my heart.

"You're so sweet. Whatever did we do to deserve you?" I say, pecking her on the cheek.

"Enough with the slickness," Caleb says. "Just start already."

"Chapter one? Or chapter fifteen?" I wriggle my brows.

"What's the difference?"

"The spice."

"Oh yes, all the spice," Crystal muses, biting her lip.

"Of course, you'd pick that chapter," I reply, winking.

"Well, if you want spice, I'll give you all the spice you desire later," Ares says, slipping his hand down her shirt. "Start reading, then. Let's see how far you get before she begs you to put it down and play out the scene instead."

"Oh …" A mischievous grin spreads on my face. "Now that's a plan I can definitely get behind."

***

CALEB

Months later

"So wait, let me get this straight … first, you tell me you want to be close again, and now you're dating Crystal *and* Ares together?" Nathan sloshes his coffee around in his cup.

I shrug and take a sip of my own. "You make it sound more complicated than it is. And I already told you I wanted to be friends."

"You *are* complicated," he rebukes.

I snort. "Aren't we all?"

"True," Nathan says, taking a sip. "But I never expected you to succumb to the power of pussy."

"Takes one to know one." I wink.

He shoves me. "Always the fucking know-it-all."

"Hey, I'm just saying, maybe we're not so different after all."

"Just say you miss me," he retorts.

I tilt my head and pout. "Fine. I miss you. Can we be friends again?" When he narrows his eyes, I add, "Please?"

He sighs out loud. "Fine."

I throw my arms around him. "Thank fuck."

"Watch it!" Nathan yells. "Almost spilled my coffee on my lap."

"Like pain ever stops you," I retort.

"True." He snorts. "But I'm normally the one dishing it out, not receiving it."

"Maybe that's why we weren't a good match after all," I say, winking.

"What are you guys talking about?" Crystal says as she sits down beside Nathan.

"Oh, nothing, just two bros hanging out," I muse.

Until I feel a familiar set of hands squeezing my shoulders, making my whole body turn to mush. "A bro that happens to be your ex?" Ares mutters.

"I'm taken. I'm taken," Nathan says, hovering off his stool like a bug scared to be squashed.

Crystal snorts from her seat. "I missed this. I missed when we were all just … happy."

I look at her and feel my heart swell with the need to smile.

I haven't smiled in such a goddamn long time.

But after losing my mother, Crystal's the only one who's managed to bring that smile back to my face. And even now, when I lean in to tuck a loose strand of hair behind her ear, the blush on her cheeks makes me feel like the world might not end today. Or ever, as long as I have these two with me.

***

Crystal

"Happy? Those two?" Blaine interjects as he places his hot cocoa on the bar and sits beside me. "Darling, those two don't know the meaning of that word."

Ares shoves him, nearly making him spill his hot cocoa.

"Hey! These are Ralph Laurens, can you not?" Blaine scoffs.

Ares raises a brow. "Watch your tongue, or I'll force it down his ass next time we have play time."

Blaine grins with slyness and giggles. "Well, that's one way to get me to never shut up."

"Well, you all seem to get along nicely," Penelope muses, throwing her arms around my neck. "The game's about to start. Are you coming?"

I look over at the gang. Lana, Felix, Kai, Milo, Dylan, Nathan, and Alistair are all sitting in a circle in front of the fireplace of the cabin we rented while Felix sorts the cards.

"Pass," Blaine mutters. Everyone looks at him. "What? Games are not my thing."

"What is your thing exactly?" Penelope asks him.

"Books. Books. Books. Hmm …" He taps his finger against his chin. "Books."

"Wow, you got yourself an actual book nerd," Penelope mutters, squeezing my shoulders.

I snort, but Blaine seems offended.

"Excuse me, reading does not constitute being a nerd. It's called sophistication. Something your lot obviously lacks, judging by that one over there nearly lighting this whole place on fire." Blaine stares at Dylan, playing with his lighter near a bottle of rum.

"Point taken," Penelope says, laughing it off.

527

"Who's talking about me?" Dylan scoffs.

"No one," Penelope yells back.

Felix grumbles as he places a deck of cards in front of everyone. "SIT!"

My brows rise. "Is he always this domineering?"

Penelope laughs. "Pretty much, yeah."

Everyone chuckles a little.

"Guess we've been summoned." Penelope snorts before she leaves.

I hop off my stool and sit down with the rest of them while Blaine and Ares drink at the bar and talk with each other.

"Who goes first?" Alistair asks.

"I'll go first," Kai says, placing down a card.

"That's not how it works. We all gotta throw the dice," Dylan tells him.

"Says who?" Kai retorts, narrowing his eyes.

"I do," Felix barks. "Now shut the fuck up and play this game like normal people."

Everyone's quieted.

"Yay for no more fighting," Milo murmurs, twirling his fingers around in the air.

Nathan pulls out his knife as he eyes Felix. "I'll give you something to f—"

"No knives!" Lana warns, giving everyone a death stare. "Can't y'all be nice for one evening?"

"One?" Alistair raises a brow.

"Thought you said we were going to do this more often?" Milo asks.

"Not if you guys keep trying to kill each other," Penelope says.

"Exactly," I say.

"So … you're part of the Death Gang now?" Milo asks me.

"The what now?" Kai asks, frowning at him.

"Well, you know, we murder everyone who crosses us. She kind of helped us kill people. To save Ares, of course," Milo explains. "Death Gang."

"I'd be honored," I say, snorting.

"Welcome to the Death Gang, apparently," Alistair says, rolling his eyes.

"What the fuck?" Caleb mutters. "No."

"What's wrong with Death Gang?" Milo asks.

"It's corny as fuck," Caleb adds.

"Guess we finally agree on something," Nathan says.

"What about Murder Maniacs?" Milo suggests.

"Oh God." Kai rubs his face.

"I'm trying *not* to associate with these fuckers at all," Felix growls.

"Well, you're here." Milo shrugs. "So I guess that failed."

Felix raises a brow. "You think I'm here because I want to be here?"

"You're here because *I* want you to be here," Penelope interjects, and she looks around the circle. "All of you."

"That's right," Lana pitches in. "And if you guys don't start behaving, we won't hesitate to punt you out."

All the men look in the other direction like they don't want to fight with their girls.

"Wow. Should call them the Girl Boss gang," I say, folding my arms.

"You mean the Pussy-whipped gang," Dylan says, snorting, and Felix smacks him in the head with a stack of cards.

"Your fucking turn," Felix growls.

"What game are we playing?" Dylan asks as he leans back.

"You're asking that now?" Nathan makes a face. "We already started."

Dylan shrugs. "Didn't want to kill the vibe."

"I'll kill something else soon," Kai mutters under his breath, and Lana throws him a death stare. "I didn't say what."

"Save the murderous intentions for later. We've still got plenty of targets to kill," Alistair says as the boys each place down a card.

"What do you mean?" I ask, placing mine down.

"Remember that woman who tried to sell you?" Lana mutters. "She sold a bunch more girls to the Bones Brotherhood too, who then sold them on to rich folks. She's a real nasty one. Guess what? We've tracked her down."

My eyes widen. "Oh my G—You're going after them all, aren't you?"

She winks and leans in to whisper, "Why do you think we rented this remote cabin in Priory Forest? That woman lives nearby, down the mountain slopes, near the road. And we're gonna make all of these fuckers pay for what they did."

"When?" I ask.

Her eyes sparkle. "Tonight. But shhh." She puts her finger to her lips. "Don't tell anyone. The boys and I are going out on our own for a little fun. But I promise we'll catch her."

A filthy grin spreads on my face. "My lips are sealed." I wrap my arms around her. "Thank you."

Even now, when the dust has settled, my friends will go to extreme lengths to secure my safety and punish those who deserve nothing less.

I used to be terrified of the mere idea of aggression and murder, but now ...

I welcome it with open arms.

Because these girls and boys are violent incarnate.

And it is their violence that makes me feel alive...

Without a single ounce of fear.

THANK YOU

FOR READING!

Thank you so much for reading Vile Boys. Please leave a review if you enjoyed! Make sure to also read Sick Boys and Evil Boys, now in Kindle Unlimited!

And if you got to this point, you're probably wondering … wait, is this series over now?

The short answer is no…

But if you want the longer answer and actually know what else I have in store, make sure to download the bonus epilogue to Vile Boys right here:

https://www.clarissawild.com/vile-boys-bonus-epilogue/

Hold on to your tits ;)

And as always, you can find teasers of my upcoming books on my Intagram: https://www.instagram.com/clarissa.wild/

Or you can join the Fan Club group on Facebook: www.facebook.com/groups/FanClubClarissaWild and talk with other readers!

ALSO BY CLARISSA WILD

Dark Romance
Evil Boys
Sick Boys
Beast & Beauty Duet
Debts & Vengeance Series
Dellucci Mafia Duet
The Debt Duet
Savage Men Series
Delirious Series
Indecent Games Series
The Company Series
FATHER

New Adult Romance
Fierce Series
Blissful Series
Ruin
Rowdy Boy & Cruel Boy

Erotic Romance
The Billionaire's Bet Series
Enflamed Series
Unprofessional Bad Boys Series

Visit Clarissa Wild's website for current titles.
www.clarissawild.com

ABOUT THE AUTHOR

Clarissa Wild is a New York Times & USA Today Bestselling author of Dark Romance and Contemporary Romance novels. She is an avid reader and writer of swoony stories about dangerous men and feisty women. Her other loves include her hilarious husband, her cutie pie son, her two crazy but cute dogs, and her adorable kitties. In her free time, she enjoys watching all sorts of movies, playing video games, reading tons of books, and cooking her favorite meals.

Want to be informed of new releases and special offers? Sign up for Clarissa Wild's newsletter on her website www.clarissawild.com/newsletter.

Visit Clarissa Wild on Amazon for current titles.

Made in the USA
Columbia, SC
20 October 2024

44775756R00319